Scalies

A Novel

by David Datz

Amazon Paperback ISBN: 978-0-9601049-4-9

Amazon Mobipocket ISBN: 978-0-9601049-3-2

Library of Congress Control Number: 2020911578

Smashwords EPUB ISBN: 978-0-9601049-0-1
Smashwords Mobipocket ISBN: 978-0-9601049-1-8
Smashwords PDF ISBN: 978-0-9601049-2-5

Cover design by Tatiana Vila, Vila Design, www.viladesign.net.

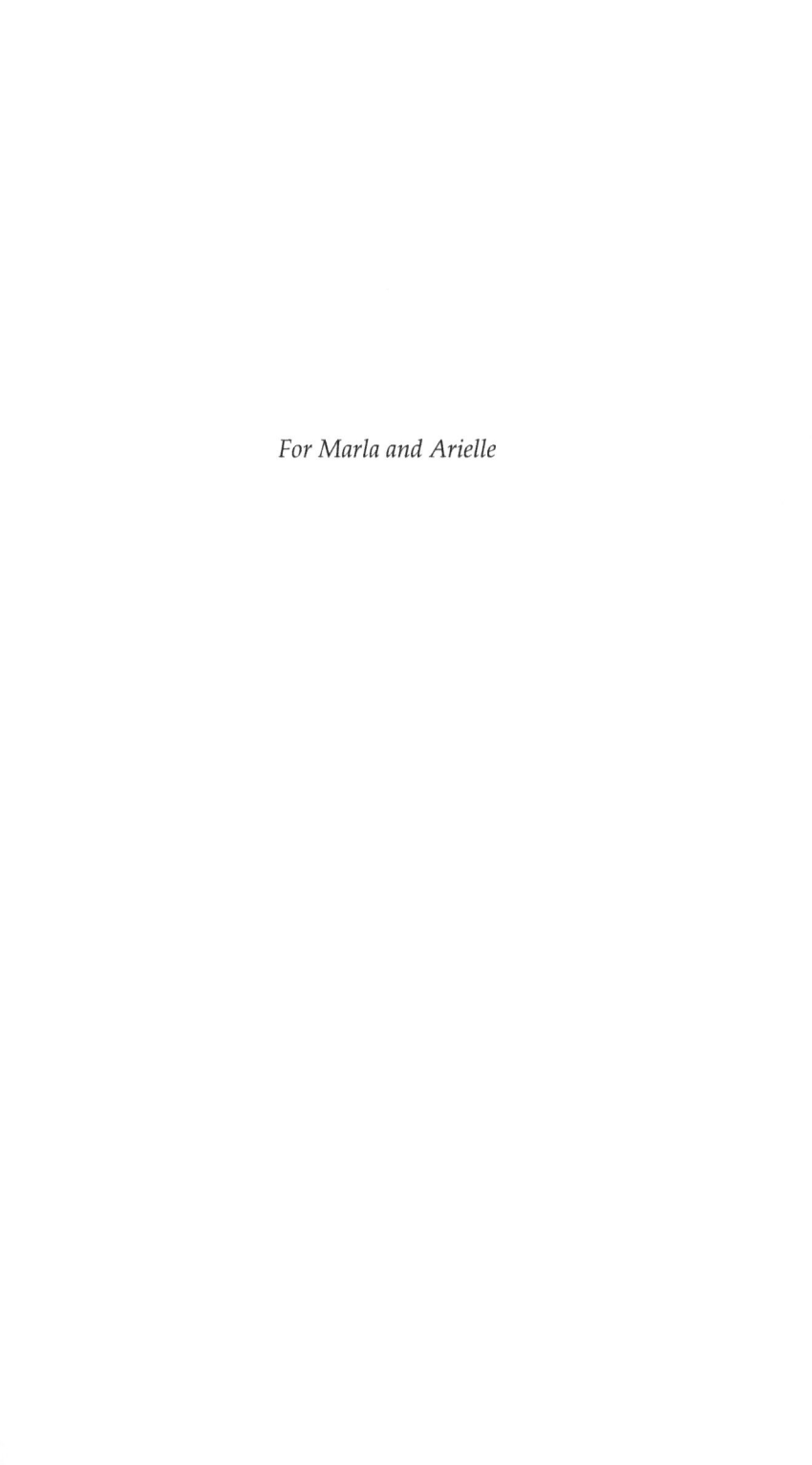

For Marla and Arielle

Prologue:
Marjorie Koehler's First Press Conference:
Transcript Excerpt

Marjorie Koehler: The government is asserting that my clients are different from the rest of us and therefore lack rights the rest of us have. And the only basis for that assertion is—well, there really is no basis. It's just an assertion.

Drew Kristopher: In the back, with the hat.

Reporter #1: But Ms. Koehler, you can't deny the difference, can you?

Marjorie Koehler: Well, we can't deny the differences between you and me, either. The differences are there for everyone to see, but I don't think anyone would assert that because of some superficial differences, our rights should be different.

Drew Kristopher: Here in the front, to my right.

Reporter #2: But given the circumstances, don't you think the government did right to detain them?

Marjorie Koehler: Detain, oh, yes, *detain* sounds just ever so much nicer than *imprison*, doesn't it. Look, the government has *imprisoned*—well, *re*-imprisoned—my clients in a secret place that even I, their attorney, have not been told about, based on so-called national security *concerns*—not *charges*, mind you—*concerns*. That's unconstitutional.

Drew Kristopher: Center, third row.

Reporter #3: Could you address the specific charges against your clients? You're talking all around them.

Marjorie Koehler: As I have said, there are no specific charges. Maybe you know something I don't. Oh, yes, there is the matter of *shoplifting*. That does not exactly warrant secret maximum security, does it?

Drew Kristopher: Right here in front.

Reporter #4: The Attorney-General says that these people knew they were violating the law from the moment they left. What's your response?

Marjorie Koehler: Violating the law? What law? My clients were imprisoned for decades with no reason other than the government's claim that they somehow posed a security risk. Unless the Attorney-General can clarify what that risk has been, he has to admit that the imprisonment was unlawful from the start, and the government, not my clients, is the law-breaker.

Drew Kristopher: Fourth row, center.

Reporter #5: What about the fact that what you call *imprisonment* was in a luxury town with amenities beyond what many Americans can ever hope to experience?

Marjorie Koehler: Granted, the facility was extremely comfortable, but it was still a prison. Ask yourself, if you were told you had to live the rest of your life in comfort in Beverly Hills but could never get out—*ever*—I think you would consider yourself imprisoned, certainly after a year or two. My clients were held for, literally, generations.

Drew Kristopher: Back row, left. Last question.

Reporter #6: But the Attorney-General says your own legal status is questionable. What about that?

Marjorie Koehler: Me? Ha. I've heard that. It's amusing. If he thinks he has a civil complaint about anything I've done, he should bring it in court. I don't think he wants to go in the criminal direction. And I think that either way, it's a loser for him, and I think he knows it.

Drew Kristopher: That's all for now, thank you very much, ladies and gentlemen. Ms. Koehler will have more for you, probably tomorrow. Thank you.

1

Drew Kristopher knew for whom the bell tolled. He also knew why, or he thought he did. Drew was due at a funeral at two that Thursday afternoon, and the alarm rang to give him four hours to jog, shower, shave, dress, eat breakfast, and drive through hot LA sunshine and traffic to the cemetery.

Drew did not need to review his lines. He knew exactly what he would say, having said it, by the reckoning required for tax purposes, sixty-three times in less than two years. His speech varied little from one funeral to the next. He sometimes wondered if he could lay claim to producing and starring in the longest running one-man show ever, not that advertising this particular show was something he relished.

He sometimes mused about how many of the deceased whose lives he glorified, without once referencing anything specific, were able to attract a hundred or more people to their funerals, but lacked even one person willing to say anything heartfelt and sympathetic about how they had lived. In his experience, the length of life or manner of death made little difference.

His first had been the unloved brother of a friend, dead from a heart attack at fifty-two. "Louise and the kids loathed him," the friend said. "Probably still do. People worked with him because they liked his money, but the truth is, they could hardly stand him. Shit, people would go to lunch with him and lose their appetites." The friend sighed. "Let's face it, he was an asshole. But he was a financially successful asshole, so there'll be a lot of people there, and somebody has to say something nice."

Drew had not seen how he could help.

"You're an actor. You know lots of plays and stuff. You can find something general, but moving, something not too religious. I don't know. Just so the damn funeral doesn't look like an accounting class."

Drew's friend pleaded a lot, and so Drew, appalled and intrigued, agreed to spend three days thinking about it. He thought about death and funeral speeches: Friends, Romans, countryman. He died the death of a salesman. Poor key-cold figure of a holy king. He rambled 'til the butcher cut him down. Good night, sweet prince. Put a twenty-dollar gold piece on my watch chain, so the boys'll know I died standing pat. For whom the bell tolls. Hmm.

He went online and found John Donne's meditation about death. After four hundred years, it could stand some revision. Drew figured that Donne wouldn't care. He pulled the Catholicism out of it to make it religion-neutral. For atheists and Unitarians, he changed "god" to "creator." He thought about using "big bang," but decided it would sound too close to humor. For the feminists he changed references to "man" to "person," "human" to "humankind," etc. He was troubled by Donne's references to his own illness, but he figured that most everyone feels really sick sometimes, figuratively if not literally. [See Drew's revision of the meditation after the end of the story.]

He composed an introductory disclaimer, about how the last word on death had been spoken four hundred years ago and could not be improved, and how he had just touched it up a little for the twenty-first century.

Then he memorized the whole thing, directed his performance to reach a crescendo near the end, the part about "an affliction in his bowels"—oddly appropriate to the deceased's IBS—and rehearsed it twenty-some times.

He was nervous at the funeral, but when he looked at the seated, well-dressed throng and saw how little they cared what he said or how he said it, he relaxed into performance. He felt good about it. He felt moved, himself, when he said, "...all humankind is of one author." He knew the "evening meditation" was good. Of course, the bell, everyone's heard that. And the final consolation, the "recourse to creation, which is our only security."

As he left the podium, he thought he heard a couple of people sob, and a couple of others start to applaud.

A few minutes later, the minister asked him if he was available next Tuesday.

Tuesday's was a younger man, from a well-fixed family, large but not large enough to hold anyone who cared. The young man's parents had already grieved more than they could bear, while he lived, for his life desolated by bad habits and meanness. After the end they had sorrow but no words. So, once again, Drew gave some meaning to a lost life.

Again the minister liked it and spread the word to his colleagues.

―――――

In the months that followed Drew discovered more dead wealthy assholes than he could have ever imagined. They all had successful careers and dysfunctional families, frequently several, with offspring ranging from pathetically homely to downright gorgeous, and most of them apparently headed for trouble and misery. Out of curiosity, Drew tallied the genders of these dead, and found that about sixty percent of them were men. Almost all had died of heart attacks, strokes, or car accidents, and Drew theorized that the suddenness of their ends gave the survivors no time for the perspective needed to summon genuine sympathy.

Preceding Drew at the podium were always a clergyperson with pieties about death, and a couple of "friends" or family who did their best to tell a story or two about the deceased. Sometimes they would give an outline of the poor soul's entire life, with notable highlights and accomplishments and absolutely no spark of sentiment, or perhaps a joke that only served to highlight the dead's obnoxiousness.

Then came Drew, who, over the months, had honed his performance to the point where he could feel the emotional catharsis of his audience. He was surprised that the various clergy seemed relieved to have someone else take up the burden. But then, they still got their fees.

Drew spoke to crowds of somberly well-dressed people, and his ability to bring tears to their eyes made him both proud and astonished. After each one, if he failed to sneak out quickly enough, someone would catch him and embarrass him with gratitude. The women, especially, would want to take hold of both his hands and weep in his face and thank him for the wonderful words. "Actually, they were John Donne's," he would sometimes say, even though he knew he should keep quiet, but he felt in himself a mix of pity and disgust that he had to deflect. These people were genuinely glad that he could speak so movingly of someone about whom they could think of nothing nice to say.

The jobs kept coming, the fees went up, and soon Drew was earning a decent living by extoling the detested dead. Even more remarkable was the candor of those left behind—Drew couldn't call them "bereaved," so absent was any sign of grief—in telling him of the deceased's faults, particularly after Drew's speech had softened them up.

There was a bond salesman, an executive with some big financial company, dead at fifty-two from a burst brain aneurism. He cheated in his business, he cheated on his wife, he cheated on his mistress, he back-stabbed at the office, he paid people to cart his kids around, always promising to be there at the next soccer game, the next class graduation, the next birthday party. He was detestable enough while he made money for his clients and his company's stockholders, but when he could no longer do that, but could still make it for himself, he became totally insufferable. Still, his funeral attracted several hundred people. From the podium they looked to Drew as if they were glad the shit was dead, but by the time Drew was through with them, they seemed affected by at least the notion of death—their own if not that of the funeral's subject.

A highly successful painting contractor rumored to be dealing cocaine. Before Drew could get away from the cemetery, a middle-aged man, looking bewildered, approached him. "You know," the man said, "not too many people liked Nick. But you made me glad I came. Thanks."

The president of a small college, who had been addressed to her face, publicly, as "the duchess" by her two angry teenaged children even before the divorce, so that the moniker became common among both the students and faculty. Her office staff used it with particular frequency, as in "the Duchess complained of too much mustard on the luncheon sandwiches," or "the Duchess wants us to order new white phones because the beige ones remind her of hotel rooms." Before the service, her bitter ex-husband, a freelance carpenter, had told the minister, in Drew's presence, that most of the attendees were people who'd been charmed by her good looks and gracious public manner into giving the college lots of money, so the service should be "nice but short." Afterwards the husband told Drew, in a softer tone, "You made her life seem worth more than a bag of dollars. Thanks."

Of course, lawyers. Clergy of a certain kind, high in the hierarchy of particularly mercenary sects, or pastors to particularly wealthy congregations. CEOs by the dozen. Show business types, not the big shots, but the middling. Drew reflected on the fact that ordinary stiffs became stiffer every day, but only the extraordinarily wealthy could attract enough people to require a speaker, much less afford his rates, which he had raised.

Drew practiced detachment. He talked to himself while driving hot freeways from one end of Los Angeles County to the other, and then down into Orange County or up into Riverside and Ventura Counties. It was only a job. It wasn't really hypocrisy because he said nothing specific about anybody. He managed to slide by, enjoying the stable if not excessive income it brought him. Still, it was hard.

Before one service, a minister invited Drew into his office to relax beforehand. As Drew sprawled in a stuffed chair, he watched the minister taking care of business: reading mail, taking and making phone calls, then sprucing himself up, humming cheerfully.

"How do you do it?" Drew asked.

"What?" the minister said.

"Preside over these things."

Straightening his tie in the mirror, the minister said, "Eh. Somebody has to do it. Somebody will have to do it for me, some day." With a smile, the minister ushered him out the door and into the large chapel. "And remember," the minister said, "even the vilest crook is entitled to a lawyer."

Drew's last girlfriend had dumped him two years previous, after four years of dating so continuous that their friends thought of them as a couple, with her finally telling him tearfully how sweet he was but how economically feckless, how unlikely to be able to pull an income, and, lord knew, she couldn't. And, damn, he was depressing. She wanted a family. She wanted stability. She wanted laughter. He had little room for argument.

Drew chased the breakup with long nights of TV, movies, drinking with friends, longer jogs. The acting auditions, always tense and desperate, became more so. He thought of Donne when his stomach ached.

Drew met women, at parties, at auditions, at friends' dinners. At some point, the conversation would veer off into ways and means of living, and Drew would feel his insides droop. How could he explain to anybody that he earned his daily bread by praising the unworthy dead?

2

The barely detectable combination of sounds should have been soporific but was not. The collective, not-quite-noise that was a blend of air conditioning, the gentle hiss-hum of a half-dozen laptops, the swallowing of coffee, the small frictional body sounds of legs re-crossing, ties placed properly on chests, or long hair being repositioned, just so, on shoulders, all combined with the voices referencing a clause in a paragraph on a page in a case file in a lawsuit that had been continuing for god only knew how long–all that homogenized background that could have induced the edgy nervousness of boredom, became, in Marjorie's brain, a discrete series of tiny irritating rasps and percussives.

Marjorie avoided what she could. She stared down at her note pad or laptop screen to avoid the eyes of others at the conference table, eyes that she thought could surely see what hid behind her own. She avoided small, two- or three-person meetings where hiding was too difficult. She avoided caffeine and refined sugar. She avoided the reading of long briefs and documents—and weren't all of them way too long? She avoided large quantities of liquid and roughage because the toilet beckoned all too frequently even without them.

But she could not avoid the sounds, which might at any time contain a certain distinctive rustling and patter, the anticipation of which gripped her belly.

Of course, a person cannot long function that way, hiding from the sounds of civilization while still living among them. Marjorie knew that. She had heard her boss asking if she were ill, in need of a rest, with a not subtle implication that she was no longer suitably productive. She had been to therapy—which carried absolutely no stigma in this place—she had tried and rejected medication, except for a glass or two of bourbon in the evening or a clandestine glass or two of wine at lunch.

Her daily run through early morning desert air, which had kept her going through her career in this miserable ultrasuburbia, was becoming a forced march.

Eating was just one of the items on her daily to-do list.

Sleep had become a chore, nearly impossible in the isolation of darkness, and only slightly less so in the glare of every light in her apartment and after more than a healthy dose of alcohol.

Marjorie needed a vacation.

———

"I knew what I was getting into," she told Boris, after confessing to having an unhappy life. "It was all written down. The fine print that most people would give up on reading? I read it. I was a lawyer. A good one, I guess, or they wouldn't have hired me."

Boris lay quietly next to her, a large, lean, exceptionally masculine presence who was apparently unburdened by imaginary but irresistible sounds. Only the bathroom light was on, because Marjorie felt safe but not entirely safe.

"Why don't you quit?" he asked.

"I can't. The fine print. That particular rule is pretty damn clear, pretty goddamned not legalese fine print, if you can wade through the rest of it to get there."

She turned to him and said, "You're the reason I can get out at all."

"You could lie," he said. "Say your dear old aunt in Cleveland is sick."

"Can't. They know everything about me. They know there is no aunt." She turned to him, said, "You're the only reason I can get out at all, for little half-night romps."

He smiled.

"You think I'm using you?" she asked.

"I don't care," he said.

"I do. I feel shitty about it, too."

"You are about the best thing I've ever seen, much less slept with," he said. "I won't complain."

She put an arm across his chest and hugged. "You're not so bad yourself," she said. "Supposed to be one of my jailers and here you are, aiding and abetting."

"Especially abetting."

They both laughed at that.

"And having you next to me is the only reason I can stand darkness—almost," she said. "So thank you. I'm going to cry on your chest for a while. Then we'd better go back."

"Yes," he said.

3.

The knowledge of being no different from his friends and all the rest of his peers, of suffering no more than a variation on the mix of eagerness, anger, fear, dread, and rebelliousness that they all felt—and probably that his parents and their parents and everyone before had felt at his present age—was of small comfort to Colin. He regarded himself passionately in the upstairs bathroom mirror, in the semi-affluent stucco house where he had always lived. His mother told him there was nothing new under the sun, but goddamn it there was or had to be, and his father told him, with a heavy undertone of unspoken knowledge, *to keep cool, just keep cool,* but what the hell did that mean?

Everything was so *nice.* The house, with his own room and the super broadband internet and the video games and the TV on demand and his weight set in the basement, was *nice.* His school was *nice.* The town with its shops and restaurants and his own credit card were *nice.* His car was really *nice*—though not as nice as his friend Bryce's.

But he did not *feel nice,* nor did he want to *be nice.* He tried not to look nice, but whether he succeeded depended on what standard was applied: Moderately long hair, one ear-ring, bat tattoo on neck, the last of which had driven his father to make Colin promise reluctantly that in exchange for continued life he would have no other body part pierced, colored, or otherwise mutilated. Colin's dread was that he was, in fact, *nice,* and doomed to remain so unless he could get his ass the hell out of this little snot pool of a town.

And there was the fear that maybe he *could* get out. It was illegal, as everyone knew. People were in prison for trying—everyone also knew that, and he had friends who said they had talked to people who knew people, etc. People were supposedly locked up somewhere, but he'd never spoken to anyone who knew about visits. There had never been a news story that he knew of, not even on the internet.

His parents told him it was *exciting*, being part of a secret government enterprise, as they were, though they did not sound excited talking about it, not to mention the fact that their jobs, per se, had nothing to do with it. Even at nearly eighteen years of age, Colin was more than dimly aware that for him and his friends, easy access to everything their culture told them was important was not the same as freedom. In their glass and chromium-plated school the teachers, sounding religious, told them to let their minds go, that they would have everything they ever needed or wanted, that they were in service to a higher goal that would someday be revealed. To encourage their minds to go where they would—the call to make-believe—the English teacher had trotted out that poem: "Stone walls do not a prison make/Nor iron bars a cage." Gerald, the smartass, had immediately told Ms. Gleason, "that Lovelace guy was a bleeping *royalist* who didn't even believe in *democracy*." She had said that whatever Mr. Lovelace believed was beside the point. The point was that they—Gerald, Colin, and the rest of their dangerous corps of adolescents—were part of something bigger than all of them. She said, "the whole is much, *much*, greater than the sum of its parts," and, "you get to be part of history without having to sacrifice anything significant." She said, of course, "some day you will understand." Even the slowest of her students could tell that Ms. Gleason herself was struggling to believe it, or, as Bryce had said, with his usual smirk, during lunch, "Her voice lacked conviction."

19

All of Colin's pals could tell anyone who asked—in case anyone ever did—that stone walls did not a prison make, nor did the occasionally glimpsed razor wire. You could be an official member of the population of their ersatz hometown, with all the endless rights and privileges accorded them, and still be in prison.

Still, scarier than the imprisonment, scarier than the unbelievable, endless, flat, dull, thrill-bereft life that he saw whenever he dared take a glance forward, scarier than the *real* prison that would, they *said*, await him, should he ever try to break out, was the possibility of actually *being* out.

Which fear was not diminished by Bryce's claims of having actually *been* out.

4

From Colin's Journal

I know I don't look it, but I'm shy. I can admit it here. I don't want to be shy, but I am. The ear stud was supposed to help me with that. Maybe it does, with other people. But it does not help me.

Our group likes me. Or I think they do. I think maybe Bryce likes me because I'm shy. Like, I don't challenge him. It's okay if he leads, I guess. He leads us into things that most of us would never get into on our own and usually it's fun, even when we get into trouble. Like the time he made Gerald take the socket wrench, with all the extensions, from the custodian's closet so we could remove all the bells. We managed to do it all during third period. All afternoon, there were no bells, so the teachers had to keep watching the clock so they could start and finish on time. It was pretty funny. But then LaTasha said that if we did not put them back that very afternoon, she would tell the principal. It was not a threat or anything like that. She just said it as a fact. Even Bryce knew she had a point, so nobody thought of her as a snitch. If she had not said it, I don't know when we would have put them back. But because she did, Elmer and I got caught by the custodian putting them back an hour after school was out.

Everybody knew that Bryce was the instigator, so we were all three in the principal's office the next morning. He made us come in an hour early in the morning and stay an hour late in the afternoon and he gave us chores to do, like helping the custodian clean the bathrooms. You could tell that both the custodian and the principal thought it was funny. Even the teachers did, once the word was out, which was mostly because of Bryce. He can smile at anyone, even the principal, and whoever it is usually smiles back and wants to share whatever the joke is.

Maybe I'd like to be a little more like Gerald, with his smart-ass mouth. He says things that are, like, I don't know. Kind of wild. Bryce listens to him. At least, sometimes Bryce seems to change his mind about where he wants to lead us because of something Gerald says.

I think people see me as being kind of like Elmer. We're both quiet. Except he's tougher than I am, and I think everyone knows that. He's not that big, but in a fight I think I would bet on Elmer. I think he might even be able to take Bryce, even though Bryce is a lot bigger. Anyway, I'm not like that. I don't want to fight anyone. Not that Elmer wants to fight anyone, but he would if he had to, and I don't think I would. I'm not sure what scares me more, the idea of being hurt, or of hurting someone else. I mean, I don't want my nose crunched and bleeding like happens to guys in sports sometimes, but I don't want to make anyone else's nose crunched and bleeding either.

It's not really size, I guess. I mean, Astrid's small even for a girl, but she's scary sometimes. She seems like this force. Any of the guys could stop her physically, but she's got some other thing about her, like she is not afraid. It's not like she hides fear or overcomes it. It's like she doesn't even have it, like fear is just not part of her like it is for most people, even Bryce a little bit. Like somebody could knock her down but could never knock fear into her.

But it's LaTasha I don't want to be shy around. I wish I knew how not to be. I wish I could be real smooth like Bryce is with girls, even with Astrid. He kissed Astrid once right on campus, during the school day, so everybody could see. I get even more nervous with LaTasha than I do with most girls. I don't know how to start.

We're talking about going outside. Bryce, Gerald, and Astrid say they went out one time, but they won't say how and they don't give details. Going out is scary. We could get caught and even if we don't, something terrible could happen to us out there. But I feel like I don't really have a choice. Bryce, Astrid, and Gerald say they are going, and Elmer is going to go with them, and LaTasha says she probably will. And if LaTasha goes I cannot not go, because I would feel weak and I'm afraid she wouldn't like me.

5

Nothing was unusual about the gleaming silver SUV with six teenagers comfortably inside, inching along Commercial Street among other cars varying in size and color but all recent models, and all owned by the riders' parents. On Saturday night these adolescents were in a wholly predictable traffic jam of their own choosing, on the main street of a wholly predictable town that provided them the best schools and athletic facilities, the highest middle-class incomes for their parents, and retail commerce offering the finest of opportunities to spend their generous allowances.

Commercial Street was the place to be, anchored at one end by an indoor shopping mall and at the other by an outdoor shopping mall, each themed to a different historical period as portrayed in the latest movies, with the fourteen intervening blocks filled with small shops showing the latest in clothing, electronics, sports gear, entertainment, and restaurants offering formulaic versions of every kind of cooking known to the world. The shops were of gleaming glass and steel—clean, cool, futuristic, and inviting—or throw-back wood, brick and concrete—cluttered, warm, carefully antiqued, and inviting. The staff in the shops and restaurants were as well-off as their customers. The ambient sound was a mélange of all the music vibrating from all the speakers in all the cars and all the shops, the mixed rhythms somehow reinforcing each other, with an underlying whirr of finely tuned, expensive automobile engines, all punctuated by the voices of boys and girls needing to shout even their laughter to make it distinguishable from the rest. The cars rolled slowly, and stopped, rolled slowly and stopped, the windows down, the kids shouting to the other kids crowding the sidewalks, the shouts of yearnings for fun, flirtation or more, the jokes displaying the inexperience the jokers tried to mask.

If Commercial Street was the place to be, it was also no place to be because it was the only place to be. The urges were too powerful, the aches too sharp, the memories too limited, the challenges at once too easy to meet and too large to comprehend, the boundaries too soft and comfortable. As for teenagers everywhere, the needs were clichés: to fly, to experience, to know, to create, to embrace, to hurt, to be hurt — and, mostly, to escape.

Which was what the six teenagers in the SUV in question were headed for, an escape not to make-believe or alcohol or drugs or sex, but to a much more expansive kind. This group did not really need to be on Commercial Street, but the driver — big, swaggering, smart-ass, Bryce Karakawa — had taken them here because it was the place to pass time before doing anything more daring, and because their parents expected them to be here, Bryce believing that if events went awry they could claim to have been here because their friends had seen them here. Nobody had objected. Bryce was not just the driver, he was the group's accepted leader, slip-streaming them behind, leading his crew in the same way he confounded his teachers and charmed his own and everyone else's parents, with his combination of maxed-out grade point average, athletic haughtiness, and blunt, humorous insolence.

Like most planned escapes, this one was to be temporary. Bryce and his girlfriend — little, wiry, blonde, hippie-hard-eyed Astrid — had done it before, as had skinny-geek-hipster Gerald with his Buddy Holly glasses. Their postures, voice tones, the very way they bobbed their heads to the music, and their refusal to speak of their experience, lorded it over the ones who had not. LaTasha, who seemed a little embarrassed

25

by her alluring body and soft brown curls, had not. Friendly Elmer, with the buzz cut hair, muscular arms, and a desire to help everyone, had not. And Colin, studious, athletic to a point that would not get him on teams, smarter than Bryce but less able to assert it, had not.

Astrid knew better, deferring to Bryce only because she craved his sex. Sharing sex with Bryce had only added to her knowing better, for *knowing better* was not so much a condition as an attitude, one which persisted even at the times when she displayed her ignorance, though she had learned to minimize those times simply by not speaking while keeping the all-knowing look on her face. Astrid could be mystified, lost, or terrified, and still she would know better. Astrid knew what was good—though she gave little effort to defining or applying any definition of goodness—and had little tolerance for those who did not.

Gerald did not *know better*. Gerald watched and chilled, alternated between earnestness and disdain, asked lots of questions, exercising no discretion at all in whom he asked and much discretion in which answers he kept. Gerald preferred vague answers to precise ones, feeling certain only in his dislike of certainty. Uncertainty, to Gerald, was cool in all things except in the certain fact that he had never had sex and wanted to.

Elmer, on the other hand, hated uncertainty. Elmer liked hard precision. He disliked school when it asked him to choose from among equally indefinite, squamous alternatives, and so, history and literature made him uncomfortable. Mathematics and computer lab lit him up. Languages—spoken or coded— came easily. The other teenagers amused him, though he was too nice to laugh. He followed Bryce, and, to some degree, Astrid, because they amused him and he thought doing what they chose could help him understand them, which would be much more interesting than understanding book characters, who, after all, did only what the author wanted them to do. Unlike the kids who followed Bryce because Bryce was irresistible, Elmer followed Bryce to find out what Bryce would do, all the while feeling comfort in the belief that if the appropriate situation arose, he was the only one who could beat the shit out Bryce.

LaTasha lacked the pretensions of either Astrid or Gerald. LaTasha knew only that she would study hard and make something of herself, that she would do good in the world, make it a better place, and that she needed not just sex, as yet as unknown to her as to Gerald, but love, believing that certainty in love, when she got it, would somehow relax her libido, make it not less, but less *acute*. LaTasha liked beatnik poetry, James Baldwin, jazz music, and, at the moment, she thought she might like Colin.

Colin thought himself more nervous than the others. If he had raised the subject—as a teenaged boy could not—he would have learned of fear beyond nervousness, of bravado based only on momentum. Colin did things because he could not think of other things. He studied hard in school because he could not see any other approach. He went out with his friends, played computer games, and followed Bryce, because, why not? He thought this outing was probably wrong and was afraid it could wreck his life, but he couldn't back out now, could he?

Seated in the back seat behind Bryce, Colin admired Bryce's eyes in the rear-view mirror. Bryce always knew where they were going and why they were going there, never seeming to doubt, winning every argument even when thwarted, knowing that eventually he would come out ahead. Colin wished he were like that but found the idea inconceivable. Colin was distracted by LaTasha seated next to him, her body pressed by happenstance against his, her curls occasionally brushing his face. To the extent he thought about her, he believed her so far beyond him as to stop thought and send it backward—especially now, dominated, as were they all, by the vague fear and excitement about the illicit thing they were about to do.

Bryce turned left at the corner occupied by City Mountaineering and Gouroma Coffee, then turned right after two blocks, and left again onto Industrial Boulevard.

"We're going to the flats?" Colin asked.

"Sort of," Bryce said.

They sped on the four-lane that became two-lane at the edge of town, into the border of desert that surrounded it and ended at the official boundary of concrete, razor wire, and god- knew-what invisible electronic barriers. The cool air rushing through the open windows felt good and smelled sweet, of desert flowers and sage, softening to a slight degree the near panic that had dampened their habitual teenage chatter and banter. Bryce turned left off the two-lane onto an unmarked dirt road on which he took fifteen minutes to travel perhaps a mile. A low, windowless, concrete structure appeared in the light of the half-moon. Bryce turned off the lights as they approached, and stopped about twenty yards from it.

"We have to be very quiet," Bryce said.

"Can we breathe?" Elmer asked from the other side of the back seat.

"Only if Bryce says so," Gerald said.

Astrid snickered.

"On the contrary," Bryce said. "You can breathe unless I tell you not to."

They sat still, waiting for Bryce to direct them. "Okay," he said, "let's open and close the doors quietly." They were able to do that because of the money Bryce's parents had paid for the car.

Bryce walked slowly to the right of the building. The others followed, in a line, Colin last. The building was about ten feet tall, of smooth concrete. Bryce led them to a mound of dirt against the building's far corner, where the wall was only four or five feet above ground level. They ascended the mound, where Bryce hiked himself up onto the roof. Gerald, though only about five-foot-six, sprang up easily, as did Astrid. Elmer gave LaTasha a boost, then easily hiked up, as did Colin. They were all in reasonably good shape, obesity being as rare in their well-mannered town as rickets.

The building roof had several large vent conduits opening above it. They followed Bryce toward one of them, which curved to horizontal, so that the grate capping it faced them. Bryce pulled a screwdriver from his jacket pocket. He removed two large screws from one side of the grate and two more from the other. He put the screws into an inside jacket pocket, which he zipped shut.

As he pulled the grate off and put it down on the roof, the kids froze as a man's voice said, "Good evening."

From behind one vent a man in khakis appeared. To his left was another, with a drawn revolver, pointed downwards, but still drawn.

The first man stepped into a lit area and stood still, motioning to the other man—the one with the gun out—to stay where he was. "I think you know who I am," the first man said.

For once Bryce wasn't the first to speak. Astrid said, "You're Chief Schmitz."

Cheng Schmitz nodded. "And you," he said, looking at Bryce, "you're Bryce Karakawa."

Bryce's stare turned to a glare. "How do you know?" he said.

Cheng smiled. "Son," he said. "You're famous. Everybody knows you." He sighed as if he were doing something he heartily hated having to do. "Bryce," he said, "you are leading yourself and your friends into more trouble than you could possibly know or understand. Now, if you stop right here, you can all go back home. I won't tell your parents, or your school, or anyone else about this. But you'll have to promise to never do it again."

"Cheng," Bryce said, "why the fuck should we?"

Cheng smiled, a response that nonplussed all of them, especially Bryce, who had plainly counted on the shock value of his answer and the use of the Chief's first name.

"I mean, what difference does it make? You'll throw us in jail? What?" Bryce, for once, was sputtering. Gerald stepped into the breach.

"On what charge," Gerald said. "Attempted escape? Everyone wants to escape. If you publicize what we do, it'll just get worse for you. Shit, I bet even *you* want to escape." With that, Gerald took four steps to the vent, hiked himself into it, and jumped. They heard him hit a metal surface, then they heard a click.

All four kids still on the roof turned to face the click, and saw the officer, slightly behind and to the left of Cheng, holding his revolver in two hands, pointed directly at Bryce. For a moment they were still. Then Astrid walked to the vent, hiked her rump onto its edge, pivoted, and disappeared, with the same metallic thump as Gerald.

"Tell them to come back down, Bryce," the officer with the revolver said.

"Put it away, Daniel," Cheng said.

"What?"

"Holster your piece, Daniel," Cheng said.

Daniel hesitated, looking puzzled, but he complied.

"If any of you want to come back in our car, you can. Same deal, nobody finds out what's been going on out here."

Bryce motioned his head to LaTasha and Colin. LaTasha followed into the vent. Colin got up on it, squatting on its edge. He paused to look at Bryce.

Cheng said, "I'm going to ask you once more, Bryce. Stop this. If you don't, you could be unleashing more hell than you have ever seen in a movie, or ever imagined."

For a moment, they were all still: Colin squatting in the vent, Bryce staring at Cheng, Cheng staring back, both hands on his belt, at Bryce, and Daniel, darting his eyes from one of them to another. When Bryce turned toward him, Colin jumped. Bryce grasped the top of the vent with his arms, pulled himself in, paused to look down, and followed Colin.

The kids were out of sight of the lawmen.

"What the hell are we doing, Chief?" Daniel asked.

Cheng sighed. "I'm no longer sure of what I'm doing. But I know what I'd do if I were them—exactly what they just did. What about you?"

Daniel said nothing.

"Let's get out of here, Daniel."

"What goes in the report?"

"I'll write it and show it to you. Don't worry about it."

"Shouldn't someone stay here for when they come back?"

"That's a harder one," Cheng said. "If we arrest them when they get back, they'll tell their lawyer that we let them go in the first place. If we don't, they sure won't tell anyone the cops let them through."

"What about the vent?"

Cheng took a long look at the vent, then asked Daniel, "Think we should lock them out?"

Daniel said nothing.

"I don't either," Cheng said. "We'll secure it later."

6

While Marjorie showered, Boris dressed in the odd, grayish, brownish, slightly bluish uniform, which he supposed had been purposely designed to make his force look official but not much different from a mall security agency. Unobtrusive, like himself.

The money was good, the rules simple, the reasons mostly hidden. He had signed a long contract that looked, he expected, much like Marjorie's. Unlike her, he had not read it, but the recruiters and trainers had soberly made plain that signing it was like swearing an oath, and that the consequences of violating it could range from very bad to catastrophically awful.

The job was a perfect, high-paying opportunity for a laid-off small-town cop with a two-year college degree and no other prospects, a man "chosen from among thousands of applicants for his intelligence, skills, and experience." The recruiters and trainers had told them repeatedly of the importance of their mission not just to America but to the entire human race (and weren't they really the same thing?). They had heard many lectures about constant vigilance, about not disclosing outside the project even the most mundane project detail, about the certain severe punishment for even the smallest violation, and about how they could never know why. Boris was no lawyer, but he could sense the emphatic lack of reference to anything judicial. Not to mention the strong implication that what they called "intelligence" really meant an outsized capacity for boredom.

So every day he sat in the air-conditioned guard booth in the desert, earning a good salary as a glorified parking lot attendant. He read all the rules and regulations. He surfed the web, read books. Nobody cared. Very few vehicles went in or out, because they were not supposed to. Supply trucks and delivery vans came in, and a few minutes later they left. Almost nobody left without having first come, and when they did, he was ready with papers to match the ones the drivers and passengers held. He took signatures, swiped identity cards, took electronic finger prints, checked his computer screen, made sure the automatic photos were taken, told folks when they were due back and handed them pages of fine print—these he *had* read, because he had the time—promising, in legalese, swift and certain retribution if they failed in any way to meet the requirements in the fine print. He made them sign receipts for the instructions.

At night, he went home to his prefab community. The promise to live where they put him, among all the other security staff, had been the only thing that had really worried him when he signed the contract. Was this organization really the military under a different name? There were some similarities, management said, but in the twenty-first century he'd like it. And he'd had to admit that the little house—not an apartment, but a house—was nice: sparkling clean, fully furnished, including two big-screen TV sets, wi-fi, modern kitchen, even a wet bar and outdoor hot tub.

They gave him a car with unlimited mileage and a bottomless debit card that he never had to think about. Of course, the closest city was a six-hour round-trip that the work schedule hardly ever left time for.

The other staff had identical perks. They were all bored, but seemed content at dissipating their off hours with the pre-fab amenities. When not watching TV, they would hunch over tables at one of the three local pre-fab bars, which, in Boris's opinion, all tried too hard—one at country honky-tonk, one at inner-city funk, and one at elite sophistication, and all with bartenders who prevented any serious inebriation.

They would soak in hot tubs, alone or with each other. They were racially and sexually diverse. Management would accept anything except illegal drugs or too much alcohol. Management called them "Sec Staff," because "security staff" was too long for government officials to say. Naturally, the staffers changed it to "sex-daft."

Boris felt oppressed. The place was too comfortable. He mused that he would have preferred to take the TV and the computer, with the wi-fi, into a three-room board-and-batten house with a plain pine floor and a fire place, for which he would have enjoyed chopping his own wood. Rustic charm to go with the electronics.

Boris felt like a highly paid prisoner. He knew that he was exactly two years, two months, and eight days into his five-year contract, when the good-looking brunette in the expensive German car stopped at the gate on her way out. She looked grim, and seemed to be working at a sort of executive brusqueness. She told him she knew she was acting beyond normal parameters, but she had official business outside, too urgent for preparation of the normal paperwork. She stepped out of her car (required), exposing nice legs below a short skirt (not required), handed him her identity card and what she said was an "exceptional permission" document, and put her finger on the print-reader.

Boris took his time reading the document. He swiped her card and looked at his computer screen, which showed a red border around the card and finger-print results.

"I know what you're seeing," she said. "It's supposed to be that way. This is not a normal situation, as I believe the document makes clear."

Boris gave her his best cop look-over.

She glanced at his badge. "Officer Feldman," she said, "believe me this is real and serious."

Boris stared back.

"You could get, I mean the consequences of your not letting me through, would be serious. This is a dangerous situation. You don't want, I mean you want to avoid severe problems for yourself," she said.

Boris knew desperation when he saw it. He did not speak, but later, he remembered that he might have raised an eyebrow.

"I also have this," she said, and reached into her brief case for another document, several stapled pages, with a paper clip on the second page.

Boris watched her face as he returned her ID card and documents, including the paper-clipped batch of hundred-dollar bills. She was trying to hold herself together and succeeding fairly well, considering. But as he continued to stare, her hard, official look vanished and her face softened.

"Please," she whispered. "I don't want to *do* anything. I *will* come back. I just need to, need, goddammit I just *need*."

He spoke for the first time. "Go back to town. Come back here at exactly six-forty-five tonight. Park behind there," he said, and turned his face toward the four-car parking shed by the road. "Stay in the car until I come."

She drove away, back towards the compound, and, two hours and twenty-three minutes later, to his mild surprise, she reappeared as he had told her. At 0700 his relief came, his buddy Sydney—who managed to drink too much despite the official vigilance, good-time Sydney, who knew about shared "sex-daft" activity and lots of other stuff. Sydney happily did not notice Boris's unusual and elaborate walks back and forth between the parking shed and whatever was behind it, or— was that another body behind Boris in the shadows as he got into his car? Who cared?

35

When Boris unexpectedly returned to the guard booth four hours later to retrieve the book he had left in the shed, Sydney shrugged, and was again happy not to notice anything unusual, such as the other car starting up and driving away at the same time as Boris's. The sex-daft had to take care of each other because who else would?

———

After the third rendezvous the operation became routine. Boris, with help from Marjorie, would tip generously for the motel room. The clerk wouldn't even smile. They would enjoy themselves for exactly two and a half hours, and return, in the same manner.

The fourth time, as they lay in bed, Marjorie took a breath and blurted a question: "That first time, why did you trust me? How could you tell I wasn't a spy? How can you tell now?"

Boris thought of how to answer. The truth was he hadn't cared, but he didn't want to say that. So instead, he said, with only a little irony, "Cop's intuition."

He did not say that at the moment when he had given her back her phony documents and her money, he had known he was falling in love with her.

He figured Marjorie already knew that.

7

Howard Sturges finished the day by installing a new oil pump in an SUV, which required further computer resets. Howard yearned for the days of computer-free cars with simple engines that a man with mechanical talent could fix without a reference manual. In his youth, before he passed fifty with relief, knowing he no longer had to pretend to be young, Howard had had the chance to work on cars like that, where he could lose himself for hours—loosening, removing, cleaning, replacing, adjusting, tightening, testing—without ever having to look at a meter or a computer screen or a manual.

Howard wiped his hands and thought about how to spend his evening. Should he sip Scotch and watch TV—all those idiots who thought they were clever? Idiotic shows, sitcoms, news, dramas, all idiotic, designed by geniuses to keep idiots watching. Better to sip Scotch and read a book. But Howard was restless.

Howard's extended family—presently he had no nuclear family of his own—referred to him as a "career curmudgeon," and Howard did not mind at all. People who met him for the first time were charmed by the way he spoke blunt, plain truths without hesitation or disguise. People who had known him for years found him tactless and offensive. Howard did not care. In his opinion they were all fools and idiots, people who could not be trusted with anything, least of all their own well-being. Not that he wanted the taxes he paid to help them. They could all rot, and he wouldn't care. He'd rot with them, soon enough.

Howard drove his pickup—which was not quite old enough to be really good, but still better than the new models—home to the two-bedroom house he owned by himself. In his immaculate kitchen, Howard poured himself two fingers of Scotch and a glass of water and went and sat in the wooden chair on his back porch, where he could see the view. Because Howard's house was on the exact edge of town, the view was of nothing but parched earth, cactus, scrubby brush, and the occasional movement of a small animal.

Howard contemplated his aloneness. He was lonely, but damned if he'd bring another woman into his life. His ex-wife lived just across town, but he managed to avoid seeing her most of the time, and he had no children—mercifully for both him and those unborn souls. Still he knew he was lonely, and he had time to kill.

He wanted to reread *King Lear*—now, there was an argument against having children. But he could not sit that long.

So, Howard took his Scotch back to his kitchen and set it on the counter while he prepared, and then ate standing up, two scrambled eggs, toast, and a small salad. Holding the Scotch, he walked back to the porch and looked at the sunset. He had to get out of there.

He went back in the kitchen and cleaned up after himself. A couple of women who had been silly enough to harbor fantasies of reforming this crotchety introvert had had their hopes crushed when they saw inside his house that he had no need of them. He would say the idea of a man needing a woman to keep a place tidy was ridiculous, since he did a better job than any three of them could. The women had to agree.

Howard used the toilet, filled a small water bottle, stuck the bottle into the back pocket of his jeans, put leather work gloves and a thirty-eight caliber revolver into the pockets of his jacket, and walked out the back door—not bothering to lock it—and continued off the porch and into the desert, in a straight line west. The moon would be out, the terrain was flat, and so he didn't worry.

After walking about an hour and a half mostly in a straight line across the unobstructed terrain, Howard saw the fence, and after only a few seconds, found the cactus next to the small boulder that, he knew, marked the opening. Two years previous, Howard had created this portal in the chain-link with bolt cutters, and then had shut it with light wire.

He put on the leather gloves and set about untwisting the wire. When he was finished, the chain link was loose, and he could get through. About ten yards beyond the fence was a low concrete barrier.

Howard looked to the right and found a log of about twelve feet in length. He examined the log carefully, then stomped on it to test for cracks and found none. He dragged the log to the concrete, carefully lifted it over, and then leaned it against the far side of the wall, which dropped about eight feet down from where he stood. He went over the wall and climbed down the log.

The ground was all just dirt for about a hundred feet— Howard believed it was laced with weed killer—and sloped steeply downward. Howard walked down the switch-back trail he had created himself from years of use, found the blacktop road, and walked west in the drainage ditch. At the faintest sound of a car or hint of a headlight he would flatten into the ditch until the car passed.

Howard veered off the road and stopped at the base of a much higher second fence. The tunnel below it was as he had last seen it, and he could see moonlight on the slope on the other side. He stopped and listened for a long while, this being the only spot that scared him into caution. Hearing nothing, he stepped into the tunnel and paused again before climbing the slope.

After another hour, he reached the four-lane, and soon after that, the truck stop loomed above him, "Fuel-Food-Rest" lit in dazzling orange. Howard always enjoyed walking by the parked semi-trailers and cars, seeing some of the older ones that only an old mechanic could appreciate. Avoiding the people was easy, though he was sometimes discomfited by the animal huffing and puffing from the back of a few of the truck cabs.

The restaurant back door was almost always open, the entry hall little used, and Howard had no problem quietly walking in, stealing food, and walking out. *Act like you own the place*, his father had told him, and it worked every time.

Just as easily, Howard sought an appropriate semi, one with California plates, on the west-bound side of the parking lot, one of the older, and rarer ones, with an easily accessible rear end. Los Angeles would be a good visit, just for the hell of it, which was what Howard wanted. He climbed into the back of the trailer.

About an hour later Howard heard the driver walk to and enter the cab. Howard braced himself for the acceleration. A few minutes later, he slept as the big rig cruised toward Los Angeles. At dawn he awoke as the trucker stopped at a diesel station somewhere in the eastern end of the LA sprawl. Howard watched and listened, and noticing nobody about, climbed off, walked quickly away from the truck, and paused by a bench. Nobody looked his way. He found a secluded spot behind a wall and relieved himself.

Around a corner of the wall, Howard just looked. The grubbiness appealed to him, nothing quite as scrubbed as everything in his hometown. Despite the early hour, a few people moved about, driving, walking, waiting at bus stops. Howard found the presence of people from, shall we say, a lower "socio-economic status" comforting. They might yearn for the squeaky-clean super-suburbs. Howard doubted that they could appreciate what they had.

Howard wanted to see more. Howard wanted downtown, glitzy Bunker Hill with skid row and the barrio close by, where the semi would be unlikely to go, so he walked in his own furtive way and looked around for his next ride.

He smelled the drunk before he saw him, the flammable breath wafting through the smog. Not a street bum, this guy was well dressed, if you liked open-collar black shirts, gold chains, and patent leather loafers. In his left hand was a whiskey bottle in a bag, no doubt just purchased from the station convenience store. "What the hell," the guy said, in a growl that matched the evil in his eyes.

Howard and the guy faced each other on the asphalt, Howard preferring to back off but not seeing an obvious way, and feeling ornery himself, not yet having had breakfast. Still, when the guy reached for him, Howard took two steps back and the drunk stumbled. Howard took a few more steps back, but the drunk righted himself with surprising quickness given his glazed eyes, and Howard tripped on something, backwards. He hit the pavement next to a car and slid under it.

"What the fuck!" the drunk yelled. "That's *my* car." Howard saw the drunk's knees on the pavement, then his groping left hand, and then his face. Howard shot him directly in his big, blood-shot, left eye. The drunk groaned and rolled over onto his right side, but he was still blowing his noxious breath in Howard's direction. Howard slid out from under the car, stood up, and shot the guy once more, in his left temple. That would probably do. Howard scuttled away. Some people had turned and looked in his direction, but as far as he could tell, nobody had seen him.

41

Despite his frustration at how fate had thwarted his plans, Howard let his better judgment prevail and found a truck headed back toward his home. He had to jump off at an interchange and walk to another fueling stop, and it would take longer than the trip out, but Howard had done it before, and he would do it again this time, with any luck arriving at his house about a day later.

Howard had never killed a man before. He was surprised at how he felt neither remorse nor regret, neither triumph nor bloodlust. It seemed only a small thing that gave him a small smile as he relaxed but never allowed himself to sleep among a load of oranges, the shiny smooth skins almost comfortable, cool where his own skin touched them, with just the right degree of give and shelter from the sixty-five-mile-an-hour wind that coursed above him as the semi rolled through the desert.

Howard climbed off at the big truck-stop convenience store, intending to steal food before trekking back to his fence hole, but as he walked from shadow to shadow on the circuitous route he knew so well, Howard saw something that stopped him.

He had met one of the teenagers, the big one with the swagger and confidence that Howard recognized as the products of youth, testosterone, and ignorance, so he was not totally surprised that this kid had backed up what had seemed to be a bluff. Shit. Howard had even told the kid what to do, given him a how-to manual for making trouble, figuring it unlikely that the kid would actually make it. Trouble was exactly what was needed, but the risks were great, and this kid and his buddies were not ready for them.

8

Gerald, LaTasha, Astrid, Elmer, Colin, and Bryce stood together in darkness on the metallic floor. Just enough moonlight filtered through the vent opening to show walls and ceiling of a hallway that stretched out into nearly pitch darkness, broken only by a hint of light through a tiny opening in the far distance. They'd jumped about four feet down from the vent.

They stood, in their jeans and khakis, t-shirts showing logos of their favorite bands, jackets more for fashion than warmth, athletic shoes never used for sport, and stared into the unknown. What they saw was nothing, which did not frighten them because nothing was what they saw all the time when they looked forward into the unknowns of their lives, and not *nothing* as in, *we don't know what's coming*, but as in, *whatever it is, it will be nothing.*

They waited for Bryce to turn on one of the small LED lights they all carried to avoid draining their phones, and then they saw more walls and floor and a faint opening in the distance. They shuffled forward on the smooth metallic floor toward the aperture ahead, which grew until after a few minutes it became just another view of the desert ground and sky, through another metal grid. They stopped where the floor reached an edge beyond which it pitched downward.

"We go back the same way?" LaTasha asked.

"The only way," Bryce said.

"And the cops back there?" Colin asked.

"They won't lock us out," Bryce said, "because they want us back."

"And it won't help us one way or the other how soon we get back," Astrid said. Her hard little blue eyes gleaming in the moonlight, she seemed more eager than Bryce.

"Gerald first," Bryce said. He pointed his light down the slope.

"Just like on the old playground," Gerald said. He sat down on the joint where the flat floor met the slope, thrust his feet out, pushed off with his hands, and slid down, stopping himself with his feet against the grid at the bottom. He pushed himself to the side and motioned for the others to follow, which they did—Astrid, LaTasha, Elmer, and Colin, while Bryce held his light for them and joined them last. The floor was, in fact, nearly as smooth as a playground slide.

Bryce moved to the side opposite the others and pulled a ratchet wrench from his jacket pocket. Tied to the wrench handle was a rope loop, which he put around his right wrist. The wire grid was quite large, and he was able to reach through it, while holding the wrench, to loosen a bolt on the outside. He removed the bolt, put it in his jacket pocket, then squatted down and removed another. Then he went to the side where Colin and the others stood, and as he removed another high bolt, Gerald and Astrid walked around him and held the grid at its center. Bryce again squatted, and as he removed another bolt, he told Elmer to go to the opposite end and hold the grid, and Colin to stay next to him.

After pocketing the fourth bolt, Bryce said, "Okay, let's lower it to the ground." The grid touched ground with about a foot sticking up into the opening in which they stood. "Now, push it out, and let go," Bryce said. They followed directions, and the grid made a metallic sound as it hit the ground.

Bryce turned to Colin and grinned. "There used to be twelve bolts, but we found that four would hold it, so what the hell. We'll use the grid as a ladder to get back up."

"And the rope," Colin said, "is so you don't lose the wrench outside."

"Right," Bryce said. "Alright folks, lets go. Gerald first."

"Wait," Elmer said. "How did you know about this, the first time? How did you know to bring the wrench? How did you know the right size?"

Bryce, still grinning his evil prankster grin, said he knew people who knew things.

Gerald sat on the opening and pushed himself off, thumping onto the ground below. The others followed, Bryce last.

The ground sloping away from the opening was mostly bare dirt, with rocks and scree about, and no vegetation except for scattered tufts of tall brown grass. The grid that had covered the opening lay in front of them.

Bryce led them down the slope until they came to a narrow, barely defined path, where he turned left. Gerald followed, and over his shoulder said, "If you haven't been here before, this trail was here the first time Bryce and I came, so we were definitely not the first."

Colin considered that others had been out before them. He thought of Vikings and Irish monks getting to North America long before Columbus.

Still on the narrow path, Bryce led the group of teenagers around a corner, then stopped when they could all see the view. He turned and grinned at them. Astrid and Gerald grinned back. The first-timers—LaTasha, Colin, and Elmer—were mystified. Searching for a clue, Colin looked from Bryce to Astrid to Gerald. "So," he said. "A gas station mini-mart. What's the big deal? We've got about fifty of those inside."

Nobody spoke. Bryce, Astrid, and Gerald kept grinning. As Colin felt increasingly perplexed, LaTasha said, slowly, "Something's weird, though. The slope, the perspective, is, just, *weird*."

"It is weird," Colin said.

Grinning more broadly, Bryce said, "Follow me."

They walked down the trail, which now made frequent switchbacks. All of them, even the three veterans of the outside, when they weren't watching the trail, were staring at the mini-mart, unable to move their eyes from its ordinary cinder-block architecture, its neon and plastic signs glowing in the desert night, and its plain gas pump bays, where a couple of cars were parked. They proceeded down the trail almost to the two-lane blacktop that led to the rest-stop oasis glowing before them.

"My god," Colin said. "It's huge. I don't think I've seen a mini-mart this big."

Bryce and Gerald laughed.

"It *is*," LaTasha said. "It's beyond humongous."

"The fuck are you kids doing here?" That last voice, a man's, came from somewhere in shadows by the roadside.

The kids froze. "Who wants to know," Bryce said.

"Lighten up, Bryce." The same voice.

"Howard," Bryce said.

Howard Sturges stepped part way out of the shadows to beckon the kids into them. With Bryce leading, they followed and watched as Howard, short and lean, did what they had seen no other accomplish, which was to intimidate Bryce, half a head taller and probably forty pounds heavier. "Guys," Bryce said, "this is Howard."

Collin, at least, understood with almost complete certainty that Howard had been the person Bryce knew who knew things.

"Well?" Howard said.

Bryce had no answer.

"I told you," Howard said. "I explained it."

Bryce, in the manner of a boy being asked to explain a transgression that was as plain as day and therefore beyond explanation, was dumb.

"How?" Howard said.

"The vent," Bryce said.

"Shit," Howard said.

"That's how you told me," Bryce said, unable to hide the whiney sound, even from himself.

Howard paused, and then said, "Go back the same way, right now. Don't wait. Don't hang around, don't explore any more. Just go back." He paused again. "Understand?" It sounded like a question, but plainly was not.

"Sure, Howard," Bryce said, and added, "Whatever," a small step towards regaining not dignity, but adolescent arrogance.

Howard stood two feet from his face and glared at him.

"Let's go, guys," Bryce said. "We'll listen to Howard."

Howard did not speak, smile, or clap Bryce on the shoulder. He just continued to glare, anger radiating from his face, as the group turned around and walked back the way they had come, with only a couple of glances back at what was, indeed, a rather large mini-mart gas station.

9

4&k3l)(n saw the messages, in and out. The fun was in figuring out the thing that tied them together, the thing that was hardly ever mentioned b36ecause all the messengers knew all about it already. Discovering the shape of that underlying unspoken thing was always the thrill that kept 4&k3l)(n going, like reverse-engineering entire lives and all the endeavors and enterprises that held them together, doing his thinking like a novelist in reverse, the real fun being that some (a little? most?) of the novel had already been written but the rest was growing before his eyes.

He had defeated the argument that he was wasting his life as a voyeur. He had never spoken to anyone about it, but he did not need to because he knew all sides of the debate too well, having heard them all inside his own head. The final indisputable point, the "deciding factor," as his internal debate monitor said, was the simple artistic beauty of the thing. *You say what I do is passive? In no way is it passive! For the essence of art is selectivity—the artist must choose what to see, and then decide what of that to expose, what to bring forward to the surface and what to leave in the background, what to emphasize with vivid color and sharp outline and what to leave muted and fuzzy, and finally what to put in the central focus.*

Was that not what 4&k3l)(n did? You say, fine, but the artist cannot simply observe, the artist has to create! But do I not create? If the occasional nudge, the shifting of a piece of furniture or re-directing of a projectile, no matter how small, is not creative, then what is? Remember the butterfly wing flap that starts a series of small events that culminate in a major event on the other side of the globe? What if I just slightly touch the wing as it starts to move—what then?

A scientist postulated the "butterfly effect." Artists and scientists share a common creative urge, the difference being that artists study reality and then create a new one, while scientists study reality to change it. So you may say I'm more scientist than artist, but the scientist has a goal of somehow improving reality—curing a disease or enabling a technology or inventing a better way to kill people—whereas I have no goal at all but to see what happens if I change one—or two or more—tiny bits of reality.

Unlike a scientist, of course, I have no control group, no way of proving a hypothesis by observing what happens with, or without, my little changes. If only I could! If only time-travel were possible, even if only in little minutes-long sprints! But, on the other hand, that would take away the fun! So there is my creative urge, based on impulse, daring to move without knowing the destination, free of any and all practical purpose—which makes me an artist, right? Q.E.D.

4&k3l)(n would watch patiently, learn what he could of reality, before nudging.

So, now, as at many other times, he watched the dialog, and examined the data that may, or may not, have prompted it.

Subject: Roaming charges
Since our last meeting more roaming charges have been incurred, though in larger volumes than before, as observed by my associate. However, the infrastructure is sound and further action beyond simple repair seems unnecessary. I will post you on all.

Subject: Re: Roaming charges
Outstanding news!
Your last status report was encouraging. Your infrastructure goals have been met, and your budget has been limited to

within stated tolerances, given the inevitability of small over-
runs. Nevertheless, more proaction is required if problems
are to be avoided. Fires do not start spontaneously, they
always have a cause. In your next status report we hope to
see better planning aimed at finding the causes before the
fires begin. Please remember our last discussion.
Subject: Re: Re: Roaming charges
Thank you for your encouragement. I assure you, I will do my
best to prevent the production of the fuel that fires need.
Measures beyond basic prevention will not be needed.

Ah! Such delightful use of trite metaphor! Such portent!
Such clumsy effort to obscure what was already encrypted!
Such nauseating bureaucratic abuse of the passive voice! Such
opportunity for creativity!

But not quite yet.

10

Samuel Giles had a normal family, a wife, a son, nine, and a daughter, six, all of whom he truly loved, and their lives together were harmonious. He had a well-paying job. With his wife's school principal job they had a handsome income. They had a television-worthy Spanish-style, three-bedroom house with all the comforts. Due to the government contract, their jobs were secure and recession-proof. Although Sam sometimes felt unease at news of Congressional budget negotiations, his program was way too secret—even from Congress—to ever get a mention, so why worry?

They chafed at being unable to leave town more, but Sam's position allowed them one vacation a year. The aftermath of the vacations, though, the weirdness of the ban on speaking about them outside the family and explaining that to their kids, was discouraging, so this year they just stayed home.

Sam's job was good: challenging, engaging, important. Sometimes too stressful, but what job wasn't?

He was afraid he was developing an intestinal problem: cramps, occasional mild diarrhea. Nothing to see a doctor about, but on his own he had started to ease off caffeine.

Loren had asked him, "How the hell does a wife tell the difference between a secretive man and a man who has to keep secrets?"

Samuel had no answer. He would evade such questions with jokes. For years he'd thought he could handle secrecy, split his life into the secret job part and the open family part. He had worked as hard at maintaining that divide as he had at the job itself, while trying to not work at the family part, to just let it flow.

So he was not entirely surprised but still stricken when Loren said they should consider therapy. "Something has to change," she said. "You've been morose," she said. "I know you are trying," she said, "but you're getting very hard to be around. I'm feeling it, and so are the kids, in case you haven't noticed."

Indeed, he had noticed.

Therapy, sure.

Project management had grudgingly sprung for a counselor, and in recent years had circulated brochures featuring color photos of good-looking, smiling families on one side, and black-and-white close-ups of worried, frowning individuals on the other, with paragraphs urging employees to seek help if they "suffered from moodiness, anxiety, or a temptation to self-medicate." But engineers didn't trust therapists, and government engineers didn't trust government, and so the brochures, and the counselor herself, who had little to do but design the brochures, served mainly as a reason for staff to vent to each other. *Oh, yeah. I'm going to go to that little tart and tell her that what I do is insane, and the way I have to live is insane, and that I sold my soul to work on an insane project. So why shouldn't I be insane?*

Samuel knew little about therapy, having taken not one psychology class in college or read a single book on the subject. But he doubted the effectiveness of therapy, as a couple or solo, where the main stressor was a forbidden subject.

So with Loren, Sam evaded.

"So, what exactly, is your job these days?" she asked.

"Infrastructure. I manage infrastructure."

"And you think an elementary school principal is smart enough to know what that means and dumb enough to accept it?"

No way. Loren was no dummy.

Having started as a network engineer, where all he did was build and maintain what the science guys needed for doing whatever it was they did, Samuel had progressed—if higher pay was the measure of progress—to managing the staff who did what he had actually once been interested in doing, all the way to "Manager of Ancillary Services"—now, *there* was a nice, tasty mouthful—at which he had to manage not only the network staff, from the degreed engineers down to the technicians who assembled the racks that held the servers, but also the electricians and cable-pullers, and the facilities managers and their maintenance crews, including janitors, who, like everyone on this project, got more money than anyone in a corresponding job could get anywhere else. Samuel knew about the Peter Principle, and figured he had aced it, reaching a level where it would be obvious to anyone who looked that he could go no higher.

But to his boss, Barry Hagenstopple, it had not been obvious. Or, maybe it had, Barry being the most intelligent person Samuel had ever known. Behind Barry's back he was called "E.G.," for "evil genius," though Samuel was not sure that Barry would object to being called that to his face, even leaving aside Sam's certainty that Barry knew most of what was said and done behind his back, or anywhere else around the project, for that matter.

In seeming deference to the Peter Principle, Barry had stopped promoting Samuel. On the other hand, he had broadened his "scope of responsibility," "enhancing" Sam's job laterally, if not vertically, "increasing his portfolio." Had Barry noticed that Samuel loathed managing people, and that he tried to compensate for the loathing by being as kind to his staff as possible? Had Barry decided that the very kindness that made Samuel's staff like him would be the perfect counterweight if Sam were given the additional authority over project security—a responsibility that required, let's face it, a dose of meanness, from which a totally mean person might go quietly berserk.

Perhaps Sam was overthinking, perhaps not even Barry had that degree of perverted wisdom, but whatever the case, "Ancillary Services" had for some time now included project security. Sitting in the guest chair in Barry's office, absorbing the news, Sam had asked the obvious: Why not the FBI or some other federal police agency? Barry had smiled—not the condescending, sneering smile, but the conspiratorial, we're-in-this-together smile, which was, of course, the scarier one. *We have to do this ourselves, buddy, we can't trust them, or anyone else. And (wink) the money won't be bad, either.* After that, Samuel had considered the possibility that Barry had simply picked Samuel as the latest object of his sadism, which would have been consistent with Barry's other behaviors, except that for Barry the project was everything, and people were nothing. On the other hand, Barry's mind was capable of embracing both, wasn't it? Barry, the once-boy-now-old-man genius, the original father of "the project," with the unbelievable and intimidating capacity to seize simultaneously both the smallest details (e.g., persistent air conditioning problems, Sam's sanity) and the grandest vision (the project's ultimate success). Barry—the combination of Henry Ford, Bill Gates, Michael Jordan, and Captain Bligh—with the relentless determination to *win*.

How could Sam tell Loren about the security part of his "portfolio"? He was afraid to even raise the subject, to even hint at his being the enforcer of all that fine print that Loren and everyone else saw but few fully understood. So, he evaded.

Barry was harder to evade than Loren, especially when Sam was in that same chair where he had frequently fought the impulse to physically squirm like a six-year-old whether

Barry was promoting or berating him, squirming being the only option when neither quitting nor resisting was viable.

"You asked for this meeting," Barry said.

Sam considered that opening statement: It was an indisputable fact, explicable in the small world of Sam's employment, but not in the larger world of good, evil, and beauty. No time for such limitless speculation now, however. "They're getting out again," Sam said. "You know I do my best, but it's like," and Sam paused, looking for *what it was like* in the photo, on the wall, of Barry with a former U.S. Secretary of Something. Failing to find it, he said, "You know what it's like."

Barry sat, his hands folded on his desk, with only an occasional glance at his computer screen. "Indeed I do," he said.

"They're kids, it's like joy-riding," Sam said. "They always come back."

"Have they been seen?" Barry asked.

"No press reports."

Barry waited.

"My friends outside have seen them. There's no other way I could know. In town, and by the convenience store."

"How many times?"

"Once in each place."

"How?"

"By accident," Sam said. "Just happpenstance."

"So you don't know totals?"

"No."

"How'd they get out?" Barry asked, his tone shifting from neutral to prosecutorial.

Sam shrugged.

"It matters," Barry said, and Sam could hear the sound of incipient boiling.

"It's always different," Sam said, trying to hide his despair. "A hole in a fence, a tunnel, some overlooked gap in a system somewhere." He waved his arms to encompass the universe.

"Bribery?" Barry said, his voice dangerously quiet.

Sam leaned forward, his elbows on his knees, and looked at the carpet. He shook his head, "The last case of that was a couple years ago." The memory was not pleasant—but then, few memories of this business were.

Barry swiveled sideways toward his window, leaned back in his executive chair and clasped his hands behind his head. The squeak of the chair made Sam look up at him.

There was a long, uncomfortable silence.

"The chips installed in them are pretty useless, aren't they?" Barry said to the window, speculatively, as if about weather.

"Totally, unless we catch one individual and scan him, or her, and then all it does is speed the identification."

"Yeah," Barry said. "The chips were another good idea that failed."

Another long silence.

"Barry," Sam said. It was a plea.

Barry sighed at the ceiling. "Only thing that works, Sam," he said.

"Only temporarily," Sam said, clutching at straws.

"Of course. From time to time we all need a dose of something." Barry swiveled back and faced Sam across the desk. "And then, after a while, we need it again."

Sam said nothing.

"What does Cheng say?"

"I haven't spoken to him lately. I expect he'll have ideas about who they are, but nothing definite."

"I don't totally trust Cheng."

Sam thought that redundant, since Barry totally trusted nobody.

"But talk to him," Barry said. "Make him give you a name."

Sam said nothing.

"Sam," Barry said, Sam knowing that the utterance of his name was always a prelude to an indisputable order, "don't make me talk to Cheng myself. I don't like talking to him."

Of course he didn't. Cheng was human.

11

Drew got a voice message from a secretary at a large Catholic church, requesting his services for a stiff named Juan Goldfarb. The paid-for obituary the secretary emailed him said Goldfarb had raised himself from poverty first by expanding his father's dry-cleaning shop into a string of franchises, "Goldfarb's Quality Cleaners," and then by successfully investing in both residential and commercial real estate. "Despite accumulating great wealth," the obit said, "Juan stayed in the blue-collar neighborhood of his birth, where he built for his family a large house. Juan loved having neighborhood kids over to use his pool, once saying that he thought of his house as not just his own home, but 'as a community center'."

Drew phoned the church secretary. "The obit doesn't mention cause of death," he said. "I was just wondering."

There was silence, and then the sound of a deep breath. "I can't comment on that," the secretary said.

"What? You can't comment?"

"No, sir. I'm sorry." She sounded like she was trying hard to be pleasant.

"I don't understand," Drew said. "It's not like I'm a reporter. Since I'll be speaking at the funeral, it's of interest to me."

"Father Henry will cover that part," the secretary said.

Drew had no argument. "But I also wondered," he said, and then stopped.

"What, sir? What else were you wondering?"

But Drew was wondering, once again, how Juan Goldfarb had come to lead such an ugly life, had become so repellent to the people from whom he should have expected love, that his survivors saw fit to pay for a professional mourner. The secretary seemed unlikely to have an answer, so Drew just thanked her and hung up.

The funeral, three days after the call, appeared to have, for Drew, a record turnout, cars filling the parking lot early and crowding the neighboring streets. After parking several blocks from the church, Drew strolled through the hot afternoon sun with people who seemed to share the attitude of bored obligation common to Drew's funeral audiences, but were of a more diverse mixture of race and class. For the most part, Drew's crowds—he had begun to think of them more as his than the deceased's—were of the classes who wore dark, warm, uncomfortable clothing to any religious service, somber or not. The current group included those, but also a large contingent whose budget or taste in formal clothing meant clean jeans and white shirts, ties optional, for the men, and business casual for the women.

Before the service, in Father Henry's office, Drew asked him about the cause of death.

"His casket is closed," the priest said. "That's probably all you need to know."

"So it was an accident?"

Father Henry shrugged.

"Suicide?"

"No. Definitely not suicide."

Drew said, "All of my, clients? I'm sorry, I still don't know what to call them, have died relatively young. They're mostly middle-aged or a little older, and mostly they have strokes or heart attacks, just a few car accidents."

"So?"

"So why did your secretary say she couldn't comment on the cause of death? Why do you say nothing?"

"I know what you do, what you'll say, so what does it matter to you?" the priest said, then took Drew's arm and said, "I'm sorry. That sounded harsh, didn't it? Of course you care. You seem like a nice young man." He shrugged again. "There's an investigation. Come on, we've got to start."

The big crowd in the big gothic church was restless, even more so than most. Drew was able to get their attention, but he saw much less emotion in them than usual. They seemed more interested in his performance as performance, even smiling at times, as if this were a play, and, a few of them, towards the end, chuckling and snorting at "If a clod be washed away by the sea," and "a begging of misery." The chuckles were short, but without any apparent embarrassment about laughing in church.

Afterward, in the buffet in the church's large recreation hall there was wine, the idea of which was just enough to make Drew stay, given that his curiosity and fascination had recently grown to compete with his repugnance for what he now mentally labeled "death festivals." Ignoring the food, he stood with a glass of red in a corner of the room, watching people who might as well have been at a wedding reception. After a time, a much younger man stood and sipped next to him. The younger man wore dark slacks, a white crewneck knitted shirt—too nice to be called a tee—with a flashy gray sport coat over it. His brown hair was longish and slicked straight back.

"Nice speech," the young man said.

Drew grunted a thanks, bracing himself for the usual expression of gratitude he got for making a wasted life seem a little less so, or for making life in general, if not the one life in question, seem valuable.

"I mean, I know you didn't write it. I read it in school. But you said it well."

Drew sipped. As minutes passed, the laughter and camaraderie in the room became almost boisterous. Adults were drinking heavily and children were running around, waiters struggling to avoid them.

"I figure you must speak a lot at things like this."

Drew was not certain what this young guy meant.

"It's a paying job, right?"

Drew, uneasy, glanced at the guy, who kept his eyes on the party and sipped his own red.

"It's okay, I understand," the guy said. "I mean, the priest gets paid too, right?" He sipped and continued, "What I meant was, you speak for money where nobody else wants to speak for free, because nobody else can think of much good to say about the dead guy."

Drew turned to look straight at this young man, wondering if he could explain what the priest could not. The man put his hand out. "Magdelano Goldfarb," he said. "Call me Mag. Juan was my father."

"Drew Kristopher," Drew said and shook Mag's hand. "I'm sorry for your loss," he added.

Mag shrugged and said, "So, you do this much?"

The words were aggressive, but in the tone Drew heard an offer, an opening to a possible trade, and his only exchange medium was honesty. "Occasionally," Drew said. "I'm an actor. Jobs are hard to find."

"Yeah, for me too," Mag said. "Actor, huh?" He paused. "Makes sense, you could say a speech like that. I could never do it."

"What do you do?"

"Fix cars. Play with computers, do apps. Go to classes at the community college. I don't know."

A group of people nearby erupted in loud laughter at some shared joke. Drew and Mag looked at them.

"My father was a shit," Mag said. "My brothers don't like to hear me say that and I wish it was a lie, but it's true." He drained his glass. "He did shitty things to people. Sometimes, really shitty. Tried to make it up by buying them things, inviting the neighborhood kids to use his pool." Seeing Drew's raised eyebrows, he added, "You saw the obit, huh? My mother wrote it. Those kids aren't really my friends. How could they be? They knew what my dad was, and I hated that they knew."

"Why are you telling me this?" Drew said.

"One time, when we were little, my little brother Rory and I were playing in that pool. Dad had left a pair of his shoes on the deck, and Rory and I splashed 'em." Mag sighed and frowned. "We knew he'd be mad, they were nice, leather shoes, but, hell, Dad had left them right where they were bound to get splashed, so how mad could he be?" Mag looked at Drew for an answer. Drew shrugged. "Dad grabbed Rory by the back of his neck, like he was a dog, and slugged him in the ass. I mean, punched, not spanked him. I was standing right there, and Dad backhanded me in the face, broke my nose."

Drew said nothing.

"So, that's just one example. People here could give you others, even worse. Not too many tears in this room, as you might have noticed. People came hoping for his money, but mostly just to see each other and celebrate."

"How'd he die?" Drew asked.

Mag snorted. "It was weird. We don't really know. But he was over in a part of town he liked. Dad had an unnatural interest in drug dealers and whores, and he liked to hang out and drink with them on the street, even though he had no problem drinking at home. I don't know, Dad was always looking for people he could impress. Anyway, I figure he was drunk. One of my cousins told me the cops said it looked like he was stabbed, twice, in the face. In the eye, I think, and in the side of his head, not with a knife, but with the point of something, like an ice pick. How do you get stabbed with an ice pick in a liquor store parking lot? One of the dealers, one of the whores maybe? No arrests, yet. His body was next to his car."

Drew, not knowing what to say, finished his wine. The party was approaching raucous.

"So, when you have a father like that," Mag said, "and you see him acting like a shit, always mean." Mag shook his head. "Well, at least in my case, it made me want to help people. But I don't know how. The priest asked me about joining his bunch, but, hell, I'm hardly even Catholic anymore, really, and I like girls. So, I saw you, and I thought, he helps people. Maybe he'd have an idea."

Drew, his old acting dreams shriveled, with no girlfriend and few other friends, in an unhappy present with no sense of future, was truly astonished that anyone, even a person more than a decade younger, could think him capable of advice. Drew, help people? Is that what he did? Is that what he wished he did? "I really don't know," Drew said. "Social worker? Teacher? Therapist?"

Without apparently noticing Drew's bewilderment, Mag shook his head. "I've thought about all those. I don't know, nothing appeals to me yet. But I'm just nineteen, so."

From the way he spoke, Drew could not tell if being "just nineteen" was good or bad in Mag's mind. Not wanting to appear helpless, and wanting even less to actually *be* helpless, Drew, on impulse, pulled a card from his jacket pocket, the one that said, *Drew Kristopher, Funeral Speaker*. "Send me an email. Maybe I'll have an idea," Drew said.

"Okay," Mag said. "Thanks a lot."

"One other thing," Drew said, and, without knowing exactly why, got Mag to tell him where Juan Goldfarb's body had been found, and where his house was.

When Drew left the church, the party was still going. He drove first to Juan's house. Obviously, Goldfarb had bought four adjoining lots, knocked down the small homes that must have looked much like the other frame and stucco one-story houses in the neighborhood, and put up an enormous frame, stucco, and marble monstrosity of a mansion, complete with second-story balconies on the three sides Drew could see. Drew stopped his car and stared at it for a few moments, noticing the enormous front door, the fake exposed wood beams, and the topiary deer in the front yard, the way the whole thing seemed intended to intimidate the people living around it. Was this piece of kitsch the home of an unloved man for whom the bell tolled?

Five or six miles from the house was the little strip mall with the liquor store. Drew parked on the street and walked the sidewalk to the store, which was at the corner of two broad avenues, lined with more strip malls and store fronts. Across one street was a gas station. Next to that was a payday lender. Across the other street was a small grocery and a bar.

He went into the liquor store, selected a six-pack of beer, and went to the counter. After paying he asked to see the manager, who was, in fact, the guy behind the counter. Drew asked about the body found in his lot just two weeks previous.

"I don't know nothing about it," the man said. "One of the ladies who frequent this street at night came in and said the guy had been lying there for quite a while, maybe just passed out drunk, but they said there was blood. I went out and saw him"—he pointed out the window diagonally across his lot— "lying right there next to his Beemer. I called nine-one-one." He lifted his hands, his shoulders, and his eyebrows, all at once, showing that he had no more to say.

Drew thanked him and walked outside. The parking lot was ordinary asphalt with no trace on it to show that one of Drew's assholes had died there.

12

The kids returned on the same route that had taken them to the truck stop, with Howard trailing them behind, watching them, at times sounding a grunt or a "go!" as if herding goats, which it seemed he was, given that they were *kids* walking among cactus and scraggly weeds, without uttering a word themselves.

At a fork in the trail, unnoticed by the kids on the way out, Howard told them to go right, which they did. Howard stood at the fork, hands on hips, watching them walk on, occasionally glancing at him over their shoulders, until they reached the far side of the ditch on the other side of the road, where Bryce, the big one, motioned the others forward, waved to Howard, then disappeared with them beyond the small rise.

The teenagers, subdued now, followed the trail back to the looming steel protuberance, against which they leaned the grate. Gerald held the it steady while the others climbed, one by one, up into the opening, and finally he followed. Bryce handed the bolts and the wrench to Astrid. At Bryce's instructions, they hauled the grate up and held it, as Astrid, reaching through the grate with the wrench, its rope looped over her wrist, attached a bolt on each side, then added the rest.

Still without speaking, they held their flashlights down and shuffled through the steel corridor to the opening at the other end, where they dropped down to the concrete roof below. Only after Bryce, with help from the rest, had replaced the other, smaller grate with its machine screws holding it in place, did they hear Cheng walking the dusty ground below them. He was alone.

"You might as well come down," Cheng said.

They all sat on the bunker-like roof and eased down the short drop. They clustered before Cheng, not confrontationally but patiently as if waiting for confirmation of something.

"See anyone?" Cheng said.

Bryce shrugged. The others were motionless and quiet.

Cheng waited.

"There were a lot of people," Colin said.

Cheng took a breath as if preparing a speech, but then said only, "Go home."

"That's it?" Bryce asked, sounding as if he felt cheated.

Cheng took a step toward Bryce and squinted at him, managing to look down on him even though Bryce was the taller. "What more do you want?" Cheng said, suddenly bitter. "You expecting a prize? A medal? A trip to the jail, which would amount to the same thing?" Cheng stopped, but Bryce had no answer. Colin watched what seemed less a conflict than a struggle for understanding. Cheng continued, "So I take you to the jail and call all your parents," and he turned his squint toward each of them, one by one, "and we'll all have that conversation that, believe me, I have already heard, taken part in, so many times that they all blend together, except for the first. And your parents will come for you and look angry or ashamed, but mostly just regretful, just wishing they could have raised you somewhere else, wishing they had more options, and now despite how hard they've tried, how they've struggled, it's too late for you, too late, and you've been ruined by this place just like they were." Cheng stopped suddenly, used up.

The kids, on the cusp between adolescence and adulthood, were unused to such emotional candor from adults, having seen it only as anger directed at them or between their parents. They had no reply.

"Go home," Cheng said again, quickly backing away and turning, almost running the twenty yards to his car, as if he, not the kids, were the terrified one. They watched him do a k-turn, throwing gravel as he sped away, turning on his lights only after covering at least a hundred yards.

Bryce started for his parents' SUV and the rest followed, finding the same seats they had occupied on the earlier trip, remaining silent until Bryce drove off the dirt road onto the smooth pavement of the highway.

"We couldn't tell them about Howard," Bryce said. "It would have been wrong."

Nobody argued.

"What did Chief Schmitz mean? What was he talking about?" LaTasha said.

Colin, sitting next to her, turned to look straight at her for the first time since she had joined them in Bryce's parents' SUV. Noticing, she returned his look, but nobody spoke for a long time. Then Colin said, addressing the car but looking at LaTasha, "He told us that we think we made a discovery, but it seems like they made it first, before us. We're not the first. And he was telling us that what it leads to is bad."

Colin broke his gaze from LaTasha's and saw in the rear-view mirror Bryce's hardening eyes.

"We're going back," Bryce said through his teeth. "At least I am," he added, leaving tacit the dare he threw at the rest of them.

Astrid, in the middle front seat, unseen by all but Bryce and Gerald, put her hand on Bryce's thigh.

Gerald smiled and said, "Cool."

"Maybe," Elmer said.

Bryce dropped them, one by one, at their homes.

———

As Colin left Bryce's parents' SUV, he wanted to tell LaTasha that he wanted to date her but instead all he said was, "Chief Schmitz was warning us. But about our parents?"

His parents were in the living room, off the hall from the front door. It was late, but not too late. Colin suspected afterwards that his pause at the front door, the act of simply standing motionless in the hallway in sight of his parents on the couch, was his unconscious cue to them to start the scene.

His father, Roberto Fairchild, on the couch, met his eyes. Roberto turned to his wife, and Colin saw their unspoken understanding.

"You've been outside," Roberto said, a simple statement of fact.

Colin stood in the hallway.

"Colin, honey," his mother Grace said, "come in."

Colin walked slowly to the armchair across from the couch. Grace turned the TV off.

His father looked at him, then down at his feet propped on the coffee table. His mother stared vaguely in the same direction, and Colin involuntarily looked in the same place, as if expecting to see the same hazy and semi-transparent picture appearing to them in the air.

"We know what it's like," Grace said.

His father now looked at him as well. "It's bad, Colin," Roberto said. "Nothing good can come from going out there."

They were both looking at him now, one face of sympathetic maternal suffering and one of paternal, masculine shared knowledge, and Colin suddenly felt pity for them both.

"We die out there, son," his father said. "They don't take prisoners."

Colin had expected a fight, but neither parent said anything more. His mother began to cry and his father put his arm around her shoulder and pulled her to him, and their eyes never left Colin's.

Colin's parents were both tall, upright, and handsome, diligent at their jobs and enthusiastic and warm in their family. When Colin thought about them, he always wondered how they could be so *certain*. And why wasn't he?

What Colin blurted next surprised even himself. "I want to go to Harvard," he said.

His mother gasped and his father snorted. "Honey," his mother said, "you can't go to Harvard."

Colin nodded, or thought he did, a movement so slight that even he was not sure of it. Slowly he rose from the chair and went upstairs to his room.

13

From Colin's Journal

What the fuck, what have we seen? Where have we been? I guess I've heard stories about what is out there, about bigger people, but until you see it I do not think you can believe it. At least I could not. Now I have seen it, but I am still not sure I can believe it.

It was just a mini-mart with a gas station like we have here, only it looked like some weird perspective shot in a movie where things look bigger than they really are for some kind of symbolic purpose. Only it was real!!! The mini-mart and the gas pumps and the cars and the trucks. And the people!!! I mean, I have never seen the King Kong model at Universal in person, just on TV, but I swear the people at that gas station looked that big. At least.

I was crazy after that, like I was on some drug. We all were, except maybe for Bryce and Gerald who were grinning in this knowing way like they had just turned us on to weed for the first time and were like, "Now you know what it's like." Astrid looked pissed for some reason I don't understand. She kept saying, "Fucking Howard," and then Bryce would say, "Don't worry about it," and "It won't be the last time," like he was trying to calm her down.

And then the cops! I thought we were going to have to phone our parents from the police station, which would have sucked royally. But the chief was really nice. I don't understand why.

And finally my parents??!!! My Dad, who had got so pissed off about my stud, and my Mom, who always worries over me like I was still a little boy, didn't get angry about this. They knew. Like they understood what happened. I guess maybe they have been outside too, when they were my age. And what was I suddenly talking about Harvard for? Like college was the first thing on my mind after a night like that? I felt just weird and embarrassed, like if they had just watched me smoking weed or losing my virginity or something.

It did not help that I was so close to LaTasha in the car, both ways. I mean it was nice but I had to keep looking down to see what was showing in my pants.

My parents were like telling me that thing adults always do, without the words maybe, about how some day I would understand. I guess maybe they are right, but it's still hard to picture myself like them, ever.

14

Just an ordinary small-town police chief, that's what Cheng was. Tough enough, friendly enough, sensitive enough, respected but not feared. Dispensing security feelings— *everything will be okay, just take two deep breaths and call me in the morning.* Or, better, *don't call me, there's nothing to see here, nothing to talk about, nothing to fear.*

And there wasn't, really. No poverty, perfect economy, low crime rate, occasional traffic violations, hell-raising teenagers or "under twenty-five, mostly male" drinking, fighting over girls or just for the hell of it. Place was a goddamn twenty-first century Mayberry, only instead of gleamingly all white, it had every color there was, every ethnic group, every sexual orientation, and all united by their sanded, polished, lacquer-coated, candy-apple red, white, and blue suburban *American-ness*.

Sher had told him not to worry, he had a "sinecure," and then she had told him what that meant. Relax, collect your pay, retire comfortably, what the hell. As if she didn't worry at least as much as he did, as if she were not as aware as he was of the stew beneath the sheen of this place, as if she—for all her professionalism—didn't crave "it all," the same way he did, although tough men cops were supposed to worry least of all about that, of all things.

He believed that people would listen if he told them about the explosion he knew was inevitable. Not too many would laugh or tell him maybe retirement time had finally arrived, because he was, he felt, maybe the most respected man in the town. Even the guys in the tailor-made suits seemed slightly in awe of him, for reasons he could only speculate about. But he couldn't talk to them, he couldn't ask them to listen, he couldn't sit the town politicians down for a heart-to-heart about what was stalking them.

Because officially, he did not know. Possibly the town politicians knew, possibly they had hints but believed Cheng knew, possibly they knew but thought they had to hide it from Cheng. But Cheng doubted any of that. He knew them, knew they ranged from genuinely good but naïve, to good but pragmatic, to home-grown greedy, but they all acted like they believed they lived in Eden with a mission of keeping it that way.

Sher, bless her, was not awed and took Cheng seriously—because, really, you don't take seriously what awes you—but Cheng dared not tell her what officially he did not know. He had brought her to the point of knowing that he knew *something*, something large and looming, and she was big enough to know it was real enough to be worrisome without poking him about it.

Cheng could tell his boss—not Sher, who was his boss on paper, but his real boss—what nobody, not even Sher, knew about. Cheng *had* told his boss, but telling Barry was *reporting*, not telling: *There are problems here, Barry. So, fix them, Barry* replied. But Barry *knew* without *understanding*. How a guy that smart could know without understanding baffled Cheng.

Cheng brooded about wanting Scotch, and so he lurched when someone tapped his shoulder.

"Hey, officer, don't shoot," Sher said. Then she looked straight at him. "I'm sorry," she added. "No jokes today, huh?"

"*I'm* sorry," Cheng said. "Just a little jumpy, I guess."

Sher slid into the booth, opposite Cheng. She smiled. It was not a smile that lit the room, not an alluring beam or a warm invitation to laugh. It was quiet and serious, and Cheng liked it better for that. Sher was an object of fantasy for Cheng. Not a fast, erotic one—he did not need that because he had the flesh a couple times a week. This fantasy was slow and long, of a whole life with her that he could not have on account of a clause in his contract.

In "The Diner"—a piece of post-modern retro bullshit, a plain cinder block box with big windows and outside steel siding shaped and coated to resemble 1930's railroad car diners that nobody really remembered or had even seen photos of, and with an interior pretending to look not like a 1950's hamburger joint but like a recent movie version of a 1950's hamburger joint—the staff and many of the other patrons recognized Cheng and Sher and maintained a friendly distance. The police chief and city manager were liked and respected, trusted with duties that nobody else wanted, and were entitled to privacy to discuss how to run things. Seeing Sher join Cheng in the far-corner booth, the waiter signaled the cook to prepare their "usuals."

They sat, sipping coffee.

"Wanna talk?" Sher said. "Not that I'll insist."

"They're sneaking around," Cheng said. "For fifteen damn years I've been holding this town in check. Lowest goddamn crime rate anywhere. Not a homicide—not one—in all that time. Just a couple armed robberies, two or three attempted rapes. People think everything's okay. But you can't keep young people from acting young. Least of all by showering them with every gadget known to man. If they can't see anything to get excited about, they'll make up something, like drugs." He paused. "Shit. I'd be absolutely relieved if the problem was just drugs."

"It's not your fault. People have been escaping since forever. They got out of Auschwitz and Alcatraz. Maximum security, whatever."

Cheng sipped coffee. The breakfasts came. They each ate a little.

"I know you can't tell me the other half," Sher said. "At least here, they come back. Usually."

"Frequently," Cheng said.

"You gonna talk to Barry?"

Cheng snorted. "That son of a bitch? The mad scientist? Yeah, I'll have to talk to him. But I'll talk to Sam first."

"You know, Cheng, I'm not completely oblivious. I've heard the same stories everyone else has. They all revolve around why people come back."

Cheng looked into the wall mirror across from the booth. "Look at me," he said, and Sher turned to see an image like a surprise photo of a couple in an unhappy mood. "Short hair, nice tan, crisp khaki uniform, typical cop." He turned back to face her, with a look that made her spill coffee. "How do I get out of this?" he said.

It was a rhetorical question.

15

Marjorie's daily routine had changed after fourteen months in town. She had needed to add motions, searches, "minor investigations," she called them.

First, perfecting her housekeeping so that her condo resembled a newly cleaned hotel suite.

At night: Turning on all lights at nightfall. Locking doors and windows, and then, a few minutes later, checking them again. Looking inside closets and cupboards. Making sure all dishes, books, tchotchkes, were where she wanted them. And, yes, looking under furniture.

At morning: Turning *off* all lights. Checking everything again. Making sure tchotchkes were in the same places. Again looking under furniture. Verifying quantities of food in the refrigerator. All that, before, during, and after the rituals of shower, grooming, and quick meals.

Scanning hallway, then elevator, then the path through the parking garage. Looking, listening, smelling. Pausing at her car door. Dropping her purse or briefcase or keys, to have an excuse to glance under the car—difficult in high heels, potentially ruinous to hosiery. Putting briefcase in trunk just to see inside trunk, purse in back seat just to look at back seat. Probing under front seats, checking glove box. All, before starting the engine.

Fitting all that into an already crammed life had required a quickening of every motion, and she became aware of behaving like small fish she'd seen darting through aquaria. Obsessive-compulsive behavior, without doubt, and it fed on itself, as she discovered more places to search, more openings to plug, forcing herself into ever more vigilance.

―――――――

The thick, convoluted prose of her contract could be summed up thus: *As long as you don't leave, you can do as you like, but we will know everything.* She could see a therapist about her compulsions, but *they would know.*

Besides, she had a reason. Sights and sounds had put the fear in her. They were real—weren't they? They had shaken her. The fear of recurrence had blossomed grotesquely in her life, but the source was real. Wasn't it?

Over the months, the memories had faded. In the constant anxiety she had come to doubt. Had she seen and heard what she remembered seeing and hearing, or had she not? Could a therapist even know? If the therapist knew, would she tell her? If not, would she simply recommend drugs she emphatically did not want—beyond the alcohol that she did?

―――――――

Saturday morning Marjorie was going shopping. She did not need new clothes, but she did need a break. So, after her morning ritual she dressed comfortably, suitably for shopping, in loose pants and shirt and sandals that were easy to remove for trying things on. She thought of Boris, and how when she saw him, usually after work, she was always wearing things difficult to remove—business suits, button-up blouses, good hosiery—did all that spice the process up or just slow it down? Maybe she should buy some more sexy garments for Boris's pleasure, except that Boris did not seem to care what she wore and they never went anywhere except to motel rooms.

But she was being unfair to Boris, thinking all he wanted was her body. Wasn't that what she wanted—his body, his muscular arms and enormous hands holding her for an hour, without any other entanglements holding her to anything else for any time at all, and finally those few pulsating moments blotting out her fears? But that was unfair too, to both of them, because afterwards they always had talk that was relaxed, disjointed, undemanding and dispassionate, talk that made her feel as human as what preceded it made her feel animal.

In the bathroom mirror she saw worry and stress, and behind that was the grief for—what was she mourning, anyway? Something lost, or about to be lost? What?

She stifled an urge to cry, shook her head like a terrier, ran fingers through her hair, and just pulled herself together, *damn it!*

After the "minor investigation," she drove to *The Atria*, the town's upscale shopping complex that was part indoor mall, part outdoor simulated small-town main street, all chock full of shops of all sizes selling any frivolous thing a woman could want to buy. This would be a diversion, yes? A focusing on garments (outer and under), shoes, cosmetics, scents, jewelry, instead of on her growing misery and loneliness and the inescapable sense of some unidentifiable but surely good thing slipping away, probably forever.

And so, after parking in the underground garage, carefully choosing a slot away from walls, doors, pillars, or drains, she emerged from the escalator into the bright, warm sunshine, her sandals clicking on the pavement, into this shopper's haven, or heaven, or whatever it was, and, good lord, how she loathed it. Maybe a glass of wine would be nice, a little buzz to make her able to think of this as fun. It wasn't too early, the cafes were open for brunch.

She chose one with outdoor tables, shaded by umbrellas, and she sat at one backed against a wall. She asked the waiter for a glass of grigio and a scone. She resisted the temptation to get her phone from her purse and check email or news—this was supposed to be recreation, away from all that stuff—and tried to simply absorb the warmth and the sights, mostly of people strolling about looking for things to buy. She worked mightily to make the scone last, breaking it into small, nibble-sized bits, and sipping, rather than gulping, the wine. *Come on, girl, you've got the money. Be nice to yourself for a change.*

The wine helped her try to be nice to herself. She walked into shops, smiled at the staff, wandered slowly among racks, shuffled hangers, pulled out sleeves or lifted entire garments and gazed at them, glanced at manikins, fingered fabrics, read care instructions and prices, and involuntarily shot her eyes into corners, under benches, behind partitions. She inhaled deeply as she quickly opened fitting room doors and exhaled when she found the rooms empty. She sat on fitting room benches for a moment before trying things on, putting them on the replacement rack, and trying more. She rejected a nice blouse because she already had one more or less like it. She settled on a skirt that would probably look nice with one of her jackets. She tried to joke about women and their shopping while paying the clerk, but the joke failed and she felt stupid.

At a cosmetics counter she tried scents, finally buying a mid-priced one because she felt she had to buy something. She started to enter a shoe store but stopped in the entry hall, knowing she was now too tense and worn out to buy anything more. She smiled apologetically at the clerk there, and turned back out into the sun, relieved by her decision to give up.

She sat on a bench aimed toward a fountain surrounded by flowers and tried and failed to think of nothing. She thought of Zen meditation, and imagined herself in a Buddhist robe, her head shaved, in lotus position on this very bench, her hands not clutching purse and shopping bags but held like a bowl, one on top of the other, the thumbs as close together as possible without touching, her eyelids half down, breathing easily, in through the nose, out through the mouth. People would laugh or drop money on the pavement in front of her. Children would point and be shushed by their parents.

Were there Buddhist temples in town? She supposed there were, there certainly was everything else. But no ostentatious public prayer, and no panhandlers, so the part about people dropping money for her would not happen.

After some twenty minutes she rose and walked to a coffee bar near the real street that crossed the fake main street. She did not need caffeine, but she wanted the comfort of the warmth and the taste of the coffee—she'd get one laced with cream and chocolate. The queue was mercifully short. With her purse strapped over her left shoulder, her shopping bags looped over her left arm, and the covered cardboard cup in her right hand, she walked down the street, not knowing a destination.

16

On the following Saturday, Colin was again seated next to LaTasha in the back seat of Bryce's parents' SUV. At school, Bryce had told them he knew another way out—or, in this case, *in*, he had said. Elmer alone had challenged Bryce. Elmer, Colin guessed, was shaken from having gotten a different treatment from his mother than Colin had from his parents.

"How the hell do you know all this stuff, man?" Elmer had demanded, the group of them clustered under a tree on the school campus. "You know people who know people? Who are they? That Howard guy? Like last time?"

Bryce, unshakeable as usual, had stared at Elmer. "What's the difference?" he said. "You can go with us or not."

"Yeah, sure, I'm going," Elmer said, out-challenged. "I just don't get your secrecy with us."

Bryce just nodded, and for the first time Colin thought he saw that Bryce was acting. Perhaps Bryce's bravery was bravado or what Colin had seen in his parents—a pretense of self-assurance so strong as to be virtually indistinguishable from the real thing, even to the pretenders. But perhaps the distinction was false anyway, maybe every soldier needed reality to push him over the line from bravado to bravery. Colin did not know that he felt either. Instead, he felt somehow pushed by his parents' peculiar stoic courage, pretended or not, their determined dreamlessness, a display of real courage clearly beyond Bryce's.

Nobody else spoke, so Bryce ordered them all to meet at the football field parking lot at ten on Saturday morning. Bryce, it seemed to Colin, looked them over like a commanding officer inspecting for mission-preparedness, and the group dispersed, except that LaTasha was walking beside Colin, by a mutual consent that neither had uttered.

"Are you scared?" LaTasha had asked.

"Yeah, I guess so," Colin had said because it seemed the sensible answer. "You?"

"I guess so, too," she had said, and they had exchanged a smile.

And now they held hands in the back seat, at whose initiative, Colin was unsure.

Bryce was driving them to a different place this time, a town district of warehouses mostly deserted on Saturday morning. This area was like the rest of the town in its spotless tidiness, but different in its nearly total lack of windows. The walls were concrete and steel painted an austere gray, with vehicle doors down and locked. Bryce parked at the dead end of an alley.

"Where are we?" Gerald asked.

Bryce, aggressively silent, walked across the street to a door with a keypad on the wall next to it. Bryce turned to them with a finger across his lips, then looked at Gerald, in an evident temporary transfer of leadership. Gerald pressed a combination into the keypad and opened the door.

"How?" Elmer whispered.

Gerald grinned and shook his head and led them into a large warehouse space, lit only by daylight through two high industrial windows, free of obstruction except for a bank of metal shelving filled with boxes. There were workbenches along two walls, tools neatly racked behind them.

They followed Gerald across the clean floor to another door with another keypad, Gerald still grinning as he opened this one too. To their incredulous looks, Gerald whispered, "Passed down from generation to generation." Colin thought that maybe Gerald had a different kind of parents than the rest of them, but it seemed unlikely, meaning that Gerald's words were just more bullshit.

"Lights," Gerald said, like a movie director, and from pockets came the LED lights, showing them a long flight of metal stairs going downward into yet another dark corridor. There was no way to keep even their rubber-soled sport shoes from making light clangs against the steel. The corridor was like the last route, except that it was lined with heavy cables of bright, multi-colored plastic, firmly zip-tied to the metal walls and ceiling. There was a faint but persistent buzz and hiss, as of steam escaping from a machine. The floor seemed to vibrate with it.

"Don't touch anything," Gerald stage-whispered. "I don't know what all of this is, but just stay away from it. Go single-file."

They obeyed him, drawing their shoulders in to avoid contact with the cables as they shuffled down a much longer corridor. Gerald was first, with Bryce last, as a sort of rear guard. To someone's question of "how far?" Gerald said only, "Far."

And it was, the darkness descending behind them as their lights opened up the unchanging space before them, for a quarter mile? A half mile? A full mile? Certainly long enough for the changelessness of it and the darkness behind them to terrify anyone not bent on escape, or even just a taste of escape.

A faint gleam appeared in their lights and grew as they walked carefully ahead until Gerald stopped them and pointed his light upward from below his chin, so that the others could see his evil grin with upward shadows. "This," he said, "is the place." Ahead of them the passageway veered off to the right. On the floor, just behind Gerald as he faced the rest of them, was an oblong panel, six feet or so in length and two and a half feet across, with two large bolts where two corners would have been had the ends not curved outward. "Stand back," Gerald said, with his hands pushing the air before the rest of them, seeming to Colin as if he were working for maximum drama. They dropped back a step obediently, even Bryce, while Gerald pulled yet another wrench from the pocket of his hoodie sweatshirt, and said, pointing downward, "Give me light." They aimed their lights to the floor as Gerald, kneeling outside the boundaries of whatever the panel was, went to work on the nut threaded onto one of the fat bolts. He removed the nut, put it aside, and then removed the other. He shoved the naked end of one of the bolts, sending the panel down slightly. He went to the other bolt and shoved it the same way, returned to the first and shoved again, and then once more on the second, until the panel swung down, evidently attached to a hinge along the opposite side, revealing daylight below. Gerald's grin showed in the dim daylight as he stood and bowed, with an elaborate gesture toward the hole.

"How did you know about this," Elmer demanded.

"Folklore," Gerald said. His grin widened. "Old papers among my dad's stuff. Refusals by my dad and others to either confirm or deny." He paused to laugh, then pointed down, where a tree grew toward the hole off to one side of it. "Me first?" Nobody said no, so Gerald sat on the opening's edge, his feet evidently on something that held him, and disappeared downward. One by one, they doused and pocketed their lights and followed him, climbing down an enormous dense hedge to the ground, where they all paused to look.

Gerald continued to grin proudly, as if he were showing them his own creation. Bryce smiled with what Colin saw as a self-conscious knowingness. The rest of them just gawked.

The scenery was not beautiful. It looked much like where Bryce had parked the car, except that it had an undeniable monumental quality, like pictures of Mexican pyramids.

"Let's go," Gerald said.

"Where?" LaTasha asked.

"Exploring."

So they walked, still gawking, down a sidewalk much like one of their own, past warehouse-type buildings in a section of a town seemingly abandoned on a Saturday morning. In the distance, down the street, they saw cars and pedestrians, looking like the edges of a larger swarm of human activity. They came to an intersection, where Bryce theatrically motioned for them to flatten against a building wall and stay quiet while he peeked around the corner. Just as theatrically, he motioned them to follow him around the building's corner to the right, and there, while still huddling against the side of the building, they walked from morning shadow into dazzling light, the sun in their faces blurring a view of a casually well-dressed horde, most carrying glossy brand-logoed shopping bags, strolling or striding purposefully among trees, flower planters, and fountains, and in and out of enticing shops, crossing streets lined with gleaming cars.

The teenagers gaped. "It looks just like Commercial Street," Astrid said.

As they watched a scene at once both weird and mundane, one of the shoppers disengaged from the throng, as if in purposeful rebellion against her tribe, notwithstanding the purse strapped over her left shoulder and the one shopping bag on the same arm and the large coffee cup in her right hand.

The teenagers stared. "She's coming right at us," Elmer said, and they all began to back away, except Colin, who continued his concentrated gaze upon this being approaching them. She wore loose beige pants and a loose white top, the billowy clothing appearing to him to accentuate rather than hide the form inside them. As he stood watching, hearing the loud slap of her sandals on the concrete, Bryce grabbed his arm, saying "Come on, man, we've got to get out of here. It's time," but Colin wrenched free.

Colin watched the figure bearing down on him, his fascination increasing as her face became more distinct and her hair shone against the sun behind her. When she was close enough so that he was in shadow, he could see the anxiety and unhappiness on the most beautiful face he had ever seen, a face that froze into blankness, as did his as they locked eyes for a long instant. Then he saw her face burst into something else, her eyes and mouth widening into something several degrees past terror, a sound between a gasp and a scream bursting from her mouth, while Colin felt something different, a rush of concern and protectiveness (he would wonder later why he wasn't terrified too), so that he moved not away from but towards her., Then the coffee cup fell from her hand and exploded just in front of him, its contents, hot but not scalding, drenching him in coffee, cream, and chocolate. Colin continued to watch as she turned from him and ran, awkward in the sandals, losing the shopping bag on the sidewalk and running faster and then slowing as she rejoined the crowd and disappeared into it.

A female voice shouted "Colin!" and it was LaTasha, standing behind and over him as he discovered he was now sitting on the sidewalk, as something—the chocolate cream coffee?—had evidently knocked him off his feet. "Are you okay?" she said, and then repeated it as he continued looking toward the coffee cup on the sidewalk in front of him.

"Yes," he said. "I'm fine."

She was now kneeling next to him, a hand on his shoulder. "We should go, Colin," she said. "More of them might come."

"Yeah," he said. "Of course," as if they were talking about being late for lunch.

LaTasha helped him up.

"Let's go!" Bryce yelled, and they went, running now, back down the sidewalk, to the hedge and up it and through the hatch, into the passageway, where they pulled the hatch cover back in place and rethreaded the nuts on the bolt ends, and then shuffled quickly and quietly back the way they had come.

Once in the SUV the tension and fear dissipated. They sat, still quiet, in the plush upholstery of Bryce's parents' SUV, in the same seats as before because changing them would require decisions, something none of them wanted to face at the moment. To Colin, it felt like shared, quiet communion, about an immensity that none could fathom. Bryce, Astrid and Gerald, who had claimed to have been out before the truck stop expedition, were as stunned as the other five, for as Bryce admitted they had never been anywhere near so close to one of *them*.

"Scared the hell out of me," Bryce said, assuming leadership even in retreat, and nobody asserted differently, but Colin did feel something different, because the woman he had seen, though her foot was probably no less than a third the size of the SUV, was plainly a person with needs and fears of her own. As he pondered how he could feel so protective of someone so much less in need of protection than he was, he felt LaTasha's arm loop through his and when he looked he saw in her face the same concern for him that he felt for the other.

"Big fuckers aren't they," Gerald said, and their collective laughter seemed to rock the car on its springs.

The laughter done, they were quiet for a moment.

"But she was scared," Astrid said.

"Wouldn't you be?" LaTasha said. "I mean, if you saw a person that looked just like other people you know except that they came up below your knee, like a doll, wouldn't you be scared?"

"But who *needs* to be scared?" Elmer asked. "The big ones generally rule, in my experience, and when the size difference is *that* big, well."

"In your experience," Colin muttered.

"Depends on how many," Gerald said.

"The only way it makes sense," Bryce said, "and I'm not sure it does make sense, is if there are more of them. I just can't see us sharing the world anywhere near evenly with them. And we're the ones who can't leave *this* place. Could you see a bunch of us keeping *them* fenced in like this?"

Nobody could answer.

"Then why go out again?" Elmer said. "I'm thinking maybe my parents are right. Mine made it pretty plain that going outside is bad."

Nobody argued that point either.

"I guess all our parents told us they went out, huh?" LaTasha asked, and all assented with a word or nod. "And so they all knew already what we know now." When nobody filled her pause, she said, "So what's the good of going again? Because what we know is that it's really dangerous out there, just like they told us. Now we know and we can't change anything." She held Colin's arm more tightly, and Colin put his free hand on top of hers.

"But we have to go out again," he said.

"Why?" Elmer said.

"I don't know," Colin said. "Why did people go to the moon?"

"*They* went to the moon," Elmer said.

"But we're *like them*," Colin said, "we're just smaller."

"Smaller?" Astrid said. "Smaller? That's like saying a coffee cup is smaller than the ocean. When something's *that* true it's not even worth talking about."

"Speaking of coffee," LaTasha said to Colin, "you smell like a mocha latte."

"The whole damn car smells that way," Gerald said.

More laughter, still nervous.

"But they're *like* us," Colin said. "It's *them* we see on TV and movies and on YouTube. They look like us and sound like us."

"Are you saying that's reason enough, to, you know, like, *mingle* with them?" Astrid said. "And if we could, how, exactly? I mean, they could step on us. They could do anything they want with us."

"Like they are now," Bryce said. "We're like in a cage. A big, nice cage, but a cage anyway."

They thought about that for a moment.

"We have to go out," Colin said. "Have to. *Have to*," he said, surprising himself with his vehemence. "I don't know *why*. We just have to."

After another moment Bryce said, "Right. So we will."

While Colin looked out the window towards what was only a cinder block wall, LaTasha looked at him. She worried about more than size.

"I got her. I know I got her." It was Gerald.

Nobody responded for a moment until Elmer said, "What do you mean you got her?"

"On my phone. I got her," Gerald said, his voice now rising in anger. "From right behind Colin, it was a perfect shot, Colin in the foreground and that woman bearing down on him, I swear to god I got it!"

"Let's see," Astrid said.

Gerald shook his head. "It's gone. I don't know what happened. I didn't do anything with it. But shit! It's gone, dammit!"

17

From Colin's Journal

If my mind was a mess after last time, it's like a total wreck now. I literally can hardly think about anything but that giant woman. Except when LaTasha is around and then I just want to find a way to hook up with her (except that I'm afraid I will come off like a total dork).

I mean, I guess I should have been scared shitless and maybe I was. But I don't think I've ever seen anyone as beautiful as her before, not even in a movie. And maybe what kept me from being so scared is that she looked scared too, maybe even more scared than I was. I think maybe she had on some kind of perfume. And then she dropped her latte or whatever it was and I smelled the coffee and sugar and the perfume. She looked, so, like stricken or something and suddenly I forgot about being scared. I just wanted to take care of her—but how could I do that? And then she totally freaked out and ran off, but the weirdest part was before that. I swear there was this thing, this sort of electronic beam that kind of leapt between our eyes. It sounds stupid even to me but I couldn't help feeling something, and I just sort of lay there feeling it until I felt hands on me, like shaking me. And of course it turned out to be LaTasha touching me. And between her touching me and the sort of electricity from that woman's eyes I was like a zombie.

I am afraid I looked weak in front of LaTasha, but she seems okay, I guess.

I am totally confused!!

18

Now, *what did we have here?* 4&k3L)(n smiled, for he had seen things like this before. An attempt to blur the trail? To destroy the evidence of an event still to happen? To erase a memory of something as yet only glimpsed as a possibility, still far from reality? Or perhaps only to deny reality?

But artifacts such as these are never completely erased, are they? They live on in reflection as in a fun-house mirror, or in the internal musings of whoever may have caught them if only from the corner of an eye, a not-memory that never dies even as it grows dim and doubt-ridden, a mere ghost impression of something that never was.

But enough poetry. In the ether things really do live on, sometimes because of carelessness that leaves remnants behind in silicon, waiting to be found by those who want to find them or others who simply stumble over them, but most often because of the compulsive record-keeping of bookkeepers disguised as high-tech wizards, which was, true to form, the case here.

But 4&k3L)(n was no scavenger, not really, no dumpster-diver, he. All one must do is lurk and watch, to see, perhaps the one gray and green paper rectangle amidst the flow of trash pouring into the truck, the thousand-dollar bill among the other discards. And 4&k3L)(n saw not just the item, but the process: a long digital network arm grabbing it from someone else not to liquidate it but to squirrel it away in a corner for some future reference, thus proving the item's value, and so he reached out and grabbed it himself, the now-you-see-it-now-you-don't willow-the-wisp.

Such a nice picture it was, too, even though the perspective was strange, the woman in the background so much larger than the people in the foreground. And there it was, floating in the same oceanic region as the prior emails.

Who knows what could happen if you pasted it on a wall somewhere, where passers-by might see?

Let's find out!

19

Marjorie ran, awkwardly in the thin sandals, her purse flapping against her side, the loops of the shopping bag sliding from her shoulder to her hand which then dropped it, leaving the merchandise on the plaza pavement, while her mind said only *yes I was right I was right to be scared I was right*, the very rightness scaring her more, now holding the strap of her purse only because of the thoughtless muscle memory that all women have of holding a purse. She ran through throngs of shoppers who paused, their faces showing only momentary concern and who looked behind the woman and, having seen nothing and nobody chasing her, resumed their own acquisitive mornings. She dodged through the crowd on the plaza, dodged more people on the escalator, and more until she was able to get into her car and fold her arms on the steering wheel, put her head down, and cry.

After finishing her cry, she remembered that she had to get out to inspect under the car and in it. Until fifteen minutes ago she had been scared of something so unbelievable as to become in her mind supernatural and therefore capable of gliding through the seals around closed car windows or penetrating the ventilation system, like a bad smell. Now that she had seen *them* again the recognition dawned in her that they were clever and probably capable of foiling even the most sophisticated electronic automobile locks if they wanted to. So she finished her inspection and re-entered and locked the car and sat in it, the closed space feeling to her like a refuge as safe as any place could be.

She *had* seen them again, as she had once before during the course of an otherwise normally boring business day. Not the same ones, but still, *them*. She had not smelled them, and certainly not touched them, but she had heard them, their startled and fearful cries. She had flinched away from them, as she would from a tarantula, but then she had run, even as she had seen them run from *her*. They were not tarantulas. They were like her, just small, doll-size, and younger, looking and sounding like and dressed like teenagers. And that one boy, different from the others, gazing back at her with some intention. He was *handsome*, that boy.

They were real, they were not mirage.

She phoned Boris. "I have to see you," she said.

"All right," he said.

————

Boris told her how and when to sneak into his car and hide on the backseat floor, and arranged for the always mischievous and cooperative Sydney to cover for him at the gate.

They did not speak in the car, even after Boris stopped to let her into the front passenger seat. His silence, sometimes irritating, an argument for never considering him as more than an expedient sex partner even as that very idea made her feel guilty, was calming, and she was grateful for it.

Now they reclined, fully clothed, shoulders just touching, on the bed looking towards the bureau with the dark TV above it and the large mirror next to it, no light except daylight from the edges of the drawn curtains.

"Why are we here?" she asked, knowing, again gratefully, that he would understand she did not mean the motel room.

"Jobs," he said.

Marjorie thought.

"But why the jobs?" she asked.

95

She waited but Boris did not speak.

"We took them knowing," she said.

"Government project, top secret," he said.

She waited again.

"Yes," she said. "But why?"

She waited more.

"Your town?" he said.

"Yes."

"I think there's another just like it."

She thought about that. "Where?"

She leaned into him, feeling his slow breathing.

"Close," he said. "Very close."

She waited for two of his breaths. "Do they tell you?" she asked.

He shook his head.

"But you notice things," she said.

He said nothing.

"They know you notice things."

He said nothing.

"Are the two towns exactly the same?"

In the mirror next to the TV, in the crepuscular light, she saw the slow, small shake of his head.

"What's the main difference?"

She saw his reflection smile faintly. He held up his hands as if indicating the size of a fish as long has his shoulders were wide, then he drew them together until the palms almost touched.

Marjorie exhaled and shuddered, and as she felt his arm around her shoulder she was crying on his chest, and then she stopped crying and her breathing and heart slowed and she stayed there and lost track of time.

After a while, he said, "You've seen?"

"Yes."

She pulled herself away to look directly at him. "Have you?"

"Pictures."

"Have you tried to learn more?"

"Less," he said and smiled again, faintly.

"Of course," she said and relaxed back into him.

"But you," he said. "You will not accept less. You'll want to know all."

Leaning into him, she nodded.

20

W hat the fuck," Gerald said to himself. For there it was, his photo of Colin from behind with the large good-looking woman looming in the background, without attribution or identification, mixed in at a website where you could randomly sift through random photos when you were bored and had nothing better to do, which was never the case for Gerald, who did not care about cute pet pictures or embarrassing drinking pictures. He did care about sex pictures, but they were distractions on which he did not allow himself to dwell, because his bigger obsession was elsewhere, *outside*.

He did allow himself, but only briefly, to wonder how his own photo had left his phone to go to where anyone could stumble over it. Weirdly random things happened on the internet, certainly, but he was not alone in seeing the *control*, or not quite seeing it, but suspecting it, because of the little discrepancies that appeared now and again, the inconsistencies that could be dismissed as chance but somehow did not *feel* like chance, and only fed the growth of his emotional certainty that they were *not* chance. He knew he was being fucked with.

"Seen it?" Gerald said on his phone.

"Gerald? What?" Colin said.

"The photo. I'm texting you a link."

Seconds later, Colin said, "Well, shit."

"See you," Gerald said, and clicked off, because there was bound to me more, just *had* to be more, and he wanted to focus on finding it.

He searched, for—what? For *outside, out there, big people, big people in malls*—what's this? Down in the hit list, under clothing ads for big and tall men and full-figured women and articles about the obesity epidemic, he saw a new item on a blog he liked to read, despite knowing it was bullshit, or maybe because of knowing it was bullshit, but probably because the bullshit was not consistent, because the texture and reek of it varied, wafting in different directions, unexpectedly.

This item, for example, about doors, about air pressure getting to be too much and blowing hatches. Said it was "a metaphor for life." Said, "When you feel so cramped that you think you might blow up, look around you. Maybe something outside you has blown up, or blown out, or just blown, leaving an opening where you can go to relieve that cramp."

Gerald stared at it until his phone vibrated and Astrid's name appeared.

"This picture? How?"

"No idea," he said.

"I poked around and found this link," she said.

Gerald clicked the link in her text that went to some site he'd never seen.

"This is fortune-telling," he said.

"Yeah, like in really old movies with beaded curtains and gypsy ladies with crystal balls," Astrid said. "Only I don't think that's what this is really about."

Gerald read aloud: "I see your future opening up in directions you have never imagined, down corridors untold. Or perhaps they are not 'untold', perhaps they are 'told', but you have not been paying attention. Wake up! Your new life awaits! But avoid excessive intake of carbohydrates and guard your money, for not everyone is trustworthy."

"Try this," Gerald said, and sent his link to her.

"Huh," Astrid said. "I'm gonna talk to Bryce," and she clicked off.

————

Colin felt dazed. He examined the photo, looking at every detail, zoomed in until all he saw were bunches of pixels, and zoomed back out to see the face.

"That her?"

He was sitting cross-legged on the bed, his back to his open door, holding the tablet up, when his mother walked in. Colin nodded. Grace stood at the foot of the bed and watched his profile, which did not turn from the photo. When he suddenly put the tablet in his lap and began typing at it, she watched him, was not even tempted to watch the screen. He paused, scanned the screen, typed more, and again scanned the screen. With each such repetition, Grace saw her son grow more intense, his eyes squint, his brows lower, his lips curling under to expose his teeth.

"Look at this, Mom," he said, and while she moved to look over his shoulder he read aloud: "Alice fell down the hole. She was too little, but then she got too big. But how big is too big? Maybe you should find out!"

"What is that?" Grace asked him.

Without moving his head, Colin said, "It's just something I like to read. Different installments once or twice a week. There are others. They all have the same theme, which is holes."

"I saw the picture," Grace said. "The back, that was you, wasn't it?"

Without turning or answering, Colin clicked back to that browser tab and made it full-screen.

"You want to talk about it?" Grace asked.

Colin said nothing.

Grace thought, *teenagers*.

————

By this time Bryce had seen the picture Astrid told him about and all the links the others had seen, either on his own or from their texts. He, too, was glaring at his screen, getting more intense, feeling like he did before a soccer match, seeing himself, his potential moves — dribble, stunt, dribble, pass, go, receive, shoot — in his mind, knowing how good he was.

Something was happening, something was changing, and he would be at the center of it. He was born for this. He knew it. He knew it scared shit out of his Mom. But she was tough, she could be there as well.

————

Astrid was in her room at her father's house with the door shut, clacking away at her internet book, seeing the picture, going to links, going back to the picture, growing more and more certain. Certain of what, exactly, she did not know, but she was *certain*. And she was not alone: she had Bryce, and Colin, Gerald, Elmer, and LaTasha. They all had each other. Her mother could stay in the tank, drying out, one more time. Her father could go and . . . she did not know what, but she didn't give a shit.

————

After LaTasha saw the picture and all the links the others sent her, she shut her notebook and lay back on her bed. She had long believed that she and her parents occupied the only sane place in the world. And maybe Colin. She wanted to think that Colin was there, somehow, in that calm, sane place, but she was not at all sure of that. She liked her friends but they scared her a little. Colin did not scare her, but liking him did.

She crossed her arms on her chest and hugged herself. She wanted things to be calm and normal. Was that even possible?

———

Elmer and his parents all huddled around Elmer's laptop, and, like Elmer's friends, looked alternately at the photo and the other links.

"Bring the picture back," Michael said, and Elmer did.

"See that?" Michael said, pointing his strong, stubby finger at something in the upper left corner. "Looks kind of like ours, doesn't it?"

"It looks exactly like ours," Phuong said, straightening her thin, straight back even straighter and leaning towards the screen.

"I've heard that at Disneyland at, what do you call it? Main street?" Elmer said. "It looks just like a regular street only just a little smaller, everything at a different scale. This looks like that, only not on a smaller scale."

"Yep," Phuong said. "Different for sure, but the same."

"All this stuff about holes," Michael said. "You understand it?"

"Oh, sure," Elmer said. "I do." He looked at his father and smiled, and then aimed the smile at his mother.

They all smiled.

"Sort of scary," Elmer said.

"Sort of!" Phuong said.

They laughed.

21

From Colin's Journal

Fuck!! If I was wrecked before, what am I now??!!!! I'm surprised people aren't looking at me and saying, like, Colin, what is wrong with you?? Should we take you to the hospital? I guess I'm hiding it but I don't know how!! That woman has been dominating all my thoughts since we met. WE MET!!??? We DID NOT MEET, ASSHOLE!!. It was not a "meeting" it was a car crash!! STOP THINKING ABOUT HER!!! But how can I do that when that picture of her—of US!!—is all over the place. I'm LOSING MY MIND!!!

What was really the strangest was when my Mom walked into the room and I showed her that blog post. I think she understood the code about Alice's rabbit hole. Actually, it was like she had already seen it and didn't care. But she had definitely seen the picture and she recognized me, even though I think from the back I look like lots of guys. She knows something. My Mom is smart.

Fuck, I don't know what to do.

22

"Have you seen the picture?"

"What picture," Cheng said.

"I'm sending it," Sam said. They waited until Cheng got it.

"How?" Cheng asked.

"I have no idea," Sam said. "The log says it was auto-cleansed within three seconds of creation."

"I guess it doesn't matter," Cheng said.

"No. Nothing to do about it now."

"Does he know?"

"I don't know. If not, it's just a matter of minutes, maybe a couple hours."

Sam listened to Cheng think, knowing what he was thinking.

"Which one?" Cheng asked.

"Later," Sam said and clicked off.

Sam remembered all five previous ones, all of them from good families because Projectville had no other kind, and all of them young, because the older ones tended to be lone wolves whom nobody would wonder about for long, much less grieve over, and all of them Sacrifices for the Cause. "We are, the two of us, together, like Abraham," Barry had said after the second one. "They're like our sons, and we have to sacrifice them with faith that the good from it will emerge at the end." Sam, dazed with guilt and grief, could ask only if they, the two of them, would be alive to see the end, which gave Barry the chance to look sadly sage as he said, "We can hope. But the end will be good, Sam, you can trust in that."

Afterwards, with the chance to think more, Sam had wondered, if Barry and he together were Abraham, and their victims were Isaac whom god had told them to sacrifice, who, in this case, was god? The president? *The president didn't even know!* And in the Bible Abraham proves his faith, making the sacrifice unnecessary. But in the *project*, proof of faith was not enough; faith had to be realized in the form of corpses. And how many would there be? How many repetitions of faith did this god need? *Anyway, Barry, aren't you god, here? And am I not just god's henchman? And in the Bible, what if Abraham hadn't had the faith to do whatever god asked? What if he'd been stupid or feeling rebellious that day? What then? Would god have killed Abraham and Isaac both? There, that'll show you! Distrust god, will ya! Poof! Chosen People, nipped in the bud! What moral would that have taught? And what would you do to me, Barry, if I suffer a lack of faith? Have me liquidated with extreme prejudice? Ship me off to maximum security solitary for the rest of my life? Do the same to my family? You, who are both god and Abraham at the same time?* Even in his own mind, Sam always lost the argument, because he knew that this god, while having no particular bloodlust, needed periodic non-judicial capital punishment to scare the bejesus out of the survivors.

Sam did his research. The photo showed the back of a young man, maybe a teen. Sam could judge height and weight from the proportions, and he had hair and skin color, all of which yielded nearly two thousand hits of high-school students. Then there were the backs of two other heads in the foreground, which, by association, brought the total below one thousand.

He sent Cheng a secure text: "Any names from the vent?"

Waiting for Cheng's response, Sam admired through his office window the view of the plain cinder-block wall opposite (which was consistent with the Spartan standard Barry set for the top echelon of project staff, Barry himself having only the additional perk of one tree to enliven his own cinder-block wall view). On the wall, Sam imagined he could see Cheng's tortured face looking, save for superficial details, much like Sam's own. If Cheng's response was slow, that would be due not only to ordinary business but also to a reluctance to face the stench.

Nonetheless, Cheng replied within ten minutes: "Bryce Karakawa." Sam found the name in his database. High-schooler.

> Sam: Could the one in the middle of the picture be Colin Fairchild?

Sam watched his phone screen and waited, suffering along with Cheng.

> Cheng: Yes.

> Sam: How fast could he catch the disease?

> Cheng: Nice kid. Never any trouble.

> Sam: Exactly what Barry would want.

> Cheng: I'll need three days.

> Sam: OK.

OK. It was all OK, everything was just *OK*, here in the front lines of the battle for human survival. With the stakes so high, what's a little sacrifice now and then? Besides, Sam *was only following orders from on high! You must have faith, man, faith in the righteousness of the cause!* Without that faith the cramp in Sam's stomach and whatever caused the trickle of blood he had seen in the toilet bowl might kill him as surely as Abraham had not killed Isaac.

23

Once again, 4&k3L)(n saw, precisely as Michelangelo saw a chunk of marble, more raw material for him to mold. How perfectly delightful that an observer could pick one from among the myriad of the world's server farms and *never be disappointed!*

He had spent days watching the doings on this one installation and here was even more reward.

Of course, the secure, encrypted messages were absolutely the best! Were not secrets the very juice of life? One need not sift through surface banalities in search of fascinating gems when the secret-keepers did the work for one. These messages were not only encrypted, but cryptic as well!

Some "kid" was to fall victim to a "disease"? Fatally, one suspected. Let's rummage through these databases, so conveniently located, like silos on a farm, to see what has happened here in what appeared to be a kind of closed community, sheltered from the slings and arrows of outrageous fortune, even apparently pampered, but subject to illness, accident, and death nevertheless. What might a little "data mining," as they called it, reveal about the least frequent cause of death among adolescents? Mmmmmmm, ahhhhhh, grind, rumble, grind—HERE! Blah, blah, blah . . . "an unnamed and medically inexplicable ailment, with always the same symptoms: Complaints of headache, dizziness and nausea, followed by sudden total bodily collapse followed by death," all within two hours. Only five instances through the decades! The medicos were stumped, stumped, I tell you! 4&k3L)(n would bet that they were about to be stumped again!

But still, this community might be hygienically sealed off from the rest of the world, but seals were never impenetrable, and nature could never be thwarted. There were diseases — real ones, not the "mysterious" ones in the secret messages — that sometimes killed people. Accidents, too, including miscarriages, sudden infant deaths, and so on. And so there were records, death records mixed with birth records. What if one were to find bureaucratic commemoration of a long-ago death so early in a life that it hardly left another trace beyond the deathless memories of the tormented parents? What if one were to insert among the secret messages a new notice of that death, and were to add some fictional years — say, seventeen — to that life? Would that satisfy whoever hungered for this new death?

As with laundered money, investigators could sift through the mix and find the truth, but that would require notice, work, and time, and much could happen while time passed, much that would doubtless be fun to watch!

24

S am stood motionless on the sidewalk area he had chosen for his call to Cheng. As security manager, he doubted that calling from outside accomplished anything in the way of privacy, but especially with the recently tightened budget, the staff could not monitor everything at once. Walking from his office to this unfrequented spot of pavement might buy Sam a few minutes to decide.

Barry might be right, maybe periodic sacrifice was, indeed, the price of survival of the entire race. *But that begs another question, doesn't it? The one about the race itself? Does a species that imposes on itself the need for such things deserve to survive?* Not a question for Darwin, with his theory's intrinsic logic. Maybe for theologians, whether they agreed with Darwin or not. Maybe for philosophers. Untouchable for politicians. But unavoidable for Sam, standing immobile and miserable and lonely on this small, barren stretch of concrete, feeling tears slide down his cheeks, feeling unable to return to his office and with almost no place else to go.

It was past two o'clock and Jennifer's school would be empty of pupils. He phoned her.

––––––––

How had Sam become number two on the Project, in charge of security? What path had led an only child of baby-boomers to this even lonelier place in which he now lived? And how had Jennifer gone with him?

His parents, while coming of age in the late last century, would have none of it, none of that stew of undefined rebellion, that tantrum against everything that held civilization together, and so they armed themselves for a long siege, the center of their bastion being their only son, who, by god, would *not* fall into that seething mosh pit. Gently, firmly, and methodically they taught him cleanliness and fearfulness, and made him know that he was special and better but needed wariness to survive, and they produced a boy who was ambitious but not bold, a dreamer afraid to step into his dreams.

In short, a bright but plodding student, driven by fear and obsession rather than curiosity, and always working just hard enough to get every "A", get into that elite university, get that electrical engineering/computer science BS, get into that pressurized graduate program, get that MS degree just, and only just, before the point where he could stomach no more and would have had to push himself away from the table until he was hungry again.

Not creative or brash enough to venture on his own, or to partner with friends to launch something new into the ocean of newness in which he lived, he found a place where his duties were to support the daring creativity of others, and where two years made clear, even to himself, that his stubborn resistance to the free-wheeling company culture was not a refusal, but an inability, to join it. His resentment of his treatment by the hierarchy, not to mention by his colleagues, turned into bewilderment about his fate in life, about the decline of an arc that should still have been rising.

Thus, after heeding polite encouragement to resign, he found himself alone in the living room of his apartment in the San Fernando Valley neighborhood called Arbor Hills (where there were few trees and the only hills were in the smog-filled distance), on his telephone cheerfully reassuring his baffled parents, who could not understand his failure in a world they had made him despise.

Having lived frugally, Sam had no immediate financial fear: his rent was low, his car was old, and his tastes where cheap. What unsettled him was the sudden understanding that his goal, or mission, or whatever it was that had motivated his life into his late twenties, was gone, leaving a void that was both scary and inviting. Which would explain how Jennifer became part of his life.

Their meeting was accidental, in a small, crowded coffee shop with only one table vacant, each of them alone and in need of a chair, she indicating in a merely helpful way that he could join her, if he liked, which he did. She was unpretentiously attractive, tall, thin, brunette. Perhaps because of his new discovery of the void, Samuel felt his shyness dissolve, and found himself hearing about her school teaching position and telling about his own career.

Samuel himself was tall, thin, and loose-jointed, and able to attract women, on occasion. Up to that moment with Jennifer, his experiences with them had generally run to five dates: first, awkward but fun; second, fun but strained; third, sex; fourth, a feeling of sadness on his part; and fifth, her goodbye. Jennifer herself, with a sort of no-nonsense friendliness, broke the pattern. Their romance actually developed and grew and remained fun, through almost a year occupying Sam's suddenly enhanced free time and hers outside her teaching schedule. Sam had found love and it had found him. The romance remained romantic after Sam moved into her apartment, and Sam saw a concrete future that demanded a job.

In job-search, Sam's plodding thoroughness turned to fire, as he tirelessly searched through every internet cranny, finally glimpsing a gem posted in a cluttered corner of a United States Government site related to "Office of Special Project (OSP),

Infrastructure Support and Development (ISAD), Information Technology Implementation Fabrication (ITIF)." OSP/ISAD/ITIF spelled out—in detailed, impenetrable repetition of acronyms and jargon—job requirements that Samuel would bet his entire student debt he could fulfill. And, of that student debt, OSP Management (OSPM) promised complete forgiveness.

Only two days later, Sam's application brought a call to interview in a USG office building in Los Angeles, where Samuel's plodding geekiness again served him well. After that, the security clearance process moved rapidly. OSP/ISAD/ITIF seemed delighted by Sam's apolitical and personally conservative life history. During the third interview, a balding, slightly paunchy man, dressed in conspicuously casual clothes, talked to him about life in general—*Any hobbies, Sam, any outside interests? None? About to marry? Wonderful! And, speaking of marriage, we have spousal employment opportunities too!* Sam listened with wonder as this man, Dr. Hagenstopple, told him of the "total environment of the Special Project" (never uttering *project* without preceding it with *special* and always enunciating the capital letters) with its apparently boundless family-friendliness and squeaky-clean living spaces, all education levels for kids, entertainment, shopping, all self-contained, and all with compensation well beyond Sam's expectations.

Switching from the glowing inducements, Barry's demeanor grew darker, though never unfriendly, as he defined requirements: life only within the Special Project confines, sharp limitations on trips out, an unbreakable twenty-five year commitment—and, above all—total secrecy. Sam could not even tell his family. Barry ended the interview with a conspiratorial, glad-to-have-you-with-us smile and a tight handshake.

Sam had returned from the interview with an offer sheet in his pocket and a pre-offer of a senior teaching job for Jennifer. Jennifer matched Sam in her disconnection from politics and added a passion for teaching young children, and so her interview and clearance process flew even faster than his.

The Special Project formally offered jobs to them both, him in the ITIF and her in one of the Special Project's elementary schools. They discussed the limitations and the commitment balanced against the benefits, looked closely at the unstable economy, and decided to go for it.

They were given a month to prepare, during which time they received forty hours of training and orientation. Their romance survived that and more—their hasty city-hall marriage and awkward visits to parents who tried not to complain about their exclusion from these rapid developments.

In the Project, their careers blossomed, Sam's to what it was, through ITIF, up to ISAD, and finally through that to near the apex of OSP, and Jennifer's to school principal. She bore their two children, who flourished in a relatively uncomplicated society with no poverty, no serious crime, and frictionless racial, ethnic, and religious diversity. There was the stress of feeling hemmed in, but for a long time it seemed no match for the safety and the comfort.

———

Sam arrived at their house first, and so was there when Jennifer charged in with flaming eyeballs.

"Divorce, huh!" she stated rather than asked, as forcefully as possible without yelling. "Well, husband, you got it."

Sam, without rising from the living room sofa, quietly shook his head. She walked to him but did not sit, and for a moment it seemed that they both appreciated her towering

113

over him, he the smaller and she the larger, authoritative in her outrage.

"What then?" she demanded. "Trial separation? Forget it. I don't need a trial."

Sam shook his head again and slowly patted the sofa beside him.

Looking somewhat intrigued if still angry, she sat, but emphatically at the other end of the couch rather than next to him. They did not look at each other.

The silence was long. Jennifer waited.

Sam took a deep breath and sighed it out. "Not you. Not us," he said.

"Not us?" Jennifer said. "Then *her*?" She glared. She laughed. "Is that good or bad?" she said. And then she was crying.

Sam did not move to comfort her. "No, there is no *her*." he said. "It's my job."

Jennifer paused in her crying, but was not appeased. "The fucking job. Sometimes I think I'd trade all the money and the house and everything." For what, she did not say.

"I have to kill people," Sam said.

Jennifer stopped crying. "What are you saying?" she asked.

"There have been five in the past. Barry will want another. He hasn't said anything yet, but I know he will. And I can't do another."

Jennifer looked at him fully and did not speak until he turned to her. "My god, what is this about?" she said.

For more than an hour Sam told her what it was about, what he had kept from her, per the contract that she understood, for almost all of their lives together: the "Special Project," its reason for being, its ultimate goal, the reason for the secrecy, his climb to its number two spot, which Sam could no longer abide because it made him kill people.

After twenty minutes Jennifer gathered herself and in businesslike fashion said, "break for coffee," and headed to the kitchen. Sam did not stop her, though caffeine was emphatically not what he wanted. What he wanted was a tumbler of Scotch, which he had been resisting to keep his head clear. She returned while the coffee-maker worked and sat again, now next to him and touching, while he told her more, pausing only after a few minutes when she returned to the kitchen and then returned again to the sofa, bearing two cups, his already infused as he liked it, setting the cups on the sofa table. He sipped the coffee once and continued.

"So you can see," he said, "that there is a great purpose to all this stuff. There is a logic to it. And it's not a war," he said, raising his shoulders that she was now stroking, "I'm not being asked to bomb villages or help some bloodthirsty tribe because they're the enemy of our enemy, or to preempt some at least theoretical future terrorist attack by killing someone who might possibly be planning one. So what am I so . . . ," and then his head was against her breast and he was the one crying, spasmodically, sobbing, his arms around her while she cradled him. But even then, wanting her to mother him, Sam felt that her body did not surround him protectively but stiffened and held back even as her arms held him.

After some minutes the fit was over and he leaned back into the sofa. "Thank you," he said. "I'm sorry. Sorry for all the years. I thought I was protecting you and the kids."

"I understand," she said. "I'd had suspicions of some of this, with people making jokes about *androids* or *robots*, or something." She paused and then said, "But they're human aren't they?"

"Oh, yes," he said nodding emphatically, "they are human. Real humans. Capable of everything we are. That's the point."

They were quiet for a while.

"What will you do?" she asked.

115

"I'll have to talk to Barry. But as you know, quitting is not easy here, it's not like a job at Bechtel. There will be stringent conditions. They may tell us where we can live, and they'll probably surveille us, maybe forever." Sam shook his head and added, "And maybe the kids even after they've grown up, and maybe even their kids. Forever."

25

B arry, Sam had learned, was most dangerous when cheerful, the good humor being a sign of confidence enhanced even beyond Barry's normal oceanic arrogance. Barry in a bad mood was indecisive and brooding, a man unsure of the best route to the goal—though never of the goal itself. But Barry in a good mood could quickly opt for anything.

And so, when Barry answered Sam's phone call with audible bonhomie, telling him to come right over, Sam knew to expect any instruction, an order to *go forth and kill*, for instance, likely to be punctuated with the manly assurance of a clap on the shoulder.

"Come in, my boy," Barry beamed as Sam appeared in his doorway, "sit, please."

A moment passed while Sam gathered himself for a struggle, but Barry did not let him start. "Don't look so grim," Barry said. "I know this will sound corny, but what you've done is for the greater good. You have done well, and you should feel assured, with faith in the ultimate."

Assured of what, Sam had no idea, and somehow *corny* was not an adjective that Sam could apply in this situation.

Barry suddenly shifted from congratulatory cheer to earnest empathy. "How did you find him?" he asked. "What made you sure that Renaldo Kim was the right one?"

Sam, feeling all substance beneath him disappear into that void he'd discovered before meeting Jennifer, said nothing. Barry peered at him, waiting, but Sam had no words, able only to summon that silent plodding that had pushed him through his formal education and now allowed him to hide his panic.

"Well," Barry said, finally looking down from Sam's face to his own clasped hands. "It's alright. I understand. I'm pleased that you made a decision, and I trust that it was the wise one, the one I would have advised had you consulted me." He raised his eyes back to Sam's. "And that's alright too, that you didn't consult me. I've looked at the system notes about Renaldo," and now Barry shifted into a condescending sarcasm, "a bold one, this young man. Overly bold, cocky, rebellious, smartass, when you get right down to it. Trouble— which you, Sam, eliminated. Thank you, my boy."

Sam held still. The decision he and Jennifer had made to quit, both of them, of course, to throw the whole thing over, even to dare Barry and the majesty of the OSP and the rest of the government to do with them as they would—now seemed wrong. There had been an "elimination," certainly no less horrible for the fact that Sam had taken no part in it. Sam, feeling a sick vacancy in his stomach and steeling himself against a whirling in his head, put one hand over his mouth.

"It's never easy, Samuel, not for me either," Barry said, "and I won't forget your courage."

Which remark was frigid water in Sam's face, pushing him back from a cliff edge beyond which lay humiliation, a plea for comfort from which he could never escape. *Courage? When had Sam shown courage?* Sam was now on his feet though he could not say how or when he had risen from the chair, and he was extending his hand to accept Barry's in a clasp supposedly marking a bargain, and he heard Barry tell him to "take the rest of the day off. Relax, go to a movie, take Jennifer and the kids out for dinner, whatever."

———

Sam did take the rest of the day off, wandering the sterile streets and alleys of the business end of the project, seeing, in every cinder block wall, one of the five expedient eliminations in which he had taken part, seeing the boys he'd never met but whose faces he'd seen in very high definition on his computer screen, remembering how with each one he had reminded himself of the greater good he was serving, a good that was knotted with the contradictory notion that *they* were not *us*, that the role of master was one *we* could never share with *them*. *We* had created *them* in our own image, as our saviors. God had allegedly created our savior as both himself on earth and as a man intended for death, so *we* had created our savior as both ourselves and as expendable lower life form.

Sam was decidedly not comfortable as god.

He phoned Cheng on their encrypted line, the one that would take the security techs just a little longer to read, if they wanted to. Their orders told them to monitor everyone, with no exceptions, not even Barry, but he figured that, being human, they would give low priority to monitoring their own boss and his boss.

"Renaldo Kim," Sam said.

"I have no idea."

"Not you?"

"No." In the one word, Sam could hear that Cheng's bafflement equaled his own.

"So you don't know how."

"Nope."

"Police record? Delinquency?"

"Zip."

"Early life?"

"Not much. It's odd, but the school records, elementary all the way into high school, are really sketchy. Almost like he was an infant, and then, presto, he's a teenager, with nothing in between."

"Reaction?"

"Strange. The word has filtered out in the usual ways, but without the usual mood change, if you know what I mean."

Sam knew: Stories inside the project on the evening TV news, in the papers, and the local blogs about how the mysterious illness has struck again, followed by a subtle and temporary change in the public atmosphere, a kind of muted grief and anger, the adults having little doubt about what the mysterious illness was, and the younger people, especially the victim's friends, smothering their pain because all the adults at home and school told them to.

"The family?" he asked.

"They won't talk," Cheng said.

That was normal. Who wanted to talk about a child dying from a sudden inexplicable illness.

"The medicos?"

"Weird. They showed me the records, but I can't find the doctor in charge, and none of the nurses will tell me who treated him. The hospital director seemed embarrassed, but he discouraged me from poking around."

"How, then?"

"No fucking idea, Sam. This one is really strange."

Sam clicked off.

Speaking of saviors, there you are: Jesus, from infant to thirty in nothing flat, unhindered by loves, frustrations, triumphs, catastrophes, and all the other ills that flesh is heir to. Only, this Renaldo made it just to seventeen.

Sam strolled, through the empty alleys and narrow streets of the project district, straying beyond his normal confines onto the more trafficked streets, the ones with the squeaky-clean tech stores and cafes, even as far as the big shopping mall, with its stores, big and small, its *boutiques*, its *eateries*, all of which he loathed. On weekends it was out of the question, a place to avoid at all cost, not fit for children, as he and Jennifer agreed, contrary to what most parents thought. After school, there were throngs of kids, from age twelve on up, wandering, eating, buying, with the jaded lusting that only the economically comfortable could manage. Once they survived the adolescent ache for life, what then? And, *why*? For years, Sam had lived and breathed the reasons, not least that he and his family were able to partake of exactly *this*, and Sam impulsively waved his hand, in conversation with himself, at the vista of comfortable consumer commerce. And, yes, they, and the other *Projectville residents*, were free of war, free of almost all crime and all disease, so that five premature deaths—now six—seemed, relatively speaking, a small price to pay for continuation of the species. Always before, Sam had reconciled himself to this necessity, but he could no more. He could not reason away the grief filling his gut for the smartass, the troublemaker, Renaldo Kim. Maybe Renaldo's parents were horrors, their warped child-rearing perhaps shaping a dangerous criminal, but even were that not belied by the absence of any record of budding criminality, and even had Kim been the first and only, the price seemed too high. Sacrifice one young person for *this mall?* Perpetuate a species that wanted only *this?*

Sam pulled out his smartphone, which, since he was the head of project security, was very smart indeed, with apps that ordinary folks could only yearn for. Projectville phones had what he had described for Barry and the crew, as "a shield," with precise protections that let the innocuous stuff in and kept the dangerous stuff—such as information about the project—out. Because he had designed it, he knew just how precise it was, exactly where the tiny holes were and exactly what could wriggle through without so much as a raised flag. He knew the kids' favorite internet places—he and his staff

121

had created some of them—and he knew the kids' coded language, the camouflage that they used to hide their plans from their parents. He also knew that the parents could see through the camouflage, so that his disguised messages would get through to everyone.

He knew even better than Barry about the "facility access system." For an instant he let himself feel the power of being Chief of Security.

Lastly, he knew how to set lags, which would let him orchestrate the messages and the FAS switches. He knew with fair certainty what the lags should be.

He had to give himself enough time, two to three days, to do what he could barely picture himself doing, which would be, besides asking Jennifer for their first date, the second totally impetuous act of his life.

He arrived home late in the afternoon, Jennifer and the kids already there, hanging out in the kitchen. He greeted them and stopped, standing in the middle of the room, looking straight at Jennifer. "We're going on a trip," he said with a smile. He saw Jennifer's apprehension and felt the moment of mutual understanding.

"Where we goin', Dad?" Kirk asked.

"I can't tell you," Sam said. "It's a surprise."

"When?" Jennifer said.

"Two days."

26

4&k3L)(n was enthralled. Ah! What have we here? A compatriot? A kinsman? A fellow artist!

4&k3L)(n saw toggles flipped, zeros changed to ones and vice versa, messages poised for sending. Someone else was nudging reality, not settling for the natural order of things, whatever that might be, or for some undefined flow pre-ordained by who knew what or whom. Someone else was using the present as a canvas on which to splatter some paint that would drip down and form the future. The splattering was fun, but watching the dripping, with its unforeseeable diversions over tiny obstacles was the most fun.

So, who was this creative soul? 4&k3L)(n knew that there were always traces, always an audit to reveal who had been there, like Kilroy scrawling someone else's name on a wall. Could this be another interloper, another digital marshal artist, like me? Or perhaps—oh, we hope not—not an artist at all, but a grubby fortune-seeker, an entrepreneur wanting only to distill potential joy into lucre.

But no! Here! An employee of the very same project that has promised so much viewing pleasure. And, uh . . . hmmmm. Oh. Oh, my! Not some key-clacking drone daily feeding data into the project maw, nor some screen-scanner working mightily to defeat boredom in the hope or fear of seeing some attention-demanding anomaly; oh, no, not this one! This is someone who rates his own box on the org chart with a misleading title.

And, yes, indeed, this was someone who knows what he is doing. There is no probing, no wasted motion, no bobbing or weaving, no need to explore and retreat from dead ends; this artist knows exactly where to go.

But what to do about this? 4&k3L)(n knew to take care, for there is the possibility, remote though it definitely is, that some art-hating philistine has stumbled over the work, and has dared the fury of the gods by trying to eradicate it, or trip me, trap me, discover me, ultimately to send jack-booted thugs to destroy me! Could that be? 4&k3L)(n considered and concluded that the thrill was in the odds.

A fellow artist, then, even if operating from within. 4&k3L)(n had seen such before. 4&k3L)(n had, in the past, been tempted to introduce himself, to get acquainted, to invite collaboration, but had not because . . . because collaboration was a bore.

However, 4&k3L)(n would engage. I shall divert some paint trails as they ooze down the canvas. This artist shows signs of daring, but not nearly enough. I shall help, I shall enhance the art. I shall push these messages out further into the frontier. I shall mate them to produce young, and the young, as the young always do, will go where they are not supposed to.

More will happen. More to watch!

27

Grace, Roberto, and Colin Fairchild ate dinner together most evenings. When Colin mentioned that fact to friends, some would roll their eyes, some would make a crack about decades-old TV shows on cable, and some—girls, usually—would say that it was nice and wish that their families did that. A few said that, yeah, their families ate together mostly.

Typically Roberto and Grace shared opinions about books or politics while giving Colin the chance to join or not, as he wished, thereby treating him as an equal instead of condescending with questions they would never ask another adult. Colin knew he had a good family and was proud of both the family and the knowledge.

But this particular evening was tough, the conversation clipped and sporadic, the eating slow and not pleasant, because Colin had broken his plan to tell them at the end of the meal and instead had told them at the start that he had been outside again, and that simple statement had flattened the normal spirit. Colin watched his parents groping for a response, each looking to the other to say something but not the wrong thing.

"Colin, you have to stop," Roberto said.

"Dad, are they the enemy?" Colin asked.

His father took a breath and then said, "For us, they are. I would have to say yes."

"I would say they're like wild animals," his mother said. "They're not bad, but they're still dangerous."

His father shrugged. "Same thing," he said.

Colin studied the food on his plate and considered his parents and the parts of their lives he knew nothing about.

He supposed his father was *average*, clean-cut, trim, athletic enough to coach Colin's soccer and baseball teams and participate in their scrimmages, authoritative without being bossy.

"I've never seen wild animals," Colin said. "Just on TV." A new thought occurred to him. "Just like them, huh? They're what we see on TV, in movies, aren't they? Like the wild animals in the nature shows?"

His parents answered by staring at the remains on their plates.

"Now I've seen *them*. Still never seen wild animals, but I've seen *them*," Colin said. Then another idea hit him: "Outside, maybe I could see the animals too."

His mother gasped, his father laughed. "We want you to live, Colin," Roberto said.

Colin replied with a line he'd heard in an old sit-com: "You call this living?"

His parents laughed, and then his mother cried.

Roberto said, "Colin, we don't know what this is all about. We don't really know where we came from, what we're doing here. But then, neither do they." He laughed at his own joke, though nobody else did. "But this is our life. It certainly has its, well, *limitations*, but many people in this world are absolutely miserable. We're not so badly off, really."

Grace gathered dishes to distract herself from crying. Roberto looked uneasily at Colin who was seeing something in a far distance.

"She didn't look like an enemy, Dad."

"Who?"

"The woman."

Grace paused at the kitchen sink to look at Colin.

"She looked *ordinary*," Colin said. "I mean, she looked like a different version of *us*. She was dressed the way women do here. She was carrying a shopping bag like she'd been to the mall, and she had a coffee. And she was *scared*. When she saw us it was like she'd seen, I don't know, a *monster*. I mean, we were scared, too. My friends all freaked. I was scared, of course, but then, I don't know, she looked so *terrified* and she was beautiful, and somehow, I didn't feel so scared because she looked like she needed help a whole lot more than I did. And then she dropped her coffee and ran." He stopped and gathered himself. "That's where the stains on my pants came from. The lid burst off her cup when it hit the sidewalk and I got splashed." Colin did not add that to him she did not look ordinary at all, that she was in fact to him the embodiment of all the masturbatory fantasies and wet dreams he'd had since he was twelve.

Grace, who had stopped crying halfway through Colin's story, stood at the sink with a hand on her hip. "Colin," she said. "You are not going out there again. Got it?"

———

At the home of LaTasha, Jerome, and Morgana Thurman, Jerome was yelling the same thing to LaTasha, but without any such narrative from LaTasha, who hunched her shoulders and clenched her hands together in the chair in the formal living room that her family hardly ever used unless they had company. Jerome was standing in the middle of the room, pounding one fist onto the other hand to punctuate each word: "Not. Again. Understood?"

LaTasha nodded.

Morgana, LaTasha's mother, sat in a chair across the room, her eyes blazing in harmony with Jerome's.

LaTasha did not want her parents to be angry at her. She did not want them to fear for her safety. She did not want to disappoint them. She respected them, and she understood what respect meant. She worked hard at being cheerful and not rebellious, unlike some of her friends for whom rebellion was all, who would speak contemptuously of their parents and defiantly of their need to burst out and have their own lives.

LaTasha's parents were strict with her, but not overly strict. They set clear boundaries. They would fight with each other sometimes, but never about how to raise her—on that they never differed.

LaTasha was trying very hard at that moment to not be rebellious, trying so hard that she stopped hearing their tag-team admonitions about how bad it was "out there." She never did hear them tell her how they knew how bad it was. She held her face up to the parent who was speaking, hearing Morgana ask, "Do you understand what I'm saying?" LaTasha nodded silently but did not hear the rest of what her mother was saying, although she was certain that she had heard it, that she got the overall message.

She wanted to be good and not rebellious.

She also wanted to go out there again, and she wanted to go with Colin.

———

Bryce heard his mother on the phone to his father, who lived with another woman in a condominium two miles from the house he had left to Bryce's mother Marissa and Bryce.

Tired of waiting for dinner, he had gotten left-overs from the refrigerator, and now he sat at the kitchen table eating cold ham and potatoes.

Marissa stood leaning against a countertop, watching Bryce eat while she argued with his father Jerry, saying, "I have *not* been too loose with him." She stared at Bryce's food. "Because that's what kids do, that's why!" Bryce watched her listen. "Oh, really? Then why the fuck did *you* do it?" Bryce got up, got a glass from the cabinet next to his mother, went back to the refrigerator and poured milk, then sat down again. "Well, then, he's a lot like you in that respect, isn't he!" Bryce finished the potatoes, saving the remaining ham to eat last, to wash down with milk. "Fine. I'll tell him to go see you tomorrow night, okay? Goodbye!"

Bryce remembered seeing old movies, before cordless or cell phones, where people would finish an angry conversation by slamming the handset down onto its cradle. Now, when all you did was push the red button, there was nothing to slam. His mother looked like she needed something to slam.

She stared at his now empty plate. She started to cry.

Bryce got up and leaned against the counter next to her. He was a head taller than she was, and when he looked down at the top of her head he felt bad for her and responsible for her.

"It'll be okay, Mom," he said. "I won't get hurt. I promise."

She turned to him and hugged him around his waist. He put his arms around her shoulders.

"Baby," she said. "You're all I've got. I don't want to burden you, but it's the truth."

"I know, Mom," he said. "I swear it will be okay."

She felt small in his arms. He kept repeating "it will be okay," but he pointedly refrained from saying he would not go "out there" again.

————

Gerald's parents had never been "out there." Leah and Mahesh Reynaud were troubled about their son's behavior, his late hours, the hipster gleam in his eyes and his big, easy grin. Where in the world had he gotten that? Not from them, surely.

129

Leah and Mahesh knew who they were and that they did not have easy smiles, that not much was easy for either of them. So, where had this kid come from, with his arrogance and his charisma?

Gerald had stopped discussing important things with them way before pubescence. Gerald knew, at about age nine, that Mahesh and Leah could not answer his questions, could not even understand his questions, did not really want to hear his questions. By age eleven Gerald had only well-hidden contempt for his parents, and by age twelve he was pretty sure he could manipulate them into believing anything possible about himself. Since what he had seen was not possible, he figured he could not explain it, and so he stayed quiet and smiled.

All they had going for them was his guilt, and he would never give them the leverage to use it.

So, Mahesh and Leah had not been able to read behind the police chief's warnings, and they managed only timid admonishments to Gerald to avoid trouble. Gerald felt a little sorry for them, but only a little.

———

Astrid's father Gilbert was swearing at her, the way he had done privately for as long as she could remember and the way he obviously, to her, worked hard not to, publicly, when she was on a soccer field, for example. While she played she could always hear him, swallowing words whole before they escaped his mouth, leaving funny gaps, as if he had some kind of weird breathing disorder, in his steady critique of her play, her attitude, her *self*. At this moment, as he drove her home from practice, he did not so censor himself.

"You have some choices, *young lady*," he said. "You can drag your lazy ass through life, like you did just now in practice and like you did in that last game—what a piece of shit *that* was—you can be Bryce's *twat*, you can go *out there* and fuck until you get dead, or you can make something of yourself. Of course, doing *that* would require some *effort*."

Astrid's father was big and hunky, like Bryce, but he wasn't nice to her, like Bryce. She watched his hair, gray but thick, blowing slightly in the wind that came in over the windshield, the top of the car down. A beautiful afternoon, and there he was, his knuckles white from clenching the steering wheel, his face red, spit flying out of his mouth on *S*'s and *T*'s.

"I want to go see Mom," she said.

That stopped Gilbert, but only for a moment. "Well, tough shit," he said, glancing at her. "I've got custody and it's not her time."

Astrid sat, quiet and sullen, watching the town pass by the car—the shiny shops, comfortable homes, carefully manicured parks, the trees that somehow looked like they were trimmed daily, like a man might trim his beard. She wasn't sure if she still loved Bryce or not. He seemed to love her, though she wasn't sure of that either. But Bryce was wild, and the outside was wild, not all tidy and neat like their town. Her father was wild too, but wild like some big movie monster bent on enslaving everyone. Bryce and the outside were wild and *free*. She understood that *free* meant *scary*, but scary like the town roller-coaster, not scary like her father.

Fuck this shit. I'd rather die out there than live in here.

————

Elmer's kitchen table was quiet, as they all sipped from bottles of beer. For a quarter hour or more, nobody spoke. That Elmer drank beer with the other teenagers was no secret, but his parents seldom allowed him one at home, and then only on special occasions, when friends and relatives came over to celebrate something and they all got loud and raucous together. This time was not like that. It was calm and quiet and somehow sad.

"We did," his mother Phuong said with a sigh. She smiled a little.

"Yep," his father said. He smiled at her, and they looked at each other and nodded a little, looking like they were sharing as secret.

His father, Michael, looked at Elmer. He said, "It would be better in some ways if you didn't. But like your mother said, we did. So."

They were quiet for a longer time.

"At some point, though," Phuong said, "it's going to happen, big. We can't stay in here, cooped up, forever."

"It's true," Michael said. "We just don't know when. And we don't know what will happen then, or how." He sipped his beer. "But some day."

Elmer did not know what to say. Knowing how dangerous it was out there, he understood why they would be scared and worried about him.

"Maybe this time will be that day," Michael said. "Whoever does it will have to be young, because once you get older and have kids," and he raised his hands and eyebrows. "So maybe you and your friends will be the ones." He took another sip. "The thing is, the only way for it to work, for anything lasting to happen, will be if we go out in large numbers, and nobody's figured out how to do that yet. They won't let us, so we have to work around them."

"It will have to be more than they can handle," Phuong said. "So if you think this is the time, but it's not, then the ones who go will be, just *gone*."

"She's right, Son. So just be careful, okay?"

"Sure, Dad," Elmer said.

"Just tell us if you think it will be long, okay?" Phuong said.

Elmer nodded.

His father raised his beer bottle, and then Phuong and Elmer did too, and they clinked together over the table.

28

They were in the motel room again, once again obviously not for sex. Boris hoped it would happen before they had to return but nevertheless found himself enjoying her, admiring her, the looker he'd first seen in the power hairdo and the sharp business suit, now looking much different. In the car she had said only, "The motel has free wi-fi," and Boris had then known how it would be.

She had opened the laptop on the bed instead of the table that was the more practical place and had said, "Please, I need your help." Responding to his shrug she had said, "This is scary. I need you next to me here." So Boris had nodded and joined her on the bed, she leaning to her left against his chest and he to his right, the laptop in the middle. He watched her browse.

"None of our stuff is there, you know. They tell us in training," he said, now assuming the official voice, *"Do not try to look for project information on the internet, which is continuingly cleansed of all mention of the project. Furthermore, searching the web for anything about the project is a punishable offense."*

"Punishable by firing?" she asked while still tapping on the laptop.

"If only that was all," he said. "You might as well do it anyway. To leaving the project area without proper permission you've now added removal of electronic equipment. If you find anything they'll hang us by our toes and skin us."

"My cousin emailed me—one of the emails that they let through, who knows why—told me that flying around the web there was a funny picture of a woman. She said it looked like a movie promo pic, a woman recoiling in horror from something. But the funny part was, she said the woman looked like me, only she couldn't find a link."

"Just as well. The link probably would have triggered the auto-censor."

Boris watched her, never hesitating as she tap-tapped away, pausing only to scroll through search results or examine an individual item. He saw the brains at work, the focus, the eagerness, the confidence bordering on aggression. It turned him on. He rubbed her shoulders with his right hand and felt her lean back into it, her small bones and muscles tense, not with fear as in their last meeting, but with purpose, her focus never leaving the screen. After twenty minutes he would have given up, but not her.

"Shit," she said.

He stopped admiring her profile and turned to the screen, where he saw her holding a shopping bag over one arm and a cup in a hand, without doubt the source of the coffee stains on the legs of her beige pants. In the photo her face was horror-stricken, and her eyes aimed down. The angle of the picture was upward.

"Facebook?" he said.

"Just some site that collects fun pictures and video."

At the bottom of the shot was the back of a male from the waist up, his head tilted backward so that they could see the crown.

They stared at it together.

"I turned and ran," she said. "At some point I dropped my coffee and then later I dropped the shopping bag. I didn't stop until I got to my car in the underground garage."

"It's a mall?" he said.

She looked at him.

"They don't let us sex daft in there," he said.

135

"But you've seen them."

He nodded. "Couple times, out on the road, in the desert."

They both turned back to the screen.

"Once there were some by my car in the street. Two or three of them. *They* ran from *me* that time. I literally couldn't believe what I'd seen. Thought I was going nuts. I thought that for a long time. Couldn't decide if I had hallucinated or really seen something. Either way, it scared the hell out of me. I became compulsive, watching out for it, real or not. You know? Checking under the bed, looking everywhere? For what? Now at least I know they're real. It's kind of a relief."

"That's when you decided to get out," Boris said.

She smiled. "Yes, that's when we met," she said. She lifted her right hand from the laptop and touched his cheek.

They stared at the photo and waited for each other.

"They're it," Boris said.

"The project," she said.

"Yes."

"Are they dangerous?"

"You know as much as I do. The situation sure is, or somebody important thinks so."

"He looked like just a boy, a teenager," she said. "A nice-looking teenager. He didn't look afraid. If anything he looked worried. Maybe my memory is off, god knows it wasn't my most rational moment, but I can't shake the idea that he was worried about me."

Boris thought, *well shit*.

29

One odd thing about the viral photo was that Marjorie could see it from her apartment.

She had never known what the project was. She knew only that she had signed a lucrative contract to work on it while remaining ignorant about it. "Do you understand clearly that ancillary and support staff are not privy to core operations?" her trainers had asked. "Do you understand that you are not even to attempt to find out?" *Yes to both*.

For years she had not cared, because of the money and the job security. But now she could not un-see what she had seen, and she was sure she had seen the heart and soul of the project, and she felt very *privy* indeed.

Internet access in Projectville was controlled, with many sites blocked continuously and others sporadically, based on content, a fact announced prominently in all Projectville employment contracts. So, why and how was she seeing not only this picture, but comments and blogs and articles about it now? At home in the evening, and even at work, there it was.

Of course, at the office people asked her about it. "Is that you?" they wanted to know. "It looks like you."

Marjorie would smile and laugh a little and say, "No, not me. I think it's a promo for some movie, but it's definitely not me."

"Not becoming a movie star, huh? Leaving Projectville for the glitz and glamour?"

Marjorie would shake her head and laugh again. "Nope. No movie stardom for me, unfortunately."

"But it sure looks like you."

"Just a gorgeous new starlet who resembles me, lucky girl."

Which was not far from what was actually claimed on some sites, in particular in one article about an unnamed film studio trying to make money not by featuring actual stars, but by creating new ones without names until the movie was released. An updated *Gulliver's Travels* maybe, with a woman as the lead. "A Hollywood source, speaking on condition of anonymity, said without sarcasm, 'In one scene she would be tied down naked with male Lilliputians climbing all over her.'" The image was a bit nauseating, but more so was the complete fabrication. She had no enemy, no angry ex-lover, who would spread lies about her, so the source had to be someone who was just making things up for the fun of it, as people frequently did on the internet.

And there was this comment:

> Giant human or mini-humans? Based on the architecture of the buildings in the background, the photo was taken somewhere in the southwest. Of course, the views of buildings are fragmentary, but the yellowish-tan pseudo-adobe walls, and the red Spanish tiles—which also could have been Photoshopped—certainly point southwest. And what else is in the Southwest? Right: Roswell, New Mexico.

But on another site, under the photo, was this:

> No, folks, this is not from some soon-to-be-released cinematic special-effects extravaganza. If it were, the pseudo-cryptic billboards would already be up, with messages like, 'On [fill in release date] they are coming out', which would encourage a lot of misguided speculation that the movie was about miniature LGBT's.

> Nor is it about space aliens. Sure, the photo location is probably in a southwestern state—judging by the architecture above and behind the big woman and what

appears to be a cactus fragment in the lower right corner—
which would make it only hours, or at most a couple easy
days, away from Roswell by car. But these ain't aliens, folks.
It's weirder even than that.

Think about it. Let's say you were moseying along with a
coffee in one hand and a shopping bag in the other, and you
came around a corner and beheld a group of little people,
leprechauns, borrowers, or whatever. You might be a bit
startled at first, but then what would you do? I know what I
would do. I would look around for the remote controller, the
box with buttons, joystick, and antenna, in the hands of a
nerd. I would be grinning, because I would know that the
nerd would be grinning, and I would be preparing for the
happy explanation of the latest in robotics.

But the big woman is not grinning. She looks terrified. And
why would she be terrified instead of bemused or intrigued?
Because she has seen these little guys, or some others like
them, before. Because she has some insider knowledge, and
she knows that these little guys are neither robots nor
androids, but something else, some new kind of being—
maybe even human being—developed for some secret
reason by some organization with lots of money to buy
scientists and the time to let them work. And who could that
be? Somebody's uncle? Named Sam, maybe?

She stopped searching to rise from her chair and go to the
kitchen to turn off the heat under the singing tea kettle, but she
did not pour the water into the pretty porcelain pot with the
her favorite relaxing mixture of herbal leaves and seeds in the
strainer. She went right back to the living room where her
laptop sat on the coffee table.

More searches revealed many stupid adolescent jokes and
numerous references to *Alice in Wonderland*, *The Incredible
Shrinking Man* and *The Attack of the 50 Foot Woman*. And then
there was this on a political blog:

139

We have, unfortunately, become accustomed to government using its secrecy classification system to hide everything from minor embarrassment to criminal activity, including some that started years ago and continues to this day, despite at least partial disclosure. And we also know that among the secrets are the government's vast technological powers.

This knowledge has propelled many people to investigate, using whatever bits of data, leaked or otherwise, they can find, to expose what should be exposed. For example, see excellent pieces here and here.

Also, naturally and inevitably, and, unfortunately, such knowledge has encouraged wild, unfounded speculation about government collusion with international bodies and even space aliens, such as this, this, and this, all of which are plainly unhinged.

However, sometimes the truth does seem crazy, for example the Kennedy Administration's attempts to enlist the aid of organized crime to kill Fidel Castro with an exploding cigar.

Our organization has gained possession of leaked government documents that seem to relate to the viral photo spinning around the web showing either a very large woman confronting ordinary people, or an ordinary woman confronting very small people. The documents clearly demonstrate that the latter would be the case—though we cannot vouch for the authenticity or provenance of the photo.

The documents include PowerPoint presentations and research papers, all referencing a project to develop miniature human beings. These are not planning documents. They clearly refer to a project known to the documents' audience and in progress for many years. They also make plain that these beings are human—they are not robots, androids, or clones, though some cloning techniques were probably used at the beginning.

The documents do not tell why the government would embark on such an enterprise, nor do they tell of future plans.

The documents are quite voluminous, and we have had time to study only a small fraction of them. As we learn more, we shall write about it.

Marjorie did not follow any of the links, but she continued searching, until she found this lying among the garbage:

You have without doubt seen the photo. You know the one I mean, the one catching more eyeballs than any pet tricks, weird animal behavior, or small children doing and saying the darnedest things.

Unlike some of those other pics, however, this one is not fake. There is documentary evidence, just revealed, about a secret government project to create undersized freaks. The documents do not say why the government would want to do such a thing, but we think we know.

The government wants to control us—of that we are certain. They can control full-sized people, but wouldn't it be much easier if people were only, say, a few inches tall? If the ruling elite can keep the rest of us from reproducing, they could replace us with these little people. The little people could do most of the work the elites need to maintain their money-making machine and would be a whole lot less trouble to control, not to mention feed and house.

Of course, the replacement could not happen all at once. It would have to be gradual. The government would start with an announcement. I imagine a TV event where the wee ones are introduced, extolled as able to do jobs we bigger folk cannot do and as less of an environmental threat than we are. There will be lots of smiles and applause.

Then there will be lots of speeches and propaganda about how we must learn to accept the wee folk, to the point where even jokes about them become politically incorrect, drawing stern, emotional lectures from the president and the rest of the administration.

Along with that will come a campaign to urge the big people—that would be us—to reduce reproduction, to make room for more of the wee folk.
Sound crazy? Well, it is, but I'm betting it's nonetheless true.

The problem for the government is, those wee folk might not be so docile. What if they decide to break out? What if their government keepers have given them knowledge we don't have? What if they decide to take things over all by themselves, bypassing this elaborate government scheme entirely? What if their very wee-ness is an advantage in a power struggle?

The government has some answering to do.

Marjorie did not imagine herself to be Clarence Darrow or Thurgood Marshall, but she did believe herself to be a pretty damned good lawyer, capable of putting up a damned good fight in pretty damned complex cases, either criminal or civil. Or at least, before recent experiences had cracked her confidence, crippled her professional performance, and—well, she could not say that they had wrecked her personal life because she had possessed hardly any, and in fact they had brought her Boris, but that was another matter. Now she knew that she had seen miniature humans, that there was a photo to prove it, that Boris had seen them too, and that she was not crazy.

So, she felt confident enough to look at what was before her eyes and know it was not internet rubbish. It was about the project—maybe not accurate in its speculations, but *about* the project. And if it was about the project, how was she seeing it? Who was allowing it, and why? And why now, so suddenly?

Top management was still opaque, guessing about it was pointless. But still.

A pre-litigation negotiation trick, perhaps? A tip that the opposition's case was collapsing? A feint to throw her off the trail? A warning from a turncoat?

———

Sydney, thankfully, answered the gate post phone. They exchanged the pleasantries of people only superficially acquainted.

"Sydney, could you please tell Boris that I phoned?"

"Of course," Sydney said, and Marjorie thought she could hear him grinning, pleasantly, through the phone.

"And tell him, please, that I won't be reachable until tomorrow morning?"

"Absolutely," Sydney said.

Sydney, rude and crude, party animal, boorish, given to adolescent sexist jokes. And always cooperative. Marjorie would have been embarrassed to admit that she liked him.

30

Barry had told his boss in Washington, the latest political appointee, that now was not a good time, that he needed to remain at the Project to deal with some unexpected problems, serious, yes, but manageable. He had considered telling fat Carl, as Barry secretly thought of him, to shuffle off to his next congressional hearing, or whatever it was that kept Carl busy, and *go ahead, Carl, fire me and find somebody else to run this thing*. That would have been fun, but Barry had been dissuaded by Carl's straightforward statement—and when, before, had Carl ever been straightforward?—that several FBI agents were ready to escort Barry if need be.

Now, in a small, plain meeting room somewhere off a basement corridor, the last of a series of corridors that began beneath an obscure Washington, DC, building but that ended so far from the building entrance that Barry could not be sure they were still even within the District's boundaries, Barry heard the president say, "So, I understand we have a *thing* here."

There followed a moment of silence broken by chairs creaking and throats clearing. Minutes before, striding down the hall, Carl, clearly panicked, had asked, in a whisper, where Barry's notes were, because Barry had no briefcase, no laptop, no bulge of pod or pad in any pocket. Did he at least have paper in his breast pocket, or something on his phone? Where?

Barry had ignored Carl. Carl may have been the assistant deputy associate under-secretary or something for something-or-other and Barry's boss, but he was still just a big jackass. The little dapper man in the hallway with them may have been more important, and then there were the three very important-looking Secret Service agents (who would stand in the hallway outside the room). But Barry led *The Project*, and he would not be intimidated by anyone, not even the leader of the free world.

The leader of the free world had, fittingly, kept them waiting, but not long enough for them to even start to agree on a story.

"Sir, it's a, it's a, um, a *situation*, sir," Carl had said, and Barry suppressed a smirk, seeing Carl's panic level rise at the apparent fact that he had just contradicted the president: Was it a *thing*? Or a *situation*?

The president glanced briefly at an aide sitting on his right with a note pad she would never use during the meeting, and then looked to the other end of the table at the small but large-nosed man in the tightly tailored suit and the bright colorful tie, who, in turn, looked at the large, hulking Carl, who sweated across the table from Barry. From that look Barry gathered that the dapper little guy was Carl's boss.

"Well, sir—" Carl said.

"Little people," the president said.

Carl looked at Barry, but Barry said nothing.

"It's a project, sir, that's been going on for, well, several decades," Carl said.

Barry was pleased to see the beads of sweat on Carl's forehead and his mouth open and close like a guppy's.

The president sighed, leaned back in his chair, clasped his hands behind his head, and spoke to the ceiling. "I've been told, but I'm not so busy running the country that I don't occasionally take a squint at the internet for my own self." He chuckled. "Little people. Right? Wee folk."

"As I said, Mr. President, it's a project that's been going for several decades—"

The president abruptly swung his chair upright and leaned down the table toward Carl. "A project? A *project?* What the hell? I've heard stuff from the sig-int folks about this but nobody can explain it to me."

Barry watched with more pleasure as Carl tried to buy time by fumbling reading glasses from his breast pocket and putting them on, pulling papers from his other breast pocket, and then saying, pretending to be searching his notes, "It is, sir, *decades old*, sir."

"Exactly *what* is decades old?" the president said.

"The project, sir."

"The *project*."

"The, uh, little people, sir."

The president squinted at Carl. "Exactly how many?"

"How many what, sir?"

"Decades! Years! Whatever! How long?" Leaning down the table the president was yelling only about four feet away from Carl's face.

Carl told him, exactly.

The president leaned back in his chair and once again became thoughtful. At the moment, he looked comfortable, the only one in the room in shirtsleeves. Barry thought of the word *affable*, but only from the nose down. The president's eyes shifted from Carl, to the little man, to Barry, and back to Carl.

"So there really are," the president said.

"Yes, sir," Carl said.

The president leaned forward, put his elbows on the table and held his head in his hands. "Uhhhh," he said.

After a moment he straightened up. For the first time, he looked at Barry. "You must be the scientist," he said.

"Yes, sir," Barry said, happy to be able to speak and smile easily, without any hesitation or forcing. "And engineer. And project manager. I run *The Project*. I am Barry Hagenstopple."

"Then you'd better tell me about it, Barry."

146

31

Michael, Elmer's father, found the place for them. Michael's job had often taken him there, in front of the fluorescent orange and black sign that looked spooky in the artificial light:

DO NOT ATTEMPT TO REMOVE

AUTHORIZED PERSONS ONLY

Every time he saw that sign Michael mused about attempting to remove authorized persons only, but not so much about why the sign was there. The big machine screws that held the big hatch required an unusual bit, difficult but probably not impossible to find, so why hadn't they put the fasteners on the other side? His boss had said something about emergencies, when, presumably, authorized persons only would show up. As foreman of a Department of Water and Sewers maintenance crew, Michael had no problem getting into the tool rooms at night. He'd allowed himself two hours to find the bit that authorized persons only should use, but he had needed less than fifteen minutes. He wondered about why authorized persons only had left it so easy to find, in a small seldom-used cabinet. Maybe because, in an emergency, even authorized persons wouldn't want to spend time punching in key combinations that they might forget, or pressing fingers into print-readers that the emergency might have broken. More likely, they were just careless, or the authorized persons' bosses were saving money.

As to why the sign was there, no authorized person, training course, or manual had told him. He knew the reason, the same way everybody knew the reason why there were certain places you didn't go, certain areas you didn't poke around in, sign or no sign. Which was why Michael was pretty damn sure this hatch was the place to go now.

When they got there, neither the bit nor his ratchet wrench was needed.

———

Just before midnight Elmer texted everyone about the manhole his father would open for them, and then he added something unusual: "My parents are coming. My dad says to bring yours too."

Bryce went to his mother's room. "Mom," he said, his hand on her shoulder, "we've got to take a trip." Bryce gave her time to turn on her back and open her eyes to him, before repeating himself.

She sat up. "What we saw on the internet last night," she said.

Bryce nodded. "We've been texting all night. Seems like it's hitting the fan."

"What is?"

Bryce shrugged. "Something. It's weird on the web, even by web standards. Elmer's dad works for the city. He says everybody's getting ready."

Marissa looked at her burly son in the light falling in from the hallway. She touched his cheek.

"We're all meeting at this place Elmer's dad knows about."

Marissa smiled. Her son, the leader. "When," she said.

"Tomorrow morning at six. Mom, it's going to be okay."

She nodded. "Wake me at four," she said, and turned back on her side.

148

Bryce, knowing his mother liked to sleep before big occasions, left her room.

————

"You've got to go," Gerald said.

His parents, both dowdy in pajamas and robes, sat opposite each other at the kitchen table, both looking at their own hands.

"To go where?" Leah said.

"Well," Gerald said, "it's not crystal clear. Just out of here."

"Why?" Mahesh said.

Gerald's usual wry, hipster, cocksure grin collapsed and suddenly he was sobbing and rocking, cradling himself in his own arms. "Aaahhh," he said, and then again, longer, "aaaaaahhhhh."

His parents gaped at him. Mahesh cautiously put a hand on Gerald's shoulder. Leah held both her hands to her face in shock. "Son," Mahesh said.

Gerald rocked back and forth, in wider motion, tears falling across his face, his nose, running into his mouth. Leah rose and went behind him and held him against her, his head just below her chin. She rocked with him until his motion abated, then stopped. He reached up and held one of her hands.

Gerald swallowed twice and gathered himself. "Mom, dad," he said. "I don't know exactly where, and I don't know why anything. I don't know why we're here and I don't know what else even exists. I just know I have to get out. And I want you to come with me."

Mahesh said, "Well." Leah and Gerald looked at him. He was clearly paused in mid-thought, his brows raised over eyes that looked out the dark kitchen window, then back to Gerald and up to Leah. "Then I suppose we should prepare," he said.

———————

Grace, in her bathrobe, was again in Colin's room, watching the internet over his shoulder. "Roberto!" she yelled.

Roberto, barefoot in boxer shorts and tee shirt, shuffled in.

"Look at this," Grace said.

Roberto looked at a blog with the header, "Emergency in Our Town???" The text below it was strange, talking about a "looming crisis" and how to escape it, while trying not to talk about it at all. Roberto said, "Sounds like astrology, where they predict your future without really saying what's going to happen."

"But, Dad," Colin said, "look here," and he read: "Look for unconventional ways out, like floating over water, or following electrons along cabling, or hitching rides on conveyor belts."

"So?"

"Elmer's dad thinks he knows what this means, about the water."

"He's a plumber or something," Roberto said.

"Ever since that picture," Grace said.

"And that death," Roberto said. "Did you know that kid, Colin?"

"No," Colin said.

"I remember others," Roberto said. "I didn't know any of them personally, but one or two were friends of friends, or someone I knew about."

"Dad, Mom," Colin said. "Our group, me and my friends, we want to go. And we think you should come with us."

"Who?" Grace said.

"Us. You."

Roberto and Grace looked down at their son, sitting cross-legged on his bed. They looked at each other and knew they

150

could not stop him and that they could not be without him either.

"We'll be like the Joads," Roberto said.

———————

LaTasha was in tears, again sitting hunched over, her hands clenched together in her lap, on a small bentwood chair next to a knick-knack table. Her parents, together on the couch across the maroon carpet, glared at her. She was pleading, on the verge of collapsing onto the floor to beg them from her knees, like in some dreadful old movie.

"It's not just this wild idea about getting out, is it?" Morgana said. It sounded like a question, but LaTasha knew it was not, so she did not answer. "It's that boy," Morgana said.

"It's both," LaTasha said.

"Without the boy?" Jerome said.

LaTasha shrugged and looked at her hands.

"I get the impression that boy does not reciprocate," Jerome said.

"I don't know," LaTasha wailed. "They're all my friends, but it's not just them and it's not just going outside and it's not for *fun*," and she veered from pain to anger that made her not fall from the chair to beg, but rise from it to demand, her fists clenched at her sides. "It's *you! It's US!*" She saw her parents' astonishment and understood it, knowing that she had never shown them defiance before. Then she heard her father laughing, heard him before she saw him, and she saw her mother looking as if stifling her own laugh, and then Morgana was laughing too, which made LaTasha laugh, though she did not know what was funny.

After they stopped laughing Jerome said, "What's funny, LaTasha, is that your mother and I had this conversation."

"With our parents," Morgana said. "We remember one of the boys who got this strange untreatable disease. They've always been boys, for some reason."

"We were angry," Jerome said. "He was a nice kid who hadn't hurt anybody."

"You knew somebody did that to him?" LaTasha asked.

Jerome sighed. "No, we didn't *know*. But we *knew*."

"The difference now is this crazy stuff on the web," Morgana said.

LaTasha, feeling weary, sat down. "There's always crazy stuff on the web," she said.

"It is different now. We figured a time would come," Jerome said, looking at his wife.

"Elmer's dad has a plan," LaTasha said.

———

Astrid did not attempt a family conversation with her father, not that she didn't want one, not that she didn't wish she had a father who would want one. She would have liked to have a conversation with her mother, in the drying tank yet again, but that seemed equally pointless as well as impractical. She knew her sadness was not about leaving her parents but about not having parents she was sad to leave.

But that had been her whole life, to date, so she threw comfortable, sensible clothes into her soccer duffel and prepared to spend the night with coffee and internet TV, the sound through her earbuds, because she would have to leave before her father woke and she could not risk the sound of an alarm clock.

The TV shows passed before her blank face. She smiled a little, thinking that none of them could match the excitement of what she was about to live, on the outside. With Bryce. Or without him.

In the dim early morning the town had the look of a place preparing for a major event, a big concert or political rally, or perhaps an invasion by a foreign army. Car traffic was less than normal, pedestrian traffic more, people with faces anxious or eager, fearful or grim, but all expectant. Strangers passed each other with small smiles and nods, not wanting to talk about what they all knew they were sharing. People who knew each other paused only briefly to say, "Something's up, huh?" The answer would be, "Seems like it," or something equally noncommittal. Friends might share hopes to meet again, but not specifics, which they were fearful of sharing without knowing why. Voices were low, nobody wanting to be overheard. The unspoken understanding was of a mass exodus, differing from historical ones in that they moved not as a mass, but separately and in small groups, each going to a different spot and respecting each other's right to keep their own spot secret.

"It's like the 'Night of the Living Dead,'" Gerald said to Elmer as they met.

"Except we're not eating each other."

They, with their parents, were the first to the corner with the manhole, not in a street but in a small slightly overgrown and unkempt corner of a park. Michael led them through a short path through untrimmed shrubbery, which was high enough to shield them from the growing crowds on the streets.

Michael and Grace introduced themselves to Leah and Mahesh, who surprised Gerald by saying, "Let us gather at the manhole," which drew a laugh from Michael and apparently drew Astrid from the bushes. As if to explain, as they watched her brush leaves and twigs from her clothing, she said, "It's just me. I've been hunkered there for an hour."

When Bryce and Melissa arrived, Bryce went right to Astrid and hugged her. Colin, Grace, and Roberto appeared with LaTasha, Jerome, and Morgana just behind at approximately 5:58, all of them beating the agreed-on time of 6:00.

"Looks like we're going," Michael said, gesturing generally at their backpacks and duffels.

"We don't have to," Mahesh said.

"Yes, we do," Morgana said, prompting a surprised and happy gasp from LaTasha. "It's been enough. We've seen enough. We stay here, nothing will change. Who knows which of our kids they'll pick off next."

"We're manipulated," Grace said.

"Trapped," Astrid said, which stopped the conversation as they all looked at this small girl whose aloneness was made more conspicuous by Bryce's arm across her shoulders.

"Okay," Michael said. "We agree." He pulled a tool from a pocket of his cargo pants and opened the manhole, which Elmer helped him move aside to empty ground. Michael climbed down a ladder into the hole and then held a flashlight while the others lowered their bags into the hole and followed. As each one reached the floor, Michael stood down the tunnel, holding the light downward so that they could see the surface without being blinded, and minimizing light that might be noticeable on the surface.

When they were all down, Leah said, sniffing the air, "Is this a sewer?"

"No," Michael said. "It houses sewers." As he led them through the tunnel, he gave them, in a low voice, a docent tour of what they were seeing, explaining that the tunnel was one of many built along with the original project town to hold electrical and communication cables in conduit clamped to the walls and the big water and sewer pipes hanging from the ceiling, pointing out junction points, repairs, locations of problems where he and his crew had needed to improvise to solve some unprecedented problem, installations of new fiber-optic cable and the old copper cable still there though unused.

"On your right," he said, allowing his voice to rise after the first quarter mile, "is one of the main valves for water shut-off in case we have to do some work downstream." He stopped and they all stopped behind him. He flipped a switch and the tunnel was lit. "I think it's safe enough now," he said. "I said *have* to do. Should have said *had* to do, since I don't expect to do more again. Anyway, there was a break downstream. Water was gushing out like a leak in one of those submarine movies, up to our knees and rising while we wrestled this thing in." He paused and gazed at the big blue wheel and the big bright red pipe fittings with attached meter dials and electric wires. The others mostly gazed at him. "Scary as hell." He took a deep breath. "See, they didn't want to turn off water to the whole town because, well, not because they were worried about our water supply, we could live without running water for a few hours, even though maybe we couldn't because not even the hospitals have an emergency supply, but because anything like that happening meant we would *know* or *think* we knew one more thing, and our ignorance was as important to them as water to us. So, my crew and I, six of us, had to get this thing in before we drowned." He paused again and smiled. "I don't think they cared if we drowned, but they let all the water drain from the tunnel before they made us come back and put in the electrical. Us frying could have shut down the whole system."

Because Michael's voice quavered and his breaths deepened, they were silent until Colin said, "So, they were giving you orders? Like, directly?"

"Sort of," Michael said. "I mean it's not like we had face time with each other, but I had my radio and cell phone. I knew who it was. They depended on us because nobody else could get into here."

"Me too," Mahesh said. "I'm an engineer. I'm probably the guy who gave you the diagrams." He returned Michael's grin.

"No more, huh?" Michael said.

"No more."

"So, you knew?" LaTasha said.

"Knew enough to keep my mouth shut," Michael said, looking at Phuong.

"You?" LaTasha said to Elmer.

"More than my Mom and Dad thought I knew," Elmer said.

Michael continued to lead, occasionally reaching out, without pausing, to flip switches to light the way ahead. A half hour later he stopped where the door lay on the floor in front of him, "Do NOT Attempt To Remove" facing up along with the machine screws requiring the non-standard bit, because the hatch was still in its frame. Michael stepped around it and examined the edges where the frame and hatch assembly had once been attached, with Mahesh following him. Electrical contacts were exposed.

"Blew it off," Michael said.

Mahesh nodded.

"Who? How? Why?" Michael said.

Mahesh shrugged. "Somebody outside," he said. "Everybody, walk around this junk on the floor. Don't touch these edges."

An hour later they were climbing down ladders made for much larger people, aided by a knotted rope from Phuong's pack, down wall brackets and conduit mountings to the floor of a large room, through a short drain pipe after easily removing a sieve covering it, from the floor to a slope outside, to the freedom of a barren desert hillside.

32

C heng saw the crap on the internet.
Cheng's job was not so much to police Projectville, which
needed little policing, but to know what was happening there
so he could tell Sam, who was not responding to secure texts
as he was supposed to twenty-four-seven. In boxer shorts and
tee shirt, Cheng had sat in front of his computer for the last
three hours, reading blog after blog, each one dumber than the
one before but not totally dumb. Blogs were always dumb,
rant alleys for ignoramuses.

Cheng rose wearily from his desk chair, his knees creaking
and his lower back sore, and took the four steps to his bed,
where he sat again, wanting sleep, feeling lonely, wanting
Sher, in the tiny studio that was just the right size for his
solitude. He had chosen both the small space and the solitude
to avoid inflicting on anyone else the unabating grief that had
begun sprouting in his belly even before his first day on the
job, decades ago, even in the early days of hope and glory
when he had believed in the great cause. God damn it, he had
known even before, hadn't he? He had seen this future, a
glimpse of it but still enough, as he had sat in that shiny office
for the video-conference interview where they had pitched this
"job of critical national security importance" to him, to prepare
him even though he had just started his first year of college.
Their manly smiles, the stress on the job's importance, "not just
to the country but to the entire human race," had worked on
him, and he had allowed an imagined picture of himself, late
in life, looking back with satisfaction on his share of the glory,
to overwhelm the small but unmistakable birth of the grief that

would overtake everything else—or would have, without Sher.

He shook his head remembering his fantasies of being honored for helping to save humanity. What was he, what had he been, in plain fact, for his whole career? *Snitch. Rat fink. Stool pigeon. Traitor. Learning about the first young male corpse after the fact, but then inevitably complicit in the rest.* How could he have dared to trust himself to fully love another person, or to beget and help raise children?

But, of course, he had needed love like anybody does, and he had shown just enough of that need so that Sher, to her misfortune, had loved him.

And now, Chief Schmitz, Mr. Bigshot, what are you going to do? The crisis is here. What will you do about it?

He phoned Sher and dressed. He decided on the street uniform, but wore the SWAT hiking boots instead of the standard street shoes and threw casual clothes into a backpack.

———

"How come we're the only ones in a car?" Sher said, as Cheng drove his cruiser through town. At two in the morning, the streets were already thick with pedestrians, but there was hardly a car.

"GPS's," Cheng said.

"This one?"

"It's at home in my garage."

"The food warehouse?" She said.

Cheng nodded. He parked at the curb in front of a brick building, two stories tall, with only small windows below the roof. At the large front doors there was already a crowd of about fifty people who moved aside to let Cheng and Sher through but did not look happy about it. A woman was trying without success to work her keys in the lock. Near the doors but away from the crowd was a young officer, looking helpless, his hands on his belt. Cheng nodded to him.

"Key won't work," Cheng said. "There's an electronic override."

"You can't stop us," the woman said.

Cheng turned from her to the crowd, which was quiet, the looks on the faces ranging from pleading to defiance, except for the small children, who clung fearfully to their parents.

"We'll break in if we have to," a man said.

"We can help, if you let us," Sher shouted, "and you won't have to break anything. Just let us lead the way, okay?"

"We'll be better off working together," Cheng said. He pulled out his cell phone and keyed in a code. "Try the key now," he said.

The woman turned the key and opened the door. Sher moved in first and held up her hand.

Cheng turned to the officer and said, "Where's your bag, Daniel?"

"In my car around the corner," Daniel said.

"Get it and come back," Cheng said, and turned to the crowd. "People," he said, "I'm Cheng Schmitz, chief of police—or maybe former chief of police. The lady is Sher Statie, city, or former, or something, city manager, and the guy coming around the corner is Daniel Talikian, one of our officers, or, I guess, we're all former now, aren't we."

Nobody spoke, but smiles began to form on some of the faces. From the back of the crowd, someone whooped.

"Sher and Daniel both know the way and will lead you out. I'll stay behind to help from the rear. There are bound to be more coming." He looked at Sher. They nodded to each other and smiled.

"Let's go, folks," Sher said. She and Daniel went into the building and the crowd followed with their bags, quietly.

Several of the people shook Cheng's hand and thanked him as they passed him at the entrance.

They moved silently and briskly through the cold food warehouse, ignoring the crates and boxes of supermarket food, to a set of doors at the back that Sher opened with her cell phone. She lit the corridor beyond, through which ran a long, wide, unmoving conveyor belt. "We'll leave it off and walk," she called. "No free rides today. Be careful."

"I'll help you up," Daniel called, and he stationed himself where the conveyor started.

And down the conveyor they went, excited but still orderly, helping each other.

After a half hour, the stream of people broke and Cheng arrived with pieces of box cardboard and tape. The cardboard had arrows hand-marked on them. Cheng taped them to the propped-open doors. "Can't wait for everyone," he said. "They'll have to make it on their own."

Cheng and Daniel walked quickly through the conveyor tunnel, and after ten minutes emerged from it where the small crowd waited for them on top of a high platform with no railings. Cheng found Sher at the far end. "I've watched the food containers come out at our end, but I've never seen this end," she said. They looked over the edge to the floor below. "What now?" she said.

"Deliveries today?" Cheng asked.

"They do them at night. Won't start again until about six."

He looked over the precipice to a concrete floor below, then he lay down on this stomach and hung his head over the edge. "Daniel," he said.

Daniel lay down next to him and Cheng pointed to a corner support. "We could tie off there if you could get to that box." He pointed to a cardboard box left conveniently next to the counter. "Think you could jump to that?"

"Probably," Daniel said. "If I had my skateboard it would be no problem, but I think I can make the leap." He grinned as he said, "But what, exactly, am I tying?"

They pushed themselves upright.

"Anybody bring any rope?" Cheng yelled to the group.

Seven people, four men and three women, shouted affirmatively, and there was the sound of zippers opening and closing before they all stepped forward, grinning, holding out varieties of rope, braided, vinyl-covered, coiled and bundled.

A teenaged girl said, "Mom? You've done this before?"

A middle-aged woman handed her coil to Cheng and said to him quietly, "Teenagers. Always think they're inventing life." Then loudly, her eyes still on Cheng, she said, "Honey, you have no idea." She winked at Cheng, who winked back.

When Cheng turned around Sher was staring at him. He laughed and said, "I was a teenager once."

Sher winced and said, "Right. But the ropes?"

Cheng raised his eyebrows as he examined the various bundles.

"Okay, I knew about this stuff. But, Cheng," she said.

"I did things before I knew you, Sher," He said.

"Not that. I'm afraid of heights."

"Must be others," he said. "We'll get you down."

Without much talk, Cheng, Daniel, and the seven others laid ropes out on the platform surface, examined them for wear, cut out worn places, knotted lengths together, made loops and harnesses.

When they were satisfied with the work, Daniel, standing near a corner, said, "Give me room, folks." Everyone stepped back. He took twenty paces from the edge, turned, and without even taking a breath, ran for the precipice and leaped. The group heard a thump, as of a heavy object landing on cardboard. Cheng, standing at the edge, applauded as Daniel waved to him from the top of the box. "Soft, really," Daniel said. "Toss me a coil." Daniel caught the coil. He leaned from the edge of the box to the corner leg of the platform, and, with his feet braced against the box edge and one shoulder against the leg, he tied a rope end through an unused bolt hole.

Some people climbed down the ropes. Some lowered others, including Sher, in harnesses. Each person, touching the solid floor, looked at those already down and felt the freedom. As the group at the bottom grew, the eagerness of those still above grew, and the group's exhilaration grew. A small boy, in a rope harness tied to his father's back, watched in awe as the two of them were lowered to the floor. "Hey," he said, "this is just a humungous countertop!" And all responded with giddy laughter.

In slightly more than an hour, they were all down, having retrieved all but one rope, which Cheng, as the last man down, had to leave behind, tied to the leg. He was the only one not smiling. He took Sher aside and whispered, "What now? This place is sealed."

"I just got over hyperventilating from that amusement park ride and you're giving me more shit?" she said. "Sorry."

They looked around: an industrial human door, a sectioned steel overhead loading dock door, all looking firmly locked and sealed to keep critters away from food distribution.

"Must be restrooms," Cheng said. "Maybe a vent?"

Sher took a deep breath and pulled her cell phone from jacket pocket. "This is for extreme emergencies," she said, "but I don't think this is what they had in mind." She opened an app and keyed a code.

Click, clack, clunk, like the sound of lock and load. The human door opened.

"I'll be goddamned," she said.

In a moment more, they, like others, were standing looking at the same immense, free, desert that Colin and his friends and their parents saw.

162

33

S am and Jennifer, their kids sleeping in the back seat, passed through the project gate just past midnight. Neither actor nor con man, Sam assumed what he believed to be an authoritative air at the gate, smiling while handing the guard his badge and ID and then making a point of ignoring the guard's authentication process while chatting with Jennifer, and finally laughing an apology about forgetting to put his finger in the print-reader.

As it happened, the guard at the time was Sydney, who noted the lack of formal exit permission and was amused by Sam's obvious act but was not about to get officious with the chief of security and didn't really give a shit anyway. "Have a nice trip, sir," he said as he handed the badge and ID back to Sam and was again amused at Sam's patronizing smile. He neglected to enter the departure into his log. Why court trouble? He mentally saved the incident as a party story for later, but never got to use it before hell broke loose.

In the early morning darkness, Sam encountered no other traffic and stayed on the official road, merged onto the state two-lane, and stayed at the posted maximum fifty-five miles per hour, past the truck stop. He pulled to the shoulder once to disable the GPS tracker. They had left all their electronic devices behind, despite protests from Kirk and Sandra.

Back on the road and then onto the freeway, while the kids slept, he explained to Jennifer that their last name was now Brookens, not Giles, a change he hoped Jennifer could make real for the kids. She said she could. He told her he had new ID cards for the two of them and that they would destroy their old ones with scissors. They also had a car, under the name Samuel Brookens, in storage in Phoenix. It was seven years old and not as nice as their current gleaming SUV, but it would attract less attention.

"I'm worried about the kids," Jennifer said.

"Me too," Sam said.

"Not ours. The ones at school. Their principal will be gone."

"Before long, most of them will be gone too."

Jennifer said nothing. Sam kept his eyes on the road.

"The word will travel. Their parents will want to leave," he said.

Four hours later, Sam stopped at a rest area. The kids were sleepy and cranky. After the restrooms, back in the car, they were hungry and whiney. Jennifer got them junk snacks from the vending machines. She got into the back seat with them, "So we can talk," she said.

As Sam drove for another hour and half, she explained to Kirk and Sandra that they were on an adventure. "It's like a game, only serious," she said. They stared at her and ate their cookies. "It's like your soccer, Sandra, or Kirk's Little League," she said. "It's a game, but when you're on the field playing, it's serious, right?" They both nodded. "So this is like that." She took a moment to let them think about it. Then she said, "Now, the first part of the game is that we all have a new name. Our first names will stay the same, but our new last name is Brookens." She spelled it for them, and then had them spell it and say it back to her. She asked them one at a time to pretend she was a stranger who wanted to know their name. They told her, accurately.

"But what's it for?" Kirk asked. "Why do we have a new name?"

"Yeah, why?" Sandra asked.

Sam winced and glanced at her in the rearview.

164

"Well," Jennifer said, dragging out the word and meeting Sam's eyes in the mirror, "this game is really important. It's more important than soccer or baseball. You know how when you lose a game, it bothers you for a while, but then you forget? Well, if we lose this game, it will bother us a lot more. Daddy has a plan for us to win, and part of that is changing our name, and other parts are changing other things, and we'll find out about them soon. Okay?"

Again, Sam's and Jennifer's eyes met in the mirror.

"Sounds cool," Kirk said.

"Okay," Sandra said.

———

Sam gave two thousand cash dollars to a gas station manager, who used his tow truck to take Sam to a long-term parking garage two miles away. The manager assured Sam that the new power train and air conditioning had worked perfectly once a week for the past three years. Sam thanked him, told him where his other SUV was and to allow forty-five minutes before taking it and doing, as quickly as possible, whatever car thieves did to mask their work.

Sam drove to where the other SUV was and found Jennifer and the kids still safely locked inside with the radio playing. He parked behind them. Jennifer got out and looked at the old SUV with its peeling black paint and red rust spots. "You could've found a worse one," she said.

"It drives great. The neighbors will never see it," Sam said.

"This is our new car?" Kirk said.

"All part of the game," Jennifer said. "Now here's another part of the game. While Daddy puts the luggage in the *new* car, we have to remove everything else from the *old* car, so that nobody will know we were in it."

Kirk, into the game, narrowed his eyes. "Remove every trace of us," he said.

"Every trace," Jennifer said.

"Every trace," Sandra said.

———

Through the bright desert day they drove and listened to music. Kirk complained about not having TV in the back seat, like in their "old" car, but Jennifer satisfied him by explaining that it was part of the "mission," which Kirk liked even better than "adventure." Sandra went along with what her big brother liked.

Sam told Jennifer about the money transfers and the new accounts and apologized for having to exclude her from money decisions. "You couldn't share even that with me?" she asked. "I brought in money too."

"How could I?" Sam said.

"All this secrecy for all these years," she said.

"It's a secret project."

"I know. And it's not like you had a mistress. But still."

"Still what?" Sam said, feeling irritated.

"I know you couldn't share with me, but I shared everything with you. You couldn't help it but I can't help resenting it."

They rode in silence for a long time.

"*Did* you have a mistress?" Jennifer asked.

Sam glanced at her. "My god, no," he said.

"What's a miss triss?" Kirk said.

"Not for you," Jennifer said.

More silence.

"So we're going to LA," Jennifer said.

"As good a place as any," Sam said. "We'll have to rent, for now. I'll find a job."

166

Sam glanced at her again, and caught her look, which seemed bitter and fearful. "It'll be okay," he said.

"You've been planning this," she said. "The money, the car, the names."

"They were contingencies, I had to. I didn't know what might be necessary, but I had to plan for anything. I was very careful."

"And those, what did you call them, liquidations?" she said.

"Cullings," he said. "I explained them."

"Yes, you did," she said. "But I don't know what to think or feel."

"Once I was in it, I was in it," Sam said.

"Like *the mob*," she said.

Sam thought about that. "Yeah, pretty much like the mob."

"And now we're *on the lam*, like in a movie."

"Please. Trust me."

Jennifer laughed. "Years of lies and subterfuge, and now I have to trust you."

"Jennifer—"

"Yes, I know, I know, you told me you had to keep secrets. Until now I never thought of that as lying. To me, it was like you walled off part of your life, and I was dumb enough to believe that you could do that without lying."

"Yes, well. My options were limited."

"Like ours are now."

Sam nodded. "Like ours are now. After lunch could you drive? I'm beat."

"Sure."

34

There was a problem the next morning, Tuesday, several hours after Sam had taken his family out.

At the gate, where Marjorie had hardly ever seen another car at the same time as hers, there were at least a dozen cars in the outbound queue, motors running. Two or three cars ahead, there were a couple of people standing outside, watching the gate. In the car directly in front of hers, Marjorie could see three heads in the back seat, three in the front. At the front of the line, a man was standing by the guard window, gesturing with his hands. She could hear his raised voice, though not the words. Inside the guard post, Boris was shaking his head. Another man approached the window waving what looked like a wad of cash. Boris glanced up and kept shaking his head, raising his hands and shoulders in a gesture of helplessness.

Two more cars arrived behind her. Between her and the gate, a car door opened, and a woman got out and stood beside it. Someone started leaning on a horn. A door opened and slammed and a man began yelling. Another car arrived but instead of joining the queue, the driver drove onto the shoulder straight to the gate and began honking. Doors opened and slammed, people stood on the road yelling at the line-jumper and at the guard, yelling something about knocking down the gates, which were nothing more than the swinging barriers common to parking garages.

The line-jumping car seemed to encourage others, and the queue behind Marjorie broke, with drivers pulling up behind the first line-jumper, while others drove to the opposite side of the road where the inbound gate stopped them. More doors opened and slammed. People formed small groups in intense conversations. Some of the groups walked towards the guard station. Voices became louder and Marjorie could hear anger and fear.

Marjorie got out of her car and stood next to it. Beside her was a heavy woman in jeans and a tee shirt, glaring at the guard post. The woman turned and met Marjorie's eyes and said, "That clown in there would do better to just open up." The woman looked back toward the gate, then quickly looked again at Marjorie. "Have we met?" she asked. "You look kind of familiar."

Marjorie quickly glanced at and away from the woman and said, flatly, "No, I don't think so."

"You sure do look familiar," the woman said.

Marjorie heard a trunk open. A moment later it closed, and to her right she saw a man with a jack handle in his hand. She looked behind and saw a free-for-all traffic jam with no escape route. She stayed with her car and tentatively raised a hand toward Boris. After a few seconds he turned and appeared to acknowledge her with a small nod.

The heavy-set woman was still gazing intently at Marjorie but her manner had changed, her eyes narrowing, her mouth starting to smile, and her head nodding slightly. "You're *her*, aren't you? The woman in the picture?" she said, with the slightly awed, slightly aggressive tone of someone meeting a movie star known for bad behavior.

Marjorie kept her eyes on the gate and said, "What picture?"

Three men in heavy work clothes, complete with yellow construction helmets and vests, walked to the car just behind the inbound gate, and spoke with the driver. A moment later, the men walked away and broke their group, with each of them speaking separately to drivers behind the first one. After each such chat, the driver backed up and re-formed a line on the shoulder and on the dirt beside the shoulder. Soon, drivers were getting the point without being told, and were cooperating.

"Shit," the heavy woman, still staring at Marjorie, said softly. Then she yelled, "Hey, everybody! It's her! Right here!" The woman held both arms straight up above her and pointed her index fingers at Marjorie, moving them in staccato bird-like pecking motions. "The one in the picture!" the woman shouted. "It's her, it's her!"

Heads turned toward Marjorie. For a moment, the movement of cars and the group conversations stopped.

Marjorie got into the car and locked it. From inside, she saw Boris exiting the guard post.

The moment of hesitation over, the semi-organized car movement started again. Quickly the inbound lane was cleared, and a large pickup truck, an elevated four-wheel-drive with big tires and a heavy duty bumper, with one of the burly hard-hats behind the wheel, rolled on the left side of the two-lane and picked up speed until it crashed through the inbound gate, which flew into the air and slammed into the guard post, cracking though not breaking the reinforced glass.

Drivers approached the opening, one at a time, cooperating enough so that each could exit in turn, and then burned rubber accelerating once outside.

Marjorie saw Boris running towards her, through the traffic, and she opened the passenger door for him and locked it after he entered. She maneuvered along with the others until they, too, were speeding down the two-lane.

"Where to?" Marjorie asked.

Boris, without seatbelt, was busy pulling at the buttons of his uniform shirt, yanking the tails out of his pants, pulling his arms from the sleeves, and finally tossing it to the floor. "Straight, for now," he said.

"How did it get in?" Marjorie asked.

"I thought you might know," Boris said.

"Me? How would I know?"

Boris shrugged. "Seems like everyone saw it, or lots of people anyway. And half the ones who did decided they wanted out, like you."

"I had more than the picture. The picture was just confirmation."

"Maybe for them too."

They rode in silence, Marjorie holding speed at about seventy, like the cars ahead and behind.

"Big secrets are hard to keep," Boris said. "The pot's been simmering for a long time. The picture turned up the heat, the pot boiled and the top is blowing off. I knew it was gonna happen since our last time in the motel." He shook his head. "Should have gotten you out sooner, avoid the rush." Before Marjorie could respond, he said, "Up ahead near those big cactuses, pull in there."

"Why?"

"Please."

Marjorie slowed and pulled onto the shoulder, then onto the dirt, the car bouncing on rocks, and she stopped behind a large clump of cactuses.

"Pop the trunk, turn off the engine, release, the hood, stay in the car" Boris said, getting out. He went back to the trunk and returned to the front of the car carrying the tool pouch that lived in a compartment of the trunk. He opened the hood and bent over behind it.

Marjorie got out and stood beside him. He was using a wrench to disconnect the positive cable from the battery.

"I said you should stay in the car," he said.

"I left my job. I don't take orders anymore," she said, holding her arms across her belly.

"I didn't mean it that way. I've got to do some stuff and you need to be able to drive away, fast."

"You?"

"As long as you're here, pick up the tool pouch and give me stuff when I ask. Oh, me? I'm with you, baby, believe me."

He handed her the wrench and asked for the Philips screwdriver, which she gave him.

He began pulling screws from a small box attached to the frame on the driver's side, letting the screws drop to the ground. As if she had asked, he said, "GPS tracking." He pulled the wire harness from the box and tossed the box to the ground beside the passenger side of the car. He took the pouch from her and said, "I need your phone and your laptop." He put the screwdriver back in the pouch and put the pouch on the ground in front of the car.

She hesitated only briefly before going to the car to pull her phone from her purse and her laptop from the trunk. She saw him on his knees leaning into the car. As she walked behind him, he said, without looking up, "Better if the laptop's out of the case." She tossed her phone on the ground near the GPS box. She unzipped the laptop case and dropped the laptop on the ground. "Might as well keep the case," he said.

Boris got up and proceeded to reconnect the battery cable. After dropping the hood, he took a flat-blade screwdriver from the tool pouch and went back to the car. Marjorie watched him kneel by the passenger door and jam the screwdriver into the CD slot and pry up, down and sideways. She heard things crunch. He rose to find a fist-sized rock by the road, which he then pounded into the radio. Bits of plastic fell to the floor and circuitry was exposed. He pounded at least six times.

He rose, holding the rock in his left hand and his uniform shirt in the other. He handed her the shirt, pulled his phone from a pants pocket, and dropped the phone near the other electronics.

He chose the GPS box first. He took the shirt back from her and wrapped it around the box in a way that would hold it, not pad it. He put the bundle on a large rock and pounded it several times with the small rock. Then he opened the shirt, examined the pieces and found them satisfactory. Using the shirt as a sling, he hurled the pieces into the desert.

He repeated the process with the two phones.

He opened the laptop , bundled it, and pounded both the main body and the screen.   As he finished the last blow, he said, "Tablet? Anything else?"

"No," Marjorie said.

"Okay." He slung the pieces of laptop onto the landscape. Then he carried the uniform shirt a few yards in from the road, kicked a shallow hole in the dirt, put the bundled shirt in it, and kicked the dirt on top.

"Have to do," he said. He returned the tool pouch to the trunk, where she had already dropped the laptop case. "On second thought," he said, and pulled the case from the trunk and hurled it off the road as far as he could. He slammed the trunk.

Once back in the car, he said, "They still might be able to track us, but," and he shrugged. As she started to drive, he turned the AC to max and took a big breath.

"Traffic's lighter but still more than usual," Boris said.

After she got up to speed, she said, "Like a movie."

He smiled at her. "You look good enough for one."

She smiled back. "You look great yourself. Especially manly, smashing electronic gear."

"About four miles up, dirt road crosses this one. Turn right."

Less than four minutes later she saw the turn and took it.

"Look out for big rocks in the road," he said. "If you see one, stop, I'll go and move it."

They needed to do that four times during the hour or so they rode on the dirt road, which wound over a low ridge that put them out of sight of the two-lane. They saw no other cars, but they did hear helicopters from the direction of the two-lane. They came to a place that had a fence with a gap allowing the dirt road through. Fifty yards beyond that was a four-lane with only a dirt center divider. Boris directed Marjorie to drive across the near lanes and the divider and turn left, which she did after only a short pause for a semi-trailer.

"Where we going?" Marjorie asked.

Boris told her, a medium-sized city in the desert near LA.

After some thought, Marjorie asked, "How'd you know about the shortcut?"

"Not really short," he said. "Actually adds distance."

"You didn't answer the question."

He smiled. "Lawyers." He shook his head. "Been on the job for years, not much to do. Other guys just watch TV, drink, and fuck whatever they can find. Sydney, for example. Me, I like to explore. Sort of wander. See a dirt road, wonder where it goes."

After five silent minutes she said, "This all seems too easy."

He shrugged. "Project goes on for years, no major incidents, they get careless, I guess. Anybody would, even pros."

More silence, more sparsely travelled four-lane. He said, "But it is kind of funny how it exploded. I figured it could happen, but not all at once like this."

"You weren't doing that, were you?"

"What?"

"Fucking whatever came along?"

Boris smiled. "I was waiting for you."

Marjorie thought about that, believing him but not really. "You say that to all the girls?" She thought more and said, "I think you might have saved my life, that first day."

"You were stretched pretty tight."

She glanced at him. "It wasn't charity though, right?"

Boris laughed, a short explosive bark. "Are you kidding me? The pleasure was all mine."

35

Barry said, "Mr. President, the project was started by a committee of six scientists of several disciplines, concerned about—" and Barry stopped as the president held up his hand and looked at the small man.

"Leslie?" the president said.

The small man cleared his throat and said, "It's one line item and it's within departmental discretionary limits, sir."

"For all these years?"

Leslie looked at Carl, who shrugged.

"Wait," the president said. "Then, Les, you haven't been briefed."

Les looked at his hands.

"Carl?" the president said.

"Sir, like Les said, it's one line item, and."

The president looked at Leslie.

"It's in the black budget, sir."

The president pointed at Barry and said, "Tell me that year again."

Barry told him.

"An inauguration year, start of a new administration," the president said.

"Yes, sir," Barry said. "Actually, it was inauguration *day*."

"So it was in the crack."

"I'm told that's what it's called, sir."

"Within departmental discretionary limits, in the black budget, in the crack," the president said to the room.

"Yes, sir," Barry said, smiling brightly.

"Congress?" the president said, looking at Leslie.

Leslie shrugged and shook his head. "I don't know every part of the history sir, but."

"So, most likely, I'm the first president to know."

"I don't really know but I would say that does seem likely," Leslie said. "Sir."

The president squinted at Barry for a moment, and then said, slowly, "Proceed."

Barry was ready. Barry had been preparing this lecture for most of his professional life, from the time the team of scientists, then nearly in their dotage, had recruited him to lead the effort. In quiet moments, before dinner while sipping his daily bourbon, or after dinner with an unread book in his lap, or in the shower or on the toilet, he had seen himself performing to a rapt audience of scientists and other scholars, of world leaders, captains of industry, and other glitterati who just happened to be there. He had not pictured himself in a room with only four other people, even if one of them was the president, but, still, he was ready. *Just try not to make it sound prepared*, he told himself now.

"As you know, sir—"

"Wait," the president said, pointing his finger at Barry. "I understand that actually, there are two."

Carl and Leslie looked perplexed, but Barry knew instantly what the president meant. "In a way sir, yes, there are two, but they are two project *spaces*, within a single *project*. There is the smaller space where what you have called the 'little people' live, and the larger space where full-sized people like us live. The larger space includes the top-secret engineers and scientists who supply what the people in the smaller space still can't do on their own—though they now are able to produce almost everything, with their own factories and fabrication plants," and Barry radiated pride as he said that. "But the top-secret people have the same ancillary needs as in any town, so the larger space also includes the support personnel—the store

177

clerks and managers, the service-providers like doctors and lawyers, and so on—that any settlement of people needs, and—"

"Okay, I get it," the president said. "Small space, big space."

"Yes, sir. And the big space has the top-secret, and the—"

"Yeah, yeah," the president said. "Go on."

"Yes, sir. Anyway, scientists have long wondered about the possibility of life on other planets, and it was more than curiosity. They had concluded that, as a practical matter, someday humans would have to leave earth. See, sir, Thomas Malthus had said—"

"I know about Malthus," the president said.

"Yes, sir. Anyway, then you know he was wrong in the long run because of technological advances, especially in agriculture and medicine, but in the *longer* run it seemed inevitable that he would prove right. Our resources—water, food, breathable air—would run out. So to preserve our species, at least some of us would have to leave earth and colonize another planet." Barry stopped.

Barry and the president looked at each other. Les coughed. Carl wiped sweat from his brow with his hand and tried to cover it by scratching between his eyes.

"Space travel," the president said.

Barry smiled. *The president may be a political hack, but he's impressed.* "Those scientists guessed, based on knowledge of the galaxy at that time, that the nearest habitable planet might be three hundred light years away. *Might* be, best case. By the way, current knowledge of the galaxy has not changed that guess much, at least not yet. But let's say it was half that, say a hundred-fifty light years away." Barry stopped again.

The president leaned back in his chair and clasped his hands behind his head and spoke to the ceiling. "So, if they could travel at the speed of light," and here the president gave

Barry a knowing nod, "it would take a hundred and fifty years to get there."

"Right, sir," Barry said. "And even *half* the speed of light seemed wildly optimistic, so we're talking about hundreds of years. And no way could they ever conceive of a space vehicle—let alone a whole fleet of them—able to carry people for that long in the numbers needed to ensure—or at least get odds favorable enough—for survival on their new home. The craft would have to be large enough to house at least six generations. And not just house, but give the people enough space to work and live, to have individual privacy and recreation. And the craft would need to carry plants and animals that could procreate and grow and feed the humans. In short, the craft would have to be bigger than even the largest of today's cruise ships."

"So you're telling me you made little ones."

The president was quicker than Barry had expected and his statement sounded like an indictment, and for an instant Barry was de-railed. He felt himself stammering. "We call them R-S-H, sir," Barry said, and then, against his will, his sudden nervousness turned defensive. Who was this guy, this *politician*, to challenge *him*? "For Reduced. Scale. *Humans*." He spat the words out defiantly.

The president let his chair tip forward, his hands going flat onto the table, a grin forming his mouth, but not his eyes. "Did that insult you?" the president said. "Me calling them 'little ones'?"

"*I* do not feel insulted," Barry said, sounding insulted. "They are *human beings*, sir," Barry said.

"Little human beings."

"Sir," Barry said, working to control himself, "they are scaled down for very practical reasons, but in every other respect, they are just like us."

"I've heard they're commonly called *scalies*."

"If you saw them on TV, in their own town, you would not know they were different from us."

"But *we* created *them*?" the president said, the half-faced smile having vanished, and with a slight upward lilt to the final word *them*, as if to leave an additional sentence ending with the same word hanging silently in the air. He continued, "And this is a *thing*, a *situation*, because they've gotten *out*?"

"Our security is very good, Mr. President. Only a few have, from time to time, and—"

"But lately?"

Barry nodded, "Just a very small—"

"So these goofy internet reports of sightings are *true*?"

"Some of them, we think might be, sir."

The president leaned in toward Barry. "You had security, right?"

"Of course, sir. But—"

"Let me guess. Over the *decades* you got complacent. These little guys are clever. Et cetera, et cetera."

"I wouldn't say *complacent* sir," and instinct told Barry this was not the right moment to shift blame.

"But in any case we cannot allow this, can we," the president said. "How valuable can they be, *really*? Because *your project* may be small enough to hide in the black budget, but the *project* to build the space craft won't be. It will be enormous. Hell, we can barely afford re-usable space craft that hold five people."

Barry felt something crumple inside him, as both his hands went involuntarily to his head. "Mr. President," he said, "you cannot."

"*You* did," the president said. "Or at least, I've read that in some of the goofier blog postings, which I really didn't believe until just now."

"Mr. President, only in isolated cases. I didn't want to, but I had to maintain control."

"*We* have to maintain control."
Barry was silent.

36

By accident, Howard, too, had seen the internet shit. To Howard, the Web was not a web, but a pot. Some geniuses had invented a virtual receptacle for metaphorical bullshit. Appropriate, but reeking just the same.

Howard had no computer except the phone, a concession to his customers who now wanted to be able to find him "twenty-four-seven" as they said, as if a sick car were as critical as a sick child. He used it to check email once or twice a week, some weeks.

As militantly as Howard avoided the web, even he could not avoid it completely, as on those rare evenings when his house, with its adjoining mechanic shop, felt too confining even for him, when the weather did not invite rambling out under the fence, when he had temporarily used up his stash of interesting books, and an unease bordering on shame, the reasons for which he did not care to analyze, made solitary drinking unappetizing.

On such evenings Howard reluctantly walked a mile and half to his favorite bar. Like everything else in this burg, it was fake: The façade that under streetlights looked old and dreary, in bright sunlight looked like it had suffered a deliberately bad paint job. The grime on the floor and window sills, and the stains on the bar itself and the tables and booths, had become impervious to cleaning not through years of neglect, but because, as was obvious under close inspection, they were painted on. Outside, Howard had seen the real dreary bars, the lonely, quiet, comfortably filthy havens for lonely people, and he knew a poor imitation when he saw one.

Still, it served the purpose, and after a drink or two, the patrons who noticed didn't care. Among them, the small but growing number using the town's Wi-Fi blanket, inescapable anyplace without lead walls, did not bother Howard—well, maybe they bothered him enough to prompt teeth-grinding, but no more. But then, management had felt compelled to add a gimmick, an attraction that Howard would expect to see in the "coffee bars" and glittery restaurants that plagued his home town, but not here: above the bar, on the corner opposite the sports TV, was another one, the *sharing* TV. Say some three-sheets-to-the-wind bozo wanted to *share* a picture of a grandkid kicking a ball, or some self-pitying recently divorced bimbo wanted to *share* a picture of her ex in flagrante delicto with a younger bimbo, or some hypocritical wine-sipper found some video she thought might elevate the rye-swiggers, or some frustrated stand-up artist wanted to show himself trying to be funny at some other bar—well then, any one of them could grab control of that second TV and just *share* the living daylights out of everyone else.

By default, the monitor showed a soundless sports news feed, but when some jerk stumbled over something he believed everyone else needed to know—say, the latest celebrity idiocy—he could put it on the big screen.

When the screen blinked from sports talk to blue to whatever, normal human reflex lifted the eyes of anyone facing it, and a picture or a few interesting words might keep your eyes on it even against your will. This time, Howard joined in a group double-take. He felt himself change from boredom to fuck-it to intrigue. The mood in the room went from placidly somber to slightly anxious.

Words about "open doors" and "gateways," a photo of an open hatch. Phrases like "one chance for freedom" and, "before they kill us all," and, "we've taken enough," and, "disbelieve this if you want to, but . . ."

Howard was wondering what this bullshit was all about, when up popped a picture of a large woman looking down with horror at smaller figures in the foreground. A voice-over, clearly electronically disguised, was asking, "Is this picture a fake, as many have suggested, an illusion of perspective, or is it real? And if it's real"—but Howard knew goddamned fucking well it was real, and he was pretty goddamned sure he knew the people at the bottom were those kids he'd seen outside. It was a tableau from a monster movie, the shot where you see godzilla face front, bearing down on the retreating humans, only it wasn't godzilla and they were all human.

Howard heard someone say, "Yep. That's the one," and he looked around and saw that most of the bar people had seen this picture before. Somebody else said, "It's out. That rips it."

At eleven that night in the bar, brains awoke from conditions ranging from light buzz to heavy intoxication. Glasses with several remaining sips of bourbon or Scotch or rye were upended down throats, or, more often, pushed to the back of the bar or the center of the table and not touched again.

"Holy shit," was what Howard muttered to himself as similar sentiments rippled through the room. Stools and chairs were slid back in unison, money was slapped on the bar, and loners who had rarely acknowledged each other locked eyes for seconds, nodded in silent assent, trooped out the door, glanced once around the street and the sky, and then walked singly, alone as always, but now with more purpose than just going home.

At his house, Howard laced on hiking shoes and put on a long jacket with enough pockets for a bottle of water, toothbrush and small tube of toothpaste, his revolver, and his semi-automatic pistol, and spare ammunition for both. He double-checked the locks on his shop and his house, gave the interiors a look, and left through the back door, locking it as well, briefly wondering why. He took his usual route.

———

In the semi-darkness of early dawn, Howard looked down the desert slope to the highway below and did not like what he saw: clusters of his fellow townspeople staggering along with backpacks, suitcases, small children. But how did these doofuses know to go towards the truck stop rather than the other direction, into miles of open desert and certain death? Had they all been out, riding on the underbellies or open beds of semi-trailers? Had the word been spread, like folklore, from the audacious few to the timid many?

Of course not. There below him, recognizable even from the back, stood the stocky figure topped by graying crew cut of Cheng Schmitz, who had apparently demoted himself to traffic cop, waving people along.

"I hope you have sense enough to put that flashlight out when traffic comes," Howard said.

"Hello, Howard," Cheng said without turning.

"And to tell them to lie down when they hear it."

"Sure," Cheng said. "Enough of them know what to do."

"You hope."

"Howard, you always know better. It's who you are, the one who knows better."

"You want them to die?"

Cheng stopped waving and turned. "What are your ideas, Howard? I don't see many options."

"You have anything to do with this?"

"No, Howard. I found out the same way you did, on the web."

Howard was disappointed. He wanted to be able to blame Cheng for ruining his solitary jaunts. Fully able to take care of himself alone, he had no idea what to do with a group, a crowd, a mob, whatever the hell they were. He looked at

Cheng, and then at the small groups of refugees struggling over the dirt and rocks. What he wanted, goddamn it all, was to head off on his own, confident of his surviving, if not thriving. He'd done it for days at a stretch and he could do it for the rest of his lonely life. What the fuck did he need with these rubes?

He took a deep breath.

"What's your plan?" he asked, still watching the refugees and avoiding Cheng's eyes.

"Plan?" Cheng said, and they both turned at once toward the source of a low sound and the vibrations in the ground. Cheng turned off his light and they both hit the ground as the headlights came into view and a big rig bore down towards them. Howard raised his head to see that in both directions, people had flattened themselves. The truck passed with the usual terrible roar they made, like a series of explosions merged into one long boom, followed by two whirring passenger cars. As the red lights sped away from them, they slowly rose.

"Gotta watch more carefully for the electrics. Just a whish. Hardly hear 'em until they're right up on you," Howard said.

"I told them to stay in small groups, keep families together. Hop trucks, scatter, go where they could," Cheng said. "Watch for animals."

Howard shrugged.

"Packing?" Cheng said.

Howard shrugged again.

"Shot anyone lately?"

When Howard said nothing, Cheng laughed.

"Chief Schmitz?"

A very young man, tall and broad, looked at the two standing older men. He had to look down at Cheng Schmitz.

"Bryce," Cheng said, and looked at the small group assembling behind Bryce. "Got your clubbies here, huh?"

"Clubbies? Oh, yes, sir," Bryce said. "And parents."

"Sir?" Cheng said.

"Yeah, well," Bryce said and grinned. "Hello, Howard."

Howard said nothing.

Sher appeared next to Cheng. "This seems like the last bunch," she said. If there's more, like you said, they're on their own." Then she kissed him on the mouth and the night was silent for a moment.

"You know Howard?" Cheng said to her.

She broke away from Cheng and looked at Howard. "Don't think so," she said. "Where's Daniel?"

Cheng waved down the road. "Maybe we'll see him again," he said.

The group looked at Cheng as if waiting for orders.

Cheng looked at Howard, and said, "What do you think? What should we do?"

Howard stared at the ground. "We," he said.

Cheng burst into long laughter. Everyone else, Sher included, looked from Cheng to Howard.

"Come on, Howard," Cheng said, still laughing. "Let's find a truck."

————

Howard showed them where they could climb up on the semi-tractor, using springs, tires, cables, bolts, mud flaps. Bryce and Elmer, the two strongest boys, held on part-way up to hoist their baggage to the top. Howard used hand signals to enforce silence and quickness.

Then they sat or lay on a steel platform made more uncomfortable by the herring-bone pattern of hills and valleys imprinted on it. The back of the truck cab partially shielded them from the wind, as did the awesome underbelly of the huge tractor above them. They held onto or lay atop their cases and bags.

At first only Howard slept. The six teenagers talked quietly among themselves. Their parents got acquainted. Cheng felt obliged to keep watch, though he wasn't sure what for. It took more than two hours for the monotony of wind and vibrations to overcome the anxiety of a trip into the unknown, and then, all of them slept.

37

The large woman who had confronted Marjorie at the gate was Adrianna Hammerfeldt, who had worked nights stocking shelves in a supermarket. Thirteen years prior, she had been a social worker in a medium-sized northeastern city before losing that job to government spending cuts, an event that had left her with mixed feelings of dread about finding another job, guilt about leaving her clients behind, and relief about losing her case load of sixty-three recovering substance abusers, recidivist homeless, and mentally ill people that nobody but her seemed to care about. In that defeated and relieved mood, she sulked in her house for months, desultorily looking for jobs online, filling out applications and attaching resumes that sank into the same black hole as herself, and neglecting her three children for whom she and her husband, an HVAC technician, could no longer afford after-school care. Zero positive reinforcement from the job search resulted, over months, in her positive revulsion at the sight of the computer and an accompanying compulsion to use the TV as narcotic. The husband, Josephus, gave her more than a year of a succession of sympathetic support, humorous prodding, and tough-love jabbing, culminating in threats of divorce.

On a Thursday night, after single-handedly getting the kids fed, bathed, and bedded while Adrianna slumped in front of the living room TV, an exhausted Josephus dropped the d-word on her, telling her to "get her ass in gear or get out." Adrianna dragged herself back in front of the computer. There, she stumbled onto an ad for a supermarket stock clerk job, which jumped out at her because the compensation package far exceeded that of the Department of Adult Welfare Services, even with its service union contract. She laughed at what had to be a mistake, but drilled down to the details: hard, repetitive work, no promise of job satisfaction, no path to advancement, very high pay, very good benefits, scrupulous pre-employment background check, unbreakable renewable five-year contract. She considered. Pro: high pay. Pro: unbelievable benefits. Con: mindless work with little responsibility. Pro: mindless work with little responsibility. Con: employment terms that sounded, under the legal gibberish, like indentured servitude. Con: a location more than two thousand miles away in a place from which she would be allowed only brief, strictly monitored leave time. Adrianna applied.

For three weeks she also applied herself to housework she hated and children she could not, despite her guilt, bring herself to love. Then she got the phone call—the first one of its kind since losing her job. A day later she cleared the phone interview. A week after that, she drove to a federal government building for a personal interview, where she was given more information than she gave. To sober, direct questions about her family, she said flatly that she was leaving them no matter what. She gave no thought to how the interviewer knew so much about her family and personal background, despite there having been no questions about them anywhere in the previous application process.

Two weeks later Adrianna was advised that she had cleared background check. She returned to the federal building, skimmed all the papers they gave her without trying to understand a word, signed in the right places, and received her travel papers.

That evening for the first time in almost eighteen months she saw her kids to bed. They met her announcement about "going away for a very long time" with indifference, which relieved but did not surprise her. Josephus, too, seemed relieved. Their last words to each other were neither hostile nor amicable. She slept on the couch and was gone before the others woke.

————

The first five years of shelf-stocking had been almost like a long vacation. She worked nights without having to think. She slept mornings and lazed through afternoons in the beautiful, modern, sunny, company-provided apartment that included a huge TV and cable to the max, four hundred and some stations, including all the premiums. She made tolerable friends with whom she exchanged no confidences. She fucked male co-workers a couple times a year. The climate was warm and non-work demands on her were absent. She had extra money for clothes she didn't need. The town was small and was almost totally crime-free. Medical care was free (and for some reason there were no really unhealthy people here).

Signing up for another five years was a no-brainer, nice for someone who had put her brain in storage.

And then at lunch one night of her eighth year a gossipy co-worker named Vidia asked her what she thought about *why*. "Why what?" Adrianna asked.

"Why any of it? Why the jobs, why the enforced isolation, why the warnings about secrecy? I mean," Vidia said, "we live better than most of the non-millionaires in America. So, don't you ever wonder why?"

Adrianna shrugged. She did not wonder why because she did not want to.

But Adrianna liked the internet. She liked the celebrity junk a bit, but mainly she liked the randomness of it, the weird stuff tucked away in corners, the anonymity, the discussions with strangers that nobody would conduct in real life without near-death embarrassment (and the invitations to onanism). And so she came to see the photo, looking like a still from a sci-fi flick showing a woman apparently scared witless by a crowd of little people. She would have dismissed it, but the woman faced right down at the camera—which appeared to be at ground level—and, god, she looked familiar. Adrianna had become unaccustomed to real thought, and so she had to summon extra will to ponder that face. Did it belong to a movie star? It was pretty enough to be one. Adrianna clipped the face from the picture and pasted it into a facial-recognition site: no hit.

Why did this particular face intrigue her? Adrianna did not know, except it was there, inside a collection of weird pictures of unlikely animal combinations and optical illusions. Adrianna tired of studying it and went to watch TV.

The next day at work, Vidia asked her, "Have you seen that picture?"

"What picture?"

"The one with the woman and the little people."

Adrianna looked up from her carton of canned vegetables.

Vidia said, "People are saying it's from here."

"What do you mean, from here?"

"Remember I asked you *why*?"

Adrianna did remember. The question had stuck in her wooly memory because she disliked Vidia, who was one of those tiny, darting women with shifty predatory eyes. Vidia could have been one of Adrianna's old unhinged clients, haunted by things nobody else could see.

"Yeah, so?" Adrianna asked.

Vidia stopped moving fruit cans to the shelf and stared at Adrianna. "You mean you haven't heard this stuff?"

Adrianna shook her head.

"We're part of a government project," Vidia said. "I mean you know that, right?" Vidia did not wait for an answer. "And it's obviously something we're not supposed to know about, why they swore us to secrecy and all that, even though we don't know anything to keep secret, right? I mean we can't tell what we don't know and we have nobody to tell anyway, so why make such a big deal of it?" Vidia moved closer to Adrianna, who nervously eyed the can of peaches Vidia still held in her right hand. Vidia now said in a raspy whisper, "So it's something weird, something dangerous, right? Like a secret disease, like a bioweapon, or a new kind of bomb, or something. I mean the government doesn't keep *good* stuff secret, right? If it's secret, it must be *bad*, and I mean *really bad*, to be *this* secret."

Adrianna had been sitting on the floor, working on a bottom shelf, and now Vidia sat down next to her, and lowered her voice even more, gesturing with the forgotten peach can still in her hand. "Well, I'm not saying I believe this, but *some* people think that they're creating some new kind of human, or semi-human, like a droid or a robot, or something, only these new guys are *tiny*, small, like what do you call them? Leprechauns or something like that, only not Irish and not cute, particularly, but made to look just like anybody else except for their size, and these little guys will be able to go places and spy on people and do stuff without us really noticing."

"Vidia," Adrianna said, "would you put that can down, please?"

Vidia paused, incomprehension on her face and then looked at the can. "Oh," she said, "sure," and she put the can on the floor.

She peered into Adrianna's eyes from no more than a foot away. "So," she said, "what do you think?"

Adrianna thought. "So, you mean the picture shows these . . . new little people?" she asked.

Vidia nodded quickly.

"How do you know it's not the other way?" Adrianna asked, feeling pleased with herself for having the idea.

"You mean big people? And we're actually the small ones?" Vidia said, and then rapidly answered the question, "How could they hide anything that big?"

Adrianna had no idea about that.

"Well," Vidia fired back in a whisper almost too low to hear, "whatever it is, I mean if it *is* those little guys, we *know* that they're bad, because they're like secret and the government is spending like bezillions of dollars on them, and so they must be *really bad*. And I'm telling you, if they get loose, who knows what diseases they might carry, or who knows what?"

Adrianna stared into Vidia's jittery eyes.

"Well, there have been reports. I've seen them on the web." Vidia paused and nodded knowingly. "And I'll tell you, this picture just sort of backs them up, if you know what I mean." Vidia thrust her lower jaw out, showing the teeth. "So if it's true, I mean if I hear that it's true—and I'm hearing things, I'll tell you—if it's true, I'm not waiting around here to find out exactly how *bad* this could be. I don't care what's in the fine print. I'm getting my ass out of here."

Adrianna stared.

"And you should too." Vidia rose, grabbed the peach can and nodded again. "You should too," she said again, and went back to work.

———

As on thousands of other nights, Adrianna completed her work shift mechanically, without any need to think about her work, leaving her mind free to fantasize about whatever had been on TV the previous day—only on this night she did not. She thought about the face, and about secret government projects, and about her life, and about little people. The face, it was someone she'd seen in the store, probably. But so what?

At home she looked again at the picture on the internet, the face that looked so familiar. Vidia had said nothing about recognizing it, but Vidia—maybe she was not crazy. Adrianna had heard no conversation like those Vidia had mentioned, but Adrianna was not so numb that she failed to recognize that she had deliberately isolated herself.

Adrianna stared at that face, and the backs of the heads of the small—regular sized?—people below that face. The sun was out, there was wine in the refrigerator, the TV beckoned, but Adrianna could not stop looking at that face, not until panic drove her from it and into her bedroom, where she threw she knew not what into a suitcase and ran from the apartment to her car.

And so, she found herself part of the mob at the gate, the presence of the mob confirming for her that her panic was correct, and then she saw Marjorie and lost all doubt. And, just like the others, she crashed out the gate to freedom.

Only, unfortunately for Adrianna, she did not even consider the possibility that her company car held a tracking device. After her forty-eight hours on the road, agents woke her from deep sleep in a highway rest area. They handcuffed her, put a hood over her head, and paid zero attention to anything she said. Someone stuck a needle in her arm and she went quickly back to sleep, to awaken alone in a cold, locked, windowless room with two tiny cameras, high on the ceiling, watching her.

38

In that night and early morning, scalies escaped singly or in small groups, not only through the passages Sam (and perhaps someone else) had opened, but also through gaps in fences left by shoddy maintenance or created by scaly bolt-cutters, through venting systems, through pipes knee-deep in sewage, through tunnels like Howard's. They made their way out through slits and crevices like common rodents—scalies being roughly the size of large rats on their hind legs, only thinner.

Families split themselves, parting with hugs and hopes, desperation, tears, brave smiles, and promises to make contact. Many would fail to maintain electronic contact, much less to regain physical contact. Parents saw their children for the last times crawling into a tunnel, or just before being swallowed by a snake or snatched by a coyote. One man was seen taken, screaming and thrashing, by a tarantula. Surprisingly few were flattened by traffic on the two-lane highway known on the few maps that showed it as Route MM.

They rode on semi-trailer tractor units, clinging to whatever they could grab between the hitch and the back wall of the cab. They road on the floors of stake-bed trucks—empty ones, between hauls, if they were lucky, but mostly sharing the space with apples as big as their children, crates of chickens three times the size of an average scaly adult, heavy machinery, trash, furniture bound for wherever the truck owner was moving. They held for dear life to the suspension of trucks, cars, buses. More reckless folks managed to climb on, into, or on top of railroad freight cars. Luckier ones sneaked inside to the relative luxury of Amtrak cars. They scurried into open luggage holds of long-distance buses, huddling in total darkness until they could sneak off when luggage was unloaded. Some made it into the cabs of private automobiles, hiding quietly under or behind seats, feeling safer if the driver had the radio blaring, stifling their own giggles at the bigs' gossipy conversations.

They discovered that stealing food was easy, especially through the loading entrances. Two scaly men could grab one packaged steak, drag it outside and away. Half of it, carved into small pieces, would feed an entire family for a day.

Luckily the weather was mild, and they quickly determined that north was the wrong direction to go, so shelter was not a big problem. Comfort was absent, but adventure was everywhere.

In cities they made camps. The easier refuges were public parks or alleys, but like rats, scalies could live almost anywhere. At first they were urban nomads, not staying in any place for longer than a few days, stealing food at will and leaving their scat in alley corners or clumps of grass. They stared at the towns, enormous, inflated versions of their own. They watched the "bigs" (full-sized humans—FSH—to Barry, "fullies" to project insiders) with mixtures of fear, hatred, and an ache to join them, as if such a thing were even remotely possible.

For the first time they saw poverty. They avoided poorer parts of towns because the pickings were better in the more affluent commercial areas, and because their aversion to poverty was the same as anyone else's.

They came to rest wherever conditions looked right. There was no specific goal, except a place to settle in relative safety where they could live by stealing. They set up housekeeping in unused buildings, or created shelters from scraps of wood, or the discarded product packaging that was everywhere:

plastic jugs, Styrofoam—excellent temperature insulation, of course—cardboard, plastic, and metal. They built homes with windows and domed skylights of the clear plastic clam shell packaging that they found to be nearly indestructible.

Within just a few weeks they had established settlements, run by town-hall meetings, some with schools for the children. They lived and worked hard together, like settlers in any wilderness, on guard against constant dangers, exhilarated by freedom, but with even less intuition about the future.

———

The top secrecy of the project helped the escaping scalies because even the people who knew about them could not speak.

Sam's staff had been smugly confident of their ability to shut-down scaly communications, whether by cell phone or internet. They did shut down the project's access to the rest of the world. Still, a sense of superiority was, as always, an occupational hazard for the staff, and so they vastly underestimated scaly ingenuity.

Twenty-two-year-old scaly Jacques Brudkepjian got to Amarillo and took up residence, alone, in the storage area at the back of a supermarket. In what he would later describe as "a manic, hell-bent, obsessive-compulsive, ninety-six hours without sleep, but with ample food and an occasional coffee bean," he first figured out how to recharge his mobile smartphone from the electrical system of a parked delivery van. He then cracked the phone's operating system, hacked his way into a local internet service provider, and then into a national cell-phone company, where he created a scaly subnetwork of his own scaly contacts. He blasted instructions for repeating what he had done, by phone text and email to all of them, hoping they would receive them before losing power.

He got responses from many, and replied with an explanation of a rudimentary coding system that the free scaly community would soon amplify into their own online English dialect. Before starting a two-day sleep, Jacques used a fake name to set up a journal on a free blogging site, as a camouflaged scaly news source. In coming days Jacques would, in brief intervals, move his blog to other sites and change account data. Then he took to the roads, never more than two nights and a day in one place, tapping high-speed lines wherever he could find them in a space big enough for his small body to wriggle into. Neither the phone companies nor the feds would ever catch up to him.

———

Just past two one morning in Phoenix, emergency room physician Celia Cohen hugged her clipboard to her chest as she gazed into the exam room where nurses had parked one George J. Tippett, officially homeless. Mr. Tippett sat on the examining bench, legs dangling four inches above the floor, arms wrapped around his torso, swaying slowly from side to side.

Dr. Cohen sighed. No longer idealistic, she felt suddenly that she had had enough: enough pathetic people doing self-destructive things, enough stupid drunks and druggies, enough vindictive boyfriends or girlfriends, enough teenaged mothers without the sense to bathe their children, enough obese wheezers, and most of all enough "special needs persons"—those special, blameless, sick, filthy, smelly people who took most of her time and were as worthy and needful of loving care as anyone else and for whom she could no longer muster even the attitude. Enough already.

She walked in front of the swaying man, steeled herself against the odor, and looked down at him. "Mr. Tippett?" she said.

He kept swaying.

"Mr. Tippett," she said again, this time not as a question. She waited while he swayed. "Mr. Tippett, you cannot have used up the medication I prescribed a week ago. I can't prescribe any more."

She bent down towards him as a teacher to an unruly first-grader, hoping to use her own eyes to focus his, but his face passed like a metronome back and forth before hers, and instead her eyes involuntarily followed him from side to side like a hypnotist's subject.

"I saw them," he said, still swaying.

She stood watching him.

He pulled a plastic bottle from a pants pocket and shook it, but she couldn't tell if the rattling was capsules or beans. "See?" he said. "Haven't used 'em up. Don't want more."

Dr. Cohen said, "Mr. Tippett, why are you here?"

"Haven't had a drink since before the last time I was here. Clean. No drugs except for what you gave me." Without ceasing to sway he began shaking his head.

"Mr. Tippett, goddamn it, sit still!" she hissed.

Suddenly he stopped swaying and looked straight at her, his eyes momentarily bright and engaged with hers. "I have seen them," he declared. "Nobody believes me but I know what I saw. Not like from the drugs. The booze never made me see anything like them. I saw them."

"Mr. Tippett, you saw what?" Dr. Cohen said as she felt the last drops of hope leaking away.

"Them!" Tippett yelled. "Don't tell me you haven't see *them*! You have to have seen them! Just walk two blocks up the street! Those little people, six or seven inches tall. Their camps are a whole lot nicer than ours, aren't they?"

Celia looked at Tippett. "Oh, shit," she whispered. "Oh god oh shit oh god." She took two steps back and bumped into the wall. With both hands she raised the clipboard to her face as a shield so that not even poor homeless addicted mentally ill Mr. Tippett could see her crack. "Lindsey!" she shouted. "Lindsey!"

A burley nurse was soon in the room and putting his arm around her thin shoulders, usually so square and steady and now shaking. "What did you do?" Lindsey said over his shoulder to Tippett, who sat still on the bench.

"It's not him," Celia said. "He didn't do anything. I'm just tired. Give me fifteen minutes and I'll be fine. Thank you."

———

At 3:50 PM In Albuquerque, three police patrol units responded to a report of a woman waving a weapon around in the front yard of her upper-middle-class home. The first pair of officers to arrive found a forty-ish woman looking trim and nice in jeans and T-shirt, like other stay-at-home moms in the neighborhood. Her hair and makeup were nice if slightly undone. In one hand she held a large carving knife and in the other, a claw hammer. She was wailing to the sky. Neighbors, mostly women and children, formed a large circle, gaping at her.

As the two officers approached her, their hands on their guns, she brought her eyes to them, smiled, and said, "Thank god!"

"Ma'am," one of the cops said. "Drop the weapons!"

The woman looked at him quizzically.

"The knife and the hammer!" the other cop said. "Drop them."

The woman raised her hands to her shoulders and seemed surprised to see the knife and hammer. "Oh!" she said, "you mean these! Oh, sure." She tossed them aside on the lawn, clasped her hands in front of her, and beamed at what was now a group of six officers. "Thank god you're here," she said. "I thought I would never get anyone's attention!"

The one female cop in the group cautiously approached her and said, "Ma'am, what seems to be the problem?"

"Oh, good heavens," the woman said. "I've called animal control, I've called the newspaper and the TV—I didn't want to call nine-one-one because it's not really an emergency. I told the neighbors, didn't I?" She directed the question to one group of onlookers, who backed away. "They've been in and out of my backyard. They've been stealing my vegetables. I've lost several tomatoes and at least two cucumbers."

"Who has?" another cop said. "Who's been stealing?"

"These little guys. And gals too! They're only half a foot tall. Come on back, I'll show you!"

———

Takumi Hilyard, Toni Ragatto, Antwan Jefferson, Terence Gomez, and Anna Minh, ages ranging from eighteen to twenty-three, had spoken to Jacques, from Las Vegas, where they were encamped under bleachers at a high school football stadium. The six of them had been pals for years back home in the project, big partyers, each busted for public drunkenness and other minor mischief more than once. The escape was a big adventure for them, a lark. Takumi and Anna had slipped into a toy store and stolen doll clothing. They texted pictures of themselves—two Kens, a GI Joe, an all-American girl, and a Barbie with blouse busts draped comically almost to Anna's waist—to Jacques and other contacts. Jacques reported that the six friends seemed happy, almost exuberant, sending photos of themselves standing under the bleachers with a bigs' football game in the background, and telling of stealing one beer bottle, enough for a daily buzz for all of them for two whole weeks, from a nearby convenience store—and then figuring out how to both open and close it. That was in addition to the airline sample bottles of various whiskeys.

Rudyard Long was a fifty-six year-old big, a bachelor. He rented a small, two-bedroom house adjoining the convenience store, which was in a strip mall also used by a store-front church that Rudyard attended twice weekly. Rudyard supplemented what he learned from the church and the pastor's Bible-study class with long hours of surfing the web during his job as grave-yard shift security guard in the lobby of an office building.

A couple years previous to the "five scaly amigos" setting up housekeeping under the bleachers, Rudyard's pastor had warned his flock that the end-times were nigh: the rapture would come in exactly sixteen months. Rudyard prepared by praying, reading the Bible, and studying rapture websites. After the stated date passed, upset by the rapture's failure to appear, the pastor told his even more upset worshippers that it was the very evil of the world that had short-circuited what god had intended. Without explaining how human failings could foil god, the pastor said that the Lord was angry, and that his True Flock should also be angry, and that they had been chosen as instruments of an ending that would be not nearly so much fun as a rapture. The pastor was vague about how and when the end time would come, but it would be soon, and the congregation's plan of action would sooner be revealed.

Therefore, one evening when Rudyard, while buttoning his uniform shirt for his coming night's work, gazed out his bedroom window and saw, running across the convenience store's small parking lot, six dolls, of several races, whispering and laughing with each other, and then huddling beside a dumpster stationed against the store's side wall, he knew exactly what to do.

Rudyard went to a pad-locked cabinet in his closet, opened it, and removed the already loaded AK-47-style rifle, equipped with sound suppressor, which he had ordered online six months previous and received two weeks after that. On receipt it had been semi-automatic, but Rudyard had ordered parts and instructions needed to change it to its current fully automatic state. Rudyard had suspected that doing so was what god intended, and now he knew for sure.

Rudyard walked as silently as he could out his back door and crouch-walked stealthily to the shrubs that bordered his yard. He peered through the shrubs at the dolls, who, judging by their giggles, seemed to be inebriated. He judged, correctly it turned out, that if he stood up slowly they would not notice him.

So, Rudyard rose to his full height and shouldered the rifle.

Sound suppressors are not really silencers, of course, but Toni, at the left side of Rudyard's steady gaze, probably never heard anything, the rifle so close and the bullet so devastating for someone her size that her death was as close to truly instantaneous as possible. But Terence, standing just next to Toni, and Antwan, leaning against the wall next to Terence, would surely have heard, and Takumi and Anna at the other end of the line of moving young-adult dolls would probably have heard and had enough time to scream before Rudyard finished spraying them.

In four seconds they were a small mound of miniature human body parts.

Rudyard calmly went back to his house, where he put the rifle back into its place and grabbed a broom, a dustpan, and a bright red plastic shopping bag. Back in the parking lot, he swept the remains of the dolls into the dustpan and poured them into the bag. Leaving the broom and dustpan, he walked up the alley behind the little strip of shops to the back door of the church, where, despite the late hour, the pastor's lights shone through a window. Rudyard knocked on the door.

The pastor, in flannel pajamas, welcomed Rudyard with a surprised but warm and welcoming smile, and told him to walk around to the front because the pastor never let other people into his living quarters. Rudyard felt slightly put out but did as he was told. When the pastor let him into the little sanctuary (previously a video rental store), Rudyard was ready and, without a word, thrust the bag forward with two hands and opened it.

The flesh had not yet started to rot, but new corpses do contain excrement, urine, partially digested food, blood, and whatnot, and so what greeted the pastor was not only the appearance of life-like doll body parts, but the worst of human smells. The pastor gaped into the bag, then up into Rudyard's face.

"What?" the pastor asked.

"What you see," Rudyard said. "The time has come."

"Yes, it has," the pastor said after only a brief moment. "Wait here."

The pastor retreated to his back room, swiftly packed his suitcase with the suit, shirts, wingtip brogue shoes, and underwear that were his only possessions, left the half-full bottle of Old Overholt, minus one last swig, on the night stand, and, still in his pajamas and slippers, ran through his back door and into his car, and then drove into the night, never to return.

Rudyard waited, standing in the church, for a quarter hour, even though he certainly heard the sounds of the pastor's departure. The bag's odor nauseated him, as did the growing fear of what the Lord would now unleash.

Rudyard left the bag in the church, returned home, retrieved the rifle and pulled the trigger once to release three mechanized rounds into his own head.

Rudyard's corpse was discovered after a week, when his mailbox, over-flowing with gun catalogs and religious publications, plus the reek of his body from under the door, alerted a postal carrier. Later in the day, police detectives decided that the unaccounted-for missing rounds from the rifle's clip were not worth searching for.

The bag of scaly parts remained unnoticed for almost two weeks until Doyle Parks, thirty-five-year-old part-time gambler and strip-mall property manager, came by to ask the pastor about un-returned phone calls concerning the rent. Once again, smells played a major role in the shaping of events. Doyle parked behind the building and, after knocking on the back door and waiting only a short moment, used his master key and entered what for a normal business would have been a stock room but had recently served as parsonage. Met by the disgusting sight and smell of soiled plates in the toilet room sink and rotting garbage beneath it, Doyle retrieved his cleaning supplies from the trunk of his car—a decades-old Oldsmobile bomber that Howard Sturges would have loved—and set to work. After two hours of moving trash, bed linens, floor mattress, and assorted detritus to the dumpster and applying bleach and Lysol to the back room and its toilet room, he noticed that a strong rancid smell persisted.

Doyle opened the door to the store-front chapel, where a more potent version of the stench clubbed him in the face. The pastor had kept the chapel relatively clean, if not dust free, and so among the folding chairs the red plastic shopping bag—the heavy-duty reusable kind—stood out as the source of the smell. Expecting a package of rotting beef or pork, Doyle, breathing shallowly through his down-turned mouth, strode to it and tried to grab the handles without looking inside, but could not quite avoid a glimpse of toy-sized clothing and tiny but swollen arms and legs.

Doyle had accepted the pastor's tenancy during difficult economic times, but had been uneasy about his so-called church. Evidence of bizarre rituals combining animal sacrifice and children's toys would not have surprised Doyle, and so in fascination he held the bag open for a closer look.

Feeling slightly dazed, Doyle set the bag on a chair, held a handle with one hand and with the other—still covered by his heavy-duty plastic work gloves—poked inside. Holding his breath, he saw what had to be a miniature female head, tenuously attached to a torso, looking impossibly human, and, though clearly either inanimate or newly dead, life-like. Doyle dropped the bag and took a step backwards, the bag falling to the floor with little body parts spilling out. In his panic, Doyle could not leave this inexplicable mess, so he squatted on the floor and pushed the pieces of flesh back into the bag, righted the bag on the floor, making sure it would not spill again, then hastened to the front door, tossed the gloves to the floor, and, in terror, fumbled with the deadbolt and lock until he was able to exit and shut the door behind him.

He sat down on the sidewalk, caught his breath, and phoned 911.

The Las Vegas Police Department dispatcher told the cruiser cops that the caller was incoherent and undeniably terrified of something or someone unidentified; the cops were used to that condition in people involved with some combination of drugs, gambling, and mayhem. The two officers found Doyle Parks, barely able to speak his name, sitting by the storefront door, moving his left hand in a circling motion toward the store. The two cops simultaneously put their palms on top of their pistols.

"Alright," Officer Lucia Vazquez said to Doyle. "Calm down and look at me."

Doyle did so.

"Is there someone dangerous inside? Someone you're afraid of?"

Doyle shook his head, somehow conveying incredulity more than negativity.

"Is the door unlocked?" Officer Harold Chin asked.

Doyle nodded.

Officer Chin put his left hand on the door handle and motioned with his head for Officer Vazquez to stay outside. Keeping his right palm on his pistol, Harold opened the door, allowing the stench to flow outside. He took a cautious step into the room where he saw only folding chairs and the shopping bag. He walked into the back room, saw nobody, walked out the open back door, and found nobody in the rear parking area. He walked back into the chapel. "Lucia?" he yelled. "Ask Mr. Parks if anyone else has just left."

Lucia asked him. Doyle shook his head. Lucia yelled, "He says no."

"Lucia?" Harold yelled again. "Come in here."

Lucia asked Doyle if he would be okay. Doyle nodded. "Don't go anywhere, okay?" she said. Doyle nodded.

Lucia entered the store to find Harold squatting next to the bag. She walked to him and bent over to see what he was staring at.

"What the fuck?" she said.

"Excuse me," Harold said, and walked to the back room and out the back door to the parking area. Hearing him retch, Lucia quickly joined him there and did the same.

Two hours later, forensic officers placed the shopping bag in a refrigeration chest.

Detective Herman Winston, holding his mobile phone, said to the closest uniform: "Ever see any of those silly sci-fi movies from the nineteen fifties—they still show them on cable—where a cop finds something totally weird and calls some scientist he knows in the federal government, and it turns out to be space aliens?" The other detective nodded. Herman said, "That's what I should be doing now. I don't know about the space aliens part—yet."

39

"Mr. President, please let me go on, sir. So that you can understand."

Carl rubbed his forehead. Les looked at his hands. Barry felt a disgusting bead of sweat between his shoulder blades. His throat was suddenly very dry.

"Go on," the president said, obligingly.

Barry fought an urge to remove his jacket and tie. "Could we get some water, please sir?"

Carl used the telephone on the conference table to ask for a case of bottled water.

Because waiting for the water was clearly not possible, Barry swallowed and pressed on, hoarsely. He told the president how the first scientific team believed that genetic cloning would be feasible in the near future. They had used the groaning room-sized computers of the day to build and run models to combine the factors of time, human sustenance, likely destinations and distances, vehicle size, fuel, and on and on, almost a hundred thousand variables, and those just the top layer, the highest level of detail. The models had yielded the optimal combinations—Barry now speaking with the awe we all feel for the courageous and resourceful early masters and pioneers to whom we moderns owe everything.

"Just think of it," Barry said, his eyes closing, his face worshipful, almost oblivious to everyone else in the room, even the president. "With only a grand vision, with only faith that any of it could ever be accomplished, they laid the foundations on which the entire project has flourished." Barry paused, opened his eyes, and plunged on, oblivious to the consternation filling the room.

"And with the advances of science in all the broad areas of space travel, computing technology, genetics—extrapolations of those advances were actually part of the original modeling!—over the decades the team achieved things. Oh, and what we achieved!" Barry exclaimed. "Using what we knew of genetics, even before we had genomes, we developed, by careful cloning, a whole new human race! But that was not enough. Under my leadership the team replicated our civilization to scale. Infrastructure—buildings, roads, houses! TVs and washing machines, telephones. Automobiles, all of it, all for the reduced-scale humans! And then, reduced-scale plants—they were easier, working with centuries of Japanese bonsai practice—and reduced-scale animals! Animals for pets, recreation, and food. You could not have six-inch humans eating beef from full-scale steers. They would need scaled down animals, for now, on earth, for the trip, and for their new home. And where has all this been happening? In one scaled-down, self-contained community! When you think of it, you cannot but be overwhelmed by its beauty."

Barry stopped and breathed deeply, selected the next paragraph from his store of arguments, opened his eyes, saw the water bottles on the table, reached for one, and noticed everyone else staring at him. Carl and Les looked alarmed, and the president looked dangerous.

"Two, actually," the president said. "Right?"

"Two what?" Barry asked.

"Self-contained communities."

"Ah, yes," Barry said, feeling the ground once more solidly beneath him, "indeed, two." He opened the bottle, drank, and re-gathered.

"But, Mr. President, before getting to that, please allow me to give you the full context."

The president nodded.

"The RSH community is actually better than what I like to call the traditional one, sir."

"Traditional meaning full-scale? Us?"

"Yes, sir. We set out—when my tenure started all those years ago—to expose them to all of our culture, but make them feel that their town was actually better. So, they watch the same TV and movies, hear the same music, and, have the same internet as we do. The team briefly considered filtering out what some of us thought were negative cultural influences, but in the end we agreed that our knowledge was inadequate to the task of what would really be censorship, so we decided to let the culture flow." Barry smiled proudly, and fiercely, leaving out the bullying that led the team to "agree."

Feeling his confidence grow, he continued. "At the same time, we did our best to make the community harmonious. As I'm sure you know, sir, we have included all racial groups and all religions. Though English is the first language for all of them, they are aware of their individual cultural heritages, as you and I are. But the community is homogeneous, and while it does have free enterprise with some people doing better than others, they all share the same basic socio-economic status. There are no economic or racial barriers or castes, and no poverty."

"They have trains?" the president asked.

"Trains? They have a small light rail—" and Barry broke off, getting the joke.

Carl and Les smiled. Only the president's aide laughed.

"Okay," the president said, relaxing in his chair but still boring his eyes into Barry, and ignoring Carl and Les. "You've produced this reduced-scale multi-racial suburban Eden. Very impressive. But I want to know about security, and first," and the president held up his hand with the first two fingers up, "I want to know about the two communities. Both."

"Of course," Barry said. "Each community—the reduced-scale human community, or RSHC, and the full-scale community, the FSC—is a self-contained, egalitarian haven. The RSH Project is committed to maintaining the highest physical, technological, and cultural standards for all inhabitants. Every structure, whether for residence or commerce, has been designed to meet current standards and all of them are updated as the standards change. And, I might add, that given the reduced energy needs that go with their reduced size, the RSH can live almost entirely on clean energy. Only two percent of their energy comes from burning anything." Barry paused. "Infrastructure, including streets and utilities, are rigorously maintained. Schools are of the highest quality. The RSHP attends to every detail of living, and, we believe, has achieved its goal of a harmonious, highly cultured, prosperous community."

Barry had spoken most of that with a smile and closed eyes, as if savoring for himself the public proclamation of his life's love. But when he opened his eyes, he saw on the president's face the look of bemused disgust of a person forced to watch a TV infomercial.

"Mr. President, what I have described is not a sales pitch. It's real. I stand behind it."

Carl rubbed his forehead. Les looked at his hands.

The president waited.

Fighting his defensive feeling, Barry said, "The FSC is the same, with some exceptions. It has the same homogeneity of SES, the same high-level of infrastructure, housing, and institutions. It does use more energy because of its traditional populace. But the largest differentiating factor is that its people have come from the country at large. For the RSH, their community is the only one they have experienced first-hand, but the FSC residents all come from the outside. They have all had to sign strict contracts binding them to stay in the FSC except in case of emergency."

"Are they GS?" the president asked.

Barry hesitated. "Oh, you mean General Services? No, sir." He then proceeded to explain that the government had formed a special entity, simultaneously capable of independent initiative and subject to government control, spelled out in three-thousand and some odd pages of classified contract, called the Independent Segment Corporation (ISC), which engaged in partnerships with private corporations—Walmart, Rite-Aid, Target, Kroger, MacDonald's, Wolfgang Puck, a couple of universities, etc., etc.—to create shared commercial subsidiaries that would in turn create enterprises in both the RSHC and the FSC, with the goal of engaging in business to provide employment and "need-fulfillment" for the communities' inhabitants. To those in the RSHC, given their education and access to news and entertainment media, the situation was entirely "transparent"—meaning that for RSH people it was simply reality as they'd seen it on TV and the web. Even "one of us traditionally sized folk," were it possible for us to be scaled down and given entry to the RSHC, would not see how the workings of commerce were any different there than in our previous experience. "And the corporations? They invested and shared their techniques, but we gave them no information about the size of the ultimate operation."

The ISC posted its job openings on the internet, with vague job descriptions and promises of high salaries. Applicants had to agree to rigorous background checks as they submitted their resumes—and, in fact, were subject to much more rigorous checks than they could have imagined, even in the modern era of reduced expectations of privacy. Personal interviews were secretly observed, recorded, and observed again, the images and sounds subject to computer and expert review. The process resulted in highly qualified, or, "frankly," over-qualified finalists, who were offered shockingly high salaries.

The quid pro quo was that those hired had to sign tightly binding contracts promising never to leave for the duration of their employment, except for a precisely worded list of emergencies including, mainly, serious illness in their families. Even though most of the jobs were not in the vaguest way related to the Project mission, hires had to promise never to speak of their work or where they lived to anybody on the outside, and they understood that all their communications would be monitored. If management determined that an employee had transgressed—and only management could make that determination, with no process for appeal—they would immediately be fired and would have to repay all previously paid earnings, plus a large penalty.

When Barry surfaced he noticed that the president was looking rather baleful. Barry was relieved to see him reach into his shirt pocket for his buzzing phone. After listening to it for a moment, the president announced that they would resume their meeting the next day.

40

C olin awoke in the dark with his back and shoulder aching, the wind battering his ears, the shriek and moan of the highway the only sound. His parents sprawled together to his right, his friends and their families on all sides, their chests rising and falling rhythmically in sleep. Bryce rolled towards Astrid and put his arm over her waist. Beyond them, Cheng and Sher were spooned together, facing out. Towards the rear of the tractor's platform, braced against the coupling, Howard was the only one sitting up, watching the roadside. Colin turned toward the small sound of a woman's cough, once, twice, and again. It was his mother. She coughed once more and stopped. Colin saw the headlights, cars passing them in both directions, flashes of utility poles and highway markers, and desert in all directions. He crawled toward the rear.

"Howard," he yelled.

Howard did not turn his head.

"Howard," Colin shouted again, more loudly.

Howard turned toward Colin and motioned at the sleepers.

Colin gripped a cable extending from the trailer coupling and with his head not three feet from Howard, yelled, "Nobody can hear us, Howard!"

"What do you want?" Howard yelled back.

"What do we do if someone gets sick?"

"Gets what?"

"Sick!"

"Who's sick?"

"Nobody. I mean just in case."

Howard grinned.

"You think it's funny?" Colin shouted.

"I think I'm hungry, and we're getting to food."

Colin relaxed and realized that he had lost nearly all his earlier fear of falling off. In just a few hours, this enormous semi had become home.

To the right front of the truck the glow of artificial light appeared in the sky.

"Wake the others," Howard shouted. "It's dinner time! But don't make too much noise."

Colin felt the truck slow. He crawled among the sleepers and gently shook each person, showing them a finger across his lips as they opened their eyes.

The road noise faded as the truck slowed more, turned right, slowed even more, turned right again and stopped.

Howard moved to the center of the group and stood and motioned them to move close to him and keep silent. Then he stood and waited.

They heard the motor die and then the sounds of a person moving in the cab ahead of them. They heard a door slam, feet hit the ground, and footsteps moving away from the truck.

In a loud whisper, Howard told them all to wait. They watched him climb down from the tractor platform. After a few moments they saw his head rise above it. In a stage whisper he said, "We're climbing off. Use the cables as handholds and scale down the tires. Do not speak." Then he descended back down.

Cheng rose and said, also in a whisper, "Howard knows the ways of the road. We'll follow him." Cheng stood and motioned for the others to go. Jerome Thurman motioned to Morgana and LaTasha, and he shepherded them out, standing at the edge to help as his daughter and then his wife climbed over. Michael, Phuong, and Elmer Cruz followed them, and then Leah, Mahesh, and Gerald Reynaud.

217

"Our turn," Colin's mother said. She walked to the edge and went down, flashing a smile at Roberto as she descended. When Colin followed her, he saw a small crowd below him, all looking pleased and slightly excited, which is how he felt when his feet felt solid ground. He looked up as his father Roberto, then Astrid, Marissa and Bryce, and finally Sher and Cheng climbed down. Howard hissed and pointed towards an area of high weeds in a shadow cast by the low wall surrounding the parking lot. Quietly, they crept there behind Howard and followed his lead by kneeling or sitting.

"Okay," Howard said quietly. "Four of you come with me to get food. The rest stay here and don't talk. If you have to piss or shit, go there," and he pointed to a patch of higher weeds. Howard paused and surveyed the group. Without talking he pointed successively at Michael Cruz, Jerome Thurman, Bryce, and Astrid. "Cheng's in charge while I'm gone."

"Wait," Bryce whispered. "I don't want Astrid to go."

"Why not?"

Bryce said, "We need strength, right?"

"We'll be carrying groceries, not car batteries," Howard said.

Bryce looked straight at Howard. "I don't want her in danger," he said.

"Cheng and I discussed this," Howard said. "You'll do as I say."

"Who appointed you?" Bryce said.

Colin watched as Bryce and Howard gazed levelly at each other. Bryce was used to leading. Even in the night shadow, Colin saw blood going to Bryce's face as he and Howard confronted each other. They were the tallest of the group. Bryce had maybe twenty pounds of muscle over Howard, but Howard in his very leanness seemed the more dangerous. Howard grimaced, a look of disgust and amusement.

"I think," Cheng said, but before he could say more, Colin heard Astrid's voice, a whisper like the others, but somehow clearer and stronger. She was looking at Bryce.

"Bryce, you listen to me. I didn't leave my bully father back there so I could be bullied by someone else out here. Howard wants me, and I'm going."

Bryce colored even more, but said nothing.

"You will find," Howard said, "that being small can be an advantage. We can get in and out of small places without being noticed, and your girlfriend is the smallest one here. Actually, I've changed my mind." He pointed to Gerald, looked at Bryce, and said, "You stay here."

"Nothing better happen to her," Bryce said.

"If aliens attack, you can defend the rest, big boy," Howard said, and motioned the designated four to follow him. They crouched as they walked quickly away.

Bryce shrugged.

"Me for the weeds," Phuong Cruz said, and crouch-walked away into the shadows. A Few minutes later she was back. "Nice broad grass," she said with a grin. "Whoever's next, watch where you step."

One by one, they politely looked at each other to determine who would follow. Colin went last. He found relief, and the broad grass leaves were indeed useful.

As the group waited, mostly sitting, for the food-gatherers to return, Colin noticed that they were all smiling, even Bryce. Had he ever seen a group, inside their town, a group of people, some having met for the first time, share—and that was what he saw, sharing—an excitement, an expectancy of—what? They had no idea where they were going or what they would do. He felt a wave of something he could not identify come over him and somehow wash away the shell of cynicism that had been hiding his hopes.

He looked at his mother and said, "Mom, are you okay?"

"What do you mean?" Grace said, smiling. Colin noticed that she was holding his father's hand.

"You were coughing in your sleep," he said.

She shrugged. "I have, seriously, never felt better in my life, except for the day you appeared," she said

"Don't forget the day you met me," Roberto said.

Everyone laughed.

"I think we all feel good," Mahesh said, sounding as incredulous.

LaTasha Thurman looked at Colin. "Maybe," she said, "this is what freedom feels like."

"Maybe we should be quiet," her mother said, but she was smiling as she said it.

The food-gatherers appeared, each carrying enormous objects. Michael, Elmer's father, had a can of orange juice half the size of all three of them together. Jerome had a carrot as long as himself. Gerald held a bar of chocolate and two soda straws. Howard cradled one apple in his arms. And Astrid held a huge package of cold cut meat. They all, even Howard, looked proud.

"Should've seen your girlfriend," Howard said to Bryce. None of them, not even Cheng, had ever seen Howard grin before. "She was able to crawl up into a box of packaged cold cuts where nobody else could go."

"Most fun I've ever had in my life," Astrid said, looking squarely at Bryce. Bryce smiled and nodded.

"Let's eat," Howard said.

41

From Colin's Journal

OUTSIDE!! I cannot believe we are outside—me and my friends and our parents (except for Astrid, and it's just as well because her father is a complete jerk). And Chief Schmitz is with us, and that Ms. Statie—what is she? City Executive or something?—who seems to be his girl friend. And Howard, the mechanic, except out here he's like Daniel Boone or Captain Kirk. We're all OUT and it's like we know we're NEVER GOING BACK!! Which is scary and exciting at the same time. I feel like in the last couple weeks someone has picked my life up and shook it and then rolled it down a hill and I'm still rolling and I don't know where it will stop. Will it ever stop?? Seriously, I'm DIZZY!!

And it's not just us. There were huge crowds of us, scurrying along quietly to get OUT. We are all in a movie where we get magically transported to a fantasy world where everything is the same as home except SO MUCH BIGGER!!! LaTasha says this is what freedom is like. Is it? Is freedom like floating over a dark hole where you don't fall unless you do one thing slightly wrong and then you fall forever? Only, if we had stayed inside it would have been worse because the word on the street was that some of us—teenagers—were going to get killed. That's why the families had to leave.

Even Bryce seems a little humbled. But not Astrid. She's like, I was born for this. I think Bryce is having a hard time handling that, and he NEVER has a hard time. Elmer is just quietly tough and Gerald is this hipster who can't ever admit that anything surprises him.

And I've never felt so good around my parents. It's like we're all sharing in this big adventure, and it's like you see in documentaries

221

about some tribal people where the parents are not just for their own kids. It's like the parents are for all the kids and the kids are for all the parents. Which is good for Astrid because she has no parents of her own.

So here we are!! Camping out all the time!! Living by stealing food. Climbing up on trucks and riding for MILES. I have never seen so much sky!! So many trees. So much dirt!! I did not know there was this much dirt—is that weird or what? Buildings like I've never seen. Stuff I've only seen on TV or online. LaTasha is right! This is what freedom feels like. Like being drunk without getting sick.

Oh, LaTasha. We hug close now. We've kissed once when we were sure nobody else could see. She does like me, I think. I hope it's not just that I'm the only guy around for her right now.

But then I look out as we're riding down this enormous highway and I see people, in cars or walking. And I think, maybe it'll be HER. I want to see her. I need to see her. I sneak looks at her on my phone. I think we'll be able to really talk to each other. Only I can't help feeling like LaTasha somehow knows I feel that way.

42

A t dusk, Sam drove them into a bright, new outdoor shopping mall, where the shops and restaurants were clustered in blocks and the alleys between them were made to look like small-town streets named for trees or numbered, except for the widest one, called "Main." All the latest chains for apparel, sporting goods, electronics, books, and food were there.

The slowing of the car had awakened Sandra. "Are we back home?" she asked.

"No, honey," Sam said. "It's just a place that looks like home."

"Can we eat at Chromium Ribs?" Kirk yelled.

"Yep," Sam said. "The sign said there's one here," and, sure enough, there it was at the corner of Oak and Third.

"It *is* just like home," Jennifer said, as Sam parked. "I don't know whether I'm comforted or disturbed."

Chromium Ribs did look exactly like the one in Projectville, down to the antiqued wood paneling and posts and the reproduction road signs and ancient advertisements hanging from the walls and vaulted ceiling. The menu was the same. The kids were excited to get the barbecue and fries that looked and tasted exactly the same. Sam and Jennifer ordered beers that did little to relax their tension. As they ate, Sam was grateful that the kids' chatter filled the silence between him and his wife.

They used the restrooms—which also looked the same. The parents had coffee, the kids had ice cream.

"And now?" Jennifer said, more of a demand than a question. She glared at Sam and he had to look away.

"There's a phone store around here somewhere," he said.

"And then?"

"There's a townhouse, a rental. We just have to get the keys from the management office."

Jennifer glared.

"I got it furnished," Sam said, "so we'd have a place to live. You can change it any way you want."

Sam waited for a reply that never came.

"I couldn't include you, Jennifer. Can't you understand that?"

"I'm supposed to just go along? You're lord and master now?"

"Oh, for god's sake."

"I should write a book. Instead of 'Married to the Mob' I'll call it 'Married to the Project'."

"Let's get out of here," Sam said.

———

The townhouse was not exactly like home, but it was close enough. Almost new, freshly painted, and furnished, with a stocked linen closet and basic toilet necessities, though without pictures on the wall. Living and dining rooms and kitchen on ground level, three bedrooms upstairs, two and a half bathrooms. The living room had a TV to occupy the kids while their parents talked upstairs.

Jennifer sat on a corner of the bare queen-sized bed in their "master suite." Sam stood behind her. They both looked through a large window at the view of two small trees between them and the next row of townhouses with mountains rising above them.

"Where the hell are we?" Jennifer said.

"They call it the 'Inland Empire'," Sam said.

"And now?"

"I've lined up a job. IT, medium-sized company. Less money, but we have a lot stashed away. I start in a week."

Jennifer twisted around to look up at him. "How long," she said, with that odd mixture of wonder and resentment, "just how long have you been plotting all this?"

Sam gazed at the far mountains, his hands in his pockets, and took several deep breaths. "There was one about three years ago," he said. "Another wild teenager not to be mollified by the usual platitudes. His parents couldn't control him and neither could Cheng—he's the police chief." Sam took another breath. "They were always boys. Could've been girls too, but Barry wouldn't touch girls. Not out of any old-fashioned morality, but to protect the breeders." He shrugged. "Anyway, this one was only a few years older than Kirk. Even looked a little like Kirk. That's when I started planning."

He glanced down and saw Jennifer's hard stare. He sat down next to her on the bed and made himself return her look. "And then, things changed. The tone of the place, somehow, got more tense. Barry was edgy, popping off more, demanding more. Cheng was sounding worn down. I'll tell you more about Cheng later."

Sam looked down at his hands. "Then a bunch of things happened at once. Another kid, only this time, I didn't think I could go along. And then that photo of the woman showed up on the internet, and a lot of other stuff too, and."

Sam hoped Jennifer would touch him, but she did not. She said, "I suppose I should be grateful. Such a good provider, you are. Finding us a place that looks so much like home—like the last place." She turned toward the window. "Except for those mountains. I like them." She turned back to him. "So why do I feel so desolate?"

"There's a good school for the kids close by, and you should be able to find sports for them."

"And what else? What am I supposed to do?"

Sam shrugged. "There might be school jobs. I couldn't cover everything. Oh, but we can buy you a car."

Jennifer looked at the mountains. "Okay. I'll make the beds and look after the kids if you'll get some groceries. But right now I'd like a little time alone, please."

"Fine," Sam said, and stood up to leave the room.

"Sam," Jennifer said.

Sam readied himself for an embrace but could see it would not be welcome.

"Are we safe?" she asked.

Sam shrugged. "I think so. Not totally. I'm going to grow a mustache. I've always loved your hair, but maybe you should dye it, darker or something. If they're onto us it won't help much, but." He shrugged again.

"Please shut the door for me," she said.

Sam nodded and left. He paused outside the door and was not sure if he heard her crying.

43

D rew's business was depressing, but it was a living. He had always wanted to earn his living as an actor, and now was he not doing exactly that, by offering the sincere pretense of sorrow and glorification over dead he had never known for the ears of people who felt no sorrow and who snickered at the very idea of glory? Now known among clergy and undertakers as that guy who could give a little pizzazz to the dreariest funeral with that "for whom the bell tolls" thing, he started rehearsing other death things, mostly poems.

From Mr. Donne himself, "O Death be not proud," for starters:

> *One short sleepe past, wee wake eternally,*
> *And death shall be no more; death, thou shalt die.*

If nightly sleep is sweet, how much sweeter is the big sleep? (Sort of the opposite of Hamlet's doubts, which were out of the question, for Drew.) Death has its fun while stalking you, but once it gets you, the fun stops, for both death and dead. It was a shorter piece, nice for the mourners who wanted mostly to get the hell out of the chapel, but when Drew tried it for a long-retired multi-millionaire ball player, drug user and peddler, liar, and slumlord, who had died by running his motorcycle over the outside rail of a mountain road, taking his pillion-riding girlfriend with him, it fell a little flat. Contrary to Donne, at that funeral the folks believed that death should be damned proud of snatching the son of a bitch on the bier, who deserved not the peace of deathless eternity, but at very least the hollow thud of a dungeon door slammed in his face.

Algernon Swinburne sang similarly of the death of death in a "forsaken garden," where

> *Here now in his triumph where all things falter,*
> *Stretched out on the spoils that his own hand spread,*
> *As a god self-slain on his own strange altar,*
> *Death lies dead.*

Dylan Thomas, self-destructively defiant as only a persistent drunkard could be, said that even the deceased could remain defiant, as death would have no dominion.

Drew could see either one of them with a guitar on his hip, bass to one side and keyboard on the other, drummer behind, shouting lyrics so hoarsely into a microphone so close to his mouth, amped up so high, that the words were distorted beyond any recognition. Lovely. Exhilarating rebellion of youth in the face of premature destruction, reducing death to the role of co-dependent with the life addict, the two of them inevitably dying together, and nobody knowing what the hell anybody else was saying.

But his audiences were not into that, and, besides, Drew wasn't ready to share his business with musicians, nor to pay royalties for Thomas.

And then a Unitarian minister phoned Drew about a war veteran and referred him to a newspaper piece:

> Before he enlisted, Rosengarten had been known as tough but warm. But, to hear his friends and family tell it, after his return, the warm part was gone. "Too many corpses, I guess," Cheryl said sadly.

> And so, even the PTSD diagnosis, the treatment, and as much support as his family could give, had not been enough for

Corporal Rosengarten. As his father Hassan said, "Some war wounds just don't heal."

The article was replete with the reporter's valiant attempts to recreate the several terrifying, gory, and dismal scenes that had so warped Cliven Rosengarten's mind. Accompanying it was what in Drew's jaded judgment was the obligatory bromidic photo of the saddened widow, Cheryl, posed with two dazed children in the kitchen of the house she had shared with Cliven, staring into the camera with sorrow and perfect hair.

The minister had given Drew Cheryl's phone number, and so, two days later, he and Cheryl talked to each other over a Formica table in a vinyl booth of a coffee shop. Cheryl Rosengarten's hair was now lank and unshining instead of perfect, and it drooped over her face and almost into the coffee cup that she sipped once only and then compulsively stirred.

"The fact is," she said, "Cliven was not much to begin with." She sighed, and spoke bitterly, hiding behind her hair and accompanying her words with the tink of spoon against porcelain. "He was big and handsome and he had one of those megawatt smiles, and he liked spending money on me, so, naturally how could I not love him? But that stuff in the story about his being a chef at the Mexican food plant? And the night classes in business? That was all bullshit. He wanted to be a chef, but the plant was close to firing him for all those absences, he'd used up what little PTO they gave him. They probably would've fired him if he hadn't quit to enlist. And the classes? He never did the homework, he was flunking."

She stirred: tink, tink, tink.

"See, the drinking and the dope were there all along. At first it was fun, y'know? Nothing like sex when you're high, right? But when he started turning up the dial on it, I couldn't keep up. I didn't like being hung-over. And then Crea came along, and Jorge, and with them to take care of, he," Cheryl said, shaking her head, "I guess he resented that I wasn't good-time Cheryl anymore, so he slugged me. Early and often. The kids too."

Tink, tink.

"This was before he enlisted," Drew said.

"Oh, yeah. It didn't start with the war. The war didn't make him an abuser. He was one already. He was drunk that night, of course, after belting me twice, when he drove our car into that monument. I'm just glad he didn't take anyone with him."

Tink, tink.

"So, anyway, I didn't intend to tell you the whole sad story. I just wanted to make clear that I don't want Cliven portrayed as some angel that the war turned into a devil. He wasn't a devil, either. But I couldn't stand to hear about some nice boy who never existed, y'know? Barbara what's her name, that Unitarian minister? I'm no Unitarian, I'm not anything really, she was just the cheapest I could find. Anyway, she said you were good at figuring out good things to say about people who maybe didn't quite deserve them. So."

"I'll have something for you," he said. "You want to review it ahead of time?"

"I'll trust you," she said.

Drew browsed poetry collections until he found Alan Seeger, who had

> . . . a rendezvous with Death
> At midnight in some flaming town;
> When Spring trips north again this year.
> And I to my pledged word am true,
> I shall not fail that rendezvous

Afterwards, when Cheryl approached him, her hair again perfect but her mascara running, she said, quietly, "That was perfect. He wasn't all bad, Cliven. I needed to feel some real sadness about him, and you helped me do that. Thanks." Neither of them said anything about Cliven dying not in combat "in some flaming town" but in a collision with a statue in the middle of an intersection.

And so, Drew had an epiphany. This was the first time anyone had volunteered to him that the deceased was "*not all bad*." So maybe he could branch out! Maybe he could say good things about good people! Maybe he could stop being a professional hypocrite!

His elation lasted an hour. He could not let go of his business, because what else was there? Temp clerical? Table-waiting? Honorable, but not so lucrative.

Drew did what modern depressives do: he stared at the internet. And there, amid the boring videos of pets and celebrities, the feverish acidity of verbally warring bloggers, and the rest of the sewage, he spied, for the second time, that photo of the huge woman evidently frightened by the little people in the foreground. Aside from the fact that she was beautiful, the picture intrigued him (as it did thousands of others, of course). But now it was linked to news stories about people seeing little people. Was this all evidence of life and hope? Or was it just more farce?

44

They were back on the semi-trailer platform again as the sun appeared behind them. Awake now, they watched horizons farther off than most of them had ever seen. The teenagers, and most of their parents, when they were teenagers, had seen only small glimpses of the outside before sneaking back into town, and now the very openness of this open road amazed them, scenes from television and museum dioramas come alive, flat desert holding their attention like a thriller movie.

Cheng watched Howard, who seemed as mesmerized as the rest. Cheng said, "Nice, huh?"

"Yeah," Howard said, "I guess it is."

Cheng watched Howard for a moment before saying, "That is beautiful."

"Why I've been coming out almost weekly for years," Howard said.

"But not the only reason."

"No."

They watched the countryside for a while. They were towards the back of the platform, far enough from the others so that Cheng believed the roar of the road would cover their conversation.

"So, Howard, what's next?"

Howard thought before saying, "You're supposed to be the leader. You tell me."

"Not out here. I'm a babe in the woods out here."

Howard did not speak.

"It's kind of a relief," Cheng said.

"Lunch."

"What?"

"What's next."

"And after that?"

"Pretty sure this truck's going to LA. Not certain, but we're going west, at least."

"Anything in particular in LA?"

"No."

Cheng looked at Howard and laughed. "Howard," he said, putting on a movie cowboy voice, "Old Howard." He laughed more.

"What's funny?"

"You are, Howard," Cheng said, still laughing.

Howard stared fiercely at the desert.

"Okay, Howard. It's okay." Cheng stopped laughing but kept smiling at Howard. After a moment he said, "So, where will this safari end? Not gonna hitch forever are we?"

"Camp somewhere that looks good, where there's odds and ends to build shelter and clean water and stores with food to steal. That means suburban probably. Strip malls, whatnot."

Cheng watched Howard move his eyes to the rest of the group.

"Look at 'em," Howard said. "Like a bunch of tourists. Kids at Disneyland."

"Their first time as tourists, Howard. It's exciting."

Howard grunted.

Cheng watched Howard watch the group, and laughed.

———

Lunch came an hour later at another truck stop. They climbed down as they had the night before but this time they took their belongings into another secluded place.

Howard chose, as gatherers, Colin, Roberto, Elmer, and, again, Astrid. "You'll all get chances, don't worry," he said. They found cheese, a hard roll, grape soda, and a peach. They relieved themselves away from the lunch site, came back, and rested in the grass, in family groups, staring at the sky, content and giddy at the same time.

"Holy shit!" It was Leah Reynaud.

The others looked in the direction she was and saw a grasshopper as large as a cat. Bryce picked up a stone and threw it, striking the beast squarely in its side, and the group gasped as it leaped over them in a spectacular arc.

No longer relaxed, they stood or sat up, looking around them for other dangers.

"Snakes," Howard said.

"Where?" Leah said.

"Not here. But they're out there." Howard gestured at the countryside. "Rats. Cats. Dogs. Coyotes. At night there are owls."

They were silent.

"You're having second thoughts, cold feet, buyer's remorse, whatever," Howard said. "Don't think that way. Those animals can be scared off easily by a loud noise or a stone." He looked at Bryce and said, "Nice throw. We do need to be watchful, but it beats being prisoners, doesn't it?"

Nobody else spoke.

"It was secure back there," Jerome Thurman said. He had his big arms around LaTasha and Morgana.

"Like hell it was," Cheng said, standing and looking over the group. "They needed us, but only a certain way. They couldn't tolerate *differences*, if you know what I mean. We could be just so," he said, gesturing with his hands as if sizing a fish he'd caught. "But if we deviated." He stopped and looked down at his feet.

They were silent for another moment.

"Incurable diseases," Marissa Karakawa said.

"I knew one of those kids," Grace Fairchild said. "Nice boy. A little crazy. Like a teenage boy, but nice. His parents were devastated."

More silence.

"You know about that all along?" Michael Cruz asked Cheng.

Cheng opened his mouth but said nothing.

"To know," Morgana said. "That some kid was going to die."

"He did what he had to and what he could," Sher said, in what Cheng recognized as her laying-down-the-law tone. "He hated it but he had no power."

Cheng was crying. Sher rose from the rock she'd been sitting on and went to him and put her arms around him while he quietly sobbed. For several minutes, with his head on her shoulder, and his arms finally wrapping around her, he cried without sound.

"You saved us, Chief," Bryce said.

"Sure as hell," Elmer added.

"Got us out," Roberto Fairchild said.

"They don't mean that," Colin said. The others looked at him and waited. "That night we went out, all of us," he said, indicating the teenagers while addressing the parents, "he caught us. At the vent. He could have busted us right there, taken us to jail. Or closed the vent after we went out."

"Could've ratted you out," Michael said, looking at his son.

"Right, Dad," Elmer said.

"Colin," Roberto Fairchild said to his son, "we've all seen cops turn the other way."

"It was a whole lot more than that," Sher said, turning back to the group, her eyes flaming at them. "One of these kids was gonna get *sick*," she said, looking at the teenagers and then at their parents, one by one. "Chief Schmitz stalled them. Put

235

them off. That's one of the reasons we had to leave when we did." She looked at Cheng, who shrugged and nodded. "For years and years he saved us when he could and suffered when he couldn't. What he knew about is the reason we—well, that's nobody's business," she said, turning to Cheng and touching his cheek briefly before turning back to the group. "But he'll still be keeping us safe when he can, if we pay attention to him." She stopped, now seeming near tears herself, and then through gritted teeth said, "And don't any one of you *dare* to blame him. Don't you fucking *dare*."

More silence. Cheng wiped his face with his sleeve.

"Chief Schmitz is boss," Bryce said.

"Da bomb," Astrid said.

"Rocks da world," LaTasha said.

"Da man," Gerald said.

"El hombre," Elmer said, at which Michael could not stop himself from laughing.

More silence.

"I think we all understand," Grace said, and put her hand on Colin's shoulder. "It will be hard out here."

"But we're *free!*" LaTasha said, smiling.

More silence.

"Leah," Mahesh said to his wife, "I've never heard you say *shit* before."

Everyone laughed.

Howard, who, through all this, had been reclining back on his elbows, stood up and said, "Okay. Enough bullshit. We have to find another truck."

"Why did we need to change?" Cheng asked.

"One we were on is going north. We need to stay south. To stay warm."

"How can you tell which way they'll go?" Cheng asked, smiling wryly at Howard.

"Plates, stickers on the back, the way they're pointed. Trust me," Howard said.

"Folks," Cheng said to the group. "Howard knows where we're going. Like he said, trust him." And Cheng again laughed and shook his head.

Howard glared at him. "I'd sure like to know what's so damn funny," he said.

Cheng walked to Howard and clapped him on the shoulder and said, "Nothing, Howard. Nothing's funny." But Cheng continued to laugh.

Howard led them stealthily across the parking lot, from shadow to shadow, under trucks, to another semi, onto which they all, now veteran tractor-jumpers, climbed.

45

M arjorie and Boris sat on the bed in another dingy awful
motel room, the curtains closed, light coming only from
the bathroom and the cheap laptop they'd bought, along with
two cheap monthly-pay dumb phones, between breakfast and
check-in after driving all of the previous night to a shabby
outskirt of Los Angeles. They'd paid for the phone service in
cash, tipping the salesman to discourage his questions.

Like the scalies, they had no plan. They spent nights in
sleep and sex, days scanning the internet for news. They
would wake, fuck, shower, eat breakfast in the chain faux-
diner across the street, return to the room and the laptop.
Later, they would get lunch from a burrito stand a block away,
return to the room and more surfing, have dinner of delivered
pizza with beer or wine from a local liquor store, watch TV
news, fuck, sleep, and then start the next day.

Occasionally Boris would announce that he felt like taking
a walk. Marjorie would say, "Okay," and would barely
manage a wave as he opened the door, his last sight before
closing the door being her face attached as if by a wire to the
laptop screen. Boris would stride around the area, through the
Mexican neighborhood into the Asian neighborhood and then
into the bland racial homogeneity of semi-urban white LA,
thinking about what he was doing with Marjorie. He would
return to find her in the same cross-legged position on the bed,
her face lit by the screen, her eyes darting across it, her fingers
resting lightly on the keyboard.

After the fourth day he returned from a stroll, closed the room door behind him, walked to the foot of the bed and looked down at her: beautiful, smart, a good lay.

"Marjorie," he said.

"Hm," she said, her nose still to the screen.

"Babe," he said louder.

"What?" she said, as she typed something.

"How about going out tonight?"

"Out," she said.

Boris sat on the bed and pushed the laptop screen down. "You know," he said. "Dinner, movie, ordinary things two people sometimes do that we've never done."

Marjorie looked at him, but her eyes seemed still focused on the screen she could no longer see.

"Marjorie?"

"I'm sorry, Boris, I just."

"You're obsessed."

"Things are happening, Boris. At any time. There's going to be news."

Boris felt an irritation but made himself speak gently: "It will happen without you. Come on, I'll show you the neighborhood."

She smiled. "I'll shower, make myself presentable."

"You look any more presentable, we'll never get out."

They walked through the early evening to the Asian block where Boris led her to a Cambodian restaurant. They ate like an old married couple with nothing to say to each other. As they left, Marjorie said, "Boris, honey, about the movie."

"Sure," he said.

Back at the motel, the laptop again burning, Boris sat behind Marjorie and watched the screen over her shoulder as she searched and clicked result links, page after page of them, one link after another usually leading to the same picture of her recoiling in horror at the little guys in front of her.

"Too many haystacks," he said. "Not enough needles."
As far as he could tell, Marjorie did not hear him.

46

For four more hours they rode their semi and watched the empty desert gradually fill with fast-food places, real restaurants, and motels. Then there were warehouses, car dealerships, office buildings of three or four stories, road signs pointing the way to an airport.

Howard, Cheng, and Sher sat together. "We're going to LA," Howard said. "Some suburb on the east. I can't remember the name. They all look the same anyway. This is a moving van. They got furniture in the back."

Several minutes passed until Sher, showing an exasperated look to Cheng, said, "So?"

"What?" Howard said.

"So, what's it matter if this is a moving van?"

"So most likely it's going into a wealthy neighborhood, because they're the ones who can afford moving vans."

They waited, until Sher again lost patience and said, with a circular hand motion, "And?"

Howard said nothing.

Cheng said, "Is that good or bad, Howard?"

Howard sighed. "Well. I suppose it's good." Then, sounding disgusted, he said, "I grew up like these kids here," raising his head to indicate the teenagers, "with the fancy shops and the squeaky-clean streets and the shiny cars and never a goddamn worry except what to do on Saturday night. But once I got out here, I saw different kinds of people, the kinds we might have seen in a movie or TV. I hid and I watched them. They have to struggle, scramble for everything, hoping in the face of reality that someday they can stop scrambling. They get up too early in the morning to be rested and they come home late, looking dirty, sweaty, and worn out. Every day, sometimes without a weekend break. But they're nicer and more generous with each other than our people. And when they have a break, they have more fun. They're just more real, if you know what I mean. I like them better."

"But?" Sher said.

"But upscale or downscale we need a place to camp and consider things for a while. The good people live on top of each other in flimsier buildings with dogs and cats running free in the streets, not to mention rats. The upscale areas are boring and full of people like us, but they're more spread out and we're more likely to find a decent, safe place to stay."

"So, unfortunately, an upscale place would be good for us," Sher said with a half-smile.

"Yeah," Howard said, catching the sarcasm. "Unfortunately, it would."

Cheng laughed.

"Cheng, you've laughed more out here in the past two days than I've seen before, and we've known each other all our lives," Howard said, not sounding the least bit amused himself.

"Yeah," Cheng said. "I think I have."

"It's fun watching somebody else have to make decisions," Sher said.

"Hah," Howard said.

The truck slowed for an interchange ramp.

"Pass the word to be ready to leave the truck at any time," Howard said, "but not to move until."

"Until what, Howard?" Cheng said.

"Until I fucking give the word," Howard said.

Cheng and Sher both laughed but Howard did not.

———

In early afternoon the clutter of occasional buildings in the desert became denser with light industry and then homes. No tourist on an Alaskan cruise has ever gaped at a glacier with more wonder than the teenagers and their parents did at the passing rows of new and under-construction homes, the finished ones all with adobe-colored walls and red tile roofs fronted by yards of green grass and sapling trees. They gasped at apartment buildings and townhouses, and actually shouted the names of the chain retail and food operations because they were the same as the ones at "home."

Cheng and Sher joined in, their arms around each other, grinning at the new world they were seeing for the first time, looking so much bigger and more inviting than what they had seen in movies or TV.

Howard sat alone and scowled in concentration, leaning out to see what was ahead, and then sat back, pondering.

The truck slowed, its right-turn signal blinked, and it rolled onto an off-ramp, then stopped at a traffic light where the ramp intersected a four-lane surface street. Howard crouch-walked among the group, his face intense, motioning for them to lie down and not talk. The truck turned right onto the large street. They saw people in cars, people shopping, people walking dogs some of which were larger than all of their group together. They saw enormous birds. They felt dread.

The truck stopped at another traffic light occupied by gasoline stations and convenience stores, where it turned left and moved onto a street with two lanes and a median strip, occupied by small shops and residences. Howard raised a hand as if signaling troops to stay down and wait, but be ready. The truck rolled to the right and parked on the street. They heard two doors open and slam, and saw two men walk across the street. Howard rose high enough to look at them all to show the urgency in his eyes, and pointed toward the ground. Quickly, they climbed off the tractor, tossing and dropping their bags as they went.

On the sidewalk, Howard motioned them toward a low hedge that fronted a large house. Holding their luggage and running, they were under the hedge in seconds. As they caught their breaths, Howard told them, "Wait here, don't move, and for god's sake stay quiet," and then he was gone.

They huddled together, sitting on the ground or on luggage, silently bonded by their fear. Moments passed, with the sounds of cars, and the sight of enormous feet, male and female, pacing down the sidewalk bordering the hedge.

"What if one of those dogs, or a cat comes?" LaTasha whispered. Morgana shushed her.

Some minutes later, they watched their truck leave them. Each person touched whoever was nearest. Like herd animals huddled together against danger, they wordlessly shared a combined bereavement at losing a last cord, no matter how thin and fragile, to what had been their home, and an exhilaration at having escaped.

After an hour Howard re-appeared. He looked pleased. "This is about as good as we're going to find," he whispered. "There's a supermarket down the street, and an office building full of doctors and dentists right near here, with a storage shed behind it. That's where we'll camp."

"Why not camp at the market, where the food is?" Bryce asked.

Howard looked dourly at him. "That's where the rats are too," he said. "Everybody just shut up and do as I say. We have to cross the street and we don't want to do that in daylight. It should be dark in about three hours, so we'll wait here. Don't talk unless it's necessary and move as little as possible. Movement attracts animals. If you have to shit or piss, go in pairs a couple feet off. Sleep is okay, but each family will have to sleep in shifts. Cheng, I'm sleeping now, so you can watch. You're as close to family as I've got." And Howard immediately lay down where he stood, settled on one side with an arm under his head and his hat over his face, and breathed evenly until he slept.

And so they stayed there, in Zen-like silence and stillness, as the afternoon grew pale and then dim, and night fell.

———

In darkness they prepared to move as a team, apportioning their luggage based on who could carry what, without regard to ownership and with hardly any talk. They had not eaten for more than eight hours, and their water was low, but they did not talk about that either.

Howard whispered to them about waiting until the traffic was sparse. He assigned himself to watch one direction of the street, Michael Cruz to watch the other, and Roberto Fairchild, Mahesh Reynaud, and Jerome Thurman to watch the two nearest intersections. The traffic on their street diminished to a car or two every few minutes, and on the cross streets there was almost none, but still Howard made them wait. When the only headlights were in the far distances on their street, Howard gathered them and gave the word, and they ran across the street to the shadows of more sidewalk shrubbery. Following Howard, they turned right, quick-walked to an intersection, paused to check for traffic, and dashed across the narrow street and rightward another half block to the entrance to a small parking lot adjoining a small two-story brick building. They walked through the parking lot and rightward again, down an alley, and stopped at the midpoint of the building across the alley from its rear wall, where there was another hedge. Howard had them duck under it to catch their breath.

245

"Nice that there are so many hedges here," Gerald said.

"Old street," Howard said. "Not like those developments we passed this afternoon."

"Old? This is ancient," Colin said, and he stepped from under the hedge to look up at it. "I can't see the top. And two of us could lie down head to toe across it and have shelter to spare."

"Get the fuck back under," Howard hissed, and Colin, looking sheepish, obeyed. Howard scowled at him and spoke to everyone. "In case you had not noticed, we live in a dangerous world that can pounce on us at any time. We have to stay in the shadows to survive."

"From what I hear, you've done okay," Bryce said.

"That's because it was just me. Now there are lots of us, and sooner or later there will be news. These bigs will be terrified of us, but they won't run. They'll stomp us if they can."

"We get the message, Howard," Marissa said. "We'll be careful." She put her hand on Bryce's shoulder.

"Fine," Howard said. "The other side of this hedge is a garage attached to an old house. The space between the hedge and the garage wall is sort of hidden by bushes at one end and stored junk at the other. We can make shelter here." Howard suddenly stopped and looked around at the group.

"It's okay, Howard," Grace Fairchild said, sounding a bit motherly. "We're listening."

"Yeah, well," Howard said. "We need food, liquid, and stuff to make shelter, so we need the most muscle power and speed out there."

"Don't bunch your undies, Howard," Sher said, sounding annoyed. She was looking behind the hedge, surveying their prospective residence area. "We ladies will stay here and *tidy*. You guys go on out and try to avoid getting stomped."

"Fine," Howard said. "But I want Astrid. She's good in small places."

"You got me," Astrid said.

"Two groups," Howard said. "One group with me to get food. The other with Cheng to grab building junk."

The men divided. Howard had Astrid, Bryce, Roberto, Jerome, and Colin. Cheng had Michael, Elmer, Mahesh, and Gerald.

"The supermarket is further up the alley," Howard said. There are a couple of dumpsters on the way. Be very careful around them. Look for any movement before you even get close and when you do get close, listen for any noises coming from inside. The rats around supermarkets tend to be large."

———————

Two hours later they sat together eating cheese and fruit. They took turns drinking from a straw in a juice can. Beneath them were two sheets of canvas, the backs from director's chairs the women had found by the garage. To either side were milk crates that Cheng's men had hauled, one at a time, from behind the supermarket, down the alley to the street fronting "their" house, and through the bushes at one end of the garage-hedge space. They had positioned the crates on their sides, facing each other, with space between them. Over the space the canvas seats from the director's chairs formed a roof, with a strip between them wide enough for a skylight of clamshell plastic packaging, all weighted with rocks and tied with string. The women camouflaged the sides and top with branches broken from the hedge and bushes, and had also prevailed on Cheng to scavenge a cardboard box for a separate latrine house, "for some privacy, goddammit," Leah had said, amusing everyone but Mahesh, and then added, "And some flatware to use for spreading the shit out and burying it."

So, finally, they felt settled, and sat in moonlight through the skylight, and conversed in free association, the way people do at a dinner party. They talked about what they would be doing were they still at "home" in the project. LaTasha said she was having more fun than she ever did cruising on their streets or shopping at their mall. Colin agreed. They wondered where others might have gone. They talked about getting more clamshell packaging to use as tubs for washing both themselves and their clothes. Astrid volunteered to steal doll toys or whatever she could from the supermarket so that they could have plates to eat from and cups to drink from. They laughed when Elmer talked about stealing beer. Morgana said they would need more cardboard boxes to create separate rooms in the milk crates, and mimicked Leah by saying, "for some privacy, goddammit," and they all laughed again. The parents stayed close to each other and looked with love on their children. Cheng and Sher relaxed against each other. Howard, while repeatedly warning them to keep their voices down, managed to smile occasionally when the others laughed.

They decided on four watches during the night. Howard volunteered for the first, Sher for the second, Phuong for the third, and Marissa for the last.

Elmer and Gerald had a separate discussion about phones. They tired of talk and found spots to sleep.

47

They did not like calling what they did "stealing," so they took to calling it "foraging," except for Gerald, who preferred "ripping off" and LaTasha, who favored "liberating." Howard declared that they would steal no more than they could eat in one day, for the simple reason that food in the camp would attract animals. Despite their growing confidence, each daily trip to the back of the supermarket was tense for both the raiders and those waiting for them in camp. So, when Bryce, Elmer, and Michael found a plastic bin that seemed safe for food storage, the rest of the group greeted them with actual cheers and applause that Howard quickly and angrily muted, and he warned them that the tub would not be safe. After he reminded them of the size of the animals in question, with laughter and fake groans they agreed to hide it halfway between camp and the market. Cheng gave Howard a good-natured slap on the back.

Bryce, Elmer, and Michael filled the tub, in one trip, with two days of provisions and sealed the lid. On the morning of the second day, Jerome and Elmer found a lid that was perforated , the container flipped over, and every sealed food package ruptured by what had to have been teeth. Bryce summoned Howard who looked at the scene and said, "Those critters can smell through plastic. Metal too. But they can't tear through metal." On Howard's orders, they laboriously gathered the garbage and hurled it into a dumpster.

That same day, Bryce and Elmer liberated a metal toolbox with a latching lid and camouflaged it in a new hiding place.

They did subdivide the milk crates with cardboard. For bathing they had plastic tubs—opaque ones, at the women's insistence—and Phuong and Marissa used a tub and a black plastic trash bag to rig a solar water heater. Once they had liquid soap, their bathing became pleasurable and the washing of their clothes and doll utensils, easier.

The end of their first two weeks found them settled and with real leisure time. Bryce and Elmer "foraged" a couple of paperback books, and a pocket music player with earbuds the size of their hands, which Colin put down on their canvas floor to function as speakers.

They wanted to explore the territory, and Howard, seeing the limits of his authority, told them to go out in groups of exactly three, to avoid drawing attention—as if they needed to be told that—and if they had to run, to never run directly back to camp.

And so, Phuong, Michael, and Marissa walked around the house backing their camp, and found it large and luxurious, if a bit run-down, in a Tudor style they had seen only on TV. Up the street they saw other large houses in varying styles, ranging in condition from old and weathered to brand new, with expensive cars parked in front. Safely hidden, they saw people leaving and returning.

Sher, Leah, and Astrid went down a street behind the supermarket and found smaller houses.

When they swapped notes, they found that what most struck them were how the people and their lives much resembled what theirs had been back "home." The only difference was size.

Defying Howard, Colin and LaTasha went out alone, though they did not notice that Morgana, at least, had seen them go. They hid in the alley behind the medical building and saw people with casts on their arms and people in wheelchairs and others, some old and some older, with oxygen tanks on the backs of the chairs.

Colin suggesting going to the big street, and LaTasha cautiously agreed. They walked quietly into a section of the parking lot where the second story covered it. Hidden under a car with a low concrete barrier in front of them, they watched. Across the street were small shops: a drug store, a small restaurant, a women's clothing shop, a hardware store.

"The shops are so small. I mean, of course they're bigger than ours, naturally, but I mean, given how much smaller we are, we don't—we didn't—have anything like these," Colin said. "Ours are all from the big chains."

"That's true," LaTasha said. She put her hand into Colin's.

They watched the people and the cars. They heard talk, though nothing notable.

"Colin?" LaTasha said. She waited until Colin turned and looked at her, then she said, "Colin, you're mostly watching the women." Before he could answer, she freed her hand from his, put both hands around his head and pulled him down for a hard kiss. She felt his surprise followed in an instant by full participation, his arms around her waist and shoulder pulling her towards him. The kiss lasted several moments.

They broke, and stood, still entwined, smiling at each other.

"Colin," LaTasha said, and then blurted out what she had promised herself she would not say. "You're looking for her, aren't you?"

"Her?" Colin said.

After a moment when she saw his eyes move back to the street, she started another kiss, and then clasped him to her, her head on his shoulder. "It's okay, baby," she whispered. "It's okay."

For Colin, it was definitely better than okay.

———————

Gerald was busy with his phone. Alone, in violation of Howard's order, he ripped off a charger from the hardware store and spliced it into his own, and then at night he plugged the hybrid device into an outdoor socket in the backyard of the house they now referred to as "next door." He removed it after an hour, with his phone now charged. None of them had seen anyone in that back yard, so the risk, especially at night, seemed minimal.

After fiddling unsuccessfully with the phone for parts of two nights—instinctively wanting to keep the operation secret,—one night while he was on watch, he crept into Elmer's cardboard cubicle, woke him, and motioned him outside. After a moment, Elmer grinned and followed him into the space between hedge and the big house they referred to as "next-door.

Gerald held up his phone. "I'm trying to surf, with not much luck. The browser doesn't respond."

"You turned off the GPS, right?" Elmer said.

"Of course, dude."

"Give it to me," Elmer said, and Gerald did.

Elmer pressed and held keys in various sequences, trying several combinations with no effect.

Excited, Gerald watched over his shoulder. "Dude, you're a genius," he said. "I didn't think of that." He watched as Elmer seemed to go from ideas of key combinations to random guesses. "Try this," Gerald said and rattled off a key combo.

Elmer tried it and the screen went black, with a small ">" in the upper left. "Ha!" Elmer said.

"Whooo!" Gerald said. "Gimme," he said, and Elmer did.

Gerald keyed in a command, and a list scrolled down the screen.

"Networks," Elmer said.

"Yup," Gerald said. "And it tells which ones are open."

"Not many," Elmer said.

Gerald pinged one with no response. Then he tried the one that happened to have been created by fellow-scaly Jacques Brudkepjian (whom Gerald would not meet until many years later). "Yikes!" he said, and went back to the browser, and found Jacques' blog. "Well, shit," he said.

Elmer moved closer so they could see the screen together. "What is this?" Elmer said.

They read on. Gerald scrolled down and clicked links to other pages. Understanding dawned on them both. "It's us!" Gerald said. "It's fucking us!"

"I know, right?" Elmer said.

They continued until a half hour before the end of Gerald's watch shift. They read of scalies camping all over, much as they had, riding trucks as they had, stowing away in cars, even on trains. They were awed.

And as they looked at the phone they could not help but press their cheeks together, and when Gerald closed his phone they rotated their heads until they faced, and kissed for a long time.

———

Early one morning Bryce, Elmer, and Colin foraged a half-liter, screw-top bottle of white wine, and Astrid wriggled into delicatessen boxes and foraged a can of smoked fish and another of caviar, while Bryce found two boxes of fancy crackers. Gerald and Elmer lifted a container of "gourmet" chocolate custard. Phuong and Leah snuck into the back of a "gift" shop and foraged a package of white fabric napkins with lace edges.

The motivation for all of that was Sher's declaration, one evening, that though they were living well, and enjoying the sights, and all that, they deserved a celebration for having established themselves. Through some miracle, nobody was sick or injured, and despite the late summer season, she said in her all-business, sober, city manager voice, "we deserve a thanksgiving, and we should have it now, today." Nobody argued.

Howard and Cheng had deputized Mahesh and Michael for security, but on most afternoons there was little need, beyond Howard's daily "don't get careless, goddammit," in which they joined in chorus despite, or perhaps because of, how much it irritated him. Howard went daily on exploratory rambles; he knew where the affluence ended, where the blue-collar started, and where the sleaze was. Despite his own misgivings, he himself "stole" — damned if he would call it "foraged" — two airline-sized bottles of twelve-year-old Glenlivet.

And so, on a hot southern California afternoon they decorated their space between the milk crates and lounged and ate and drank. The teenagers, as pampered as they had been back in the project, had never tasted caviar, and now they pronounced it good, except for Astrid, who said that had she known what it was like she would have foraged some salami instead. Roberto remarked that after a life of rising for work every day, he had no idea what day of the week today was.

After a couple hours, the banter gave way to contented silence. The parent couples — Roberto and Grace, Jerome and Morgana, Phuong and Michael, and Mahesh and Leah — one by one nudged each other and retired to their cardboard rooms. Marissa, the lone adult with the kids, sniffled. "Don't mind me," she said to them. "Wine makes me maudlin." Seeing the eyes of Colin and LaTasha, sitting next to each other, she waived her hands as if warding off mosquitoes and said, "all of you, just, whatever. Everybody knows."

Colin and LaTasha, holding hands, went first, toward the shrubbery by the side of "next-door." Gerald and Elmer went off in the opposite direction.

Which left only Marissa, Bryce, and Astrid, the latter pair looking uneasily at the softly crying Marissa.

Bryce rose from his spot on a lacy napkin and sat next to his mother, the two of them leaning against one side of a milk crate. "I'm okay, son," Marissa said. "Just lonely. You two can . . . whatever," and she did her backhanded wave again.

Bryce shifted his uneasy look from his mother to Astrid, who sat on the ground by herself, drawing figures on the ground with a stick.

"Not such a couple anymore, huh?" Marissa said. "Well, it happens. Lord knows I can testify to that." She took a breath. "Astrid, too. Too bad there's nobody else around, but." She shrugged.

Bryce put his large right arm over his mother's shoulder, but he kept his eyes on Astrid, who looked up from her dirt picture and cast an unmistakable no at him. After a few minutes Marissa put her head on Bryce's arm and fell asleep. Bryce looked pleadingly at Astrid, but she rose and left, apparently for her own cardboard room.

––––––

Colin and LaTasha were into heavy necking when LaTasha said, "I started the pills two months ago, Colin," which stopped him for a moment. "Don't look like that," she said. "They're for you. I've never done it before either." Colin, a bit flustered but nonetheless eager, hugged her. Over his shoulder she said, "Colin," and he said, "LaTasha," and she said, "Colin, wait," and pushed him away.

"What?" he said, and then turned from her in the direction she was looking, through the bushes, and saw the dog, a white

Labrador, or a mix, five times his size, its eyes fixed on them, tail wagging, just a few yards away.

"Shit," Colin said.

The dog advanced and lowered its snout, sniffing them from a distance.

"We should run," LaTasha said.

"If we run it'll chase," Colin said. "Stay behind me." He looked at the next-door house and scanned the street. Seeing nobody, he stepped from under the shrubs into the sunlight of the lawn. "Sit!" he shouted.

The dog, clearly male, stopped his slow movement towards them and raised his head. The tail stopped wagging.

"*SIT!*" Colin shouted again.

The dog sat. Colin and the dog looked at each other.

"*LIE DOWN!*" Colin shouted.

The dog lay down.

Colin stared at the dog. "*GO HOME!*" he shouted.

The dog raised his head quizzically.

"*GO HOME!*" Colin shouted again.

The dog did not move.

Colin picked up a stone and threw it over the dog. "*GO HOME!*" he shouted again. He picked up another stone and threw it over the dog. "*HOME!*" he yelled fiercely, and threw yet another stone, this time hitting the dog in the nose. The dog recoiled, his eyes widened, and quickly, he rose to his feet and ran off, as Colin watched.

"My hero," LaTasha said behind him. He turned to her and grinned, and then noticed that she held her cell phone.

"You took a picture?"

"Got both of you," LaTasha said with a smile.

They were both laughing as he went to her in the shadows.

48

From Colin's Journal

Would we have done it if we weren't free? If we weren't all running from our homes toward—what? We don't know. I can't stop thinking that if we were still back home, I'd still be a virgin.

Was it fantastic? Fabulous? All those other words? Goddamn right it was!!!!

The first time was hard, especially for her, with the pain and the blood and all, which kind of scared me. But she said it was okay, and then just a little while later we did it again and it was like the Pacific Ocean (which I've never seen!) came pounding down on us and lifted us up at the same time. After, LaTasha cried a little, but it was a good kind of crying. I cried a little too and I wasn't even embarrassed about it.

What's really cool is that our parents know and are good with it. It's not like we made an announcement, but we could tell that they knew from the minute they saw us coming back to camp. At first that embarrassed me, but now it's just like we are all family. And Elmer and Gerald have hooked up, and their parents are cool about that too. Bryce is hurting, I can tell. Astrid doesn't want much to do with him. Seems like the one she likes is Howard, but not in that way. They both seem to need lots of alone time. LaTasha and I leave camp and find a nice spot under a bush to hang out. Gerald and Elmer do the same, and even the parents, and the Chief and Ms. Statie. Astrid and Howard are into going off alone. Astrid is sort of going native, wearing leaves for clothing. The ones I feel bad for are Bryce and his mom. Bryce because he wants Astrid but she doesn't want him, and his mom because she's sort of glad and sad at the same time about having her son but seeing him unhappy.

Our camp is so beautiful it's unbelievable, like one of those resorts you see in movies.
We're living in nature—even though there are houses and supermarkets and stores right close. And we built the camp ourselves, which is like the ultimate, with a shower and a toilet. We go out on "liberating" trips, as LaTasha calls them, and come back with all kinds of great food stuff to improve the camp, and then we just relax in the sun and eat. Wow!!!!

And Gerald and Elmer have found these websites where people like us can tell each other stuff. We have our own little community online. It's exciting knowing we're not all alone in the world.

We're always alert to danger, and if we ever forget, Howard or the Chief or Ms. Statie reminds us. We take turns as sentries at night.

LaTasha knows I'm always on the lookout for that woman. She tells me it's okay, but I know it's not. I can't help it. I guess I'm a little crazy.

49

4&k3L)(n watched the traffic, lines of IP addresses and communication packets, a river of information flowing down his screen for him only. Those boyish bureaucrats in their cubicles, with their giant vacuum cleaners and their philistine brains, looking in their "haystacks" for their "needles," could not see the beauty of what they were watching, and therefore they missed it, the spectacle of human beings speaking to each other: buying, selling, yearning, wishing, begging, cajoling, demanding, suffering, laughing, worshipping, sneering, scorning, fearing, hoping, despairing, lusting, loving, hating—not to mention reporting what they ate for lunch today or how hung-over they were from last night. Like a painting by Bruegel, humanity baring all, from triumph to catastrophe.

But he could see. 4&k3L)(n embraced it all.

The picture, the one of the big woman and the small adolescents, 4&k3L)(n had plucked and planted, and from it a vine had grown, creeping, climbing, and sticking, and it had fed little bunnies, hippety-hopping from one IP address to another.

Like this Jacques Brudkepjian, a young revolutionary—4&k3L)(n had to assume he was young, no old fart would behave this way—who had grafted his own shoot onto the vine and fertilized it and released it to spread like kudzu across the land. And then had come those boyish bureaucrats—what did they have against vines, anyway?—snipping and grabbing and no doubt wondering, *is this the needle? This? Or this?* But Jacques was an artist, like 4&k3L)(n, and the exuberance of art can never be repressed or contained, and so Jacques had hopped to another IP, another MAC address, and planted a twig from the vine, and in virtual no-time, the twig had recreated the vine anew. And again, god-like—for were artists not strivers for the divine?—Jacques had *created* a *new* address, a new source, and grafted it onto the vine and it had likewise grown! Etc.!

But not without difficulty. This poor, young Jacques, living his hobo life! He needed help. Which is what 4&k3L)(n was here for! For his own vine blossomed with notes and pictures. There was not only the beautiful woman with the little people, there were also delightful photos of five happy twenty-somethings, three boys, two girls, having such a wonderful time, for they had escaped the confines of their narrow world and were ecstatic in a land of milk and honey—or, at least, beer and pretzels. Theirs was a wonderful series of pictures of a carefree daily life, which had suddenly and without warning, vanished. No IP trail, no packet crumbs, nothing. But the vine had persisted.

Someone, or some *two*, identified as Gerald&Elmer, had posted their own pictures of subjects ranging from the pedestrian—literally, pedestrians on a sidewalk with perspective chosen to show just how enormous they were—to the idyllic, people lounging in sun and shadow, and sitting on—what? Plastic margarine tubs? How could *that* be? And then there was the one featuring the back of a boy or young man with a gigantic dog lying on the ground beyond him, facing the camera, the huge dog head cocked to one side, the big canine eyes straining to understand.

Hmm. The young male back looked familiar. 4&k3L)(n quickly opened the other photo, the one similarly showing the backs of several young people with, instead of a gigantic quizzical dog, a gigantic terrified woman in the background. But one of the male backs in the woman photo definitely resembled the one in the dog photo. One back recoiling away from the woman, the other standing tall and straight and commanding, in different shirts, but could they be the same? Head shape, cut and color of hair, shape of torso: could they be the same?

Well, really, who cared? What was the difference? For *art*, 4&k3L)(n would think of them as the same. For real life, whatever *that* was, well, whatever.

The important thing was to protect the vine. For there, in the stream, came the packet prints, the foot prints, the finger prints, the *nose* prints, of the boyish bureaucrats with their pruning shears and their magnifying glasses, bent on picking and examining vine specimens to add to their collection of *might-be-needles*. 4&k3L)(n could not stop them, but he could divert them by leaving his own packet prints for them to chase, so that they would never even notice Gerald&Elmer, who could continue in their idyllic way to enhance 4&k3L)(n's living work of art.

50

For weeks Samuel commuted daily to his job with a small engineering company, creating circuit diagrams for small construction projects and diagnosing problems in buildings so old that their diagrams existed only on rolls of yellowing E-sized paper. The twenty-two-mile commute could take an hour in the morning, meaning that Sam had to leave the house while his kids and wife still slept. At first he had kissed each sleeping figure on the cheek or head, whatever was above the covers, before leaving, but after a week, he had stopped that ritual, partly because of his own distractions and partly because nobody else seemed to notice or care. The return commute in the late afternoon was generally at least thirty minutes longer than the morning, leaving him tense and incommunicative at home.

Jennifer's search for work at local schools had failed, and she had begun, resentfully, to look for "administrative assistant" or retail jobs. Kirk reported that his new fifth grade class was okay. Sandra liked her third-grade class because it was so much easier than the previous one, which distressed Jennifer. Both kids made some friends, which was good. Jennifer fought hard against the void that seemed to be growing around her, but the feeling she was losing angered her, and the anger naturally directed itself toward Samuel, who deserved it, and Kirk and Sandra, who did not. Jennifer carried on as a housewife, feeding her family, clothing them cleanly, maintaining the house, and filling the remaining time with trashy novels. Once, she turned on Sam's laptop to see if she could follow his browser history, but, of course, he had erased it.

She tried to stop the retreat of Kirk and Sandra away from family, but she felt herself failing at that too, and, besides, how could she blame them? At least they seemed to have each other. She imagined them as adults, meeting at one of their apartments, having dinner and swapping darkly humorous stories about Mom and Dad. In those imaginings there was neither in-law nor grandchild.

Their dinners became more silent, more taut, leading to arrival of a guest previously banned from their table: a TV set, a small one that Jennifer had bought cheaply. She announced, brightly, that she thought it might lighten things up. They could watch sit-coms or old movies and laugh a little while they ate. On the second night after its arrival, Sam rose from his seat at the table, and moving slowly and in Jennifer's eyes looking as if he'd planned each move (which he might have), took the remote from where it rested on a kitchen counter, sat down again, and switched to news, ignoring the kids' protests. Not eating, he stared at the coverage of a state political scandal, a U.S. Senate argument about taxes, a controversy over school curricula. At the commercial break, he switched to another news channel, this one with local stories of car crashes and drug arrests and disgraced city council members. Jennifer, Kirk, and Sandra, also not eating, watched Sam. At the next commercial break, Sam muted the TV and returned to the dinner Jennifer had made. As if that were a signal, the others also ate, though without enthusiasm. Sam kept the remote, but he did not touch it, letting the news run without sound, until the next break when he switched to another, still without sound. After finishing perhaps two thirds of the food Jennifer had served him, he left the remote on the table and excused himself to the living room.

From her chair in the dining nook, through the doorway to the living room, Jennifer could see him in profile, sitting on the sofa. He turned on their big TV and tuned it to a news station, but he kept the volume very low. Then he turned on the laptop computer that had been on the coffee table since their second day here. He leaned into it and quickly tapped keys, stopping to look at the screen, then tapped again, twice shifting his eyes up toward the TV. A wall hid the TV from her and the laptop was sideways to her, but she could see the light flicker from both of them, casting rapidly changing colors on her husband who moved only his hands on the keyboard and his eyes up and down from one screen to the other, his eyebrows lowered in concentration, his mouth in a frown, sometimes biting his lips.

Jennifer sensed something start to come apart inside her and around her, a feeling of disintegration so intense that she could nearly see the image of it superimposed over her husband at his screens. Where was he? Where was she? Where, in what, were they all floating?

She heard Kirk saying, "Mom," and was aware that he had said it perhaps two or three times before she reacted. She turned toward him and was surprised by the solid reality of him, and as if to confirm what she saw, she reached out and caressed his cheek, and then she saw fear in his eyes and, remembering that she had to be solid for him, she smiled. "Mom," he said, "can we watch the movie?"

"Yeah," Sandra said, so quietly that Jennifer could barely hear her, "can we watch the movie?"

"Sure," Jennifer said. She punched the remote buttons for the movie channel and raised the volume. She started eating again, mostly as a cue for her children, who took it. The only sounds were of their flatware against the plates, the voices, music, and cartoon clashes of the movie, and the barely audible drone of the big TV in the living room. She looked again at Sam, in his electronic pastel colors, who seemed to be aware only of his screens. The voice fragments from the big living room TV clashed with the movie sound, so she reached out and swung the door between them closed.

As she resumed her meal, she watched her children desultorily eating theirs while they focused on the movie, which held no interest for her. She saw only them, and soon even they were covered by that same barely but clearly visible lack of solidity, that void, which came between her and them, until she roused herself and began kitchen cleanup.

———

Sam did not feel totally secure on the laptop. The internet account was for Brookens, not Giles, and Sam knew that there were hundreds of Samuel Brookens's, and he even knew that there were several families of Samuel, Jennifer, Kirk, and Sandra Brookens. He had a new IP address, and he applied enough security to ward off average hackers and not enough to call attention to himself. He avoided web sites with controversial politics and hoped that Sam Brookens could hide in the internet crowd. Still, he knew he was pursued and he knew of the scalies' break-out, and he wasn't sure which was more depressing.

On one such night, Jennifer stood behind the couch.

"I'm reduced to looking for morning waitress jobs. Like when I was in college," she said.

"You don't have to," Sam said, looking from the laptop to the TV and back again. "You write the checks, so you know we're getting by."

"I need to be doing something."

"Why not volunteer in the school."

"Because, as I told you weeks ago, they do background investigations of volunteers. The Brookens family has no background."

Sam's attention stayed with the laptop and TV.

"I thought it might be romantic," Jennifer said.

After a moment, Sam said, "What might?"

"Hiding together. Us against the world. I thought we'd get closer."

Sam said nothing.

"But it's just more of the same. Secrets and more secrets. And your obsessions, none of which is me."

Sam leaned toward his laptop.

"Sam, goddammit, did you hear me?"

"They're here," he said.

"Who?" she said, reflexively turning toward the front door.

"Scalies."

Jennifer looked at the laptop, and then kneeled down behind the couch to see better over his shoulder, as he clicked through a collection of photos. There were young people who looked like kids at a college party. "They look like the Village People," she said.

"It's doll clothing," Sam said, and moved the pointer to one of the boys. "GI Joe."

"My god, Barbie and Ken? Where are they?"

"Don't know. See in this one? That's a football game in the background. I'm not sure, but it looks like they're actually under the bleachers." Sam clicked another browser tab. "Look at these people."

There was a group apparently picnicking, only they appeared to be sitting on standard size food containers and in the background was a huge wine bottle. Jennifer squinted at the photo. "I've never seen them before," she said.

Surprised, Sam turned his head towards her. "I've never shown you pictures?"

"No. They remind me of the borrowers."

"The what?"

"Children's books. My mother and I read them together. I thought they were too old-fashioned for our kids."

Sam clicked through more pictures. There was one of walkers on a city sidewalk, but the camera seemed to have been mounted at shoe level. Then Sam typed a URL, and there was a picture of the back of a boy or young man, with a huge dog in the background. "See here?" Sam said. "Now look at this one." He clicked another tab, and there were several young-looking human backs, with an enormous scared-looking woman looming over them. "This one you're looking at, I think it was taken before the break-out. These are kids. One of them was on the list, but I think it might be the same kid as this one," and Sam switched back to the photo with the dog, "and so it looks like he might be okay, for now."

Jennifer studied the picture. "And us?" she said.

"What about us?" Sam said.

Suddenly she was angry again. "Are we okay?"

"The same as him," Sam said flatly, without intonation, as if not hearing her anger. "We're okay like he is."

"For now," she said.

Sam shifted his attention to the TV and turned up the sound, which had been a barely audible drone behind their talk.

> . . . when local police successfully defused what appeared to be a dangerous situation. As you can see in this video, the woman was brandishing weapons at a circle of people, her neighbors, one of whom called nine-one-one while another one took the video. You can see here, officers approaching with their weapons out, and you can hear her saying what sounds like, "Haven't you seen them?"

The female reporter stopped talking so the audience could hear another female voice saying what could have been:

"Haven't you seen them?"

The reporter resumed:

But here, fortunately, you can see the woman dropping her weapons.

The scene changed from the slightly fuzzy cell phone video to a crisp TV view of the reporter with her microphone and a young woman next to her.

Reporter: Are you Renee DeKalb?

Renee DeKalb nods.

Reporter: You know this woman?

Renee DeKalb: Yes, we've been neighbors for years.

Reporter: Can you tell us what happened?

Renee DeKalb: Well, I was in the backyard, doing some yard work, and I heard Gwen yelling—

Reporter: That would be Gwendolyn Tompkins, the woman in question?

Renee DeKalb: Right. Anyway, I looked over the fence, and she had a hammer in one hand and a big knife in the other and was yelling about seeing *them*, and she had this crazy look on her face, so I went around to her yard, and other neighbors were there and she looked scary, we were all scared. We just kind of tried to calm her, but she was, like, hysterical. Fortunately, the police came and she sort of came to her senses.

The scene changed again to the reporter talking alone now, with an ambulance in the background:

So, that's Ms. Tompkins, being taken into the ambulance—

Sam muted the TV and was now typing quickly, searching. "Here," he said, and there was the phone video, already on the web, of an ordinary looking middle-aged woman swinging a hammer and knife around while she yelled at a circle of people looking at her fearfully. Sam turned the laptop sound volume to the maximum and replayed the video. Jennifer could hear people's voices, a jumble of *it's okay, Gwen it's us, Gwen you're safe you don't need the hammer or the knife*, and the woman repeating, "haven't you seen them? They're here. Right over there." Sam replayed the video several times.

"I have to talk to her," he said. "I'll have to take tomorrow off, find her, talk to her."

"Sam," Jennifer said.

"But I can't go directly to her. If she's in a hospital, and someone not family comes to see her they won't let me in. I have to do it without attracting attention."

Jennifer walked around the couch and sat next to him.

"How can I do that?" he said.

"Fuck, Sam, *look at me!*" Jennifer yelled. "We've been having this conversation and you haven't looked at me. You hardly looked at me or the kids since you got home, which, I don't know why I should be upset now, it's like every other night."

Sam looked at her. "It's them. I'm responsible."

"For us too, Sam."

Sam turned back to the laptop. "I have to find her. I have to find them."

51

Astrid discovered she was not in love with Bryce not when his touch ceased to arouse her, but when her mind stopped lurching towards him while they were apart, which times were increasing, as he went scavenging and she went wandering, which she knew she was not supposed to do. Howard had confronted her about it and Marissa had expressed a motherly concern, but after a couple of weeks even that stopped, as their lives became routine. How fast could weird become regular? Pioneers on new continents, people locked in prisons, scalies among the bigs, people going willingly or unwillingly into the strange quickly turned it into the ordinary.

Astonished at her boredom, Astrid drifted outside to see this big world, only to find that it looked a lot like the little one, except it included people who looked poor. Still, she drifted, and she found in herself an ability to blend, without trying, becoming one with the scenery. She gained confidence and drifted farther, always remembering the way back. She saw insects as big as one of her legs, but they did not scare her, even the spiders. She would bat them with a stick and they would depart. She smeared dirt on her face and peered at the big folk from the leaves of shrubbery, which she would climb to get a better view. She stopped washing her outer clothing to let the dirt mute the colors.

She remembered her studies about immigrants to America who still yearned for the "old country," talked about it as "home," just like the scalies in camp talked about "home." Did they want to go back? Hold reunions? Designate some annual day of festivities, a scaly version of St. Patrick's Day? She didn't think so, but they talked that way sometimes.

She eyed the big people, wondering what their lives were like. Were they bored too? They didn't look it. Most of them looked harried, rushing about. Back "home" she and her friends had never felt harried, only trapped. Was harried better than trapped?

She skulked the edges of streets and alleys, skillfully avoiding cats and dogs. She saw human couples of all sorts, some openly affectionate, some in that comfortable way of people who are supposed to love each other, and some in the furtive way of people who are not. She became particularly interested in the variety of partings: fond and matter-of-fact, the years of goodbyes and hellos as expected as morning and evening; hungry and desperate, uncertain of the next meeting; angry and relieved; thoughtless and inconsiderate of any but the self; caring; totally uncaring. She could see that in their emotions bigs were no different from scalies.

She thought of her father. Maybe she should have left a note: *Sorry it has to be like this, but good luck and maybe we'll meet again*. What would that have cost her? At the time, the idea had not arisen. Her departure from "home" had not been a parting, really, because she had avoided seeing her father. Now she watched carefully when people left a house alone, but she never saw anyone who appeared to be running away.

More anthropologist than spy, she became skillful at finding secluded watching places. Hitching onto wi-fi, she also browsed. She hardly tired of looking at the backs of herself and her friends looking up at the giant woman. Reading the latest internet comments on that photo was actually a pastime in the little scaly colony; the bigs' cluelessness was hilarious. Over dinners, her fellow scaly colonists talked about how to survive in the world of bigs, and the consensus seemed to be that they needed to figure out how to get a safe corner of the world to live their lives apart, which is where the discussions stopped. Astrid did not participate, afraid that nobody would accept her desire to join the feral animals that lived among the bigs, and just *be*. She didn't want to say that because she didn't know how to argue the point and she feared a challenge.

Her furtive little treks began as escapes from boredom, progressed to curiosity-driven expeditions, and then, over weeks, became her life. In camp, she avoided Bryce. She didn't want his affection, and his longing looks made her feel guilty. Soon, she began avoiding everyone. She left camp early, most often before dawn, and returned in the evenings after dark. Howard, with a scowl, told her she was risking not only herself but the rest of them by going out after dark. When she responded with silence, he told her she was a fool but had no answer when she reminded him that she was doing what he did. Several times they found each other in the night just outside camp and silently acknowledged what was common and different, the common being that they were both loners, and the different, that while Howard went exploring as a scout behind enemy lines, armed and belligerent, Astrid went as one whose only chance of survival lay in finding harmony in the strangeness.

"You look like you've joined a jungle tribe," Marissa told her once when Astrid appeared suddenly in camp wearing leaves over her clothing and in her hair. Astrid recognized Marissa's usual wry kindness, but, unable to think of anything to say, just smiled and went to her room.

Astrid pondered her condition as the only teenager in camp without even one parent. Any of the families would take her in if she wanted. They would hug her, teach her, even love her. Marissa seemed to want that more than anything, next to loving Bryce. Astrid also felt, and saw in Bryce's face, the lack of a couple friend, in contrast to Elmer-Gerald and Colin-

LaTasha. But she sensed in herself a love of loneliness and the sweet-sad pleasuring of herself among the leaves.

She assumed that her mother remained back "home" in Projectville, her mind a victim of substance abuse, living in comfortable oblivion in the clean, briskly run institution there. Their alternate weekends together had, for Astrid, gone from hopeful to cloying to frightening, as her mother's mind followed its own journey away from her and everything else. The idea of her father was her only emotional flare, fueled by guilt at fleeing him, fear that he would find her, and fear that he might not want to find her.

She was aware that everyone in camp had to contribute to their new life, and so, she brought them useful things: sample sized-containers of toothpaste, first-aid and other medications, a compact with a mirror they could all share, airline-sized bottles of liquor, toy clothing and implements of various kinds. The thrill of stealing, which she had discovered under Howard's teaching on the night of their escape, had never left her, and she was confident of her talent at sneaking into shops and leaving with booty, and most confident that she would do it best solo.

After a few weeks she found that except for the creature comforts they had built in camp, she need not return at all, and took to spending entire nights away.

Over time the camp adjusted and settled into life in the world of the bigs, and accepted, with good humor, that Astrid was a "forest creature" whose roaming they had neither reason, ability, nor will, to control.

In her leafy camouflage, she saw families sharing laughing pleasure and sullen mutual distaste. She saw women shopping in fun, boredom, or compulsion. She saw men and women, well-dressed as at "home," driving cars and hustling along streets; teenagers in cars or on foot, cruising just like at "home." When she saw a shop door left open and unattended, she would sneak in, just far enough to a hiding place behind a chair, a table, a packing case, a potted plant. She was fascinated by the mundane: office routines, people at computers, opening mail, talking on the phones to customers. She watched mechanics fixing cars, and crews of people fixing streets, painting walls, cleaning.

The regular drill for scalies was to retreat at the sounds of bigs, but Astrid did just the opposite. She followed the sounds of conversation into a back yard, to an early evening party with drinks and casual food and a swimming pool. There were children in the pool and chatting clusters of adults on the deck. Astrid crept into the house through the open back doorway. Allowing her curiosity to overcome her caution, she followed more voices down a hallway and into a bedroom, where she saw two teenaged boys smoking pot and occasionally spraying the room with air freshener. They kept their voices low as they spoke with sneering contempt of their parents and the bunch outside, before they put on what they called their "game faces" to fool the adults with their cheerfulness.

She also saw scenes of genuine love, where families ate dinner in tidy alcoves and talked about their days, where parents read books to toddlers and everyone laughed at the jokes. And, she saw, and heard through open windows, the sounds of verbal and sometimes physical violence, with shouts and screams and slapping and broken glass.

She saw what she had only read about in school—poverty. The shopping area bordered a small park, and there, just before dawn, she walked by a heap of blankets and old clothing piled against the stucco wall and under the eave of a storage building. The heap smelled bad, and just as she had passed it, it swelled once, then contracted, and at the end of it she saw the top of a head. She lay down behind a large tree root to watch. The wall faced east, and as morning sun struck it, the heap moved again, and from the heap a person appeared. It was a woman, who shifted herself into a sitting position, her back against the wall. She raised her face to the sun, breathed deeply, and smiled.

This was one of the homeless Astrid had seen only on the internet. This woman was filthy, her skin rough, scorched by the sun and scabbed by injury or scurvy.

She did wonder about her life as a voyeur and what all this compulsive observation could bring her. As if in the controlled space of an art museum, she was constantly fascinated but never shocked, until, one day, she was.

Moving furtively in a commercial alleyway, on hearing a rustling from the direction of a garbage can, reflexively she crawled under a parked car and saw, instead of the expected cat, dog, or rat, the figure of a man, not much larger than herself: a scaly. He was out in plain sight, in the bright sunlight on the concrete pavement, biting ravenously on something he held in both hands, not caring about mess or being seen. He was unshaven, thin and dirty, but when he paused eating to take a breath, an expression of desperate satisfaction on his face, Astrid recognized him.

"Daddy," she said quietly, to herself, as if to confirm what she saw. His condition shocked her. She was relieved that he was alive. She was afraid of him. "All I can do," she said to herself. "Daddy!" she shouted.

The man looked in her direction, what looked like blood dripping from his mouth.

"Follow me," she said, and dashed from the car into a narrow space between a garage wall and a fence, into a place deeply shadowed by weeds. She heard his footsteps behind her, and when she turned he was there, in front of her, the pizza crust still in his hands, the tomato sauce still looking like blood on his face. His clothes—blue jeans, tee-shirt, jacket— were filthy and torn. He stank. She could see food stuck to his lips and gums as his mouth hung open. She saw in his face incredulity and accusation. "Stay here," she said, and disappeared from him.

She knew where the restaurant's open door was and where to find what she wanted inside. She returned to him with a small paper cup loaded with ice. He held the pizza in one hand and grabbed a small ice chip and licked it, then put it whole into his mouth and closed his eyes. Some of the water dribbled down his chin and mixed with the tomato sauce and other dried, unidentifiable food in his beard. He winced and put his free hand to his face as the ice seemed to chill his head. After a moment, he looked straight at her.

"I figured I'd never see you again," he said.

"Mom?" she said.

"Still in the junk joint as far as I know," he said.

Astrid watched him and waited.

He looked down at his clothes and spread his arms, the pizza fragment still in his left hand. "Not much to look at, huh?" he said, with a grin that looked forced and disappeared quickly.

He sighed and the smell of it pushed Astrid back a step.

"I'm alone," he said. "I was with a group, but we didn't get along, so I haven't had a chance to bathe, or anything else, really."

Astrid watched him.

He reached for one of the leaves that hung from the string around her waist, and she backed off another step.

He looked at her the way he habitually had, before. "You look like a savage," he said.

"Meet me here tomorrow at sunrise," she said, and she slipped away from him, as she could from anyone.

A strid was in the weedy shadows by the garage before dawn. She had a small plastic pill bottle filled with water, and a plastic bag with doll clothes, a soap fragment, a small half-used toothpaste tube, and a toothbrush from home. The sun was well above the horizon when her father ran across the alley to her.

He stood, panting, looking down at her.

"For you," she said, indicating the bottle and the bag.

He hesitated, then opened the bag. "Looks like doll clothes," he said, laughing.

"Yes. Plus some homemade underwear."

"Thanks," he said. He glanced up at the weeds. "Look, that group I was with, they were. Well, we didn't get along, like I said. But it's tough out here alone."

Astrid had no chance to ask if he thought she too was alone.

A very loud male voice reverberated in the alley as from speakers in a movie theater: "There! I swear to fuckin' god!"

Another loud male voice, deeper than the first: "Really?"

Then Astrid and her father saw the huge face, framed by the huge hand pushing the weeds aside.

"With me!" Astrid said, grabbing her father's hand and pulling him behind her as she ran, through the weeds, under shrubbery, slowing to squeeze through small gaps in fencing, pausing to peek around corners, listening for the pounding of enormous feet. Her father panted and struggled to stay with her. She led him into a carefully kept formal garden, through tall flowers and into the low-lying branches of a jade plant, where they sat on the ground.

Gilbert started to speak, but Astrid stopped him. She whispered to him, "We have to run across the street. Stay with me."

Her father nodded.

She pushed out through the branches so she could see that there were no cars. "Now, fast!" she said, and she ran, graceful as the athlete she was, letting her father follow on his own, clumsily, stumbling slightly. She allowed him to catch up with her under shrubbery.

———————

They walked through the bushes and into camp in the midst of breakfast, all of the colony gathered in the space between the milk crates to enjoy the sun and food foraged only that morning. They were eating and lounging on overturned plastic tubs and on the ground. With her father, who looked much like the homeless woman in the park, standing beside her, Astrid had to smile at the sight of all her friends enjoying a relaxed meal, the couples together, and Howard, seated alone, as usual. She felt proud. These were her people and she was proud of them. She might be a jungle girl, but she belonged with them, as they all belonged with each other.

"Mister Martin?" Bryce said.

"Gilbert," Marissa said.

Gilbert stood silently, having eyes for only the food.

Sher made him a plate and gestured for him to sit. The others watched him eat rapidly and without pause until he couldn't any longer. He looked up at them and said, "I have to."

"It's back there," Bryce said. "I'll take you," and led the way to their privy.

Once they were gone, Marissa said, "Astrid's father."

Everyone looked at Astrid.

278

"I had no idea he was even out," she said. "I saw him in an alley yesterday. He was, like you see. I told him to meet me at the same place this morning. I brought him food, some clothes, water. A big saw him cross the alley."

Gasps and groans.

"I thought if I left him, he'd just bring the bigs down on us anyway. Besides, he is my father."

Marissa went to Astrid, standing alone at the edge of the camp, and hugged her. "You did the right thing, honey."

"She did, but shit," Elmer said.

Bryce and Gilbert returned.

"Meeting, now," Sher said. "Cheng, what do you think?"

Cheng, who was sprawled on the ground, said, "We always knew we couldn't stay here forever. Howard?"

Howard took a deep breath. "I like this place a lot," he said. "I didn't think I would, but I do. But Cheng's right. We should hitch out of here, go miles away."

"Far," Cheng said.

"Okay, let's pack," Sher said. "Whatever you can stuff into your bags. Can't carry more luggage than we brought. Final potty trips, and we go."

"And we follow Howard," Cheng said.

"I want Astrid with me as a scout," Howard said.

————

A half hour later they assembled with packed bags.

Howard said, "Leaves."

They all looked at him.

"Who leaves, Howard?" Cheng said.

"Not who. What. Astrid," Howard said, "show us."

And the Astrid they knew as the slightly sad outsider grinned and said, brightly, "Like this," and broke a stem of leaves off a shrub. She looked at each of them and chose Bryce, around whose head she wound the stem, expertly twisted the leaves together, and draped them down his back. Then she stretched out her arms to present him to the group. "The latest camo style," she said.

Bryce grinned as if seeing the return of Astrid's affection.

The others followed her example, decking each other out in leaves. Marissa, after she and Bryce were covered, helped Astrid's father. "This does not mean I like you, Gilbert," she muttered.

Then they were moving, leaving the camp behind (dismissing Phuong's and Grace's fretting about the litter) and following Howard and Astrid. Howard knew the way to a main road where they could find semi-trailers to ride. Howard told Astrid where they were going and relied on her to pick the way through gardens and hedges and broken fences along side streets and through back yards. Walking swiftly on their athletic shoes, in their backpacks, and carrying their wheeled suitcases to minimize noise, covered in leaves, to a big they might have looked like small shrubbery branches blown by the wind. To another scaly, they might have looked like Burnham Wood approaching Dunsinane.

———

They moved in single file, with Howard leading, Sher in the middle, and Cheng at the back. They went several long blocks, always on side streets, pausing in shadows and under flora while cars, bicyclists or big pedestrians passed before them. They crossed open streets swiftly. Their weeks in camp, with daily foraging and other physical work, had put them in good physical condition and bonded them into a unit, so that they moved nearly as one, knowing as a group when to rest and when to run.

Only Gilbert struggled in bewilderment, hindered by poor nutrition, sleep deprivation, and misanthropy, quietly resenting the guidance and help that others gave him.

In camp, once Howard had taught his group how to forage, his work had been to explore, to look for threats and for escape routes he knew they would need eventually, though over time and against his will he had grown as attached to the camp as any of them, as he watched them with fatherly pride. Now, he steered them through one of the routes, while Astrid scouted ahead. She came back more than once to warn him that they would have to detour to avoid gardeners or a street construction crew or some other group of bigs.

This time, she returned to confer with him only briefly, as they moved through shrubs bordering two back yards, about the residential alley they were approaching. "It's quiet," she reported, "just like you said."

Without stopping the group's movement, Howard nodded and gestured for Astrid to stay with them. Between two old garages they reached the edge of the alley, its concrete in bright sunlight and empty except for several small dumpsters and a couple of parked cars.

Howard repeated his standard instruction: "Together, quiet, and fast." At his signal they walked rapidly, directly across the alley towards the opening between two garages on the other side.

They were in the middle when they heard the cinema-loud female voice yelling, "I see them!" and they all turned to see a big woman in a blue police uniform where the alley intersected a street. She was pointing towards them and yelling down the street at people they could not see, and then she was yelling into a radio.

For a moment, they froze and stared at the cop. Howard yelled "Drop and run forward!" and they dropped all the hand-held bags and kept the backpacks, per their emergency

281

procedures, and sprinted for the other side of the alley, and they were there, in shadow, shielded by two dumpsters, and moving forward when Astrid called, "Daddy!" The rest of the group turned and saw Astrid facing back towards the alley and her father still in the middle of it, facing towards where the cop had been.

Gilbert stood still, turned to look once at Astrid for a second, and then turned his back on her and yelled, "This way! This way! Over here!" and he ran back towards the alley's other side and he was nearly there when they heard an explosion and Gilbert's body was propelled into the air and then came apart into pieces leaving only bloody splotches on the pavement and a garage wall.

They hesitated, stunned, for an instant. Astrid began to wail and Bryce covered her mouth with one hand and lifted her around the waist with the other arm. He carried her as they all turned and ran through bushes into a backyard, where Howard pointed toward a gap in metal mesh that covered the opening to the crawl space under the house. They ran there and wriggled through the gap, where Cheng helped Bryce put Astrid through, to the center of the house and, on Howard's order, flattened themselves face-down on the dry earth. Next to Astrid, Bryce looked into her crumpled, unbelieving face. "He saved us," Bryce whispered. "He diverted them so we could get away. He saved you."

53

Prone on the ground, with their heads together, beneath plumbing and wiring, the eighteen scalies heard the bigs' voices all around them, the squawk of radios, the low growl of cars, and the wail of distant sirens getting louder as they approached. The voices were urgent, first in shouts, then lowered as if the speakers did not want to be heard. A low soft roar that Howard thought sounded like a Harley-Davidson started, and soon after they saw lights aimed in their direction so that small objects cast huge shadows into the musty crawl space where they lay. "Generators?" Michael Cruz hissed at Howard, who nodded.

They whispered about what to do next. Mahesh said, "I think we've bonded in the last few weeks, but we should at least think about splitting up. I hate the idea, myself, but maybe we'd be safer. We could keep contact with our phones and meet again later."

They looked at each other, trying to control their breathing and heartbeats to stave off the panic that seemed to float on the massive light beams aimed at them. Howard, the natural loner, muttered that Mahesh might have a point. Sher angrily rasped, "If we all want to die, that would be the best way, in my opinion. No offense, Mahesh, but think of what we've done together."

"No offense taken," Mahesh said. "I feel the same."

LaTasha said, sounding as flatly unyielding as a whisperer could, "Colin and I are not splitting up, so that means my parents and Mr. and Mrs. Fairchild have to be together with us."

Colin, speechless, looked at LaTasha in awe, as if, despite the passion and the sex, he had seen something that he previously had not known existed.

Gerald said, "Elmer and I neither, so that means our parents have to stay with us."

"Right," Elmer said.

"That's two thirds of us," Cheng said.

"So we stay together," Sher said. "We need a plan."

"We wait here until dawn," Cheng said. "With those lights, I think they'll see us easier in the dark than in the light."

"Okay," Sher said. "Then what?"

After a moment Bryce averted his eyes and said, "I could make a run, divert them so the rest of you could get away in a different direction."

"Like hell!" Marissa said, and put her hand on Bryce's head. "My brave baby."

Morgana, lying next to Astrid, put her arm over the girl's shoulders and said, "Your father, Astrid. He saved us."

Astrid continued crying quietly and said nothing.

"Not a bad idea," Howard said, "but I should be the one to do it. I won't let myself get blasted, and I do have my own side arm."

"Me too," Cheng said. "We can defend ourselves, to a point, at least."

Phuong Cruz said, "No more blood, please. Maybe we should just surrender. Hope for the best."

Another silence.

"Honey, they'll put us in cages," Michael said.

"And then they'll kill us," Jerome said.

Colin, feeling LaTasha's body next to him, said, "Even if they don't, we'll be locked up forever. No way should we surrender."

"I agree," Howard said. "I've seen what they do to each other."

Sher spoke to Cheng, across the circle from her: "What about Sam and Barry? Would they help?"

Cheng shrugged. "I could try to call Sam. He's a good man basically, except that he does what Barry tells him, and Barry's a lunatic."

Their whispers were killed by the thunderous, unmistakable chopping roar of a helicopter overhead. They could see two spotlights moving about on the ground outside their haven. They waited for the lights and noise to recede, which it did, but replacing it was a light whirring sound, too steady and continuous for insects.

Gerald got everyone's attention with a shake of a forefinger that he immediately put over his lips. When the whirring was gone, he whispered, "Drones, probably with cameras, sound and heat sensors, and infrared."

They allowed another moment to pass.

Sher said. "So how do we get out of here together?"

54

In D.C., in the back seat of a government car after the meeting with the president, while considering what he would say about security the next day, Barry received a call from his staff saying that a group of RSH had been cornered in a backyard near Los Angeles, and one of them had been shot. A bit more than an hour ago, the caller said, though they had known within fifteen minutes and she had left five messages on Barry's cell. Local police, she told Barry. Yes, she said, the local chief had followed the recent security directive, had told the neighbors and the press that it was a dangerous stray dog, probably a pit bull. No, he had not spoken to the press and probably not to the FBI or other agencies, though they could not be certain. Project Security had quarantined the area. Yes sir, they were maintaining low-profile isolation. Home residents had been evacuated, with no resistance, to a nice hotel. Not much left of the body. Shotgun. Group reportedly including both sexes were now surrounded in a large backyard of a big house. Yard was overgrown with weeds and had a lot of hiding places. Yes sir, they would do their best to capture them without injury, if possible, but it was mostly local law enforcement there, so the project had little control. No sir, they didn't know the identity of the dead RSH. Yes sir it was possible that some or all of them had left the yard, but not likely. Yes sir, they would hold action until he arrived.

After ending the call, Barry asked the driver to get him to his hotel, which was in Arlington, as fast as possible. There, he went to his room, put his cell phone on the bureau, grabbed his alternate phone along with his alternate wallet, which was

286

stuffed with alternate government ID, driver's license, credit cards, and family photos, and his alternate passport. He phoned the desk and told them he would be staying in his room and did not need housekeeping for at least three days— yes, that was right, three days. Then he took stairs down the seven floors to a back exit, walked to a shopping mall where he used cash to buy underwear, several shirts, two pairs of pants, a sport coat, two pairs of shoes, other necessities, and a small suitcase. He took all that into a men's room and into the large disabled-accessible stall, where he unpackaged all his purchases, used his pocket knife to remove those ridiculous zip-tied tags, changed his own clothing for some just purchased, carefully packed the rest of the new items in the suitcase, and stuffed his old clothes and the packaging trash into the merchandise bags. At the sink, he used a disposable razor and hand-soap to remove his mustache. He tossed the razor and his pocketknife into the trash. Behind the mall, he tossed the merchandise bags into a dumpster. On the main street in front of the mall, he found a cab to take him to Dulles International Airport, where he was relieved to hear from a ticket seller that he should have just enough time to get through security and make that next flight to Los Angeles, by way of Phoenix, scheduled to leave in less than forty-five minutes.

———

Sergeant Herman Winston, the Las Vegas police detective who had arranged freezer storage of the remains of the six scalies that Rudyard Long had pulverized, had not been candid in his official report. Some instinct—simple incredulity? avoidance of involvement in craziness?—had steered him into hiding what he had seen with his own eyes. The forensics guys had seen only a white trash bag, sealed with duct tape, containing the red bag of scaly remains. Officers Vazquez and Chin had agreed without argument that they had seen body parts of exotic animals that, due to their wildly colorful fur, had appeared almost human. (In a largely successful attempt to erase their memories, Vazquez and Chin had gotten drunk together that very night.) Doyle Parks had readily, and gratefully, agreed to whatever story Herman Winston told him. Herman regretted his offhand sci-fi quip to the anonymous uniform at the scene, but that guy—Lopez? Luchinski? Logan?—had probably dismissed it as another lame cop joke.

Herman had, however, felt driven to tell *somebody* about the weirdness. Not trusting the chain of command, he managed after several attempts to test the Chief's professed open-door policy. "What can I do for you, son," the Chief had said from across his desk.

Herman had recoiled momentarily from the expected but still breath-taking condescension, the Chief being only a couple years older than Herman. After recovering, Herman had plunged straight ahead. "Sir," he said, "on a call a couple days ago we—that is, I—recovered some, um, animal remains."

"So," the Chief said affably.

"Well, the animals must have been very small, about squirrel-size. I say must have been because the bodies, I mean the carcasses, had been somehow dismembered."

"And," the Chief said and glanced at his computer screen, the back of which faced Herman.

"Well, sir, they looked very human-like, like some exotic monkeys or something, and they had clothing."

The Chief pecked at his keyboard a few times and Herman watched his face change, as if something on the screen had confirmed a fact.

"That's probably what it is," the Chief said, smiling at Herman. "There is international dealing in exotic animals, monkeys, birds, reptiles. It rivals the drug trade, in terms of money."

The Chief leaned forward, which, in combination with the smile, struck Herman as conspiratorial. "This is hot information, Sergeant. I do know some things about it, but not enough. I want you to continue to investigate it—but it should not, and I emphasize *not*—interfere with your other work, okay? Only as time permits. And, it should be our secret, just between you and me. Okay?" And the Chief actually winked.

Herman had gotten the message and departed the office, feeling confirmed in his instinctive desire to distance himself from whatever it was he had found. That was until he saw the official email bulletin about the cordoning off of a house in a suburb of Los Angeles, where a federal agency was trying to catch several apparently escaped and possibly dangerous non-native animals, although one report said there was at least one pit bull dog.

————

4&k3L)(n watched guarded law-enforcement emails floating, this way and that, through the ether. Oh, my goodness, were they ever *guarded*. Electronically encrypted, of course, but even upstream from that, written in *code words* about "small exotic animals escaped from a research facility." Or were they dogs? Or about "avoiding abdication of federal responsibility to ill-equipped locals," about "non-lethal exterminators dealing with the problem humanely." But still, "timing was critical." Good grief! So little trust in the small band of people with encryption keys! Encryption! *Bah*! Encryption, like locks, was for honest people with nothing to hide. *If you're dishonest, or have something to hide, well, then—keep it to yourself!* Yet, here they were, their encryption, and their "lead-lined" browsers (a nuclear reality borrowed as metaphor—oh, how software people *loved* metaphor) brushed aside like cobwebs, and their transparent code words—*oh, how stupid could smart people be!* Probably they thought, like everyone else, that there was anonymity in numbers, that among the zillions of emails, encrypted or not, who would single them out? Well, 4&k3L)(n would, because 4&k3L)(n was absolutely *hooked* on this "RSH" drama—who wouldn't be?—and once you were hooked, all you had to do was follow the fishing line.

Anyway, what have we here? Law enforcement bulletins! *Calling all cars! Calling all cars! Things have escaped and whatever they are, they are wearing clothing and are extremely dangerous, possibly armed! Clothed and armed! If found, form a perimeter and call federal authorities! Do not approach directly! Repeat: Do not approach directly!* Or words to that effect. Oh, golly, let's approach as directly as possible!

In the RSH drama, 4&k3L)(n knew the lead players, or at least some of them. They would enjoy receiving those emails, wouldn't they, and they would not care that they were *really* anonymously forwarded—*You want anonymous? I'll show you anonymous!* And those delicious *bulletins*, well they would be just scrumptious scoops for news services, wouldn't they? So, let's dump them into this inbox, and that inbox, and—*oh, so much more fun!*—let's jump over *this* inbox and just post them directly to the "Salacious and Conspiratorial News Service," or whatever it was called! And, what a headline: "Secret Government 'Bulletins' Confirm Existence of 'Little People'"!

———

Samuel had avoided his encrypted email since departing the project because he knew that just logging into it would reveal his location to Barry and his security minions. He was, therefore, shocked to see, in his new email inbox (which he had named not even for Samuel Brookens, but for Fil Pistachio, and which he had created not for communication—he was not emailing anyone—but because some internet services required an email address) a series of emails between Barry and his security officers. In consternation, before even looking at the content, he studied the headers, which left him with only two possibilities: either Barry had found him, wanted him to know he had been found, and had information for him; or some highly skilled third party had hijacked the emails, unencrypted them, and forwarded them on for some unknown reason. The first seemed plausible, the second, highly unlikely.

Before reading the messages, Sam sat and considered. It was five-thirty on a weekday afternoon, and the family was together—or at least all in the same house, as Jennifer was hardly speaking to him and the kids were avoiding both their parents. He put his laptop aside and found Jennifer sprawled on their bed watching TV. She did not look away from it as he said, "Jennifer, you and the kids have to leave this house." She focused on the reality show, but he could tell she heard him. He told her what hotel she should check into. "It's four-star, suites. We have the money and you'll be comfortable."

"Great. Why?" she said.

Without looking at him and with exact precision, she spoke in unison with him as he said, "I can't tell you."

Sam sighed. "Please," he said. "Just go."

When she finally looked at him, her hostility shocked him. "And you?" she said.

"I'll take the other car. I have to go somewhere else. I'll contact you and meet you later."

"Sweet of you," she said. Without another word she clicked off the TV, rose from the side of the bed opposite where he stood, walked to the closet and pulled out her suitcase.

———

Drew had an email from Magdelano Goldfarb:

> Since talking to you at my dad's funeral I've been thinking about what I want to do. With my life, I mean. I know I won't be a mean fuck like my dad, but I don't want to be nothing. You know? A guy who just gets by without hurting anyone else? I want to make a difference. But I still don't know how.
>
> I've also been following this stuff about the little people, you know? And this thing that's happened? I kind of think those guys could use some help. I don't know what I could do, but I want to be there. Maybe I could help. And with one of them maybe dead, I thought maybe you could help too, since death is sort of your thing.
>
> Anyway, I'm going there tonight. Thought maybe you'd like to come. Please phone. I tried to phone you but didn't want to leave a message.

Drew phoned.

"Hey!" Mag said. "You wanna go there?"

"Mag, I have no idea what you're talking about."

"Really? Seriously?"

"Seriously."

"Man, you must live in a cave. I'm sending you a couple links right now."

Drew put his phone on speaker, went to his computer and opened Mag's note. He clicked a link and read, hearing Mag's breathing.

"What do you think?" Mag said.

"Wait." Drew read more, then clicked the other link. "Mag," he said. "This sounds a little weird."

"A little weird? It's totally weird!"

"But this is like space aliens."

"Well, yeah."

Drew wanted to be careful. With his hand on his head, he said, "Mag. You don't believe in space aliens, do you?"

"No! I don't! But this, just, I don't know! It seems real!"

"Mag."

"I know, man, it might all be a hoax. But what if it's not? Those guys need help, and this would be, like, history! I can hear you laughing."

"I'm sorry, Mag."

"No, it's okay. I guess it is funny. Little people?"

Drew said nothing.

"Please, Drew. I don't want to go alone and I can't think of anyone else to ask. If it's nothing, we'll just turn around and go home."

Drew laughed again, but what the hell? He had nothing to do that evening. "Who's driving?"

"Great! I'll drive, I looked up the location and I know exactly where it is."

"I'm at—"

"I know where you are too. You might want to pack a bag. I'll be there in forty-five minutes."

"Mag, are you thinking overnight?" Drew said, but Mag was gone.

———

"Boris Boris Boris!" Marjorie yelled. She was at the motel room's little table, hunched over the laptop. Most of her burrito was uneaten on the table. Boris was on the bed, plugged into an iPod, moving with the music while eating his burger and fries. It was their fifth cheap motel, but they were all the same, all in the same kind of neighborhoods on the same noisy streets.

"Boris!" Marjorie yelled.

Boris removed his buds. He had become bored with the whole scaly thing and bored with Marjorie's outbursts, which were usually because of some strange thing on local news somewhere about alleged sightings of little people. Boris was annoyed that Marjorie seemed not to understand why the local newscasters mocked the reports—most of which were undoubtedly invented by people who would say or do anything to get on TV. He was also finding it hard to love an obsessive person. She'd been exciting and as hungry as he was, and she was smart, but as far as he could tell the intelligence was drowning under the obsession, which was dominating both their lives.

"Boris!" Marjorie yelled again, louder.

"Coming," Boris said. He swung his legs to the floor, careful not to spill the paper plate of fries, walked the three steps to the table, and looked over Marjorie's shoulder.

"See?" she said.

"I'm reading," he said. He folded his arms.

"This one's different," she said, seeing the doubt on his face.

"More detail," he said.

"And the dead one?" she said. "I haven't seen anything like that before."

He heard her pleading in her voice.

"So?" he said.

"Let's go," she said. "Please."

Boris rubbed his head.

"Now?" she said.

Boris shrugged. "Why not?"

55

The usual miserable early evening rush-hour traffic was not what worried Barry Hagenstopple, trapped on the freeway in stop-and-go. That, he had expected. What rasped at his nerves, tightened his chest, and raised his pulse was the worry about the zoo he might find at the location, despite his orders to project security, his entreaties to the feds, and his warnings to local law enforcement. In his heart—or actually, in his gut, which was starting ominously to cramp—he did not believe that security people, either singly or collectively, had the brains to understand and react properly in this situation. Which thought brought him round to that smarmy little son of a bitch nerd Giles and his incredible disloyalty and utter lack of thought for the greater good, turning on Barry and the project itself, in disregard of all Barry had taught him, at this critical moment, a crisis point not just for the project but more than likely for the very survival of humanity.

With relief, Barry exited the freeway to a normally flowing boulevard, two lanes for each direction, nicely planted median strip, left-turn lanes to minimize traffic impediments. It was quite nice, really, almost as nice as the project streets, even the ones for the RSH, and Barry allowed himself to remember Projectville with some pride. He smiled a little at the thought of that town, such a perfectly scaled improvement on the messiness of most real towns—of *any* real town—and he nodded to confirm for everyone who had no idea about it— including the president—what he, Barry, had accomplished. Three miles, per the rental's GPS, to the site, and already the traffic was clotting. And what was that ahead? *Good lord, what in the world? A checkpoint?* Six cars ahead of him were stopped, their drivers waiting for the uniformed dolt standing between a barricade of saw horses and black-and-whites, who appeared to be asking for licenses that the drivers took endless minutes to fumble for, only to be ordered to turn away from the site. In his mirror Barry saw more cars, stacking up, some drivers impatiently making U-turns across the beautiful grass in the median to get away from the worsening jam. And then, to his left, across the boulevard, corralled by more uniforms, *what the hell? News vans!* With their stupid proletarian crews and their even stupider nattily dressed *reporters! How the fuck?* In the cold air-conditioning Barry felt sweat rising from his skin. He breathed deeply, in and out, relaxing himself so he could think through this crisis as he had hundreds of others during the project's life—though none of those others could ever compare with this one.

Finally it was his turn at the checkpoint, and he made sure he simultaneously squared his grim face and his U.S.G. buzzer at the young cop, who was properly intimidated and pointed him into the heart of the action.

And then Barry groaned as, *oh shit*, there they were, the dark navy-blue uniforms on the bodies weirdly over-inflated by Kevlar, and the goddamn "SWAT" stenciled on their backs, clustered around an armored Humvee. *What the hell did they think RSH were?* Barry saw not crisis, but disaster.

He parked, ostentatiously blocking the Hummer, and exited his car. One of the SWATs pulled off his helmet and yelled, "Sir!" but Barry led with his left, holding the federal shield, and calmly asked the SWAT guy who was in charge and where they were. The SWAT guy hesitated, his resentment showing, but then pointed to a group of people at a cruiser fifty yards further down a small residential street. Barry strode to the group, who were clustered around a tablet computer, and interrupted their discussion to announce, "I'm

Hagenstopple, U.S. government special project and who is in charge?"

The six or so individuals turned to him in unison, nobody speaking, as if waiting for him to explain what he had just said.

"Well?" Barry said.

A tall, fit-looking, fiftyish redhead in a ranking blue uniform, said, "I'm Chief Wondolowsky."

"So it's you," Barry said.

"I'm Rondeau." That was a short fat man with an insolent face.

As nobody else spoke, Barry looked one by one at each of the other four faces and discarded them as of no immediate importance. "Chief, Mr. Rondeau," he said. "A word."

The Chief led them back up the street toward the Humvee.

"Not in the Hummer," Barry said.

"It's the most private place we've got," the Chief said.

"Fucking well is not," Barry said.

Chief Wondolowsky glared at him. Rondeau looked amused.

Barry pointed at the trunk of a large live oak just across the street. They walked there together and stood for a quiet moment beneath the tree's spreading boughs. Dusk had fallen and the streetlight next to the tree was on, giving them dim light.

"Couldn't keep the press away?" Barry said.

The Chief looked at where the news vans were parked and shook his head. Rondeau just looked amused. Barry waited.

"We really don't understand it," Wondolowsky said. "This was as tightly wrapped as we could make it. Guess things just get out."

"Just get out," Barry repeated.

"You think you could do better?"

"Looky-loons?" Barry said, ignoring the question.

"They're here," Wondolowsky said. "We've got a perimeter of almost a quarter mile." He shrugged. "More will come. Like trying to stop water from running down a hillside."

"This is the street, right?"

"Yes. It's all been evacuated. The house is about a block down."

"Let me explain some things," Barry said.

"Shit-can that," Rondeau said. His voice was a low resonant growl that made people listen to him. "We know. We know who you are and we know there are some critters—"

"Critters!" Barry nearly yelled but fought his voice back down. "These are not—"

"Whatever the fuck they are," Rondeau said. "We get that it's important," and he raised a hand to stop Barry. "We *know*. Okay?"

Barry suppressed the impulse to explain just how the whole human race could be affected here, and said only, "What's with the heavy armor?"

Rondeau looked at Wondolowsky, who was almost a foot taller and looked over Rondeau's head rather than back at his eyes. "There's danger, right?" the chief said. "And besides, the SWAT presence impresses the public, makes them more likely to keep their distance."

"Like the water on a hillside," Barry said.

The Chief ground his teeth.

Barry looked at Rondeau and said, "Who told you?"

"We got the usual bullshit brief from a crat. Vague outlines, no details. These, whatever they are have escaped. Huh?"

"Nothing else?" Barry said.

Rondeau looked up at the Chief.

"Okay," Wondolowsky said. "I'll leave you lovers alone," and he walked back towards the group at the car.

"Lilliputians," Rondeau said.

Barry waited for more.

"I'm not supposed to know, I guess," Rondeau said. "But your security guy gave me some details. Not too much." Rondeau cocked his head. "Don't you look at the internet?"

Barry felt his gut cramp again. "My what?" he said.

Rondeau looked surprised. "The internet?"

"The *guy*," Barry stage-whispered.

"Oh, the *security* guy. I forget his real title, if he ever said it. You didn't send him?"

"Where is he?" Barry said.

Rondeau laughed.

"Where?" Barry said.

Rondeau laughed again, harder, and stared at Barry. "Feeling out of control, are we? Keep walking down the street, you'll find him."

He was still laughing as Barry left him.

Barry walked past uniformed officers and unidentified, non-uniformed people, scurrying around, doing things, laying cable like on a movie set, or standing still and trying to look important. Radios squawked. Birds sang.

Sam Giles stood on a street corner, his hands on his hips, looking toward a sprawling ill-maintained craftsman-style house on the opposite corner.

"In there, huh?" Barry said.

Sam turned his head to Barry.

"Is that the place?" Barry said. He pulled out his phone. "The GPS says so."

"Fuck you, Barry," Sam said.

"Oh, Sam," Barry said, and put his hand on Sam's shoulder.

Sam spun away from him.

Barry put on his best fatherly smile, the one that always before had made Sam come round, but Sam spoke first.

"No more," Sam said.

Barry held the smile. "No more what, Sam?"

"No more bullshit," Sam said.

Barry laughed. "Bullshit? Sam, did you do this?"

"Do?" Sam said. "Do what? Do *somebody*?"

"Oh, Sam," Barry said again.

"Shit can the *oh Sam*."

Barry took a breath. "What did you tell Rondeau?"

"The feeb? Just a taste."

"Sam, why don't we go somewhere to talk. Man to man, okay?"

Barry moved toward Sam, who took a step backward and pointed a finger at Barry's face. "I'm going nowhere with you, Barry," he said. "Not ever. I'm done with you."

"Son, you know you may have to be, um, restrained?"

"Right. Have me arrested? That taste I gave Rondeau? I can feed him—them—a lot more. I don't think you want me arrested."

"I trusted you," Barry said.

"Sure, Barry," Sam said, and he laughed humorlessly.

That was the second time in a quarter hour someone had laughed at Barry, and he could not imagine what was funny.

"So," Sam said. "I'll be around here tonight. You can do what you want." He looked back towards the craftsman house. "The cops think they're around that place, somewhere. They're good at hiding so they could be anywhere, on the grounds, under the house. Might even be gone. But we have a shared interest, huh, Barry? We both want them alive. Don't we? Alive?"

"Yes," Barry said. "Alive."

"This time? All of them?"

Barry's face reddened.

Sam said, "No examples, right? No lessons. All of them."

"Yes. All."

"Those SWAT guys, they're not so good at that part, are they?"

"Probably not."

They stood eye to eye for a moment.

Barry broke first. "Any toilets around?"

Sam pointed to a house across the street from the target house. "Coffee there too. Maybe some donuts left." He did not watch Barry cross the street.

56

Over and over, Drew had to protest that he needed more time to finish the blog he was on before going to the next one, with Mag weaving through heavy freeway traffic and gesturing with his right hand and trying to glance at Drew's phone, until the traffic stopped him completely so that he could grab for the phone and Drew had to pull it away, the two of them like teenagers sharing porn.

"Forget those links," Mag said. "Just go where I'm telling you."

"Okay," Drew said. "Done with this one, now what was that other place?"

Mag told him.

While Drew waited for the site to fill the screen, he said, "You believe all this?"

"One blog, no. Two? Still no. Three, I started to believe. Now this stuff is everywhere, and it's hard not to believe. I don't see how you missed it."

Drew scrolled as he read. "I ignored it." He read for a moment. "You too young to know about Roswell?"

"What's that?"

"Place in New Mexico. Legendary for UFO sightings."

"What's a UFO?"

Drew looked at Mag, who inched forward a car length after the driver behind him honked. "You really don't know?" Mag looked vacant. "'Unidentified flying object', like a flying saucer."

"Saucer?"

"Starship. Whatever. Alien spaceship. Tons of articles in magazines and newspapers. Aliens landing, actually meeting people. All of it bullshit."

"When was that?"

"Before I was born. I read about it. What's next?"

Mag gave him another site. "Okay," he said, his emotions dampened, "maybe this is bullshit too. But it just feels right, you know?"

Drew read more. "I'm trying to believe, Mag. It just seems like one of those internet things that people latch onto because they don't have lives, and people start adding details, some plausible speculation, and some lies to keep it going."

"Maybe you're right."

"I'm sorry, Mag. Who knows?"

"Our exit," Mag said, and began inching to the exit lane. "If I dragged you out here for nothing, then *I'm* sorry."

They did not speak as Mag joined bumper-to-bumper traffic on the off-ramp. Getting to the traffic light at the end of the ramp took several minutes, and when he turned at the light, they saw a circus of cars, pedestrians, irritated cops, news vans, and two helicopters overhead.

"Good lord," Drew said.

Mag grinned. "Lots of other fools out here, huh?" He laughed.

"Whatever this is," Drew said, "it's *something*."

His excitement restored, Mag turned off the boulevard several blocks before the intersection where a cop was stopping everyone. He drove several more blocks on a side street until he found a parking space. As they got out of the car he popped the trunk, from which he pulled one of his two backpacks but told Drew to leave his. "This one has sandwiches," he said. "No point in carrying clothes." Then he handed Drew a camera case and a photo equipment case. He took others for himself.

"What?" Drew asked.

"We're news photographers. I made these myself," Mag said and gave Drew a laminated five-by-eight press identity badge with a lanyard attached. "I actually take photos, kind of a hobby. You didn't notice my safari shirt?"

Drew looked at the camera cases, which, did in fact look professional. He shook the one Mag had given him. "Is there really a camera in here?"

Mag nodded and told Drew the proper way to shoulder the cases and hang the ID lanyard around his neck. "You're the actor," he said. "You'll have be the guy, and I'll be your assistant."

Drew considered his doubts, sighed over the situation, smiled, and accepted his role.

They walked briskly with the crowd, all going in the same direction, sharing the anticipatory air of people going to a pop music concert or a football game. To Drew's amazement, there were even slogan T-shirts: "Small is beautiful," "Size Does NOT Matter," etc. He overheard bits of conversations, mostly stories of sightings of tiny humans or of government conspiracies involving them, and allusions to Jonathan Swift and Mary Norton, who had, perhaps, not totally invented their stories after all—and Drew could not decide which was more amazing, that people still read those authors, or that they believed the stories to be real. *They are totally space aliens. Seen those 'Twilight Zone' shows, where in one U.S. astronauts go to another planet and find giants, and in another one they are the giants? Not like those shows were real, but they still said something.*

They were now a block from the boulevard at an intersection choked with crowds, both cars and pedestrians, and three cops were trying to maintain order and their own equanimity.

"Photos," Mag said and took his camera from its case.

"I don't know how to use a good camera like this."

"You're an actor, fake it. Just remember to remove the lens cap." Mag moved forward in the crowd and turned, quickly snapping away as he walked backwards. Drew walked through the crowd to the opposite side of the street, unsheathed his camera, and began faking. At the boulevard intersection the crowd thickened and then flowed right and left, around yellow tape, sawhorses, and police officers. Drew looked around, thought *what the hell?*, got Mag's attention, strode purposefully and confidently towards a police officer, and, with a half smile designed to project both friendliness and entitlement, held up his press ID and said "Press, officer."

"No press," she said, and pointed back across the boulevard to a clot of press vans and milling people with press passes dangling from their necks.

"Just pictures," Drew said.

"No press inside the perimeter," she said.

"Boss," Mag said and pulled Drew by the arm. Drew followed him between cars caught in the check-point jam, and they agreed to walk around the barricaded area, looking for weak spots. But they were not alone in that, and there were cops every few yards sending people across the street, away from their boundaries.

"Hopeless," Mag said.

"Sandwiches?" Drew said.

57

The scalies finished their planning and were left with nothing more to whisper. They listened in silence as the noise around them diminished as their hunters seemed to settle for the night.

"One thing to remember," Howard said. "I've been out here more than most anybody, mostly unseen by them. If we stick to our plan and keep our heads, we have a chance because they're more scared of us than we are of them. We know them, but they don't know us. That makes them dangerous, but also stupid. So we can get out of this."

Cheng chuckled. Nobody else said anything.

LaTasha took Colin's hand and when his eyes found hers she glanced around. Across the circle Colin looked at his parents, Grace and Roberto, and LaTasha looked at hers, Jerome and Morgana. The pairs of parents each looked at each other and back at the teenagers. Colin and LaTasha stomach-crawled, he to his parents and she to hers, and then the two groups of three joined together. Elmer and Gerald followed the example and brought themselves and their own parents together. Cheng joined Sher. Bryce and Marissa crawled towards each other, arriving where Astrid lay. Marissa tried to hug the girl, but Astrid, her weeping done, stiffened and glanced at Howard. Marissa turned to her son, taking him into her eyes, beholding her boy, who smiled back at her.

Astrid remained a short distance from Howard, her buddy-in-arms. He looked at her and said, "We're the watch." To be doing something, he unholstered his sidearms and rechecked the loads.

58

From Colin's Journal

LaTasha and I went to sleep, holding each other. When I woke just now, she was sleeping next to me. I can hear snoring all around. The amazing part is that we could sleep at all. I can see Howard on one side of the house and Astrid on the other, keeping watch. They don't seem to need sleep.

We don't know what's going to happen. Maybe they'll just take us back home and this time make sure we can never get out again. Maybe they will put us in cages on display in a zoo. Maybe they will kill us. Maybe they'll kill us right here on the ground, or maybe they'll capture us and then kill us out of sight, so nobody will know.

But there are other scalies out there. I know from this genius Jacques's crazy inside internet that there are more of us. Maybe some of them will stay free, even if we can't.

I feel like I'm in one of those corny scenes in an old movie where the people finally have no place to go and they agree that whatever happens, it was all worth it, they would do it all again if they had to, and they will all love each other forever. But that's how I feel. I love LaTasha. I love my parents. I love Gerald and Elmer and Bryce, and all their parents. I love Astrid and Howard and Chief Schmitz and Ms. Statie. I'm crying. I can't stop. I can't stop cropping. My gingers are muddling the kites. And I'm laughing and can't stop crying.

LaTasha's waking up and shushing me. She's putting her arms around me. Howard and Astrid are signaling. It's time now. Whatever happens, I love my people.

59

This guy was a shit. Nobody, not even his own family, for chrissake, cared enough about him to want to know what exactly killed him. I said to them, to his family, *ice pick?* How does someone get close enough to him in a public parking lot—okay it was a bad part of town, but still—to stab him twice in the head, once in the eye and once in the temple, with an ice pick? And who walks around carrying an ice pick? Sure, it makes a good weapon, but it's not real convenient to carry, you know? I mean, it's gonna poke a hole in your pocket, your purse, whatever it's in. You're more likely to hurt yourself before anyone else, your front pocket and you risk your balls, your back pocket, your ass, your purse, your boobs." Herman Winston paused to bite his burger and then continued with his mouth full. "They just shrugged. Maybe a hair pin, they said. He'd pissed enough people off, hung around with baddies too much, and finally the inevitable happened. Ice pick, hair pin, shotgun, what's the difference."

Past eleven at night, Herman, Marjorie, and Boris were in a twenty-four-hour burger place.

————

Two hours before, they had been part of the crowd around the police perimeter, shunted away by tense cops. Hanging around at the same place, they'd started to talk and Herman had said he'd seen a fast-food dump nearby, why not go together. Marjorie wondered what if it happened while they were away, but Herman said he had some experience in such matters and he doubted that "it," whatever that might be, was going to happen for hours. And, besides, he needed a men's room. As they walked five blocks, Boris asked him what his "experience" was, to which he said "law enforcement," to which Boris replied, "me too," and that was all they said until they got to the restaurant, which was mobbed, with as many people queuing for the restrooms as for the food. They squeezed into a tiny table, and Marjorie and Boris watched as Herman, a thin, average-looking middle-aged guy in jeans and a windbreaker, flashed a wallet to jump the line to the men's room.

When Herman returned, Boris asked to see the badge, which Herman casually showed him as he took his seat. Boris replied by displaying his own Project Security badge.

"We're even," Herman said.

Marjorie said, "So why aren't we inside?"

"Me? I didn't want to push it," Herman said, "and I just don't think much is gonna happen till dawn. You?"

"We're supposed to stay outside," Boris said, truthfully.

Herman stared at Boris but said nothing.

They ate in silence. Boris used Herman's technique to get to the men's, then slipped the badge to Marjorie so she could use the ladies'. Back together, they continued, slowly, to eat.

"What do you know about this?" Marjorie asked Herman.

Herman took a deep breath in and let it out, looked through the plate glass at the milling people outside, and shrugged. "Couple of peculiar crimes happened around here and in Vegas. Some of this stuff, the crap people find. Look at them." He motioned at all the people inside and outside the restaurant. "Half of them surfing and the other half talking about it. Something's weird. I mean, I'm sure it has an explanation, but." He shook his head. "And you?"

"I've seen them," Marjorie said.

Boris, sitting next to her, stopped chewing and turned and stared at her.

"Oh, what the fuck," Marjorie said to him. "What's it hurt. Herman's right, just look at all these people." She looked back at Herman. "I'm an attorney. I worked at the project."

"Project," Herman said.

"To develop little people, wee folk but without the pointy ears. Just like us, actually. I'm a lawyer on the project. I mean, people who work on the project need lawyers too. It's complicated, but I do have first-hand knowledge."

"Government project," Herman said and looked at Boris. "And you're security on the project."

Boris nodded and dipped fries into ketchup.

Herman laughed. "Wow," he said. "We're all characters in a bad novel. Not exactly Stephen King, but sold at airports everywhere." He sipped his coffee. "So, you're here in official capacity?" He looked at Marjorie and at Boris, but neither spoke. "Well. If the novel goes the way they usually do, you're not supposed to be here." He waited. "In fact, you're not supposed to have left the project at all." He waited longer and looked them over. "You're on the run. Which means, mister you-ass-government-project-security, your badge is worthless."

Boris raised an eyebrow and dropped it and ate more fries. "And you're?" he asked.

"Out of jurisdiction," Herman said.

"What else was peculiar?" Marjorie asked.

"Huh?" Herman said.

"You said there was a peculiar crime," she said.

"A bag of doll-sized body parts," Herman said. "In Vegas."

Boris and Marjorie both stopped eating.

Herman looked up at the ceiling. "They turned up, wouldn't you know it, in a store-front church, one of those places where a con man preaches to loonies about the rapture or Armageddon or whatever big thing is supposed to happen next week. The preacher was gone, vanished, with this bag of smelly little torsos and arms and legs in doll clothing in the middle of the chapel or sanctuary or whatever. They're now in a box in an official evidence freezer. The two cops who found them came to believe they were monkeys, but that was just because their brains couldn't see reality. I'm the only other person who saw them and I didn't want to believe either. I wrapped the bag up before the techs got there, so nobody else knows. Or wants to."

"Or is supposed to," Marjorie said.

Herman nodded. "You've actually seen them." he said.

"Live ones," Marjorie said. "I wasn't supposed to see them either. It turns out, they *are* just like us. They don't like being cooped."

"And they're sneaky," Herman said.

"Which is why I saw them in a shopping mall. And before that on streets," she said.

"There was a large break-out," Boris said. "Most of the project staff, even security, wasn't supposed to know about them. But something happened." He shook his head. "We could see it on our screens, there were big cracks in the security. Word got out. People panicked."

"And lots of them got out, or so it seems, and lots of us too," Marjorie said. "For once, a lot of the internet crap turns out to be real."

"Lots of you?" Herman asked.

Marjorie and Boris said nothing.

"Ah," Herman said. "I get it."

For a few moments they ate in silence.

"Do they have weapons?" Herman asked Boris.

Boris shrugged. "They might."

"So, the stabbing," Herman said.

And that was when he told them about a police bulletin describing a stiff named Juan Goldfarb, and about the ice pick theory of why he had one tiny hole in his left eye and another tiny hole in his left temple.

"See, I work in Vegas, but I follow homicide cases all around the southwest because sometimes they get connected, and I just guessed that this stabbing might be connected to the little bodies I saw. On my own time, I came here to poke around, quick-flashed the badge and got the stiff's neighbors to talk about him. Just another dead creep. My friend in the local coroner's said they didn't see any point to the expense of sawing open the guy's head, particularly if the family—and this family has money, by the way—didn't care."

"You saw one dead guy and those little bodies and you naturally thought about tiny guns," Boris said.

"Yeah," Herman said, wiping his mouth. "But you're the first ones I've discussed it with."

They sipped their coffee.

"You think the tiny shooter might be here?" Marjorie asked.

Herman shrugged.

"Well," Marjorie said. "If one of them might be a crime suspect, he'll need a lawyer."

"Two cops and a lawyer," Boris said.

Herman grinned. "I like it. We'll get in."

60

There will be no dogs, understand? *No dogs!*" Barry had pushed his red face into Wondolowsky's. The Chief, though half a foot taller than Barry, stepped backwards. They were in an area between streetlights a block from the target house. Rondeau laughed.

Sam watched, still feeling like a junior partner. Knowing better than to let Barry out of his sight, he had overcome his disgust and followed him to this meeting of the minds. Maybe he could mediate. Lord knows he had done it before between Barry and scalies. "Mr. Rondeau," he said with exaggerated calm. "I cannot say how crucial it is that these, ah, creatures, be captured unharmed."

"Why is that?" Rondeau asked.

Barry wheeled from Wondolowsky to Rondeau and shouted at him, "Because I am the federal official in charge, that's why, and because you have no idea about any of this. These beings are charges of the United States government!"

So much for mediation.

Rondeau, though shorter than Barry, did not back off, as the taller Wondolowsky had, but only raised his eyebrows and hands in mock surrender at Barry's face, not three inches from his own. "You should brush your teeth," he said.

Barry, seething, turned and walked a few paces away.

"So? What's your plan?" Rondeau said.

Without facing either the amused Rondeau or the consternated Wondolowsky, Barry said, "When we find them, just make damn sure you don't do anything without me. I'll get back to you."

"You know, Hagenstopple, my bosses are feds too," Rondeau said, and he laughed as Barry walked away.

Sam followed Barry into the two o'clock darkness, caught up with him and said, "Barry, what *is* the plan?"

Barry silently kept walking until Sam grabbed his left arm and spun him around. "Tell me, Barry. Huh?" Sam said. "Tell me what you intend to do?"

Barry started to turn away but Sam did not let him. Barry looked at the hand that held his arm. "Get your hand off me, Sam," he said.

"What, Barry? Tell me."

"You'll find out in time," Barry said quietly. "Now take your hand off me."

"Barry, I've worked with you for a very long time. When they got out and wouldn't come back, I killed them for you. Sometimes even if they did come back I killed them for you."

"Let go of my arm, Sam," Barry said.

Sam gripped harder on Barry's left arm and pushed his own left hand into Barry's throat and shoved him against a parked black-and-white. *"No more killing, Barry,"* Sam said in a hoarse stage whisper. *"No more!"* Sam saw Barry's eyes shift from side to side and noticed three or four uniforms watching them. He released Barry.

"As I told you before," Barry said, instructing a small child, "I want them alive."

"So, how?" Sam said. "Butterfly nets?" He watched Barry's eyes. "Oh, no," he said, "you didn't really bring butterfly nets, did you?"

"I didn't have time," Barry said as he rubbed his throat. "Some kind of nets might be useful."

"Even after all the years you still surprise me," Sam said. "They're really just zoo animals, huh?"

Barry gathered himself and cast his best imperial glare. "How dare you?" he said.

Sam snorted. "Oh, stop, Barry."

"Ask me how many conversations I've had with them. With that *city manager*, and, what's his name, the *police chief*."

"Sher and Cheng," Sam said.

Barry's tone shifted. "Are *they* here?" he asked.

Sam could not help smiling. "I have no idea," he said.

"Huh. They could be."

"It doesn't really matter who's here."

"So, what's *your* plan, speaking as head of security?"

Sam ignored the sarcasm. "We have to talk to them. Promise them safety. Persuade them."

Barry raised one eyebrow. "Might work," he said. "But they have to come to me."

Sam looked toward the target house.

"You know I'm right," Barry said. "If somehow they stay out they won't survive. Wondolowsky's crew will exterminate all of them, and we don't want Rondeau's boys to get them, do we?"

61

At two-thirty that morning, Herman, Marjorie, and Boris approached a couple of uniformed police at an intersection blocked by both sawhorses and parked cruisers.

"PD," Herman said, and showed his badge to one of the uniforms, a tall woman with icy eyes and dark hair pulled tightly into a bun, who seemed unimpressed.

"If you're supposed to be in here, you would already be in," she said.

"Actually, we were in," Herman said, "but we had to leave for a bit."

The cop showed them the side of her face as she looked off into the crowds milling across the street.

"Excuse me," Boris said, opening his own ID. "We *are* supposed to be in there."

The cop studied the project badge and seemed to waiver. Her partner, a large man who looked like he could have been a linebacker, moved to her and looked over her shoulder at Boris's badge.

"Fed, huh?" The big man said.

"Project," Boris said with clearly suppressed irritation. "*The* project."

The big cop said, "Our orders—"

"We *give* the orders," Boris said.

The big man stepped away and pulled his radio. "Three frank, Chief" he said into it.

"Chief here. Go ahead three frank," the radio voice said.

"There's a Vegas cop here, name, Herman Winston," the cop said and gave Herman's badge number. "Says he was inside and had to go out, now he wants back in. Over."

"That's all? Over."

"With him's another guy with *project* security ID. Over."

"So?"

"So what should I do?"

"The fuck do you think?"

"Our orders—"

"Guys go out, guys come back. We're busy here, just do your job."

"But Vegas, sir?"

"We've got cooperation from other jurisdictions, this is national, goddammit."

"Yessir."

The big cop put his radio back on his belt and motioned with his head.

"Wait," the female cop said. "What about her?" She pointed at Marjorie.

"She's an *attorney*," Herman said with disgust.

"Attorney?" the big cop asked.

Herman nodded and shrugged.

Marjorie found two business cards in her purse and handed one to each cop.

"Why?" the female cop said.

"That would be between me and my clients, who may be inside your cordon," Marjorie said, with iciness to match the female cop's.

As the two officers studied the cards, Herman said, "Won't do any good to argue with her."

"We tried already," Boris said.

The two cops looked at each other for a moment, and then stepped apart.

"Thanks," Herman said as the three of them walked briskly through the check point. They had not slowed when, moments later, Herman said, "Nice job."

"Now?" Marjorie said.

"Keep moving," Herman said.

"Look official," Boris said.

———

Drew and Mag had found food and restrooms at a Mexican restaurant across the cordoned area from the burger place where Marjorie, Boris, and Herman had eaten. They sipped iced tea over the remains of their rice and beans.

"I'm beat," Drew said.

Mag smiled. "You won't leave."

"How could I?"

"You wouldn't if you could."

Drew sighed. "You're right. Good thing I don't have a job tomorrow."

"Lull?"

"A break in the usual steady stream of dead rich sociopaths. Sorry."

"It's okay. I told you, I know what my father was."

"Sad."

"Reality. I've dealt with it all my life."

"Shall we go back to reconnoitering?"

"Why not?"

———

Nobody under the house had slept when dawn began to neutralize the big generator-driven floodlights. Re-adorned in their leaves, the scalies crawled to one arbitrarily chosen side of the house. Per their simple plan, Astrid led. Behind her, the others watched as she rose ever so slowly, like a ball of leaves pushed by the softest breeze, from flat on her stomach to a kneel. She beckoned once for them to follow, and then she crouch-walked slowly, one smooth step followed by a pause. Howard followed, one scaly car-length behind her, moving as much like Astrid as a middle-aged man could. The rest followed one by one, at the same distance from the one ahead, so that they formed a loose troop of crouch-walkers, moving when Astrid moved and stopping when she stopped, and never speaking, with Cheng at the rear.

Slowly the chain moved, from shadow to shadow, pausing longer in beds of shrubbery or flowers. Around them they heard big voices and big movements. From under a hedge they saw two pair of big shiny black shoes below navy blue pant legs, not two scaly car-lengths away. They heard radios squawk. They were amused by bigs' stupid attempts to lower their enormous voices, confirming how their ignorance limited their advantage. They wondered about the effectiveness of the low-hovering helicopters, and feared the drones more.

After a half hour, they were into the next yard. They were in an area of old homes with much mature planting that made good hiding places. At each pause, Astrid and Howard watched the big hunters, who seemed to be forming a loop tightening around the house where they had spent the night.

Two hours later, with the sun still below the tree line, they came to a major street. From a flower bed ringing a large live oak, they could see that they had reached the bigs' perimeter, where they beheld what they had previously seen only in movies. There were people in uniforms, navy blue and khaki, standing on guard where black and white cruisers or sawhorses or yellow tape blocked entry into the place the scalies wanted to exit. There were people who appeared to be press, and there were knots of other people, and the knots were becoming a crowd.

Freedom was on the other side of a two-lane street, but for the scalies it might as well have been the Mississippi River. Howard, Astrid, Sher, and Cheng conferred.

And then, a large armored vehicle, the mine-resistant ambush-protected (MRAP) kind, big enough for sixteen personnel and equipment, arrived. It came slowly down the street, pausing as people dashed in front of it to take phone photos, and pausing again as uniformed officers walked ahead to clear the way. The vehicle slowed and parked diagonally across the intersection. The scalies were on the driver's side of the MRAP, beneath which they could see feet in combat boots exiting the door.

"Under that car," Cheng whispered. "Now."

The word went down the scaly line, and Astrid led the way, smoothly, in her athletic way, from the flower bed, down the curb and under the large vehicle, and then, still crouching, toward the MRAP's rear and the possible safety of the other side of the street. The others followed.

Astrid had reached the back end of the vehicle when a drone the size of a full-sized human frying pan suddenly swooped down and hovered next to the vehicle, just above the pavement, like a giant dragonfly.

———

The drone hovered just above ground, next to the MRAP. The operator, miles away at a police substation, followed his orders and sent his text messages and broadcast the video through the secure network. Days later he would point to records to prove that he had done so, but the stored video was gone.

———

4&k3L)(n, of course, had been watching the story unfold in emails, texts, social media, from the totally unsecure to the allegedly completely locked down and locked up, so much more dramatic than any episode of any TV drama. The wee folk had run and hid, enjoyed idylls, basked in freedom, eaten at leisure, explored, obviously delighted at this big world with all its dangers. They had created their own communications too, safe from the authorities though not safe from—but still safe *with*—4&k3L)(n. Those little guys were smart!

A lot of their keepers had run too, from who knew what. They had hung it on the limb and busted out. That woman of the famous picture, for instance, she was out. He had followed her electronic tracks as she followed the same story. And the project security chief nerd had bolted with his entire family, though 4&k3L)(n had somehow lost them; the nerd must be very clever.

All the while, their big masters had huffed and puffed, like overlords always do when their powers fail them, when the world gets out of hand, as is its wont. The project overlord had flown to the nation's capital to confer with the big boss-in-chief, whose staff was smart enough to have the conference in some lead-lined chamber that even 4&k3L)(n could not penetrate.

Everyone flailed, everyone wanted the scalies!

But, oh my, what a world of not just text and audio, but video! Great, swooping special effects of *real* things in *real* time, all so fascinating that 4&k3L)(n had to resort to contraband to stay awake, eating sporadically, unbathed, in his hideously cluttered, smelly, and unsanitary apartment, in anticipation of the unknown climax *where the artist might intervene!*

And, *ah! Here! Now! There they were! On clone video! The wee folk dressed in foliage! Not a split second to waste! Hijack that video! Short-circuit those messages!*

Buzzing from hunger and sleep-deprivation, his eyes as big as old Kennedy half dollars, 4&k3L)(n held to the view of the aerial drone before him on one monitor, the text communication on another, phone audio instantaneously translated into text on another, 4&k3L)(n like a TV director with all before him!

————

At sight of the drone, the scaly band froze in terror. "They got us," Gerald said.

"Run!" Cheng shouted as he pulled his semi-automatic pistol and fired two quick shots into the drone, which fluttered once and then collapsed to the ground.

They ran, crouching under the military vehicle until they emerged onto the street opposite the cordon, where they faced a wall of big sneakers and boots belonging to the churning masses of big civilians the police had kept at bay. The eighteen scalies froze again. The crowd of bigs froze as well, though slowly, subsiding into silence at the sight before them: walking human beings, male and female, in clothing just like the bigs' own though it was badly hidden by leafy camouflage. For several seconds the scalies and bigs gaped at each other in shocked discovery, and then cell phones appeared and pictures were snapped, recording for posterity this first large encounter probably not much unlike the first encounter of Native Americans and Spaniards centuries before, except for the contrast in size.

Three more drones appeared and hovered thirty feet above the pavement, a helicopter chopped its way higher above, and the scalies heard the pounding of big feet, like a buffalo stampede, growing louder as it approached them.

Drew and Mag were among the bigs who were pushed back by the camouflaged soldiers, all holding assault rifles. From inside the cordon, police of different agencies in navy blue and khaki stormed into the intersection, stopped, and pulled their side arms to shooting position.

The scalies whirled and saw that they were now surrounded on all sides by uniforms, but the uniforms came no closer than about twenty feet, everyone now tensely quiet.

Sher decided to act. She stripped off her leaves, shook out her long hair (hoping for an effect), raised her hands and shouted, "Everyone calm down! It's okay! We won't hurt you!"

At the same time, Bryce looked up at the guns aimed at them, at *him*, and he saw his future, a lifetime of imprisonment, humiliation, and loneliness, his sense of his own entitlement to leadership crushed and degraded. And so, he too stripped off his leaves and faced that future, and strode defiantly towards its personification as uniformed giants with firearms.

Marissa saw her beautiful son and knew what he was doing and ran to him and threw her arms around his neck, wailing, "No, baby, no baby," but Bryce was on a mission and she was way too small to stop him as he walked resolutely toward the guns.

Officer L. MacBride, twenty-nine years old, veteran of only five years, had a sterling record that included facing down gangbangers, drug-dealers, and pimps, while still earning the trust and admiration of the community he patrolled. He had remained composed during the last thirty-six hours of no sleep, bad food, bad coffee, high alert, vague orders, and no explanation of what the fuck was going on here. Chance had put him where he could hear the small cap-pistol pops and see the subsequent drone crash, and now he was thoroughly pissed off at his commanders and the entire situation, and truly, as he would say later during an official inquiry (and at the advice of his lawyer), he "feared for my safety" as with shock and incredulity he saw this young man, tiny but looking to be in good shape and possibly armed with whatever had downed the drone, approach him.

Officer MacBride expertly squeezed off one round that instantly penetrated and destroyed the torsos of both Bryce and his mother behind him, ricocheted off the pavement, and grazed the shoulder of a man in the crowd before embedding in a tree trunk.

Howard, who had seen enough and was tired of his role as shepherd, pulled his own weapon and just as expertly fired at and hit the neck of Officer MacBride, who dropped his pistol, clutched his neck, fell to his knees, and gasped for breath.

In the next instant, another shot obliterated Howard.

Marjorie, Boris, and Herman were there amidst the commotion. They saw the destruction of Bryce and Marissa (though Marjorie had not yet matched them with faces she'd seen on the internet), and as Officer MacBride continued his collapse, Boris plunged through the line of cops and put himself between the them and the scalies. He pulled out his wallet, which contained his now canceled but still impressive-looking Project Security ID, waved it over his head, and shouted "Stop! Stop!." From among the exhausted and tense ranks of police officers, the dark object in Boris's hand was enough to prompt three more rounds, all of which found Boris's body. Scalies ran to avoid him as he fell and missed crushing the bodies of Bryce and Marissa by a foot, and that of Howard by another.

Marjorie followed him quickly and fell to her knees beside him, crying and shouting, "*No! No shooting! No! Boris, my god, oh Boris.*"

Cheng dropped his gun and gun belt and shouted, "There are no more guns! None of us has any guns," and he raised his hands in surrender.

The soldiers in the camouflage suits at that moment understood why they had been given small animal traps, the cage type designed to fall on an unsuspecting animal that went for the bait under it. As instructed, the soldiers worked in threes with the cages. One soldier would hold a trap bottom open while another lowered the trap over groups of the scalies, who were in shock and easily herded, and then the first soldier would slide the bottom into place, all while a third soldier held his rifle in firing position. As the soldiers carried the cages away, the scalies could see through the mesh sides and bottoms the destroyed bodies of Bryce, Marissa, and Howard, on the pavement—and that of Boris, too, though he meant little to them as his blood flowed and mingled with what was left of the three dead scalies.

Beside Boris's corpse, through her tears, Marjorie could not avoid seeing the dead scalies, and there, quite clearly, was the real flesh face of one of the young people who had frightened her into dropping her coffee that day in the mall. Then she saw the soldiers carrying the cages, and from one of them, her eyes found Colin's and shared an unmistakable recognition.

———————

The scene became a melee of screaming crowd being pushed back, with varying success, by panicked cops and soldiers. Paramedics appeared. Two of them performed an emergency tracheotomy on Officer MacBride. Two others verified that Boris was dead.

Barry and Sam had been at the target house when they heard the shots, and they had sprinted to the scene in time to see the cages of scalies being taken onto the MRAP. Barry, horrified, ran to the soldiers shouting, *"Those are mine! Mine! You have no right to take them!"* The soldiers ignored him.

Sam saw the four bodies, put his hands to his head and wailed, and then bent over and vomited.

At the edge of the crowd, Drew and Mag found that by showing their fake press IDs, they could now filter through the phalange of cops and crowd. Drew had seen the dead but had never seen true grief at their funerals, and he had never seen the dying, and now he saw four, and a woman grieving over all of them. Magdelano began taking photos.

Barry watched as the soldiers loaded the cages onto their vehicle. Then he turned and saw Sam, and also Chief Wondolowsky and Rondeau, who had just appeared. Barry approached Rondeau and pointed to Sam, still heaving onto the tarmac, and said, "Him. He's the cause of all this. Arrest him."

Rondeau looked bemusedly from Sam to Barry and watched Chief Wondolowsky himself put plastic cuffs on Sam. "What's the charge?" Wondolowsky said.

"Theft of government property. Disclosure of classified intelligence. Probably violation of the Espionage Act," Barry said.

"We'll hold him for you in our jail," Wondolowsky said, and yelled at a uniform to take Sam, adding that the medics should have a look at him.

Rondeau snorted.

Magdelano moved about the scene taking pictures.

Herman Winston stood behind the line of cops and stroked his chin.

Drew crouched to examine the remains of the three scalies. Then he moved slowly toward Boris's body and Marjorie, who was now gathering herself.

Marjorie rose to her feet, and said as loudly and firmly as she could, "I am Marjorie Koehler and I am the attorney representing the people who have just been taken away in cages. As their lawyer I demand that the authorities announce charges immediately and grant them the due process to which they are entitled, including my access to them." She stood there as officers with bullhorns ordered the crowds to "disperse" and others scrambled to clear the crowd, most of whom had recovered, with renewed fascination, from the sounds and results of the gunfire. The first reporters arrived in Marjorie's face.

"As far as I know, my clients have committed no crime," Marjorie said to one and then two microphones. "The man who unfortunately shot the officer, who, I fervently hope will recover from his wound, is dead, as are, tragically, this woman, this young man, and this security officer at my feet, all of whom were unarmed."

An officer approached her and told her she needed to clear the crime area.

Marjorie said, for him and the press to hear, "I will stay here to make sure these bodies are properly cared for."

As she answered questions for the press, who ignored orders to leave, Drew watched. In the months of his career as funeral orator, he had seen only fake piety in such quantity that he had come to doubt that real grief even existed, and the sight of this woman clearly feeling it and fighting through it held him. And then, through the changed hair and the makeup, he recognized the face.

Drew moved his fake press ID from his neck to his back pocket. He strolled to Mag, as press, civilians, and cops milled about. "It's her," he said.

"Who?" Mag asked.

"The picture you showed me yesterday, the woman with the small people."

Mag looked toward Marjorie. "Yeah? It could be. You know, I think it is."

"Put the press pass in your pocket and stay with me," Drew said. He slowly moved through the now thinning crowd to Marjorie, who was now protesting loudly to several cops that she would not leave the bodies until the medics properly gathered them.

A sergeant looked into Drew's face as he now stood next to Marjorie. "Who might you be?" he said.

"I'm Drew Kristopher. This is Magdelano Goldfarb. We work for Ms. Koehler. We're assistants. That's why we have the cameras."

The sergeant turned to Mag.

"That's right sir," Mag said.

As Marjorie turned towards them and fell into the act, Herman Winston, his PD badge now clipped to his jacket, walked past the uniforms and to her. "It's okay," he told the sergeant. "The medics will be here once they're finished with the wounded officer. My card, Ms. Koehler," he said, and handed her his business card.

As she took it, she saw writing on the back. "Drew," she said, "do you have a business card for the Lieutenant? I seem to have used mine up."

Drew pulled out his wallet and from it gave Herman one of his own cards, which Herman pocketed without looking at it.

The medics came with a full-size body bag for Boris. One of them said to Marjorie, "Um, we don't have, uh, in that size."

"Get some evidence bags," Herman said. "The plastic ones, and also some brown paper ones, to put the plastic inside."

Which is what they did.

62

"Take Mag's offer. Don't worry about the car." Detective Winston had referred to Marjorie's BMW, which was technically the project's BMW. Seeing her start to protest, he had said that he would "take care of it."

And so, she was in the back of Magdelano's car when Drew asked how she was doing and turned to see her curled up across the seat. "Out," Drew said. "Where I'd like to be."

"Some of those, what did she call them?"

"Scalies," Drew said.

"Scalies. Some of them looked like my age."

Drew said nothing. He was thinking about the three dead ones and the other dead one that Marjorie had called Boris.

"Yeah, this is the place," Mag said as he slowed the car. "I knew I'd been here before." It was an all-night taco truck in a parking lot. As he cut the engine he saw Marjorie's worried face in the mirror. "Hungry?" he asked. She shook her head. The car clock said it was twenty minutes to midnight.

Drew and Mag ordered tacos and horchatas, Marjorie ordered a coke. They took their orders to a picnic table and were starting to eat when Herman drove up in his unmarked. He got a large coffee and joined them. "How's everyone?" He said.

"Wiped," Drew said.

"Me too," Herman said. He sat next to Marjorie, with Drew and Mag on the opposite bench. "I just wanted to sort some things out and this seemed like a good place to talk privately. Not far from your apartment," he said to Drew.

"You're a police officer," Marjorie said slowly.

"And you're a lawyer on the case, I know," he said. He unzipped a side pocket of his jacket and from it pulled a six-by-nine-inch brown envelope that he put in front of Marjorie.

She looked at it without touching it.

"Just open it," Herman said.

Marjorie picked it up, opened the clasp and squeezed the sides to see inside. She turned it upside down and onto the tabletop fell a small re-closeable plastic bag, which she picked up by a corner and held up to her face. It contained a tiny object. "A pistol," she said. "A revolver."

"Probably the one that shot the officer," Herman said.

Marjorie looked at him.

"It's an offering. So that you trust me. When you give it to them, maybe they'll trust you. Make sure the press knows."

"Where did I get it?"

"The pavement. You were nearby with the press when the techs finished scouring the scene. They missed it. You noticed it and picked it up."

"Why didn't I give it to them then, right away?"

Herman shrugged. "You meant to, but you were distraught and exhausted and dropped it into your jeans pocket, where you found it tomorrow and knew you had to do the right thing. So you put it in the baggie and took it to them."

"Prints?"

Herman snorted. "I'm doubting they have prints on the scalies, but if they do, what's the difference? They got one other gun like it, an automatic in a belted holster. I'm pretty sure this is the only one that shot the cop, and they know who fired it. No mystery. Oh, and tell them where you left the BMW, which is government property, right?"

"Thank you," Marjorie said. "And how can I help you?"

Herman shrugged. "Not sure. It's just something that feels right." He sipped coffee and thought about it. "You're finding out, from a totally anonymous and untraceable tip, about a box

330

in a PD evidence freezer in Vegas. Inside the box are." Herman stopped, then began again, "Body parts. Small ones. I don't know what you'll do about them, but since you represent the bunch they just hauled away in cages, I thought you should know." He shrugged again. "Maybe some kind of class action." Herman put his coffee down and put both hands to his face. "I'm tired too."

"Like the ones today?" Marjorie said.

"Worse, I think."

"You're crying."

"Like I said, I'm tired." He took his hands from his face, which was wet. "One other thing, from the same anonymous untraceable source, discovery, or full disclosure, or whatever. Just a wild guess. But it's possible that little revolver is actually the ice pick. Remember that?"

Marjorie did.

"Ice pick?" Mag said.

"Yeah," Herman said. "Guy was killed in LA not long ago, apparently from two tiny wounds to the head. Investigators thought it was most likely an ice pick."

"Left eye and left temple," Mag said, and he started to laugh, and then he was crying too, without covering up. "My dad," he said. "My dear old dad. Shit. He was probably drunk and trying to stomp that little guy. Oh dad oh shit."

Drew had his arm across Mag's shoulder.

"It's okay," Mag said. "He was an asshole. It was probably self-defense. Whatever, he deserved it." He gathered himself, cocked his head toward Drew and, smiling at Marjorie, said, "This guy spoke at the funeral."

Marjorie and Herman both looked at Drew.

"A friend?" Herman said.

Drew shook his head.

"Preacher?"

Drew looked deeply into his horchata.

"Professional funeral speaker," Mag said, smiling at Drew. "He actually made my father sound like a worthwhile individual. Don't be embarrassed, Drew. Ms. Kohler, we're going to have a funeral, right?"

Suddenly, Marjorie was crying.

"Boris wasn't just a guy, was he?" Herman said.

Marjorie shook her head. "Also," she said.

They all waited.

"I'd seen those kids. The dead boy. The other young people, the scalies."

"The picture of you," Mag said. "Their backs to the camera."

Marjorie nodded and cried into her napkin. "Somebody is going to pay for this. Somebody is going to goddamn well pay for this. And I'm sure there are others needing protection."

"Think you should find someone with a little separation?"

"Another attorney? No. This is me. This is why I went to law school." She blew her nose. "And while we're on the subject of paying," she said to Drew, "how much do you charge?"

"For a funeral?" Drew said.

Marjorie nodded.

"I'm already working for you. You can give me a percentage bonus."

Herman said, "I should go," rose from the bench, waved once as he walked to his car, and in a moment was gone.

"Mag can drop us," Drew said. "I'll take the couch, you can have my bed. I'll change the sheets."

"I'm sure they're okay," Marjorie said.

"They've had a couple weeks use," Drew said.

63

A splatter of blood and body fragments from Bryce and Marissa struck Gerald, Leah, and Mahesh Reynaud and Morgana, Jerome, and LaTasha Thurman, and Colin Fairchild, who was holding LaTasha's hand. Pieces of Howard hit Grace and Roberto Fairchild. They and all the other scalies, in shocked immobility, were an easy harvest for the soldiers with their cages. Mahesh, Leah, Gerald, and Elmer were the first in one cage, and then the Fairchilds and Elmer's parents, in another. Colin and LaTasha were gathered with her parents. Cheng, Sher, and Colin's parents were last. Cheng kept repeating, as a mantra, "No guns. We have no guns. No weapons of any kind."

All of them, throughout their lives, when they talked of their capture, would agree that the motion and the view through the steel mesh as they were carried away was like a nightmare ride on the roller coaster in their town (which, in fact, had an amusement park), and that it was the ultimate humiliation. They would remember the abrupt loss of the bright sunshine, of the trees and flowers, and even of the sight of the weird tourist-like crowd of onlookers, all as part of their loss of freedom as their cages were placed on racks inside the windowless poorly lit back end of the MRAP. Exhausted and defeated, they sat on the steel trap floors apart from each other, guarded by two armed soldiers whose cold gaze stopped their natural desire to huddle together.

For hours—was it three, four, more?—they rode in the cages in the MRAP, which was driven directly into the belly of a military transport plane. As the plane ascended, they slid across the cage floors until they were jumbled in a heap together at the back, momentarily finding comfort in the group touch, but then again separating under the eyes of their giant guards. Turbulence during the flight bounced them up and down, fortunately causing only bruises. The plane was cold. Some of them lay down. They kept their eyes away from the guards. They did not speak to each other. None could sleep. Several, in desperation, relieved themselves in corners of the cage; the stench filled the space. On landing, they braced to avoid sliding, but slid nonetheless.

The MRAP carried them for another couple hours before backing up to a loading dock. The cage containing the Thurmans and Colin was taken first, with a black cloth draped over it, to a small brightly lit room where it was placed on a table and the cloth removed. Against every edge of the table soldiers formed a barrier, hip to hip, shoulder to shoulder. The bottom was pulled from the cage, and one of the soldiers used a gloved hand to sweep the four scalies into another cage, on the floor of which was a small lidded jar, apparently glued to the floor, and a heap of clothing.

"Change," one of the soldiers said.

None of the scalies moved.

"You have to change clothing," the soldier said.

Jerome Thurman looked at his wife and daughter and Colin, and shook his head. "Let's have a seat," he said to them. They sat in a square, facing each other, away from the clothing.

"Well, shit," the soldier said. "Take the cage to the cell and leave it there."

The cloth was replaced over the cage and it was carried to a larger room, also brightly lit, where it was placed on the floor. The door to the room was slammed, and they were alone.

The procedure was repeated for Cheng, Sher, Grace, and Roberto. When the soldier ordered them to change into the clothing, Sher said, "Fuck you." Cheng had to stifle a laugh.

Next came Grace and Roberto Fairchild and Phuong and Michael Cruz. "Take your clothes and shove 'em," Michael said.

When the turn came for Mahesh, Leah, Gerald, and Elmer, Gerald said, "I'd like to see the room first. Have the beds been made?"

————

Together, but still in four cages, placed in a row against one wall of a cell intended for one ordinary human, the scalies shivered. They sat quietly for a time none of them could gauge.

Phuong stood and looked around. She walked around her cage so that she could see into the others. "Where is Astrid?" she said.

Her question roused everyone at once, and they all stood and looked around.

"I haven't seen her since," Elmer said.

"Hope she's okay," Roberto said.

After some time, Morgana Thurman said, "We need to say goodbye to our dead. I don't think there will be a funeral."

"They're watching us, you know," Gerald said.

"Yes," Cheng said. "There are bound to be cameras."

"So?" LaTasha said. "Let's show them we care about each other."

Jerome smiled. "Yes, let's." He held out his hands. The others stood. Morgana took his left hand, LaTasha took his right, and Colin took LaTasha's right. They faced the other cages and smiled. In the next cage, Cheng, Sher, Grace, and Roberto formed a similar line. Beyond them, Mahesh, Leah, Gerald, and Elmer did the same, as did Michael, Phuong,

Roberto, and Grace. In their separate cages, they maneuvered so they could all see each other.

"Without Howard's bravery, we would probably all be dead," Grace said.

Sher said, "Cheng, you knew him the best."

"Yes," Cheng said. "We raised hell together as kids." Cheng took time to look at the teenagers, who all smiled. "But he was always a loner. Until we gave him the need not to be. And then he did what he had to. He gave his life for us."

Phuong was crying. "Bryce and Marissa," she said. "Such a fine young man. Such a giving mother. How they supported each other."

There was more crying, only some of it audible. There was much hand-squeezing.

"Rest peacefully, Howard, Bryce, Marissa," Michael said.

The cell door opened with solid mechanical clicking. Each group of scalies dispersed in their cages, as if on command.

Four soldiers entered, one carrying a stack of covered hospital-style plates, and another with six-ounce bottles of water. Each plate was a scaly body-length wide. A soldier shut the door. As two soldiers watched, one soldier raised each cage top while another slid a plate, without lid, into it, and added two open bottles of water with straws in them. When they were finished, the soldiers left without speaking.

The plates held very small pieces of what seemed to be chicken, and finely chopped vegetables. There were neither utensils nor napkins.

"I guess this is lunch," Elmer said. "Or is it dinner?"

"I think I need to use a jar," LaTasha said.

"She needs some privacy," Colin said, and raised his hands to Morgana and Jerome.

"Nice idea," Morgana said.

With LaTasha leading, they walked to the jar. Colin, Morgana, and Jerome clustered around her, then turned their backs to her so that they were facing out, while she opened the jar lid and made her deposit.

64

When Drew awoke on the couch, he could see Marjorie, barefoot in a pair of his shorts and tee-shirt, her hair sticking out in all directions—looking, in total, altogether desirable—puttering in the kitchen. She turned her back to him and opened the refrigerator.

"Not much in there, I'm afraid. Eggs and bread, I think," Drew said.

She let the door close and turned to him. "I need your wi-fi. You do have wi-fi, right?"

Her face, though pretty in a no-nonsense kind of way, was puffy from sleep, her eyes were red, and she still wore smeared eye make-up and a tense expression.

"Sure," Drew said. He rose from the couch, letting the sheet fall away. "Sorry about the boxer shorts," he said.

She shrugged a little as if she hadn't noticed and cared less.

At a computer desk, Drew and wrote the wi-fi name and password on note paper for Marjorie. She took the paper into his bedroom and came out with her laptop, which she opened on the kitchen table.

"You really should consider a tablet," Drew said. "Much lighter and easier to use."

"I like my laptop," Marjorie said.

Drew watched her focus on her screen as if he weren't there. "I'll start some coffee," he said. "You can shower. I put towels out for you last night."

"Do I stink?" she said, still watching the screen.

"Not worse than I do," he said as he switched on the coffee maker. "If you don't mind, I'll go first."

Marjorie, sitting still, began to cry. When Drew moved towards her, she held up her hand to stop him. "For weeks," she said, "with Boris taking care of me, feeding me, all I cared about was this screen. Except for sex, I pretty much ignored him." She smiled a little. "But Boris made me shower. I was obsessed. Must have smelled bad and looked worse." She looked evenly at him.

Drew said nothing.

————

"Habeas corpus," she said, her mouth full of the scrambled eggs Drew had made. "We need to see them and we need to know the charges. And our contracts. Government, classified, oaths, all that bullshit, more fine print than a thousand mortgages. Can't be legal. There's precedent. Can't keep people from coming and going even if they sign a paper saying you can."

Drew watched her talk, eat, and drink at the same time, all in a hurry.

"In fact, I think there was some unlawful imprisonment going on. And then the bodies." She stopped herself. "Have to see them." She let a moment pass. "I'm sorry. Tell me again about you and funerals?"

"Actually, I'm an actor. Speaking at funerals is my day job."

Marjorie looked at him.

"Somebody dies. Nobody liked him. Lots of money, people still want a funeral. They're embarrassed that nobody can think of much nice to say. They hire me." He explained about Donne's meditation on death and his succession of unloved corpses. "Be nice to speak for a nice person, at least once."

"We'll get to that. How old is Mag?"

"Nineteen, I think."

"Old enough. Smart. Energetic. Idealistic. Almost perfect."

Drew smiled.

Looking sheepish, she said, "Oh, I'm sorry. You're."

"Fine."

They drank coffee.

"Thanks for breakfast," she said. "I'll clean up."

Drew let her gather the dishes.

At the sink, her back to him as she began cleaning, she said, "About money."

"Don't worry about it," Drew said.

"Well, there may very well be some. A lot, I'm thinking. Civil suits. You and Mag would definitely be in for a cut."

"Whatever," he said.

———

When Mag showed up a half hour later Marjorie told them what she knew about the scaly project and its two towns, which, she admitted, was not a great deal. "We worked there, but very few of us knew why." She told them how she had believed she was losing her mind when she first saw scalies, and how the famous picture came to be. She told them about how everybody there was forbidden to leave during their contract periods, except with special permission, and about how people found ways out anyway. She told them what she knew about the panic and the break-out by "us regular people." She knew little more than they did about how the scalies got out, or how many, or why, and she didn't know how much of the internet stuff on the subject was true. She told them she traveled with Boris, but not why.

When she stopped talking, after three cups of coffee, Mag asked, "So you're gonna be their lawyer?"

"Yes," Marjorie said. "I'm guessing they don't have another, at least not yet."

"So how can we help?"

She took a moment. "I'll need a lot of help," she said. "Boris told me I was obsessive. I think he was right." She looked out the window at an ordinary sky. "If I get bossy, that might be why."

"Boss away, lady," Mag said.

She smiled at Mag. "Well, I'll need you to run paperwork errands. We can't do it all online. For now, please, start cataloging whatever you find about scalies on the web. Drew, please start contacting press. Set up a conference for day after tomorrow. And please find a location."

"And you?" Drew said.

"I'm going to try to find them, in between researching the law. And I better buy some clothes."

———

Drew, on the couch, and Mag, at the kitchen table, heard Marjorie's voice rising from the bedroom: "What do you mean, you don't know? You have to know where federal prisoners are." Pause. "I'm not asking about *every* prisoner, just these, and they aren't exactly garden variety prisoners, are they?" Pause. "That's what your other office told me." Pause. "Well. I guess I'll have to find out in court. Thank you very much." Then: "*Fuck!*"

"She's hot," Mag said in a low voice.

"Yeah," Drew said.

"I mean, you know, as a woman."

"She's too old for you."

"But not for you."

"Thanks, Mag. If I need a wing man I'll ask."

"Who do you think Boris was? I mean, to her?"

"We have more important things to think about, Mag."

"Seems pretty important to me."

Marjorie came storming into the room. "Unbelievable! Nobody will tell me where they are. The fuckers won't even tell me where the bodies are. Not even Boris's."

"Mag got us a church for the press conference," Drew said, "and the press is coming. Sounds like you'll have something to tell them."

"Oh, yeah. Mag, you'll be going to the courthouse tomorrow."

"I phoned Herman Winston," Mag said. "He's looking for them."

65

Army Intelligence Lieutenant Colonel Seamus Nguyen sat at the head of a long metal table with a plastic top in a conference room bare of anything else except twelve uncomfortable metal chairs that were occupied by his staff. Even though he knew it would look bad to his troops, he could not resist the need to massage his temples. His head ached.

A thin young blonde woman with sergeant's stripes remarked that their wards needed better sanitation facilities, a way to bathe, and decent places to sleep. And they needed to be coaxed into changing their clothing. "We did get what seem to be cell phones from their pockets," she added.

"Cell phones?" Nguyen asked.

"Yes, sir."

"How did you get them?"

"They wouldn't undress so Lars held each one individually while Muhammed used tweezers to go into their pockets."

"Does their new clothing include underwear?" Colonel Nguyen asked.

"No, sir," the blond sergeant said.

Nguyen sighed. "Why couldn't they just bring us some ordinary terrorists?" he asked nobody in particular.

————

Colonel Nguyen and Sergeant Eliza Adjaye now sat on hard wooden chairs in an interrogation room facing a pretty young woman or adolescent girl with a dark complexion and dirty black hair, in a very dirty sweatshirt ("University of

Chicago" for god's sake?), jeans and a defiant attitude. She sat alone on the floor of a cage on the table.

Sergeant Adjaye (the skinny blonde with the logistics report) had not wanted this particular assignment, but neither had anyone else on Nguyen's staff, not even the ones who had successfully interrogated people who, on good evidence, had conspired to plant bombs in public places. Nguyen saw her trying, with only some success, to stifle her consternation at the sight on the table. How could he blame her? It was tough on him too. He could forget that the subject was less than six inches tall only by imagining he was seeing her on TV.

The colonel had chosen this woman for the first interview because he thought her youth might make her an easier subject. To Adjaye's first question she had readily stated her name, "LaTasha Thurman," but had answered the second, about her age, with, "What difference does that make?"

An adolescent, Nguyen thought.

To Sergeant Adjaye's third question, "Why did you leave your project town?" LaTasha answered with another question, "Are you free?"

"We're not here to talk about me, LaTasha," Adjaye said.

"It's okay, Sergeant," Nguyen said. "Ms. Thurman, we do need to know about your motivations."

"Are you free?" she said again, this time to him.

Nguyen held up a hand to silence Adjaye. "I'm as free as the army allows me to be," he said, smiling a little.

"So when you're on leave, or when you go home for the night, you can go wherever you want, right?"

"Sort of," he said.

"But you're not hemmed in. And you're not scared you might get killed if you go out, right?"

"There are always limits, and people do get killed."

"Well, I don't know much about the army and I know people get killed everywhere, but you don't know what it was like for us."

"I've been told it was pretty nice."

LaTasha gathered herself. "It was *very* nice." she said. "We had everything. But it was still a very nice prison. And then, like, there was a sort of panic and we got scared that more of us were going to get killed, and so a bunch of us decided to get out." And then she spilled. Nguyen let her roll on, with only an encouraging nod or grunt, as she told about how she and her friends had gone outside a couple of times, and how it had been scary but exhilarating, like a roller-coaster ride, and then how all their families had gotten together to break out on a night when it seemed as if everyone else was too. She told about how Howard, "one of the guys you shot?" (Nguyen again held up his hand to stop Adjaye) had shown them how to climb onto big trucks and ride, and how they had stolen food, and finally about their encampment. "It was beautiful, you know?" she said. "It was tough, but it was all *ours*, you know?"

Nguyen nodded.

"Where's Astrid?" LaTasha said.

Nguyen shook his head and shrugged.

"Little blonde thing. Cute. Like her," she said, pointing at Adjaye.

"We have no idea about anyone outside your group," Nguyen said.

"Her father got shot," LaTasha said. "Days ago."

"Oh," Nguyen said. "That one."

"And then we had to leave our camp. But you know about that," she said, and then she was crying. "Bryce and his mother. Why?"

"We don't really know," Nguyen said.

"We weren't hurting anything or anybody. We were just trying not to *be* hurt."

And then Adjaye surprised Nguyen by saying, in a soft voice, "You're in love with that tall thin boy with the brown hair, aren't you?"

LaTasha looked at her sharply. *"Don't you goddamn touch him!"* she said through more tears. *"Just—"*

"It's alright, Ms. Thurman. That's all we need for now," Nguyen said. He ordered Adjaye to have the guards take the girl back, and to have them bring the guy in the police shirt.

———

"Explain," Nguyen said when he and Adjaye were alone in the interrogation room.

"We've been watching," she said. "I know what two kids in love look like."

Nguyen said nothing.

"We're supposed to watch, right? It's what we're taught, to look for whatever can give us leverage."

"Sure," Nguyen said.

Two guards entered with another cloth-covered cage, which they unveiled on the table, revealing a man in a khaki police shirt and jeans, as dirty as the girl's had been. The man rose from his sitting position to face them with his hands behind his back at parade rest.

"Name?" Adjaye asked.

"Cheng Schmitz."

"Spell?"

The man spelled his name.

"Age?"

"Fifty-two."

"Who's Astrid?" Nguyen asked.

"Do you have her?" Cheng asked back.

346

"No," Nguyen said.

Cheng smiled and said nothing.

"Tell us about yourself," Adjaye said.

"I am, or was, the police chief in Projectville."

"Police chief?"

"Yes, ma'am."

"So, how—"

Nguyen interrupted her. "You're the man Dr. Hagenstopple told us about."

"Barry? Could be," Cheng said.

"He told us about talking to the police chief."

"I wouldn't know what he said."

"So the weapon you dropped on the pavement when you were captured, that was official police issue?"

"Yes, sir."

"You shot the drone."

"Yes, sir."

"Tell us about leaving Projectville."

Cheng shrugged. "Everybody wanted to leave. I didn't see how I could stop them, even if I had wanted to. Which I didn't."

"So you abandoned your post."

Cheng looked up at the ceiling and exhaled, and then he looked squarely at Nguyen and said, "Yeah. I did."

"How do you justify that?"

"Well, suppose you were asked to kill this, ah," and Cheng took a step back so he could see Adjaye's stripes. "This sergeant here."

"What do you mean?"

"What I said. And suppose she wasn't the first and wouldn't be the last."

Nguyen was quiet.

"After a while," Cheng said, "maybe you'd start to think about abandoning your post."

Nguyen said, "Go on."

Cheng hesitated again. "If you've talked to Barry, you should know."

After a silent moment, Nguyen said, "Tell about the escape."

Cheng chuckled. "Well, actually, there were a lot of them."

"What do you mean?"

"Over the years. Teenagers, mostly." Cheng told about the various holes in the project's perimeter—the big air vent, the fences, about how he and Howard ("one of the ones who got shot") as kids used to sneak out and steal beer from the truck stop. "We had beer inside, but it was more fun outside, if you know what I mean. The outside was supposed to be a secret from us, but we weren't stupid. Nothing is air-tight, not even this place. Barry knew."

"So, the big escape?"

Cheng took his time and told the same things LaTasha had but with different details, such as the conveyor belt. He did not mention Samuel Giles.

Nguyen reached into his brief case and pulled an eight-by-ten color photo of all the scalies in their cell. "Can you tell us who each of these people is?"

"So you are watching."

"You knew that."

Cheng shrugged and identified each person.

Adjaye said, "The middle-aged woman with the long brown hair, the one—"

Nguyen again interrupted her, saying, "That's enough, Sergeant."

"It's alright," Cheng said. "That's Sher Statie. She's—was—city manager. We worked together a lot. And, yeah, we're a couple."

"Thank you, Chief," Nguyen said.

"How's that cop?" Cheng asked.

348

"The one your friend Howard shot?"

"Yeah. The one who blasted the boy and his mother."

"The woman was his mother?"

"Yeah."

Nguyen looked at his hands. "The cop will be okay. Thanks for your cooperation."

———————

"Was the big escape your first time outside, Colin?" Adjaye asked.

"No."

"You'd been out before?"

"Sure. A couple times."

"Tell us about them.

"Well, it was a bunch of us. Elmer and Gerald, the two guys in the box—"

"The box?"

Colin shrugged. "Yeah. That place you keep us. The box."

Nguyen smiled as Adjaye continued her questions. "I see. Who else?"

"Astrid." Colin stopped himself.

"We've heard about Astrid," Nguyen said. "We don't know where she is."

Colin took a breath. "Okay. LaTasha. And, uh, Bryce."

"Bryce was your friend?" Adjaye asked.

"Yeah."

"Inside?"

"What do you mean, inside?"

"Before you left home."

"Oh. Yes, he was." Colin smiled. "Everyone was Bryce's friend. He was a good guy. He could have been a snob, but he wasn't."

"Why could he have been a snob?"

"Jock. Top student. You know."

"Jock?"

"Yeah. Football and baseball."

Adjaye changed her tone. "Football. So he was tough?"

"Yeah, I guess so."

"So you think maybe he was doing something?"

"Doing something?"

"Yes."

Colin raised his hands in bewilderment.

"When he was walking toward the officer."

"You mean the cop who blew him and his mother to bits?"

"Yes, the cop one of your friends shot."

Colin snorted. "What the hell could he do? I mean, look at me. Are you afraid of me?"

Adjaye was speechless for a moment.

"If I were outside this cage, would you be terrified?" Colin raised his hands like claws and yelled, "Waaargh!"

"Very funny," Adjaye said, "but my questions are serious."

"So was mine," Colin said.

Now clearly irritated, Adjaye said, "LaTasha implied that you two are in love."

Colin went quiet.

"Are you?" Adjaye asked.

Colin made himself taller. "You were asking about when we were outside, together. Well, it was Bryce, Elmer, Gerald, Astrid, LaTasha, and me. Twice. If you've been doing your job, Miz Military Investigator, you've seen us."

"What do you mean, seen you?"

"What I said. I mean, you've seen the picture, right?"

Nguyen said, "What picture?"

"The one with the big—the woman. She spilled coffee on me."

"That was you?"

Colin grinned. "Yeah. All of us. You saw us from the back. Cool, huh?"

"Thanks, Colin," Nguyen said.

_____

"So, you stole?" Adjaye said to Elmer.

Elmer, who seemed more relaxed than the others, shrugged. "Sure."

"You think that was okay?"

"Well, ordinarily I don't steal, but we had to live. What was it Ms. Statie called it? _Foraging_, that's the word." Elmer smiled.

Elmer's story jibed with what Nguyen and Adjaye had already heard, but she had another question.

"Elmer," she said, smiling, "you seem to have a relationship with another young man."

Nguyen cleared his throat and said, "Elmer, Sergeant Adjaye just broke up with her girlfriend. Would you have any relationship advice for her?"

Elmer thought, and then said, "I don't know. It's tough. Find someone else?"

_____

"You know," Gerald said, as he sat Indian style on the floor and studied his fingernails, "you wouldn't have to ask half these questions if you went online more. Start with the simple stuff, you know, Twitter and Facebook. Once you're at home with them, you can go onto the more sophisticated sites, like PonderThis and others. And lots of news sites, of course."

"Gerald, if you could just—"

"By the way, who are you?"

"Excuse me?" Adjaye said.

"Who _are_ you?"

Nguyen smiled. "I'm Lieutenant Colonel Seamus Nguyen, and this is Sergeant Eliza Adjaye, United States Army Intelligence. Congratulations on being the first to ask."

The stories did not vary significantly. The parents were in shock at losing their freedom, as they had been elated at experiencing it. They all expressed grief and bitterness, but not surprise, about the deaths they had seen. They wanted to know about the bodies. They wanted a funeral. They wanted their own space where they could live and come and go as they wished, and could have good futures for their children. They did not understand why their kids could not do what other kids did.

"Other kids?" Nguyen asked Leah Reynaud.

"The ones on TV," Leah said. "TV shows, movies, news." She shrugged.

"TV," Nguyen said.

"Of course," she said.

She said, "At the time, I wanted Gerald not to go out. But he's a smart boy, you know? My husband, Mahesh, was upset, but I think fathers naturally worry more, don't you?"

Mahesh said he was appalled but not surprised at how they were being treated.

The parents uniformly described being worried but not surprised when their kids sneaked out, just as their own parents had worried about them. Some were more worried than others, but they were all proud of their kids' strength. Michael Cruz said that "kids need to let off steam." His wife Phuong agreed, saying that "mothers worry more than fathers, I think, it's natural, but the kids were bored, what else could they do?" She felt sick every time she thought about Bryce and Marissa . "Marissa was a sweet person and she just adored her

SCALIES

son. I suppose it's better for her than surviving without him would have been."

Grace Fairchild started and ended her interview angry. "You just try living the way we have to," she said. "Just try it for a while. You think nice things are enough? Do you?"

Roberto Fairchild told them to keep their hands off the kids. "Okay? Think you can do that? Think you can keep from killing more of them? I'm glad my boy's alive but I don't understand why Bryce and Marissa had to die. Not to mention Astrid's dad. What was accomplished, can you tell me? It won't surprise me if you kill more, just for the hell of it."

Jerome Thurman limited his answers to *yes, no, could be, maybe*. Nguyen would not press him. Morgana Thurman controlled her need to cry. "I'm not surprised at how things went," she said, "but it still hurts. You should be able to understand that."

"Yeah, I was City Manager," Sher said. "Cheng and I were good bureaucrats, keeping things going, keeping the anger at a simmer instead of a boil, you know? So we had some freedom. Now it's over. Won't surprise me if you put us in solitary. Save you from seeing us fuck."

Nguyen was impressed by how these people were never surprised by bad things.

———

"What do you think?" Nguyen said. He and Adjaye were in his office, talking across his desk, after interviewing the rest of the scalies and getting the same tale from all of them.

"Sir, we gave them time to get their stories straight."

"All fifteen of them? We've been watching them. They haven't talked much. You think they could have all come up with stories this close?"

"Sir, if I may?"

353

"Sure."

"We should have kept them separate."

"To discover what?" Nguyen asked. When she didn't answer, he said, "See, the people we get here are generally suspected of doing something bad, you know? Besides escaping, what exactly do we suspect of *these* people?"

"Shooting other people, for one thing."

"Under very threatening circumstances. And we found only two weapons."

"Still, sir."

"You think they were plotting to take over the country?"

"I don't know, sir."

"Me neither."

Nguyen thought for a moment, and then asked, "You have the packs from their camp?"

"Yes, sir."

"Give them their underwear, and any jackets or sweaters you find. Tell them they have to wear the GI-Joe suits. Let them out of their cages. Work on those issues you mentioned, the toilets, washing, sleeping. Use our credit card to buy what you need. When Hagenstopple comes I'll talk to him about other supplies from back at their project. And tell them we have to watch them, but we don't really care about their intimacies. That's the best we can do."

66

B arry could not tell which irritated him more: Lieutenant Colonel Nguyen, with his spit-shined combat boots and his crisply ironed camouflage fatigues (camouflage in an office to hide from what, for god's sake?), or Rondeau, with his way of seeing everything as a joke.

Nguyen answered questions in the same way that he sat behind his military-issue steel desk, crisply and precisely.

"So you've questioned all of them?" Barry asked him.

"Yes, sir."

"Together or separately?"

"All separately, sir."

"And you learned what?"

"What's in the report, sir."

"Yeah," Barry said. "Except, they had to have help, Colonel, wouldn't you say?"

"With, sir?"

"With getting out," Barry said quietly, suppressing an urge to yell.

"We asked them, sir, but were unable to ascertain that, sir. There were numerous escape routes, sir."

"What he means," Rondeau said to Barry, "is that your project perimeter was a sieve."

"And what have your guys gotten from Giles?" Barry asked him.

"Not a word. He won't even say good morning," Rondeau said.

"You've kept him in solitary?"

"Oh, yes. With some sleep deprivation and irregular lighting periods. We haven't started sensory deprivation yet, but my personal opinion is, that yields ravings." Rondeau grinned. "You'd probably like to water board him personally, wouldn't you, Barry?"

Barry turned back to Nguyen. "Weren't you told to isolate these people?"

"Yes, sir," Nguyen said. "But we're not currently able to do that, sir."

"Oh?" Barry said.

"Our cells, sir, are built for regular people, sir. It made no sense to use fifteen full-sized cells to separate them, sir."

Barry sighed. "Surely you could build boxes, or whatever?"

"We're working on it, sir. But, uh, plumbing is a major problem, sir, and your project has not provided us—"

"Yeah, yeah," Barry said. "They won't let me take anything out of the project."

"We did keep them in this one room, but separated in the cage traps, for a while, sir."

Barry raised an eyebrow. "And?"

"Well, sir, we've had real terrorists here, sir. Very bad people. Humiliating them can work. But with these people, the humiliation of seeing each other in separate cages, knowing we're watching them, well, it seemed counter-productive, sir."

"How do they know you're watching them?" Barry asked.

Rondeau said, "Shit, Barry, everybody locked up in these places knows they're being watched. Sometimes you tell, them, right Colonel? Lack of privacy helps break people down."

"Yes, sir. But it has not seemed to have that effect in this case, sir."

Barry ran out of questions, so for a while they gazed at the forty-inch flat screen on Colonel Nguyen's wall. The fifteen scalies were in one large, gray, featureless cell from which the full-sized human bunk bed and latrine had been removed. In one corner was what appeared to be a small improvised toilet, but without privacy walls. The scalies were all dressed in GI-Joe doll fatigues. Mostly they were still, sitting or lying prone on the floor. Two or three paced from wall to wall. In one corner, a woman was leading several others in yoga exercises. They sometimes nudged each other and exchanged brief smiles or grimaces. They seldom touched, and even more seldom spoke.

"They behave like fucking zoo animals in cages," Barry said.

"That's what we have observed, sir."

Rondeau chuckled.

"What's funny now?" Barry said.

"Role reversal," Rondeau said.

Barry glared at him.

Rondeau said, "In the movie, the scientist is supposed to be humane, and the law-enforcement and military are supposed to be the hard asses."

"They were not supposed to even try to leave," Barry said.

Rondeau laughed. "What you'd like to do to Giles is nothing compared to what you want to do to these little guys, is it, Barry?"

"I—we—need for them to talk, goddammit."

Nguyen said, "The thing is, sir, except for shoplifting, which wouldn't justify all this, we don't know what these people are supposed to have done wrong, or what they plan to do wrong. They have admitted to escaping, and everyone saw their gunshots, but the shooter is dead and we cannot determine any other bad intent, sir. Even the illegality of the escape is questionable, since they had never been legally charged with anything, let alone convicted. So besides the collaboration you want to know about, we don't really know what to ask them. And I must admit frankly, sir, we have not gotten over the weirdness of this. It's been very painful for my staff. All of us have needed counseling."

Rondeau looked at Nguyen with some concern. "You did know about these people before, right, Colonel?"

"No, sir."

"But all that internet crap? Most of which turned out not to be crap at all—you missed it?"

"For us it was banned, sir."

Rondeau leaned back and laughed. "Well of course it was."

"All the information was classified, so because it had been leaked it was blocked from all military computers and we were ordered not to look at it at home."

"So everyone in the world knew, except for you," Rondeau said.

"Yes, sir. But we know now. And we believe there are others." Nguyen pulled a key from his pocket and unlocked a desk drawer, from which he took a box. He opened the box on his desk. Inside, on soft white cloth, were what looked like a dozen very tiny cell phones.

Rondeau grinned.

Barry said. "I oversaw the contract for that work myself. RSH people made those."

"We haven't gotten very far, it's difficult, but it does appear that these people had developed a very sophisticated and rather secure network of their own. A sort of VPN."

They watched the quiet TV screen. One of the scalies raised her hand and walked to the makeshift toilet. Four others gathered around her, facing outward, as if to shield her from sight.

"This thing has sound, right?" Barry said.

"Yes, sir. They don't speak much," Nguyen said. "That behavior you see is common, sir."

After another moment of watching, Barry stood, walked to the screen and pointed closely at two of the scalies. "I want to see these two."

"I can arrange that, sir."

"Now."

"Yes, sir. One thing, sir."

"What?"

"Those two, in particular, did independently and voluntarily express extreme dislike of you, sir."

Barry whirled from the screen and said, "Dislike of *me*?"

"Yes, sir. The woman used the word 'evil' and the man said you were, uh, 'a syphilitic prick' was the phrase, I believe, sir."

Rondeau roared.

————

A half hour later Barry sat in an interrogation room. On the table, standing in separate cages, were Sher Statie and Cheng Schmitz.

"So, this is what Barry looks like," Sher said to Cheng.

"I guess so," Cheng said. "Sounds like him."

"You violated our trust," Barry said.

"Yeah, that really does sound like him," Cheng said.

Sher laughed.

Barry wanted to say that he was heartily sick of being laughed at, but instead he said, "Did Sam Giles help you?"

"If you want to know if he conspired with us, the answer is no," Cheng said.

"So what did he do?"

Cheng shrugged.

Barry lowered his head. He removed his glasses and massaged the bridge of his nose. "I have to say," he said huskily, "I am very disappointed in you."

"Oh, for chrissake, Barry," Sher said.

Barry looked up at her. "What do you mean?" he said.

"The fake emotion," she said.

"Fake?" he said. "Fake? The project—*you*—are my life's work. Without *me*, *you* would not exist. In your town I gave you everything, you lived better than ninety-nine percent of the world's population, and yet you ran away from me." Barry felt tears welling from his eyes, and he did not care.

"Barry," Cheng said, "you know why we ran."

"No," Barry said sincerely. "I don't."

"Oh, good god, Barry."

Barry thought—for what, the hundredth time?—about the breakout, and still he could not understand why, why then, why suddenly, had they all turned their backs on him? There was only the one thing, and it wasn't really one thing, was it? "The need to cull?" he said. "It could not have been that."

"Barry, have you ever wondered why Sher and I didn't have kids?"

"Well, yes, actually, I have," Barry said. "You do seem perfect for each other and I know you'd make great parents."

Sher laughed again.

"*goddammit!*" Barry bellowed. "*Stop laughing at me!*" The tears were now streaming down his cheeks and his nose ran.

"Barry," Sher said sternly, "Cheng and I *knew*. Others suspected, but we *knew*. How could we bring a child into the world, knowing that our child might someday be *culled?*"

Barry was genuinely shocked. "You knew it was necessary."

"*You* knew it was necessary," Cheng said. "But we had to endure it."

"Without me . . ."

"Sure, Barry," Sher said, sarcastically, "without you we wouldn't exist. We owe you our lives."

"You have no idea how much you've hurt me," Barry said, sobbing.

Sher and Cheng looked at each other, and said nothing.

———

Rondeau and Nguyen watched through the one-way glass.

"Some piece of work, huh?" Nguyen said.

"Those cages are nauseating. Let's see if we can get those people some comfort. Some privacy at least. And let them be together, can't you?"

"I'm working on it."

67

'Scalies' Attorney Files Habeas Corpus Writ
Los Angeles Times, September 14, 20__
By Carmen Keo

The lawyer who last week announced her pro-bono representation of the 15 reduced-scale humans now in custody, today said that she is taking her first action on their behalf by filing a writ of habeas corpus in federal court.

Attorney Marjorie Koehler told a press briefing that the Justice Department had failed to respond to numerous inquiries from herself and her staff. "We've contacted the U.S. Attorney, the Attorney General's office in Washington, and the local and Washington offices of the FBI," she said. "So, far, nobody has told us what my clients are charged with or when they will appear in court. They won't even tell us where they are. Nor will they tell us where the dead bodies are. So the writ is our main course of action now."

Koehler brushed aside national security concerns. "These people are a biological creation of the government who have been basically imprisoned for their entire existence. The idea that they pose some kind of national security threat is ludicrous." When asked where they would go if released, she said that was an open question. "But the government created them, and so I think it's up to the government to help them."

The notion of six-inch tall people was broadly dismissed as an internet hoax until five days ago when many witnesses reported seeing what some described as a "fire fight" or "gun battle" between them and local and federal law enforcement.

One unidentified man is believed to have been killed, and witnesses said they saw at least two "scaly" bodies. A police officer suffered a minor wound to the neck.

A source at the Justice Department in Los Angeles, who spoke on condition of anonymity, laughed at the idea. "It's amazing the bilge that sloshes around the internet," he said. "There was an altercation at that intersection, and the details will emerge appropriately."

Albert Leonetta, an accountant at a large downtown company, says he took that day off work. "I burned PTO to see what was going on, along with hundreds of other people. I can tell you that I saw two, maybe three scalies get killed."

Stories of "scalies" started to appear early this year . . .

———————

Dead Man in Scaly Fight Identified
New York Times, September 15, 20__
By Feodor Hurston

The man killed in the so-called "scaly gunfight" eight days ago has been identified as Boris Feldman, an employee at the RSH Project where the "reduced-size humans" (RSH), commonly known as "scalies," were allegedly developed. Drew Kristopher, a spokesman for attorney Marjorie Koehler, who has said she is representing captured RSH, told a press briefing today in Los Angeles that Ms. Koehler knew Mr. Feldman personally and had withheld his name out of respect for family. Mr. Kristopher said that an exhaustive search had yielded no living family of Mr. Feldman. He refused to speculate on why local, state, and federal law enforcement had not released Mr. Feldman's name. He said that Ms. Koehler and Mr. Feldman had worked together at the RSH Project.

The Times has confirmed the identity of Mr. Feldman.

Mr. Kristopher repeated his claim that the government is holding, illegally and without charge, at least 15 RSH at an unidentified facility.

Mr. Kristopher claimed that he himself had seen three "scalies" killed in brutal fashion. He said it is true that a police officer was shot by a scaly, but added that the alleged shooter was himself killed by law enforcement and therefore no longer posed a threat to anyone.

Mr. Kristopher said the government should "come clean" about this whole matter, and that its imprisonment of scalies without charge and without allowing them contact with counsel was "outrageous."

The Times has yet to confirm even the existence of RSH . . .

———

Attorney Says Government Illegally Holding Scalies
NonOfficialNews.com, September 15, 20__
By Ladislav Khan

Scalygate just got scalier. Marjorie Koehler today filed charges in federal court alleging that the government is violating the sixth amendment to the Constitution and the Civil Liberties Act of 1988 by holding her clients incommunicado, without charge, and without even naming the place where they are detained. The Civil Liberties Act was passed specifically to apologize and pay reparations for illegal internment of Japanese Americans during World War II, but Koehler says it set a precedent than can be applied to any illegal mass imprisonment.

Matthew Lopez, a spokesperson for the Los Angeles US Attorney's Office, told me by phone this afternoon that the charges were "without merit" and that the government expects them to be dismissed "very soon." When I asked him if his statement did not at least imply that scalies do, in fact, exist, he said, tellingly, "The government has many scientific projects underway all the time. Obviously, the government can't tell everybody everything about all of them."

NON has been trying, without success, to get confirmation or denial of the so-called "RSH Project" from the Administration for days. So far, we have been unable to get even off-the-record comment . . .

————

Administration Accuses Man of Illegally Releasing Subjects Who Don't Exist
Pokeprysnoop.com, September 18, 20__
By Bradley Brownwell

Each time I think I've seen every kind of dodge and deceit the Administration is capable of, starting with, you can't sue us for illegal acts when law forbids even discussion of whether those acts exist, to, we have solid legal basis for what we do but for your own good we can't tell you what it is, I get surprised once again.

The Administration in Washington today said it had arrested one Samuel Giles, former Director of Information Technology and Security at the Reduced-Scale Human Project, and was charging him with the illegal "release of subjects from a government project." In its formal indictment, the government admits, at least by implication, that the RSH Project does exist (emphasis added):

Mr. Giles knowingly and maliciously released information and **physical subjects**, contrary to law and his contract with an entity known as RSHP . . .

365

When asked about "RSHP" at his briefing today, Press Secretary Ernest Still said that "the reference in the indictment is to Mr. Giles' contract, not the entity he damaged through his releases." And then, to a follow-up question, Still said, "I am, unfortunately, not able to tell you about RSHP." So, he is telling us that Giles actions violated a contract that had nothing to do with his work for the government, and, by the way, he can't tell us who the other party to that contract is, except that it's called "RSHP."

And then, in answer to another question, Still said, "At this time I cannot tell you anything about the released subjects, except that they have nothing to do with the rumors and innuendo you may have seen on the web, and in fact, may be only virtual subjects and not real ones at all. And, I would add, that we live in perilous times and sometimes people have to trust their public servants to do the right thing."

In other words, the government accuses Samuel Giles of doing a terrible awful thing by releasing these "subjects," but the "subjects" are nowhere near as dangerous as you think they are, and might even be "only virtual."

Now, it may very well be that this Samuel Giles has, in fact, done something to Endanger the Homeland. But the Alice-In-Wonderland arrogance and presumption of the government, in telling us we must Trust Them, continues to be breathtaking . . .

————

RSH Attorney, ACLU, Demand Access to Giles
Washington Post, September 25, 20__
By Gillian Rostropovich

Marjorie Koehler, now widely known as the "scaly lawyer" for her representation of so-called "Reduced Scale Humans" (RSH), the existence of which has yet to be confirmed, has been joined by American Civil Liberties Union (ACLU) attorney Saleem McConnell in demanding access to Samuel Giles. The Justice Department has detained Giles under the Homeland Operational Security and Technology Act (HOST). HOST allows DOJ to detain subjects "deemed" by the Attorney General to pose a Homeland risk for up to 18 days without public hearing, according to DOJ spokesperson Martha Gray. "HOST is clearly the authority in cases like this," Gray said, refusing to elaborate because "releasing more information would create an imminent public danger, thereby violating section 7385 of the act."

At a press briefing with Koehler, McConnell called the DOJ's assertion "Kafkaesque," saying "They cannot, on the one hand, tell us that Mr. Giles has endangered national security, and on the other hand, say that the 'subjects' he released information about aren't really that dangerous and may not even exist. This is exactly the sort of thing the English wanted to stop when they made King John sign the Magna Carta more than nine hundred years ago, and is further prohibited by the sixth and fourteenth amendments to the Constitution."

Koehler expressed frustration at the government's "refusal to even acknowledge the existence of my RSH clients, while they now hold Samuel Giles for releasing them. This is as opaque as anything I have ever seen." In response to a question about her involvement with the RSH Project, she said, "Yes, I have done work for the RSH, so, yes, I do know it exists. As for the maps showing the project's alleged location, I have no knowledge."

Government officials remained tight-lipped about the so-called "scaly affair," claiming "national security concerns" as the reason for their secrecy. Even off the record . . .

Editorial: Scaly Affair: Allow the Government to Function
New York Times, September 27, 20__

The scaly furor continues to grow. The internet noise is deafening, and street demonstrations have erupted in several large cities in America and even abroad. Indeed, we agree that the Administration owes the public answers to many questions. What in the world are "scalies", anyway? Has the government actually created real-life leprechauns? On one day the Administration says, yes, there is a "Reduced Scale Humans" project, and on the next they say, maybe not. Are they joking?

We continue to be skeptical about the existence of six-inch tall humans supposedly developed in laboratories. Yes, there are "eye-witness accounts" of them, but we would remind people in general, and some of the land's more hysterical commentators in particular, that there have also been "eye-witness" accounts of mermaids, the Loch Ness monster, bigfoot, and flying saucers (why are there never any flying cups?).

While the government's lack of explanations is troubling, let's remember that we continue to live in dangerous times. We should allow the people to whom we have entrusted our safety to do their jobs and give them the benefit of the doubt.

Regarding Samuel Giles, the Administration says it has good reason to hold him. If he has, in fact, violated the law—including his own employment contract with the government—then the HOST Act allows him to be held. Emails in which Giles expresses doubts about his work assignments appear to support that position.

The government should not have forever to disclose what it knows. The truth will out, and, when it does, we believe it will be much more mundane then many people seem to think. Until then, those wanting to demonstrate should do so in an orderly way, and we should all keep the rhetoric civilized, and not rant about the impossible until we see it.

————————

Scaly FOIA Request Denied
National Tribune-Ombudsman, October 2, 20__
By Sven Baghdadi

This morning a federal judge ruled that in the RSH case, the national security exception for Freedom of Information Act (FOIA) requests trumps the public's right to know. Judge Indira Rosenthal's decision sided with Justice Department attorneys who argued that section 7334 of the HOST Act prohibits any public discussion of what they referred to as "the project in question." Dismissing the arguments of Marjorie Koehler, the attorney claiming to represent the so-called "scalies," and ACLU attorney Saleem McConnell, that "the project in question" is publicly known as the "Reduced Scale Humans Project," Judge Rosenthal agreed with the government that even the naming of the project in open court is forbidden.

In her 73-page decision, the judge stressed repeatedly that both HOST and the contractual language that established "the project in question" absolutely bar acknowledgement of its existence. Further, the judge said that because the "submitters of the request" could not even establish the existence of "the persons they claim to represent," the very substance of their request is questionable and "the grounds for it are ephemeral."

Outside the court room, Koehler and McConnell expressed frustration at the judge's decision. "For god's sake," Koehler said, "the government has admitted that RSH exists. I know personally that it exists. Our request rests on solid ground, as

Judge Rosenthal's decision does not." A disconsolate McConnell added, "When the government pronounces that something does not exist, it is very difficult to proceed in court. We will have to carefully consider our next steps."

———————

"It's hot out here," Mag said. "You really think they're listening in the apartment?"

"It's easy for them to do it, so we should assume they do," Herman said.

"What difference does it make if they do?" Drew asked. "They say everything we say is fiction anyway."

"And they could be listening here," Mag said.

"They could," Saleem said, "But it's much less likely. Everyone's phone is in the cars, right?" The meeting at the picnic table in the middle of a city park had been his idea, though with six feet in height and a fifty-four-inch girth, he obviously suffered in the heat more than anyone else. His clothes were already half-drenched, and he panted almost like a dog. "Lieutenant?"

Herman said, "I can't find anybody. I can't find the fifteen, I can't find Giles, I can't find Boris or the other three corpses, and the bag of body parts from that church is missing from the Vegas freezer. So I risked my job being anywhere near you folks to tell you I've got nothing. Even less than I had before, actually."

For several minutes, they were quiet.

"So what's our strategy?" Drew said.

Saleem took a long, loud breath in, and a longer, louder one out. Sweat dripped off his nose and chin.

Nobody spoke.

"What do you think?" Drew asked Marjorie, across the table.

Marjorie did not respond.

"Marjorie?" Drew said.

She did not respond.

He put his hand on the spot on the table where her eyes seemed to fall. "What should we do next?"

Still no response.

"Marjorie. You okay? Marjorie?"

68

Who cares what they see?" Colin said.

"I do," LaTasha said.

They spoke in a whisper, close to each other but not touching.

"They know we," Colin said.

LaTasha nodded and smiled. She cupped her hands around her face and mouthed, "I love you."

Colin grinned.

They stood smiling at each other until LaTasha broke away and sat, with exaggerated demureness, on one of the new toy beds. Colin walked across the room and sat on the floor. Across the sparsely crowded room they gazed at each other.

————

Elmer was finishing his shower in a metal enclosure sized for scalies. He turned a small valve to stop the water, which was uniformly warm if not hot. He dried inside the stall, dressed in the small anteroom attached to it, emerged into the fluorescent-lit cell, and turned to see Gerald, leaning against the outside of the stall, smiling.

"We can't go on meeting like this," Elmer said.

"People will talk," Gerald said.

They both laughed before they went their separate ways in the cell.

————

"Young love," Mahesh said to Phuong, who nodded and smiled. They were sharing a toy couch.

Morgana, who was on a nearby chair, said, "At least they have that."

Sher, sprawled on the floor said, "Nice that somebody figured out that they don't have to treat us like Al Qaeda."

Across the cell, Jerome was poking at a tablet computer that was as tall as he was, propped on an easel. "Who wants a movie?" he said.

From another corner, Roberto called, "What are the options?"

"There are two. Hoosiers, or Hoosiers."

"Crap," Colin said.

"Think the white kids will win again?" Morgana said.

"Maybe this time Norman and Myra will really get it on," Gerald said.

"We can hope," Sher said.

————

Nobody was really interested in the movie, but they watched, or talked in front of the tablet, because there was nothing else to do. Couples took it as a chance to lean against each other. They took a break at mid-day when guards brought lunch, which was slightly improved, with some spice and a stack of scaly-sized plates.

Soon after lunch the cell door was opened and a large voice ordered them to "proceed through the doorway, please."

The scalies looked at each other. Families hugged, groups of families hugged, couples embraced.

Sher said, "Barry."

373

They filed through the doorway into a cage in the big-sized corridor, but the cage had both ends removed, and was the first in a series of similar ones, end-to-end, forming a steel mesh scaly-sized hallway within the hallway. On either side of them there was a single big guard. "Proceed down the hallway," the big voice said, and they did, turning right when the cages forced them that way, and then they stopped, awed by the sight before them, which was nothing more than an open door exposing blue sky, sunlight, and a patch of green grass.

"You'll have an hour out here," the big voice said.

The scalies walked slowly into an interior courtyard with grass, shrubbery, flowers, two wide trees, and a small decorative fountain. On all four sides were walls featuring closed windows and doors. At each corner a big guard sat on a chair.

Cheng approached one of the guards. "What is this?"

"Officers' outdoor lounge, sir."

"*Sir?*"

"Yes, sir."

"Colonel Nguyen's doing?"

The guard shrugged. "He runs the place, sir."

The sun was warm. The grass was soft. The shade under the trees was pleasantly cool. The manicured flower beds were lovely and fragrant. The water sound was soothing. The scalies laughed like small children let loose in a park. They strolled across the lawn and among the flowers. Couples held hands. All of them looked at the sky that days ago had ceased to exist for them. They sprawled on the grass, took off their shoes, and lay on their backs.

Sher, seeing Elmer and Gerald next to each other, partially in the tree shade, said, "Eight eyes watching us, folks." She looked up to the second and third stories and added, "At least."

"We demand sunscreen!" Gerald yelled.

Even the guards laughed.

69

4&k3L)(n was angry with himself. He should have seen the catastrophe coming. The signs were there. He knew the players, their histories, recent events, and he should have known, in broad strokes at least, what would happen. That he had actually believed that playing with the data from one drone would accomplish anything was ridiculous. Stupid. Unworthy of him. Artistically speaking, a flop.

The artistic structure now called for a dramatic build to the decisive battle, a climactic scene followed by a resolution, for which the artist must decide whether to buttress the audience's hopes that the good will out, or to caution them that frequently it does not. But 4&k3L)(n gloomily had to admit to himself that his control of events was dubious at best and that he had no more time to observe what would happen if he nudged, opened some doors, closed others, directed the flow. The crisis was here. The fools might continue to kill each other, but the artist disliked disappearances. What was art if characters could be arbitrarily pulled from the scene and the stage went dark?

Emails, spreadsheets, PowerPoints, all this *stuff* lying around for the taking by the skilled artist. Add some spice, take in some here, let out a little there, skim off the fat, add a detail or a flourish, stir the pot, bring to a boil, mix the metaphors, decant the liquid, divvy into smaller piles, repeat and replicate, and finally plop the portions down on websites, oh so many hungry websites yearning to be fed! *Contact us*, the websites said, or maybe, even better, break and enter and leave the goodies on the conference table! Good might not out, but maybe a cosmic truth would!

70

Polling Shows Anti-Scaly Sentiments
Washington Post, September 16, 20__
By Coraghessan Horowitz

Public polling by the Post and the Center for The Study of
Public Responsiveness at Romanov College indicates that the
public overwhelmingly believes that the so-called "scalies"
are the products of science gone awry and that any of them
loose in America should be rounded up and destroyed.
Seventy-four percent of respondents believe that scalies pose
a threat to American society while only 16 percent believe
they might be beneficial. Seventy-two percent said they
thought scalies should all be killed, compared to only 14
percent saying they should be controlled but protected.

Additionally, nearly 80 percent believe that any project
employee found to have aided in scalies' escape from their
project site should be severely punished.

While only a small handful of Americans claim to have seen
scalies, that number is growing. A large majority of
respondents expressed "fear" or "extreme fear" of scalies,
while a somewhat smaller majority alleged to have witnessed
scalies engaged in criminal activity . . .

————

Scaly Project Director Defends Work, Accuses Security Officer
New York Times, September 21, 20__
By Issachar Chu

In an exclusive interview with the Times, Dr. Barry Hagenstopple, Director of the Reduced Scale Humans Project, defended his work and accused his former head of security of "exposing classified information, releasing laboratory subjects, and nearly destroying the project."

Dr. Hagenstopple asserted that the RSH Project was "essential for the preservation of the human race" but declined to give specifics, citing security concerns. He said that RSH—he dismissed the common moniker "scalies" as "a frankly stupid oversimplification"—posed little or no danger to society at large. He said, "Members of the public should immediately report sightings of RSH to law-enforcement," adding that he would soon be sending "guidance to first-responders about how best to apprehend RSH without injuring them." He further said that "RSH pose absolutely no threat to society at large, although, of course, as in any group, there might be problematic individuals."

When asked if RSH were, as the project name implies, humans distinguished only by their smallness, Dr. Hagenstopple stopped short of full agreement, describing them as "work in progress—and unfortunately that progress has been imperiled by the behavior of one man," a reference to Mr. Giles.

Of Mr. Giles, Dr. Hagenstopple said, "I trusted Sam, thought of him as one of the best staffers I'd ever had. He was practically a son to me. But he went off the rails in a totally irresponsible and reckless way that endangered decades of painstaking research, and I intend to see that he pays for it."

Dr. Hagenstopple insisted that the secrecy surrounding the RSHP was appropriate. "The public," he said, "sometimes needs to be protected from knowledge that might hurt them." He declined to elaborate . . .

———————

New Leaked Documents Should Change Minds About RSH
Pokeprysnoop.com, October 1, 20__
By Bradley Brownwell

Pokeprysnoop has received a trove of thousands of documents from the Reduced Scale Humans Project that seems to thoroughly debunk most of the prevailing views of the project. Although the source of the documents is anonymous, PPS has verified their authenticity.

The mainstream media, echoing public opinion polls, generally deride the project as a hare-brained scheme, cooked up by crazed scientists running amok in the Defense Department. A loud chorus of mainstream pundits calls for shutting the project down totally and destroying whatever it produced—that being, of course, the Reduced Scale Humans commonly called scalies. Accusatory fingers almost universally point to Samuel Giles, the former project security chief, as the culprit in letting the scalies out. The project's director, Barry Hagenstopple, is the object of both admiration and scorn, the former for his "genius" as the prime mover of the project, and the latter for letting it go on in the first place.

I have no opinion about the value of the project or how "essential"—Hagenstopple's word—it is for survival of the human species. I'll leave that to others.

What I can say is that scalies are not droids or monkeys. They are human. I can say that because that's what these documents tell us, in the words of project participants from Hagenstopple on down. Countless emails and planning documents refer to scalies as "human." They are just like everyone else in everything from how they procreate, how they grow from infants to adults, how they grow old and die. They eat the same foods and are subject to the same diseases, and they have the same yearnings for independence.

If that view is true—and these documents support it—then there is no moral or legal justification for exterminating scalies. On the contrary, they would have the same rights as everyone else. In particular, there can be no argument about their American citizenship because generations of them have been born and raised inside the United States.

The documents also show that the accusations against Giles are, to say the least, misguided. Numerous emails show that he tried repeatedly to warn Hagenstopple that his practices were, far from preventing scalies from escaping, giving them even more reasons for trying to do so.

But there is an even darker side to all this, which should surprise nobody. Over the years, when the pressures of confinement became too much, scalies would find ways to leave, some acting more boldly than others. Oppressive regimes, faced with such defiance, have always resorted to violence—i.e., killing the worst troublemakers as examples to everyone else. And, as the documents show, that is exactly what Hagenstopple did . . .

———

Released Documents Change Opinions on RSH
Los Angeles Times, October 5, 20__
By Carmen Keo

The release of documents from the Reduced Scale Humans Project, reported by the Times and other publications, appears to have radically changed perceptions about the project and the so-called "scalies" it produced.

Just two weeks ago, almost all opinion polls showed the overwhelming majority of the public favoring total eradication of scalies. Now, opinions have flipped, with polls showing that most people agree that scalies are human and worthy of protection. There even appears to be broad acknowledgement that scalies' smallness might be useful in the miniaturization of electronics and medical devices . . .

––––––––––––

Judge Frees Giles
National Tribune-Ombudsman, October 13, 20__
By Gwendolyn Baghdadi

Federal Judge Guadalupe Lieu today ordered a bail hearing for Samuel Giles, who had been held under terms of the HOST Act without charge or legal representation in a secret location. The judge said that government lawyers had failed to show that the circumstances of the case rose to the levels required for application of the HOST Act.

Judge Lieu's ruling comes in the wake of her previous ruling ordering that captured scalies be moved from a maximum security facility to their homes in the scaly project, with the added proviso that they were be freed as soon as the government could put in place measures for their physical protection.

The court room atmosphere became tense as Judge Lieu lectured government lawyers on what she called the government's "high-handed treatment" of both Giles and the scalies . . .

––––––––––

The Whitley Huang Show
October 14, 20__

Well, folks, we don't know what to believe, do we? In the last couple weeks we've been told that there are these things called *scalies*, and then we were told that they don't exist, and then we were told that they *do*, but they aren't human, and now we're told that they *do* exist, they *are* human, and the persons who created them then turned around and killed them. But they didn't kill all of them, no sir, no ma'am, because these *documents*—and I use the word *documents* because everybody else is, though who knows what in the world they really are—also say that they've been *escaping*, wriggling out of that *project*, like puppies climbing out of a box, and who knows how many of them are out there.

I tell you, folks, I'm scared, and you should be too. We don't know anything about these scalies. There are people who will tell you they're just like us, that they even watch the same shows we watch, but we don't know *who*, or, really, *what* they are. Might they carry disease? Might they be associated with *terrorists*? So, some mad scientist creates them, like some new microorganism in a petri dish, and now they're scurrying around in our America, maybe *in our homes*, and they've been cooped up for so long, and maybe they're bitter about that, so who knows what they might do? And folks, they do have firearms.

Now some nutcases might argue that, sure they have firearms, why not? The rest of us have them. Well, folks, *the rest of us* are *us*, and those *scalies* are not part of *us*, they are not citizens, they are scientifically created *creatures* and as far as I'm concerned they have *no* rights. *None*.

The guys who created them should get them under control. Now. If that means killing some of them, fine. The people who leaked the classified information should be locked up. And if I see one of those little monsters wandering around *my* home, or *my* neighborhood, or, for that matter, anywhere in *my* America, I'm going to stomp him, or her, and *then* I'll call the authorities.

383

————

President Says Scalies are Citizens
National Public Radio
November 5, 20__
By Alemnesh Tudor

At a hastily organized news conference focused on the rapidly changing RSH situation, the President today declared that reduced-scale humans are citizens. In prepared remarks he said that "scalies are human beings." He went on to say, "Using the awesome power of genetics, scientists created a new race. This new race is smaller than our other races, but scalies look like us, act like us, talk like us, think like us, and share the same yearnings as the rest of us. I've consulted with Attorney General Geoffrey Gozalian, the Office of Legal Counsel, and Health and Human Services Secretary Akra Adornetto, and we have concluded that there is no legal or other justification for not treating scalies as full-fledged citizens."

The President added that he has ordered Secretary Adornetto to immediately begin plans for creating new reduced-scale living areas beyond the city built for them in the RSH project.

In response to questions, the President said that he and Ms. Adornetto were searching for new leadership for the RSH Project. In appearing to skirt questions about whether the Project had "run amok," he said that there "may have been some irregularities," but that he would leave the answers to the newly created RSH Commission that he announced last Thursday.

He refused comment on the newly formed investigatory committees in both the House and Senate, and he said "absolutely not," to a question about whether a special prosecutor should be appointed, although he left open the question of whether the RSH Commission would have subpoena power.

In concluding remarks, the President said, "Let's face it. These are people. Justice demands that they have the same rights as anyone else. Though they arrived in a different manner than other groups, like those other groups, I believe they will enrich and enhance . . .

71

The fourteen scalies met Marjorie in a conference room of her old law firm in Projectville.

Instead of sneaking out through a ventilation duct or under a fence, they had driven their own cars in single file through a newly constructed interchange connecting the two towns. At a gate that was no more than an observation post with a guard as traffic cop, they stopped, as planned, so they could fall in behind a black Homeland Security SUV. Another SUV trailed them, and security motorcycles were on either side. The odd convoy of big and little cars moved slowly through the bigs' town, stopping frequently at intersections.

In the scaly cars there were many flip comments: *Hey, that's where we were that night when . . . Mom, you mean you and Dad were there? We were there . . . Oh, yeah, that's the place where Arnie almost got run over . . . he was drunk . . . we were all drunk . . . I can't believe the bigs didn't see us . . . they* did *see us . . . they just didn't believe it . . . how dumb could they be? . . . now, honey, they didn't know . . . they didn't* want *to know . . .*

After several blocks they had begun to notice the bigs lining the streets. *Look at them . . . they look glad to see us . . . they're waving . . . what is this, a parade? . . . that guy, I think he's the one I saw that time . . .*

Stopped at an intersection, sitting beside Cheng in the lead scaly car, Sher grinned at him and rolled down her window, ignoring his protests that they had agreed to keep them up. "Stop being chief, Cheng," she said, and she waved out the window and yelled, "Hey, folks, how are you doing?" A clump of bigs started cheering and applauding, and Sher said,

"Well, shit," and before Cheng could stop her, she was unbuckled and out of the car, and the cheering got louder. Through his headset Cheng could hear a security officer yelling at him.

Just behind, Colin jumped out of the back seat of the Fairchild's car. He grinned and raised his hands as if he'd just made the winning score, and the bigs' cheers grew louder. Grace and Roberto were next, and then down the line of scaly cars everyone, teenagers and adults, were now out in the street. Cheng was the last, as he heard the screaming through his headset: *WHAT THE FUCK THIS IS NOT SAFE THIS IS EXPRESSLY AGAINST WHAT* . . . But the rest of it was drowned out by a unified cheer erupting from the crowd of bigs: "*Sca-LIES! Sca-LIES! Sca-LIES!* . . . "

Gerald sighted Elmer, and they ran to each other and jumped up to bump chests, and then raised their fists and ran around the cars screaming. LaTasha struck a cheerleader pose and was surprised to feel herself leave the ground as Colin grabbed her around the thighs and lifted.

Other scaly couples hugged and waved. The tense motorcycle security men parked their bikes and waved the crowd of bigs back, and the bigs stayed back but did not stop cheering. A big woman reached out to Phuong and for a second they touched fingers and a second later they were both beaming and crying.

Cheng surveyed the scene and laughed.

After more than a half hour they got back in their cars and waved as they proceeded down the street, with the cheers following them.

————

At the office of Marjorie's firm, she and Mag and Drew watched the convoy become a parade and their jaws dropped.

They watched from a fourth story window as security officers met the scalies at the curb and helped them into the firm's Danish mahogany refreshment trays, which had been fitted with small chairs with seat belts, all of which had been Mag's ideas.

"If anything happens to them now," Marjorie said.

"I've briefed these guys," Mag said. "Nothing's gonna happen."

Two security officers carried each of the three trays into the building foyer and the elevators. "How are you guys, doing?" Cheng asked.

"We're not supposed to speak, sir," an officer said.

"Sure," Cheng said, "but you're human like us. And you're law enforcement like me."

"You the chief?"

"Sure."

"Weirdest assignment I've ever had, sir."

———

The scalies now sat in their chairs on the trays on the conference table, with Marjorie on one side of the table and Drew and Mag on the other. Mag had provided water bottles and pastries, appropriately sized, for all of them.

"Well," Marjorie said, "I'm Marjorie Koehler, and it's a pleasure to finally meet my clients." Sher stood and introduced herself and the rest of the group. "I recognize you from pictures, and some of you, from a day that seems to have become history," Marjorie said.

"Did you ever get the coffee stains out?" Colin said.

Everyone laughed.

"Did you?" Marjorie said.

"Badge of honor," Colin said.

"We scared you nearly to death, didn't we," Gerald said.

"She sure as hell scared me," Elmer said.

"I felt bad for you," LaTasha said. "After. At the time I was in shock."

"You guys are like rock stars," Mag said. "Everybody on earth saw you."

"We'll always have that to remember," Marjorie said. "We should have a party later. These gentlemen are Drew Kristopher and Magdelano Goldfarb, who work for me. Mag does logistics and Drew deals with the press."

"You know, I'm not much older than some of you teenagers," Mag said. "We should party together."

The teenagers laughed. The adults groaned.

"Well," Marjorie said. "Some business." She went on to explain the legalities and answer their questions. The charges against them would be dropped: leaving their "compound" without authorization, theft, destruction of government property, assault on a police officer, and some misdemeanors including whatever legal code sections kept people from surreptitiously hitching rides on semi-trailers. In exchange, the scalies would not press charges against the government for: illegal imprisonment, excessive use of force, and a few others. "No," she said to Cheng's question, "the killing of scalies by project staff is outside this agreement. I made sure of that. In fact, Dr. Hagenstopple's entire case is separate from yours." And to Mahesh's question, "Yes, this agreement applies to all RSH, without restriction. That means scalies—I hope it's okay if I use that word," and it was, "whether they stayed in your town or broke out, and no matter where they are now. It applies to all." The government, she explained, promised to get the word out to all law enforcement, federal, state, and local, that they were to treat scalies as they would other citizens, and to all scalies that if they came forward they would be treated well, and they would no longer "need to steal to stay alive. And, by the way, the government will compensate any merchant who files a reasonable claim of loss by scaly," and at that she smiled and drew a laugh.

Colin sat next to LaTasha, and through Marjorie's briefing, he and LaTasha held hands. As he listened, he split his attention between Marjorie and LaTasha. Each time he turned to LaTasha, her eyes were on him and in them was a stew of pleading and longing and anger.

Marjorie told them that while the citizenship of scalies was settled—"over the continued protests of some loonies"—how they would live was not. Here, Marjorie took a breath and became more serious. "You must understand that this is for your own safety, because there are crazy people out there. We," and she gestured to include herself and her staff, "have special security arrangements ourselves. Actually, we're bigger targets, but you're."

"We understand," Cheng said.

"As long as we're not prisoners," Leah Reynaud said.

"The position I want to press, with your permission," Marjorie said, "is that in exchange for the suffering and loss of liberty you have endured, the government owes you special security. The downside is that with security comes restrictions. You won't be able to travel on your own, or even make travel plans without consulting the security people."

"She's right," Cheng said. "There is no other way."

Nobody objected.

"And how are your homes?" Marjorie asked.

"The way we left them," Sher said. "It's amazing. Nobody touched our houses or our things, our cars, everything's the same."

"If the project does anything wrong to you, please contact me immediately. I'm on top of this."

There was a silence.

"Okay," Marjorie said. "I'll be in touch. You'll get emails about security arrangements, and new developments about where you could move, if you want to."

Mag left the room to summon the security crew.

Colin looked at LaTasha, and now held both her hands. He said her name. LaTasha said, "Okay," but the word held more of permission than acquiescence.

Colin stood and faced Marjorie. "Could I have a moment alone with you, Ms. Koehler? It's—well, it's sort of a legal matter?"

Marjorie hesitated and then said, "Yes, it's okay with me if it's okay with the others."

Nobody spoke.

Roberto and Michael looked at each other with half smiles and shrugged. The look between Morgana and Grace was a bit tenser.

Mag prevailed on the security guys to make two trips.

The scalies buckled themselves in their seats, except for Colin, who walked off the tray onto the tabletop. As LaTasha left with the others, she and Colin exchanged another look.

———

Marjorie sat while Colin stood before her on the table, alone in the room. Marjorie broke the silence. "I hope I didn't scald you," she said.

Colin shook his head. He looked at the tabletop, and then out the window. "Never been up this high," he said. "Nice view."

"I think in your life you'll see nicer ones."

"None nicer than," and Colin stopped speaking.

Marjorie looked at him for a moment and then said, "You have the same handsome, sweet face."

Colin let out a breath and grinned. "Thanks. You—you're still beautiful."

Marjorie felt herself redden and she had to look down. One laugh exploded from her and she covered her mouth with her hand. How could she be embarrassed before this boy?

"I guess something happened besides spilled coffee," she said, and hurried on before Colin could reply. "You know, you—all the scalies—were prisoners, but we were too. And I—I was ready to burst. I was on edge—well, terrified, actually—because I'd caught glimpses of some of you. Scalies, I mean. And you've probably seen the reports of early *scaly sightings*," she said, making a wide-eyed face at the phrase. "People who said they'd seen *little people* were considered crazy. I thought *I* was crazy." She took a breath and looked at Colin. "All that is by way of telling you that in that instant when we, when you and I first saw each other, I was in need of some, I don't know, some resolution or something. You know, you may have heard that old line that's in the magazines—the women's magazines, anyway—how you meet *someone* when you're *ready*? Well, I was ready. And then *bam*, there you were." And suddenly she was crying and saying, "I'm sorry."

Colin had so often wondered if this woman could ever care about him, and now it seemed she could. "But then along came Boris," he said, and immediately regretted it. "I'm sorry. I should not have said that."

"I know. I follow the web. I've seen it. It's okay. You're right."

"I'm sorry about him."

"Yes, and about Howard and Bryce and Marissa, and Gilbert."

They were quiet for another spell.

"I mean, it could never have worked out between us," Colin said.

Marjorie looked at him.

"It's just, you know, the difference in our ages."

And they both burst out laughing for what seemed a very long time.

"LaTasha seems very nice," Marjorie said. "And extremely pretty."

"LaTasha is great, the best," Colin said. "We know we're really young. But right now, she's exactly what I need."

"I think you're what she needs too," Marjorie said, though she had no real idea it.

After another quiet moment, Colin said, "I guess I should go now."

72

Mag had secured a big Unitarian church for the funeral, but after he sent out the press release, he could see that the sanctuary would not be adequate. He phoned the office of a company that arranged outdoor celebrity galas and asked for the head, telling the receptionist, "I need help with the event of the century. Tell her she'll hate herself forever if another company does it." Seven minutes later he told the CEO about the event, and when she asked for more details to create an estimate, he said, "You do this event, you can plaster your name—what is it? CorpGalas?—everywhere you want, on top of every tent, on the back of every waiter and security guard, wherever the TV cameras can see it, as long as it's, you know, tasteful. But that's it. We have no money." She told him her company couldn't work for free, not even for a presidential inauguration or a Super Bowl. He said, "Your compensation will be that you won't be sitting at home watching some other company doing the biggest TV event maybe ever."

And so, after several more of Mag's relentless phone calls and prodding, CorpGalas had set up four enormous pavilions in the park near the site of what was now known as "the scaly gunfight," to shield the attendees from another day of blistering December Los Angeles basin heat. There were two additional tents with football-stadium-sized TVs, and another TV screen in the open, to accommodate overflow. The rest of the park held catering trucks, a security center, a communications hub, and an emergency medical unit. The security in the surrounding streets was similar, though not as restrictive, as it had been the day of the gunfight.

The VIP tables spread across the front of two of the tents gave the feel of an international diplomatic summit. Ambassadors of several countries claiming ethnic DNA connection to one or more of the scalies arrived in limousines. The area seemed flooded with burly men with dark suits, grim faces, and headsets.

The president's staff had wanted him to arrive last, as the guest of honor, even if he wasn't. "So you didn't actually lie to them," Marjorie had said to Mag.

"Nah. They thought they intimidated me, which they actually did, but I just didn't, you know, tell them everything."

"You let them believe."

"Yeah."

"Tell me again why."

"Because, goddamn it, the focus should be on the people who matter."

Marjorie had been unable to disagree.

When the president's party arrived, the platform for the scalies was still empty, as were the chairs for Marjorie and Drew. A distraught presidential staffer was caught on camera whispering up into the ear of the tall, lanky chief executive, who could be seen fighting back an angry scowl before he solemnly strode through the VIP crowd where he paused to shake many hands, his face now set in friendly grief, on his way to the raised platform assigned to his group. Trailing him were the first lady, the vice president and her husband, the Secretaries of Health and Human Services and Homeland Security, and the Director of National Intelligence.

Saleem McConnell, Herman Winston, and Sam Giles were seated at the front row of a small section of semi-VIP bleachers behind the tables. With them, at Herman's invitation, out of uniform because of his suspension, was Officer L. McBride. At the other end of their row was Barry Hagenstopple, released on bail, and his attorney. Security surrounded them all.

(Jennifer Giles, now barely speaking to Sam, was at home watching TV with Sandra and Kirk.)

Mag, wearing a headset as he watched a TV monitor, gave the signal to one of his crew of fourteen. ("Who are *these* guys?" Marjorie had asked him. "My friends," he said. "Don't worry about it, they're okay.") The sound of one muffled drum beating a slow cadence rose from a distance and the crowd slowly silenced. The press, held back by security, pointed their cameras in the sound's general direction.

First came Sydney and seven other current or former Projectville security guards, in uniform, bearing Boris Feldman. ("And how did you find *them*?" Marjorie had demanded. "Internet. Not one of them hesitated," Mag said.) Trailing the coffin were Marjorie and Drew. The bearers took their burden up a short set of steps to a platform with a bier and only two seats. The guards took standing positions, at parade rest, on the ground below.

Scalies followed.

The bearers for Howard Sturges were Cheng Schmitz, Michael Cruz, Jerome Thurman, and Mahesh Reynaud.

Bearing Bryce were Colin Fairchild, Gerald Reynaud, Elmer Cruz, Roberto Fairchild, and Phuong Cruz.

Bearing the petite body of Marissa were Leah Reynaud, Grace Fairchild, and LaTasha and Morgana Thurman.

Last was Sher Statie carrying a small brass urn with "Gilbert Martin" engraved on it.

As the drummer continued her cadence from beside the platform reserved for scalies, the silent crowd, including the presidential party, stood on toes and craned necks, to see the procession. The scalies, all dressed, by their own agreement, in their now cleaned and well-pressed GI Joe jumpsuits, grimly carried their tiny coffins down the center aisle. There were gasps and cries from the crowd, nearly all of whom had never seen a scaly except on TV. The scaly party struggled a bit up the stairs and ramps designed for them, to the platform with three biers and fourteen seats.

At a word from Mag into Drew's earpiece, Drew rose from his seat, walked down stairs from his platform and up to a smaller platform with a podium and a microphone.

He stood for a moment and looked at the crowd. "Good afternoon," he said. "I'm Drew Kristopher. The scalies you see to my left"—and he named them all—"along with their attorney, Marjorie Koehler, to my right, have asked me to preside today." He paused, and when he resumed, he spoke in a voice calm and low. "Today, we are celebrating four lives. One of them was Boris Feldman, who, while working as a security officer at the Reduced Scale Humans Project, came to see a higher good than what he had sworn to when he took his job. He saw humanity, on a reduced scale physically, but humanity nonetheless, and on an enormous scale morally. And he saw inhumanity. And unlike many of us, he had the courage to do something about it. He was not deterred by fine print on contracts or by the bullying of his bosses and their crude attempts at indoctrination, or their exhortations to see no evil even when it was right before their eyes.

"Before he came to the RSH Project, Boris had been a police officer, sworn and dedicated to fighting crime and protecting citizens. He was a good, hard-working cop, but as the budgets got smaller and the cameras and activity detectors started replacing people, he got laid off. He needed a job, and the RSHP was recruiting. He didn't like what they told him about the job, and he liked less what they wouldn't tell him. He disliked the threats about what would happen to him and his fellow trainees should they depart in any way from any rule. He disliked most of all the fact that he would be, like all the full-sized project employees, a prisoner, free—or sort of free—only for occasional furloughs. But the pay and benefits were beyond anything he had ever hoped for, and, a man without a family, he agreed to the terms, and took the job."

Drew's voice began to rise. "But Boris saw things. Boris knew things that he could not help but know. And he started to wonder about that oath he'd sworn. Did it supersede everything? Did it mean ignoring or forgiving everything? Did it have precedence over his conscience?

"Boris doubted. And then he met Marjorie Koehler, and her courage combined with his, and his doubts met her passion, and together they embarked on a mission to find those human beings—those *scaly* human beings—in that photo that we've all seen."

Drew dropped his voice again, as he'd planned, into a tone of mourning, but the reality exceeded what he had directed himself to do. "And at that moment when Boris and Marjorie found them, those scaly humans, and he saw them in danger, he did not doubt. He did not hesitate. His courage and his sense of rightness took charge," and Drew's voice rang loudly as he said, "and Boris did what a good police officer, what a good security man, what a good human being would do, and when he saw those scaly humans in danger his decision was instantaneous, and he *saved them, by throwing his own body between them and harm*, and in the act, gave his life for theirs."

As Drew paused, Marjorie, who had seen Drew's speech even before he had memorized it, clenched her hands together in a vain attempt to stop her tears.

"Boris was a hero. I know, because I was there. I'd never seen a live heroic act before. Boris not only saved the lives of these fourteen human beings to my left. His act, and my privilege to be there and see it, gave meaning to mine. Whatever the courts or the bureaucracy, or the national security people or the pundits or the politicians say, Boris was a hero."

Drew stopped speaking amid total silence from the crowd. When he heard the first rustle and cough, he spoke again. "To speak for the three other human beings who died on that day, and for the one who died the day before, Sher Statie."

Sher rose from her seat among her fellow scalies and walked down the stairs and the ramp, and up another set of scaly-sized stairs to the platform. Once on the platform—all of this per Mag's plan, in full view of the audience—she sat in a chair mounted on a two-foot square tile of polished mahogany. Drew dropped to one knee, grasped the specially made brass handles attached to the wood tile, and slowly lifted it to the top of the podium, just as they had rehearsed. Sher rose from the chair and walked to the microphone, which Drew lowered for her before he walked off to re-join Marjorie.

Marjorie clutched Drew's hand, leaned into him, and whispered, "I used him."

Startled, Drew looked at her.

"Boris. I used him. For me, sex, protection and obsession. For him, love, bravery and sacrifice."

"Hush," Drew said.

"I don't want to use you."

Drew looked at her, speechless, and then Sher began to speak.

"I'm Sher Statie," she said, as if introducing herself to a luncheon of a civic club. The crowd alternately gazed in wonder at the doll-sized woman standing not *at*, but *on*, the podium, speaking without notes or teleprompter, and at her beautifully strong face on the big TV screens.

"I am, or was, city manager in our little RSH town. You may have seen my name in some recent news stories, along with the names of my dear friends to my left. That big man—well, big for us—is Cheng Schmitz, who was our police chief. And, yes, he and I are lovers."

Mag, in the production trailer, held on Sher's adoring smile and then cut to Cheng's big grin, split the screen to show both for five seconds, and then switched back to Sher alone.

"We lived in a town not much different from many of yours. We had schools and theaters and nice restaurants. We had money and some of the same stores to spend it in that you have. We were comfortable. For generations.

"Like Boris and his colleagues and all the other full-sized workers that made our town run, we were also prisoners.

"But we knew about *you*," she said, gesturing to take in the crowd with her arms. "We saw your TV and your movies, and your sporting events. At times we could overlook just how different we were from you, but we knew about that difference too. And how did we know? Because we snuck out. We saw you. Sometimes, one or two of you would see us, but nobody would believe their stories. Usually, those witnesses came to disbelieve themselves."

Sher sighed. "But we knew there was a big world out there, and we knew we could never enjoy it. Unlike even Boris—wonderful, brave, life-saving Boris—we had no furloughs. What we had were tiny illegal excursions, fleeting peeks and glimpses, usually when we were teenagers because, as everybody knows, sneaking around and breaking rules are what teenagers do."

The crowd laughed and Mag cut to them so they could see themselves laughing. The people with faces on screen waved. The president forced a smile.

"But then, folks, we got punished. Some of those teenagers died. Some outside, and some—by mysterious, unnamed, incurable diseases—inside, after returning from some mischievous expedition into your big world. Parents knew the risks, because the parents had been teenagers once, and they had gone out there, and they had seen friends die.

"Now, Chief Cheng and I were lovers, but not parents. But we knew—well, everybody knew, but *we* knew because we had it from the horse's mouth. Because Cheng was the police chief and I was the city manager, we were the contacts. The Project Director or one of his staff would tell us that something bad would need to happen to one of us. I think that you can tell that we're not stupid. We knew what that meant."

Sher paused and when she resumed, her delivery went from matter-of-fact to angry. "So, after generations of grieving parents and confused kids, enough was enough. I won't go into all the details now, but one day we couldn't stand it anymore, and *a whole lot of us just busted out!*"

And now, suddenly, Sher beamed. "And for a while, it was *glorious!* We ran, we hitched rides on trucks, we stole your food, we stole your doll furniture and clothing. Yes, I admit it, we stole. We were terrified, we were goofy, and *by god we were free!*

"But four of us didn't make it. Gilbert Martin, Howard Sturges, Bryce Karakawa, and his mother, Marissa Karakawa."

As Sher paused, Mag cut to the audience watching her, and back to her.

"I don't blame the people who shot them," Sher said sadly. "They were doing their jobs and I suppose they were scared. We knew we scared you. This is not a time for blame."

Officer McBride grimaced.

"Who were they, those four now dead scalies? In our town, Cheng and I were acquainted with all the other folks you see to my left, but we didn't get to really know them until we broke out.

"We did not know Gilbert Martin. He was not with our group until the day before we were caught. But purely by accident, he and his daughter, Astrid, found each other, and in that meeting, were discovered by some of your police officers. Astrid took her father to us, and we knew then we had to leave our encampment, which had become home to us. But as we left, we were seen, and Gilbert, acting bravely, like Boris without thought for himself, drew attention away from us. In giving us the chance to escape, Gilbert died by one of your officers' shotguns. Which is why he has only an urn instead of a coffin."

As Sher's voice grew low and somber, Mag ordered her camera closer.

"We salute you, Gilbert," Sher said. And then, looking directly at the camera, said, "And Astrid, honey, I know you are somewhere, watching. Contact us. You will be protected."

Smiling a little, Sher pressed on. "Howard Sturges, Cheng knew. Long, lean, lonely Howard. He fixed cars—yes, we do have cars, pretty much like yours. He was a good mechanic. Most people who knew him would describe him with words like crabby, crotchety. For Cheng and me, he was a pain in the ass, because he didn't stop his outside excursions when he grew out of adolescence. He kept on, always by himself. We worried that he would cause trouble.

"But at the moment of our break-out, because Howard had that outside experience, he became our Moses. He led us out of bondage, into the wilderness. He taught us how to hitch those rides, how to steal that food, how to make camp, how to avoid detection. And then, like Moses, when we got to the promised land—I don't know if it's really promised or not, but the story fits—he died. For us, Howard was a great man, as brave as we've ever seen.

"The Karakawas were just us. Just folks. A Single mother and her adored son. Bryce was a cool teenager, in the best sense. The other kids looked up to him. Smart, a good athlete, big, and handsome. A born leader, I think. He walked into his death because, I think, he didn't really believe that anybody would harm him.

"And his mother, trying desperately to save her beautiful son, pierced by the same bullet. Maybe, this way is better. She won't spend a long life grieving.

"We're really like you, my friends. We don't always get along. We argue, we bicker. We love. I hope the awful tragedy of these deaths will allow us to do it in the light."

Sher looked at Drew and nodded, and returned to her chair. Drew returned to the podium, lifted her down—again on one knee, the gesture at once practical, gallant, and respectful—and she joined her fellow scalies, who, one by one, embraced her, Cheng last and longest. Mag made sure everyone saw every detail up close.

Drew stood silently until the scalies settled in their chairs. Mag spoke into his headset, and one of his crew raised a hammer and struck the bell—a big, brass one, mounted on a plain wooden frame, obviously an antique ("Where the hell did you get *that*?" Marjorie had yelled. "Stop worrying," Mag had said)—*bong*, pause, *bong*, pause, *bong*, pause, *bong*, pause, *bong*.

"Perchance," Drew began, "he for whom this bell tolls may be so ill, as that he knows not it tolls for him; and perchance I may think myself so much better than I am, as that they who are about me, and see my state, may have caused it to toll for me, and I know not that."

The words of Donne's meditation on death, as Drew had edited them, filled Drew and flowed from him, for once not as generalities to stir emotions the mourners could not muster for a despicable deceased, but for Drew's new friends, for the moment, and for himself. He was telling them, *this is what I feel. It me hurts but it cleanses. Maybe it will for you.*

"*All that happens to humanity belongs to all. When a child is born, that concerns me; for that child is thereby connected to that body which is my head too, and ingrafted into that body whereof I am*

403

a member. And when a person dies anywhere, that action concerns me: all humankind is of one author, and is one volume . . ."

(A man seated behind Barry Hagenstopple would later shake his head as he told a friend, "At that point, I heard this guy mumbling to himself. 'It's *me*. I am the author of *these people*.' And then he swore.")

When Drew reached the part about the bells, he allowed his voice to soar, and his own tears to fall: *"Who bends not his ear to any bell which upon any occasion rings? But who can remove it from that bell which is passing a piece of herself out of this world?"* He paused, and from among the rapt audience came a small sob, and Mag, on instinct, told his number three camera to focus on the scalies and *bingo*: he split the screen between Drew and a weeping Phuong Cruz. The audience heard, and saw, on the big screens. From among the crowd of bigs another sob erupted, and then another, female, male, until the sound of crying became background. Mag clicked from one view of crying to another, across the crowd of bigs where tissues blossomed. Drew held his pause. Mag filled the screen with a shot of the row of scalies, hands clasped to one another, all shedding tears, bowing their heads but lifting them again as Drew resumed speaking. Mag himself was flowing through the moment, in a kind of exhilaration he had never before known (his own grief would surface afterwards, in a group embrace with Marjorie and Drew).

Drew continued, exhorting: *"No person is an island, entire of itself; every man is a piece of the continent, a part of the main. If a clod be washed away by the sea, the world is less . . . any woman's death diminishes me, because I am involved in all humankind . . ."*

The scalies and Marjorie wept for their dead.

Sam Giles wept for these dead and the other scalies in whose deaths he had shared. He wept for his estranged family. He wept for his own life wasted and resolved to devote the rest of it to pay for what he had done. He gave up any effort to stifle the crying and he shook violently, and his sobs turned to a spastic hiccupping. The shaking spread to his entire body. He found enough presence of mind to rise from his seat and stumble over the feet of Saleem McConnell and Herman Winston, to stagger through an aisle (Mag saw a camera view of him, but decided against cutting to it) to the intense sunlight outside the canopy and to a portable toilet, mercifully empty, where his cramps gave way to a hot splattering flow that contained (he noticed) a fair amount of blood.

"*. . . never send to know for whom the bell tolls: it tolls for thee.*"

Herman Winston did not cry. Instead, he allowed himself to feel quiet, sickly sadness over human foolishness and evil and the premature deaths they brought, a deep depression that cops spent careers covering with cynicism.

Officer McBride wondered about his impulse on that gunfight day. Was it right? Was it wrong but excusable? Would he ever know?

Barry Hagenstopple seethed at the soft-hearted, soft-headed naivety of these fools who could not see that in a grand effort to save the human race there must be casualties. Regrettable, certainly, but necessary nonetheless.

The crowd cried because some among them cried, and not crying became impossible as impulse and general sympathy carried them away.

Drew finished, in sorrow: "*. . . this bell, that tells me of her affliction . . . applies . . . to me: if by this consideration of another's danger I take mine own into contemplation, and so secure myself, by making my recourse to creation, which is our only security.*"

For a long moment there was complete silence. The applause began from one corner of the pavilion, and then it quickly swept the area, until the entire crowd rose.

Mag cut to crowd shots and stayed with them until he saw that Drew had gathered himself and was thanking everyone for attending (the burials would be private).

405

The president stopped stewing over the mess he faced and the political attacks from every direction, and started thinking out his strategy.

Astrid, who had watched the whole while, unseen under the president's chair (she had not known it was his chair), in her green leafy camouflage that was no longer camouflage but just the way she always dressed, slipped away, crying silently for her mother (who, oblivious to all around her, was still fighting her demons of drugs and mental illness in a Projectville institution), her father who had tried to love her and had saved her, for Bryce who had loved her, for Marissa who had mothered her, for Boris who had saved them, and for Howard who had taught her how to come and go unnoticed.

73

From Colin's Journal

I can't believe we got our phones back. It was that Colonel Nguyen, I'm pretty sure. There was a hand-written note, from some big, saying that nobody had gotten the contents. It had to be him. We can't be sure, but the SIMs have the same change that Gerald did to them to protect them. Those government guys could probably still get the stuff and we'd never know, but it's still really cool that we have them.

So here I am writing in my journal again. Do I care if somebody else saw it? I don't think so. I'm ready to shout the whole thing from a rooftop, or put it on the web, whatever. I just got through reading the whole thing myself, and thinking about who I was, who we all were. We're the same now but we're different.

So we're going back home, but not for long. The families are all going to that new development they're building for us near San Diego. For the kids, it seems like every university wants us. Our schools were pretty good back home, I guess. But they're all talking about how they want to help us get the best education we can and how they will learn from us too. It's going to be weird, though, sitting in some class of mostly bigs. I think we'll get used to each other though.

I guess now I'm over Marjorie. I feel like I was an idiot about her. Really stupid. It embarrasses me to think about it. I'm not sure I'm totally over her. She said if I wanted to study law she would help me, and she is really nice and friendly, but I still feel weird about seeing her again. I don't know if I can. I guess it's like having a crush on a movie star, though. Should disappear over time.

The hard thing is that I'm going to the U of Chicago and LaTasha's going to Berkeley. My mom tells me we're young and that a lot will happen to us. We can't know what will happen. And thinking back over the last few months, man, is that ever true! We leave in a few weeks but it seems like I already miss her. We know we can do video chats and all, but still. LaTasha is really the best and I worry about her and the scaly guys at Berkeley.

But the stuff Chicago is sending me looks so cool! Scalies will be in a new part of an old dormitory, and we'll share the cafeteria, and they already made some really cool ebooks available to us. I can't help being excited.

We're free, it seems like. We'll always have to worry about the bigs. I think they'll always be a little scary to us. Without protection, any one of them could stomp us. By accident or on purpose.

But we are free.

74

The exact terms of the settlement of *RSH v. RSH Project* remain secret to this day, but they were said to have resulted in one of the largest per-participant awards ever. Common press rumors had Marjorie's share in eight figures, but she wouldn't receive it for more than a year.

In the days following the funeral, Marjorie and Drew tried to hole up in his apartment, but quiet withdrawal from the spotlight, even temporarily, soon became impossible. Marjorie remained the lead scaly attorney, contributing her work to the cases of other scaly groups around the country. Drew's job in press relations demanded almost all of his time, and Mag continued doing logistics and planning.

As the death threats accelerated, the Los Angeles Police Department, backed up by Saleem McConnell, Herman Winston, and Rondeau—the latter two having moved to Los Angeles and joined Marjorie's firm as investigators—advised moving to a secure building. After Sher was able to convince a reluctant Marjorie to accept their fee payments, there was enough money for Marjorie, Drew, and Mag to rent secure apartments in the same building (Marjorie and Drew in one, Mag alone in another).

Still, the continuing housing costs would have been a problem without the numerous TV interviews and the book and movie deals that Mag orchestrated, until Drew, with Marjorie's blessing, began accepting the movie acting deals that started within months of the funeral, and culminated in a starring role as a superhero.

Mag would later become chief operating officer of CorpGalas (where the CEO gladly deferred to him on all substantial decisions), which he began expanding into one of the premiere event-planning and public-relations consultancies in the world. After his first year, he took the company public. Its IPO tripled in value after just three hours of trading.

Marjorie's passion remained with helping scalies with their continuing legal problems, but soon she would become an advocate for all individuals and groups who, as she told a TV interviewer, "had suffered genuine injustices and faced enormous odds against righting them. I guess I want to help the little guy—and not just scalies." In coming years, she would work with Saleem McConnell on many civil rights cases, and would hire several young lawyers as staff.

At no charge, Mag would arrange semi-annual vacation retreats for Marjorie and Drew where nobody could find them.

———

Samuel and Jennifer Giles' divorce became final within eight months of the funeral, with Jennifer getting full custody of Kirk and Sandra. Jennifer also legally changed hers and the children's last name to Brookens. She would have gone back to her maiden name, but she thought that might have been one change too many for the children.

Sam received treatment and medication for ulcerative colitis. After the president pardoned him for the many charges still formally on the books, Sam, in misery and despair, joined a small monastic order in Big Sur, where the other monks found him excessively reclusive even by their standards. When he was not doing his daily chores, he read every religious book of every kind that he could lay hands on. The

410

abbot, fearing for Sam's health, ordered him to sit rather than kneel, and "for heaven's sake stay off your knees, okay?"

Sam spent his daily hours of prayer trying to find a way to forgive himself.

————

Barry Hagenstopple also lived a life of solitude and menial tasks, in a minimum-security prison that he shared with various low-level white-collar criminals. He was allowed to use—well, actually, required to use—a virtual private network, with video and audio, so that he could advise the new director of the project, a former chancellor of a major state university system. The two despised each other, but he understood that any chance of freedom during his lifetime depended on his complete and honest cooperation, and that any deviation from that would result in his transfer to a facility of utter darkness.

————

4&k3l)(n surveyed what had occurred, all the data, documents, photos, audio and video, on all the servers, in what he named, to himself, as "my ethereal domain." He was proud. The spectacle had been entertaining, no? Without his deft shoves, his fertilization of the internet, would not this whole affair have been just another boring tragedy, soon forgotten except in the occasional academic treatise? He had pushed it to heights and pulled it to depths, given it color. A few deaths, yes, but, after all, one lacked *complete* control—and was it not the uncertainty that made it all so much fun?

And now on to the next thing, and no blank page or canvas for him! Forget your *tabula rasa*. This *tabula* ain't *rasa* at all! It's teeming with documents and metadata, all linked to real people! The boyish bureaucrats think they can use the data to control the real people, but all one need do is add a little data here, subtract a little data there, to reveal that boyishly bureaucratic control as an illusion, blowing in the ether! And then the forces of nature and humanity will blossom, and *I, 4&k3l)(n, get to watch!*

————

The Thurman, Fairchild, Cruz, and Reynaud families moved to the new development in San Diego.

After a competitive recruiting process run by Health and Human Services, Morgana became city manager. She supervised the election that resulted in Roberto Fairchild becoming mayor. Roberto soon would harbor thoughts of running for the California State Senate.

Grace Fairchild found work, telecommuting, as a compliance manager for a health insurance company.

Jerome Thurman resumed his accountancy practice, which he expanded to include bigs, whom he served, mostly but not exclusively, via video conference.

Michael Cruz and Mahesh Reynaud, along with several hundred scalies, were hired by a start-up company, with multi-billion dollar backing, to design and implement miniaturized electronics for business, consumers, and defense.

Jacques Brodkepjian brought in a seven-figure starting salary at a telecommunications firm, a position he accepted on condition that he would have his own staff, complete autonomy, and the ability to live and work wherever he pleased.

A scaly doctor reversed Phuong's tubal ligation (required at the project after one child) and she and Michael would soon be expecting another child, which Phuong decided to enjoy at home.

Leah Reynaud, who held a doctorate in comparative literature, was hired by the University of California at San Diego, which wanted her to teach in person, and so arranged her commute. She would stand on a desk and lecture to a large hall, always filled to capacity, and preside over seminars in smaller rooms. The students loved her. She started writing a novel about a love triangle of three scalies who lived among bigs.

Gerald Reynaud would attend Stanford University, where after one semester he would be elected president of the LGBT Student Alliance.

Elmer Cruz went to UCLA, where he became the first scaly to join a fraternity.

Sher Statie and Cheng Schmitz also moved to the San Diego development, but they used some of their award money to have a small cabin built apart from it, secluded by trees. They consulted for Marjorie's firm. Sher appeared occasionally as a commentator on a TV news channel. Cheng became a consultant to law enforcement agencies and made speeches at conferences. Their best days were the ones they spent alone together in their cabin, and after a year they were surprised and delighted when they learned of Sher's pregnancy.

―――――――

Congress Demands Answers on Scaly Funding
Los Angeles Times, January 13, 20__

―――――――

Head of NSA Reveals Chinese Attempt to Hack RSH Genome
New York Times, February 1, 20__

————

President Implores Scalies to Reject the Lure of Large Salaries Abroad
PBS News Hour, March 9, 20__

————

The Whitley Huang Show
June 3, 20__

Well, folks, they are at it again. You know who I mean. The people the world over who envy what we Americans have gained through our own sweat and hard work, who say they hate our freedoms but try to steal from us at the slightest opportunity.

Well, I've got news for them. You cannot have our scalies.

You've heard me talk about scalies before. You know how I felt about them when we first found out they existed. I don't apologize for that. I was right.

But let's face it, they're here to stay. And they give us some advantages. Sometimes being tiny helps, as in electronics manufacturing and surgical procedures.

Which is why those other countries want to take them from us.

What the president needs to do is take any means necessary and possible to prevent spies—who are out there, believe me—from stealing our scalies. He should prohibit scalies from traveling abroad, and Congress should pass a law prohibiting them from even working with foreign governments or companies over the internet.

This is serious, folks. America's future is at stake.

———

Astrid Martin's life was feral. She kept no electronic device. She befriended bigs who fed her, talked to her, and watched her recede into the shrubbery and weeds where she lived. She consented to only one press interview, unrecorded, where she said, "I'm living the only life I can. It's beautiful. People have been very kind to me, and I do not fear anything."

###

Drew Kristopher's Revision of John Donne's Meditation on Death

Perchance he for whom this bell tolls may be so ill, as that he knows not it tolls for him; and perchance I may think myself so much better than I am, as that they who are about me, and see my state, may have caused it to toll for me, and I know not that. ~~The church is Catholic, universal, so are all her actions; all~~ All that ~~she does~~ happens to humanity belongs to all. When ~~she baptizes~~ a child is born, that ~~action~~ concerns me; for that child is thereby connected to that body which is my head too, and ingrafted into that body whereof I am a member. And when ~~she buries a man~~ a person dies, that ~~action~~ concerns me: all humankind is of one author, and is one volume; when one ~~man~~ person dies, one is not torn out of the book, but translated into a better language; and every must be so translated; ~~god~~ the creator employs several translators; some pieces are translated by age, some by sickness, some by war, some by justice; but ~~god's~~ the creator's hand is in every translation, and ~~his~~ that hand shall bind up all our scattered leaves again for that library where every book shall lie open to one another. As therefore the bell that rings to a sermon calls not upon the ~~preacher~~ minister only, but upon the congregation to come, so this bell calls us all; but how much more me, who am brought so near the door by this sickness. There was a contention as far as a suit (in which both piety and dignity, religion and estimation, were mingled), ~~which of the religious orders~~ of who should ring to ~~prayers~~ meditations first in the morning; and it was determined, that they should ring first that rose

416

earliest. If we understand aright the dignity of this bell that tolls for our ~~prayer~~ meditation, we would be glad to make it ours by rising early, in that application, that it might be ours as well as ~~his~~ theirs, whose indeed it is. The bell does toll for ~~him~~ her that thinks it does; and though it intermit again, yet from that minute that that occasion wrought upon ~~him~~ her, ~~he~~ she is united to god. Who casts not up his eye to the sun when it rises? but who takes off his eye from a comet when that breaks out? Who bends not his ear to any bell which upon any occasion rings? but who can remove it from that bell which is passing a piece of ~~himself~~ herself out of this world?

No ~~man~~ person is an island, entire of itself; every man is a piece of the continent, a part of the main. If a clod be washed away by the sea, ~~Europe~~ the world is the less, as well as if a promontory were, as well as if a manor of thy friend's or of thine own were: any ~~man's~~ woman's death diminishes me, because I am involved in humankind, and therefore never send to know for whom the bell tolls; it tolls for thee. Neither can we call this a begging of misery, or a borrowing of misery, as though we were not miserable enough of ourselves, but must fetch in more from the next house, in taking upon us the misery of our neighbors. Truly it were an excusable covetousness if we did, for affliction is a treasure, and scarce any man hath enough of it. No woman or man hath affliction enough that is not matured and ripened by and made fit for ~~god~~ creation by that affliction. If a man carry treasure in bullion, or in a wedge of gold, and have none coined into current money, his treasure will not defray him as he travels. Tribulation is treasure in the nature of it, but it is not current money in the use of it, except we get nearer and nearer our home, ~~heaven,~~ by it. Another ~~man~~ person may be sick too, and sick to death, and this affliction may lie in his bowels, as gold in a mine, and be of no use to him; but this bell, that tells me of ~~his~~ her affliction, digs out and applies that gold to me: if by this consideration of another's danger I take mine own into contemplation, and so secure myself, by making my recourse to ~~my god~~ creation, ~~who~~ which is our only security.

Acknowledgements

My thanks to Paul Zarou and Kristine Hurst for their candid, supportive, and helpful comments about this book as well as for their constant friendship. Thanks to Arielle Datz for lovingly pointing out problems. Thanks to Tatiana Vila for her great cover art and great attitude. And enormous thanks to Marla Knutsen for her editing and comments, but mostly for being there for me always.

Afterword

I thank you for reading my book. If you liked it, please help me by telling your friends and by writing an online review.

Thank you again.

David Datz

About David Datz

David Datz is a writer and actor. He has written several novels and stage plays. As an actor, he has performed in TV shows, films, and stage plays. He has also had a career as a systems analyst, computer project manager, and group manager. He lives in southern California with his wife.

Connect With David Datz

For more about David Datz, please see his Facebook page: https://www.facebook.com/David-Datz-Author-102112348194088

You can also email him at: ddatz.writer.actor@gmail.com